THE GUEST

Charlotte Cory was born in 1956 and studied English at Bristol
University. After a D.Phil. in Medieval English at York University
she worked as a freelance artist specializing in woodcut illus-
tration. She is the author of *The Unforgiving* and *The Laughter of
Fools* which were published by Faber and Faber to critical
acclaim. She is married and lives in Manchester.

CHARLOTTE CORY
The Guest

faber and faber
LONDON · BOSTON

First published in Great Britain in 1996
by Faber and Faber Limited
3 Queen Square London WC1N 3AU
This paperback edition first published in 1997

Phototypeset by Intype London Ltd
Printed and bound in Great Britain
by Mackays of Chatham PLC, Chatham, Kent

A CIP record for this book
is available from the British Library

ISBN 0–571–19057–X

2 4 6 8 10 9 7 5 3 1

For Bob, Mr Chicken and Rufus.
And in memory of my beloved grandmother
Ella Harriet Everest (*née* Binham) 1899–1992
with thanks for all her kindness
and encouragement

The Guest

PART ONE

Death of a Stranger

Hester Jones

You ask me who I am, and how I came to be here. You want to know if I can have anything to do with the death of your stranger . . .

Rest assured. My name is Hester Jones. I too am a stranger. I came quite by chance so I cannot be connected in any way with your mystery. Until yesterday morning – it amazes me to realize this even as I write, so much has happened since – I had lived all my life in the same small house in the same quiet respectable street in which I was born. Not that anyone could have guessed after the disruption and chaos the night of my birth what a steady quiet life I would lead till now: a violent thunderstorm rent the sky, lightning flashed, rain pounded down and every so often volleys of slates crashed with loud reports from off the roof. My father, banished by the midwife to sit out the storm and the hour of my coming in a cold kitchen, cradled his old grey head in trembling hands and feared for my life. When day broke and the storm subsided, how surprised the poor man had been to wake and find the house still standing. Convinced some cataclysm had been postponed, the end of the world but narrowly averted, he crept upstairs to my mother's bedroom and found *me* lying there, washed and wailing, looking suspiciously like any other new-born baby, in my crib.

My mother recovered quickly, considering her age and ordeal. She held me up to the cold morning light and, with my father looking on gingerly from the doorway, she named me 'Hester': Hester Jones.

Most people like to think their own children special – but, as *I* was growing up, what amazed *my* parents most was my ordinariness. However hard they gazed into my plain little pancake face, I never showed signs of precocity or waywardness. However fast they turned round or entered rooms unexpectedly, they never caught young Hester doing anything she shouldn't. I did not soil my clothes, or make outlandish demands. Nor was I blessed with good looks liable to prove dangerous, or an endearing disposition designed to deceive. My chief desire in all things was always to please. This made the pair of them nervous. Unable to forget the heavens bursting apart, unleashing something incalculable on an unsuspecting world, they regarded their little girl warily. They felt too old to cope. Had I been a handful they might have found me easier, but my ready compliance with all adult ridiculousness caused them to wonder what I was stubbornly storing up. Their greatest wish, I think now, was not to live long enough to find out.

I was sixteen when my father died. I'd been about to take the exams that would have taken me away from my quiet upbringing. I liked the orderly conclusiveness of arithmetic and nurtured a safe, solid, ambition to teach. I could see myself standing in front of a class, wearing a long blue skirt, relentlessly chalking up numbers on the blackboard. My own teachers had expected me to do quite well. With few natural talents and no desire to make friends, I'd been content to spend my evenings hunched over books but when my mother told me my father was dying, I immediately abandoned my studies and stayed at home to help her nurse him into his grave.

One day, his last, when she was out of the room and I sat gazing into space, my father suddenly opened his eyes and demanded to know what I was thinking about. I told him the truth – which was that I was too tired to think about anything – whereupon he gasped with pain and exasperation, and declared that I had always been a puzzle. He and my mother had never known what went on in my funny little head, and he could not regret that now he would never find out. Then he laughed till he choked, and he choked till he died and my mother, who had heard the noise and come running back into the room, took his old grey head in her arms and looked over at me accusingly as he breathed his last.

She clung to me afterwards. How could I leave her? I let the little schoolroom of my dreams float away. I let the years drift past. And then my mother also died. So there you have me – in less than two pages! – orphaned, alone in the world and ready for whatever might happen next. My parents had had no relatives, or friends. They barely ever spoke to the neighbours. They had lived

4

for each other and I had lived with them, and now they were both dead.

If I felt sorry for myself, I was not entirely sorry. My mother had become very difficult and tetchy towards the end. She kept wanting to know what I had said to my father to kill him. And she accused me of waiting for her to die. 'You are waiting for me to die before you make your move!' she would shriek when all I'd been doing, night after night, was to sit beside her while she slept, keeping her company and silently darning sheets. She tried her utmost to provoke me but I refused to be provoked. One day she went further. She asked the doctor if he was married, which he was. Then she told him I thought this a pity as I had designs on him myself.

'Little Hester has designs on the whole world!' my mother said. 'She is bent on causing havoc. Always has been.'

This was totally untrue, of course, and caused me no little awkwardness but the doctor took it in his stride. He tapped his pen on his prescription pad and looked me up and down. It was a hazard of his profession, he remarked, elderly patients trying to foist unmarried daughters off on gullible physicians before it was too late. Young men were warned about the danger at medical school. My mother laughed uproariously and, like a desperate clown who hits on a new trick, she lay there with her puffy white face and garish overbright lips and said exactly the same thing to the parson who came, a worried-looking fellow called the Reverend Philip Peebles. He asked her if she was frightened of dying and she immediately replied that *dying* could scarcely be more terrifying than *living* with me. 'Don't let that plain little pancake face fool you!' she said. The Reverend Peebles glanced – somewhat cautiously, I might say – in my direction but my mother cackled happily. Then she asked him if *he* was married and he told us he was not. He lived with his older sister who was devoted to him.

'Your sister had better watch out then. The young inherit the earth, as I'm sure you're aware, Mr Peebles. The moment I'm gone, Hester here will be able to do as she pleases – I am only too glad *I* shall not be around to see the consequences.'

I did not know where to look. I certainly did not look at the

5

Reverend Peebles, and I did not see him again until after she was gone.

'Well now, Miss Jones! And what are you going to do with yourself?' The parson had invited me back after the quick quiet funeral to the rambling rectory he shared with his sister. He offered me cheap sweet wine from Spain. There were rows of other, more elaborately labelled bottles on his sideboard, but he had clearly designated cheap sweet wine my desert. The Reverend Philip held my hand as he handed me the glass. We could hear his sister moving about upstairs. Everything became quickly blurry, the double chin less doubly defined.

'I intend to enjoy myself,' I answered, withdrawing my hand and sipping hastily. 'I want to get out and about a bit, see something of the world.'

I was surprised by my words which had been liberated, I supposed, by the cheap sweet wine, but the man nodded. 'Good, good. And you have been left well provided for? You are able now to do as you please?'

It was my turn to nod. I had inherited the earth, I reminded him, thanking him for his interest. I had also inherited enough to live on so long as I was not extravagant and extravagance, fortunately, had never been in my nature.

'Good, good,' the Reverend Peebles said again, beaming at me through the thick glass of his spectacles. He ran a trembling finger up my arm and was about to say something further when we heard his sister coming heavily downstairs.

'I didn't know we had visitors!' Clara Peebles remarked, as if she did not know who I was or what I was doing there, when only the day before I had called to check on the funeral arrangements and pay what was due for these services, in advance. The Reverend Peebles had been out but his sister had invited me in. She was kind enough to take my money and ply me with milky tea and conversation.

A large bossy woman in clumpy sweater and pleated skirt, with enormous front teeth and clear shining skin, Clara Peebles insisted on making out a receipt in big careful handwriting even though I said I did not need one. 'Best to get these things out of the way,' she said, shaking her head sorrowfully over the tea-pot. At first I thought she meant my parents and I was about to agree that I would probably manage very well on my own, but then she appeared to be saying something else, 'Funny their not wanting a plot for *three*, what with you being on your own now. It wouldn't have cost a lot more to dig down a bit deeper.' She eyed me searchingly for a moment and chomped her big teeth. 'I dare say they expected you to marry, Miss Jones?' she asked sharply. 'Or move away?'

I shrugged. It was impossible to say what my parents had ever expected. They had probably been frightened to have me with them in their grave the way they had been obliged, in late middle age, to let an alarmingly well-behaved child share their small quiet house. I arrived with considerable commotion at the last minute, I explained, and could only presume that my elderly parents' fears *for* me during that stormy night had contrived to make them fearful *of* me. Miss Peebles seemed to think I was referring somehow to her brother's absence, and his lateness coming home. 'The Reverend Peebles is a busy man!' she declared, breaking a Nice biscuit in two and dunking one half in her tea. She cleared her throat. 'I am not a selfish woman, Miss Jones. I would never stand in the way of my brother's happiness. He is a little inclined to get too involved in his work. Women like to cry on his shoulder,' she disclosed in between bites at her biscuit. And then, probably because I was staring at her in open-mouthed fascination, or perhaps she thought Miss Hester Jones likely to want to cry on his shoulder, Clara Peebles started to tell me about a girl called Swan who had recently taken a foolish fancy to her brother. 'Where will I go if he marries the creature?' Miss Peebles cried, swallowing the second half of her Nice biscuit whole. I watched as it made its lumpy way slowly, but surely, down her waggling throat.

'Is there any question that the Reverend Peebles may do so?' I asked. A telephone sounded just then in the distance. My hostess made no move to answer me, or it.

'That will be *her* now,' she hissed frostily. 'Whenever I pick up the receiver there is nobody there. *I* am not the one she wants to speak to. Miss Swan will not cease till she has my poor brother firmly in her clutches.'

'Oh dear!' I said.

'I only know of her existence because I once found the name

scribbled down on a piece of paper by the telephone. Philip has never kept anything from me before . . .'

The ringing stopped.

'There you are!' Clara Peebles grasped my arm urgently. Her eyes were hollow. She had not been sleeping. 'I have always looked after my brother, Miss Jones. It is the only life I know. The only life I want.'

'I can't see what *I* . . .'

'If dear Philip were to marry somebody I could trust, somebody like you, Hester – you are on your own now and, from what I understand, have inherited enough to do as you please. He has said such nice things and I'm sure we could all get on . . .'

'I don't know *what* your brother can have said about *me*, Miss Peebles,' I resisted her hastily. 'He does not know me – nobody does! There can be no question . . . He was kind enough to call when my mother was dying. She told me to let him in. I think she wanted company. I was not enough, you see. I never provided any excitement and after the thunderstorm that accompanied my birth, I dare say they expected . . . They probably had a right to expect. I – I had better go . . .'

'It's Hester!' The Reverend Philip attempted to remind his sister now about my mother's funeral that had just taken place.

'Good heavens, why so it is! Hester Jones – back again!' Miss Peebles flashed her large teeth at me and encompassed us both in a broad emphatic smile. 'I hope Philip has been looking after you.' She flew enthusiastically across the room, seized the open bottle of cheap sweet wine, and returned to liberally top up my glass. 'We had *such* a nice chat yesterday,' she told her brother. 'Why, Hester and I came to *quite* an understanding!' She splashed the back of my hand which I was obliged to lick, like a dog with a wounded paw.

'I must go,' I said.

'Go!' Clara Peebles placed a restraining hand on my sticky wrist. 'Go where? Just when we . . .'

But for the Peebleses, standing there together smiling in unison, you might never have met me. I would probably have gone on living in my parents' dreary house. I might even have found light work and learned to enjoy myself in my own quiet way. I would not be sitting here writing this – and I would

8

never have heard of the death of your stranger. As it was, though, I put down my glass. 'Thank you both so much,' I said resolutely. 'You have been very kind.'

I ran from the room, and I ran all the way home. When I got there I found two burly men sitting in a parked van outside the house. 'We've been waiting for you, Miss,' they said, climbing down from their cab. 'We heard someone died. We have come to pay our respects.'

'Thank you,' I mumbled politely.

'You'll be wanting the place cleared then?' They jerked their thumbs over their shoulders in the direction of my parents' house.

I glanced at their van. 'House clearances, by appointment' was painted in red and gold letters on the side. It would have felt churlish to point out that they had *not* made an appointment, so I asked them instead how much they charged.

'We do it for free,' one of the men said. 'As a favour.'

'Fifty quid!' interposed the other. 'To take it off your hands.'

We settled part way. For twenty-five pounds they set to at once and within hours had completely emptied my parents' house. I watched them dismantling the wooden bed in which my mother had died and in which I'd been born. 'Firewood,' the sharper of the two told me, indicating a sizeable crack in the mahogany frame. I giggled, and helped pile things into boxes to take out to their van. It was as if I were moving house but did not have the responsibility of taking everything with me.

When the men had gone I sat on bare floorboards like a toddler with no toys. All my mother's knick-knacks, her photograph albums, even my father's walking stick and pipe had been jumbled together and consigned to oblivion in a dangerously loaded-down van with red and gold lettering on the side. I hugged my knees to my chin. 'Little Hester has designs on the whole world,' I said out loud. 'She is bent on causing havoc. Always has been!'

The Reverend Peebles and his sister came several times to the house. They came separately, and then together. On each occasion I crouched very quietly in the empty room in which my mother had died, waiting until they gave up ringing the door bell and went away. When the landlord's agent called for the rent, I came out of hiding and explained that I would soon be leaving. He told

9

me rather curtly that I must pay to the end of the next quarter and be sure to touch up any paint that was chipped and leave the place spotless, ready for the next tenant.

It took me three days, and three cans of paint. I worked all day and right through the nights. I scrubbed and swept and painted until you would not have known anyone had ever lived there. Then I slept solidly on a blanket for forty-eight hours, and at last, early yesterday morning almost before it was light, I closed the front door of the house in which I had lived all my life and posted the key back through the letterbox. I paused long enough to hear it clatter to the floor. Then I walked to the railway station, a small cardboard suitcase containing all my possessions scarcely weighing me down. I had resolved to purchase a single ticket to the furthest destination I could see on the departure board, which turned out to be Penzance.

'You'll have to change twice,' the man beyond the small pane of glass at the ticket office said as I counted out the money. I had no time to inquire further because a train on the platform immediately behind me started to pull out of the station. It wasn't going very fast as yet so I seized the ticket and ran, flinging myself into the end carriage just before the train gathered speed. What bliss to have a compartment all to myself! I put my suitcase up on the rack and sat down feeling as light-headed and light-hearted as if I had changed trains a couple of times already.

We rumbled down the line for I don't know how long, long enough for me to doze off and dream of seagulls and sandcastles and wander among the whitewashed houses that I imagined lined the winding streets of Penzance. I was about to purchase a colourful paper windmill from a vendor on the quay when the train cranked abruptly to a halt, and I came to. I felt stiff all over and knew at once that I had been asleep for some time. After sitting quite contentedly for a while, yawning, it occurred to me to put my head out of the window. There was nothing to be seen in any direction except empty countryside, scrubby fields stretching far into the distance. I breathed in the cool, late autumn air and rather fancifully regretted that I had not acquired that pretty paper windmill. It would have been company for me, turning brightly in the breeze. Then I noticed that the train had been shunted into some sort of siding. I banged the window shut and sat down again, angry that my endeavours had only come to this. It was hot and fumy in the carriage, the engine's heater had been left on. Soon I fell asleep again but this time did not dream.

'What the . . . are *you* doing 'ere?' A railway official shook me roughly by the shoulder. He threw down a bucket and mop.

'Er – aren't I . . .' I stuttered.

'Aren't you what?' he demanded angrily.

'Isn't this the train for . . .'

'No, it ain't! And you've no business in 'ere – it's out of service, for cleaning. You gave me a jolt, I can tell you. Sitting there like some ghost.'

'A ghost?'

'People *die* on trains, you know. They forget to get out at their stop and then they're found years later, still riding the network, an out-of-date ticket in their pocket. Other passengers and officials assume they are asleep and don't like to wake them.'

'How macabre!' I sat up and blearily contemplated the bucket and mop. I was about to tell the man that – as I was neither asleep, nor dead – I would shortly be looking for work and did not in any way consider myself above cleaning out trains, when he began swooping about the carriage like some demented cage-bird and returned waving a cluster of discarded tickets and scrunched-up newspapers in my face. 'Vermin, that's what you lot are!' he shouted. 'All coming and going as you please, leaving droppings . . .'

One of the newspapers fell to the ground. I bent down and picked it up. Someone had drawn a large circle in red ink round the heading, SITUATIONS VACANT. I stared at the words; my situation surely as vacant as any I could conceive.

'You can't stay in 'ere readin' papers,' the man said briskly. 'This isn't a Ladies' Waiting Room for Madam to take tea in till something better 'appens along – I've work to do, even if you 'aven't!' He emptied his bucket, slopping filthy water across the floor so that it ran around my shoes. 'You'd best make your way straight back up the track and get a connection at the next station. Where did you say you was going?'

'I didn't say,' I said, producing the ticket to Penzance from my purse.

The man flicked it aside. 'All right for some!' he grumbled, but then something made him pause and lean thoughtfully on his mop. 'There was this kid sat beside me at school. Told me *he* was going to Penzance.' The man stared for a while, nodding thoughtfully to himself. Then he spoke again. 'He never came back. I've always wondered what happened to him. If the teachers knew, they never said. Maybe his mum ran off with a sailor and he stayed in Penzance with her. Or maybe he went out in a small boat lobster potting, the waves got up and he was drowned. Dragged down into the deep, he'd 'ave been, with his lobster pots. His parents didn't think to tell the school. Can't remember his name, only the empty seat beside me, and sitting sucking my pencil, trying to recall what he'd looked like. Or anything about him. I didn't know he'd go missing so I never paid him much attention, until after he was gone. I have never forgotten 'im though . . .'

It was late afternoon. The sun was now low in the sky and dark thick clouds were gathering menacingly overhead. I had spent the whole day on the train going nowhere. While the man addressed his audience of empty seats in the empty train, I lifted my suitcase down from the rack and released the brass catch on the carriage door. It was a steep drop to the ground without a platform and I landed awkwardly. As I steadied myself, the door slammed shut above me. I stood for a moment looking across the desolate fields. It had not occurred to me to ask where I was and when I glanced back up inside the train I could see the man now intently at work with his mop. He appeared to be cheerfully singing. Hester Jones on the ground just below the window was far less an object of curiosity than a nameless boy who had disappeared many years before from the desk beside him at school.

I turned and began to walk back along the track as the man had advised. The light was failing fast and I made slow, undignified progress over the weeds and stones. I kept losing my footing. It was a long way to Penzance, I told myself drily. I was probably not even going in the right direction. My suitcase that had seemed so light that morning grew heavier and more unwieldy with each step. I stumbled and slipped. I grazed my hands and knees. Then the strap on my best shoes broke, and I stubbed my toe.

I started to weep. I raised my plain little pancake face to the darkening skies and wept like the heavens had wept at my birth, noisily, angrily and without restraint. So, this was the cataclysm so long postponed! The end of the world, as I knew it. I laughed aloud then. Hester Jones had been a goody-goody all her life, complying with all adult ridiculousness until she too had become a ridiculous adult. I shivered. A cold wind had got up; it began to rain heavily. Dead leaves swirled in wet clusters from the trees, slapping against my face and clinging to my hair and clothes. By now I was dragging my suitcase along the stones, howling with rage like the heavens around me, making my way as fast as I could – though I could not know it yet – towards you . . .

2

Cayke's Timing

When I looked up and saw a brightly illuminated, downy white creature with a yellow beak and watchful eye staring down at me, my first thoughts were of the girl, Swan, who had foolishly set her heart on the Reverend Peebles. For a brief, startled moment I thought she had followed me, and found me out, but then I realized that this was only the painted signboard of a public house I had come to. And, as I peered through the rain-washed windows into a cosy crowded room, my own heart lifted at the prospect of refreshing myself and drying off. I reckoned I'd easily be able to slip in and out again, unnoticed.

I was mistaken. The moment I appeared through the Swan's swing doors someone grabbed me purposefully by the sleeve. 'You knew him?'

A glass was thrust into my hands. I was tired and thirsty. I drank gratefully.

'Your good health!' A young man in a brown baggy suit, leaning against the wall just inside the entrance, saluted me heartily. He wiped froth from his beer off his bushy ginger moustaches using a large grubby handkerchief which he then stuffed back into his breast pocket. Though people were already turning to look, he waved his glass eagerly in my direction. 'Here she is!'

'Is it raining outside?' someone asked.

The whole room convulsed with laughter. I looked down – my clothes were soaked through, I was dripping all over the carpet. I caught sight of myself above the bottles in the mirror behind the bar. There were dead leaves tangled in my wet matted hair. I looked what my mother would have called 'a fright'.

'Are you staying over?'

'Of course she is!' The man with the beer and bushy moustaches winked encouragingly. 'She can't go back out into all that rain.'

'We won't let her!'

'She'd die of cold.'

'There's been death enough round here already!' A towel was draped round my shoulders and my glass refilled.

'Are you related?' someone close by inquired earnestly. By now a crowd had sealed me off from the door. People began pressing about to get a better look. 'I'll swear you weren't in church!'

'She was probably hiding.'

'Behind a pillar.'

'Veiled.'

'Shamefaced.'

'Weeping into a black-edged hanky. . . '

'I saw her!'

'You knew him, dear?'

'You were his mistress?'

I gazed at the unknown faces ranged before me. They all gaped eagerly back. There was a buzz of excitement and nervous laughter. 'I have only come in for a quick drink to refresh myself,' I tried to say. 'And to get out of the driving rain.' No one was listening. I shivered, though the heat in the room caused a light steam to rise from my sopping clothes.

A man pushed bluffly forward. 'And do *you* have hopes, Miss?'

'Of course she has!'

'I . . . ' They saw me hesitate. How could I deny the little schoolroom of my dreams, and all those other foolish fancies Hester Jones had hoped for so fearfully over the years. Had I not set out that very morning, even, full of joyous but apparently senseless expectation? 'I am naturally hopeful,' I began to say. 'I have had to be. I took the wrong train. I was on my way to Penzance – the name on a destination board at the railway station furthest away. I intended to start afresh. A clean break. A new life. A bit of a holiday – beside the sea. Lobster potting, maybe . . . '

'But you came *here* instead.'

'We are miles from the sea!'

'What were you hoping for?'

'There are no sailors here, Miss!'

'I told you so. She *does* have hopes. She can't help herself. Any more than we . . . '

A woman in the crowd clad in a bright orange dress turned angrily on the man speaking. 'You and your *hopes*, Mr Matchett!' She put her hands on her large bulky hips and gave a long loud disapproving sniff. 'Not *everyone* in this world is as greedy and grasping as you!'

'Aren't they now?' the man Matchett retorted. 'We all have our hopes, why else are we here?'

'Speak for yourself!' The woman sniffed again but Mr Matchett drew himself up, undaunted.

'I *am* speaking for myself,' he declared stoutly. 'And I speak for you an' all, Beryl Laffety! There's no one here in this room today without hope pounding in their bosom. No one who doesn't expect . . .' He paused and looked about him.

There were murmurs of 'True . . . true enough.'

'And not just in *here* neither,' he went on. 'Everyone in the town stands to benefit. The whole of Knibden is *alive* with expectation.'

'Knibden!' I exclaimed. Was I in Knibden then? At once the attention reverted to me. People stepped back to get a better look.

'You have been here before?' they wanted to know.

'Not exactly . . .'

'How then?'

And so I told them. How I had once set out for Knibden as a child. My elderly parents who'd always felt too old to cope though I had never been a handful, or in any way wayward, had taken last-minute cut-price seats in a coach which was meant to break its journey in Knibden but broke down half an hour from home, going up a steep hill. We passed the whole of the afternoon we should have spent in the town huddled at the side of the road in the drizzle waiting for a breakdown vehicle to effect repairs. Eventually the party had been led to a miserable wayside café where we had eked out a pot of stewed tea and a stale tea-cake, courtesy of the coach company, until replacement transport could be found to take us home. I sat between my two tight-lipped parents, glancing from one to the other, picking at the crumbs and dry currants on my plate. For a child who desires, above all things, to please, there was little pleasing to be done that afternoon. When everyone else from the coach started singing, the three of us stared straight ahead, refusing to join in. The venture had been a mistake, my father pronounced grimly. He was a careful man. He needed to be. A growing child is an expensive business, he would say whenever my mother needed to buy me clothes or shoes. The one indulgence they'd allowed themselves after I was born had been a tight little grave for two, purchased from the Reverend Peebles, a parson who had recently got himself entangled with a girl called Swan. She was intent on marrying him, but his toothy sister wanted me . . .

My audience listened respectfully. Someone refilled my glass.

'Now there's a coincidence!' the man behind the bar broke the uncertain silence that followed my speech. 'We are in the Swan now.'

This was greeted with a loud burst of merry laughter but the small, rather leathery man called Matchett who had spoken before, bent towards me and coughed confidentially. 'Pardon me, Miss, and don't mind my asking, but how do you *know* this particular lady was called "Swan"?'

I tried to think. 'The Reverend Peebles's sister once found the name scribbled down beside the telephone . . .'

'Ah!' Matchett snapped his fingers and called out for another whisky. 'As I thought!' he said, with a grin. 'In her agitation she'll have misread her brother's writing. I am a printer, I know about such things . . .'

'He's *the* Mr Matchett! Of Buckworth & Matchett's!' the large brightly dressed woman, Beryl Laffety, put in impressively. The man in the brown baggy suit, who had greeted me when I first arrived, belched.

'Buckworth & Matchett's?' I inquired.

'Printers of the *Knibden Bugle*, incorporating the *Knibden Gazette*, the *Knibden Daily Bystander* and the *Knibden Globe*. All now well and truly defunct.'

'Gone for ever.'

'Famous newspapers, in their day.'

'Not enough *new* ever happened in Knibden,' Mr Matchett said defensively, tipping his head back and draining his whisky. 'You can't have *news*papers without any news!'

'We've got news enough now . . .'

'There hasn't been a Buckworth in Buckworth & Matchett's for years,' someone observed. 'Not since old Godfrey . . .'

'Godfrey Buckworth who first encountered his natural son while handing out prizes at the Knibden Board School. A hundred pairs of keen young eyes looked on as father and son met for the first time, gazing at each other over a presentation copy of Mrs Esmerald Dean's *The Good Path*. When the boy died of TB a few months later, his mother sent *The Good Path* back to Mr Buckworth. With a nasty note telling him he could keep it!'

'That's just gossip.'

'That was not what I heard.'

'The old Buck had bastards all over town. Mister Godfrey couldn't have given out school prizes in Knibden without encountering at least one.'

'He never had anything to do with the printing. Henry Buckworth paid his brother to stay away from the works. Poor Godfrey used to wander aimlessly round the town all the time. No wonder he got into mischief . . .'

'He drowned in the canal.'

'That was all a long time ago!' Mr Matchett heaved with impatience. 'Godfrey Buckworth would have been dead by now anyway – I can't see *he* can have any bearing on this present business.' Matchett turned to me. 'And as for *your* little matter, Miss – your "Swan" should have been "Susan", of course. Susan would look like Swan, scribbled hastily, and an infatuated man does not always inscribe his letters carefully. This Reverend Peebles would have no cause to correct his sister's misapprehension – so while she would be on the look out for a Swan, the parson could cunningly carry on with his Susan right under her – and your – very noses.'

'Well, I never!'

'It's shocking what goes on.'

'You're well off out of it, Miss.'

'You're better off here! With us.'

As I stood staring at Mr Matchett and the other speakers, a woman dived towards me, grabbing me by the arm. 'I know you!' she screeched. 'It was *you* what put him up to it. *You* know more about this than you're letting on!'

'Who knows who put him up to it?' someone else asked airily. 'Who can say what drives a man to such extremes?'

'The Reverend Philip Peebles . . .' I began, but it was useless.

'Forget the fellow!'

'We know no one of that name here, dear.'

'We have our own problems that need solving. And someone will have to hurry up and solve them.'

'Who are you?' a voice interrupted. The voice of a man I now know to be Michael Milady. He had been standing to the side looking on ever since I arrived. When his question boomed out, a hush descended. The crowd around me fell back to clear a passage between us.

'I am Hester Jones,' I said, speaking firmly and as calmly as I could.

A juke box in the corner was playing scratchy old dance tunes. *Hold me tight, my baby sweet, as we round the rocky coast, Kiss me light when we meet* ... The words hung in the air, tinny and inappropriate as Mr Milady looked at me and I looked back at him. He was a man of slight build, elderly, nimble, with wispy white hair and watery eyes so clear that he seemed to see right through you. *What a sight for sore feet* ... Everyone else in the crowded room stood quietly now, watching the two of us closely as they sipped from their glasses and tapped their toes to the tune. *Breaks my heart when we part, Right from the start I* ...

At last the music stopped and Michael Milady advanced towards me. 'Am I to presume, Hester Jones, that you are staying in Knibden tonight? At the Gallimore Hotel?'

'I ...' I glanced down at the sodden cardboard suitcase that had lain all this time at my feet. 'I don't know where I'm staying,' I admitted. 'I took the wrong train – I ... I shouldn't be in Knibden at all.'

'Come, come, Miss Jones! That is hardly for *you* to say.' Michael Milady now stood but three feet from me. '*We* will surely be the judge of that.'

'I had a ticket for Penzance ...' I extracted my purse from my pocket and fumbled for a while. 'It must have blown away when I was struggling along the railway line,' I said.

A pause ensued. Someone coughed.

At last, Mr Milady began to speak. 'I listened with interest to your account of how you once nearly came here, Miss Jones. You see, I too was brought to Knibden as a child. A lifetime ago. By my mother. Like you, I remember every detail of the journey but, unlike you, alas, *we* reached our destination. No pots of tea and stale tea-cakes to detain *us* along the way – how different things might have been if they had! How well I remember riding up from Knibden station in an open carriage. The faces turning in the street, my mother holding me close and telling me not to look so that, as I peered out from the warmth and sweet softness of her arms, I did not understand what I was not meant to see. Nor could I comprehend the calamity about to engulf my happy little world. No child could. I thought it was some sort of holiday – in a way it was. A holiday from another life, and one that has never ended. My mother took the best rooms they had available in the town's best hotel. She paid for a two-night stay. Then she put me to bed, kissed me goodnight, and abandoned me there, alone in the darkness, upstairs in the Gallimore Hotel . . .'

'She went home?' I asked.

'No! Alas!' Michael Milady sighed, a sigh of such sorrow I felt myself shudder. The whole room shuddered. He shook out his mane of wispy white hair. 'My poor mother died. We had no home. Melinda Milady had come back to Knibden to make her peace. It cost the poor woman her life. That is not what others will say. They have an interest in saying otherwise.' He paused. 'My mother's family felt tricked into bearing the expense of my upbringing. You said yourself, a child is an expensive business. By chance, however, another resident of the Gallimore at that time, the great actor/manager, Montague Cayke, no less, took pity on my plight. He happened to be on tour in England just then, playing that week at the Knibden Alhambra. Picture the scene, Miss Jones, enacted that morning before the great Montague Cayke in the foyer of the Gallimore Hotel: see there!' He pointed: we looked – at a cigarette burn on the carpet across the floor. 'See the orphaned boy clutching his woollen toy rabbit, sobbing piteously on a hard oak settle while his dead mother's relations squabble above his head, each bitterly disclaiming responsibility for the whimpering offspring of the poor girl's unfortunate marriage. "I knew it would end in tears!" Melinda's eldest sister is saying. Over and over. She was right – the tears were mine. I have been weeping those tears ever since. This story wrings your heart; it wrung Monty Cayke's. You weren't there that morning, many moons ago, in the foyer of the Gallimore Hotel – *he* was. Such is fate. While accusations flew and the unwanted child wept, Cayke stepped in with the timing that made his Imperial Players famous worldwide. *Cayke's Timing* they still call it in the trade. My mother's relations could only stand with their mouths wide open, Melinda Milady not yet in her unmarked grave, as the great Montague Cayke removed his plumed hat with a flourish and offered to take me on in his Imperial Players, to tour the British Empire as Aladdin's younger brother . . .'

'Aladdin's younger brother!' a woman in the crowd clustered round the bar yelled out. Michael Milady glanced over his shoulder, graciously acknowledging his audience's astonishment. Then he continued, 'I worked for dear Monty over fifty years. It was a good life, as good a life as any. Across India, South Africa, Australia, Canada, I graduated through the ranks of the Imperial Players. We were a happy, close-knit company. Closely knit around Monty. The great man reached a great age, in harness to the end. At Moose Jaw he managed his most magnificent Hamlet, but by Medicine Hat Cayke could scarcely raise the feeblest ghost. "Remember me!" he croaked, as if anyone could ever forget Montague Cayke. We buried him there, amid the wigwams and totem poles. And although I, young Michael Milady, then took over the Imperial Players and we went on posting up playbills before indifferent natives of one shade or another across the globe, it was never the same without Monty. Or an empire any more, by then, to tour. We did our best but the world had changed under our feet. We had become an anachronism. Pale relics of a past, painted pink, that no brushing of any magic lamp could ever conjure back. Eventually those few of us left went our own separate ways, and I came home to Knibden, having nowhere else to call home . . .' Michael Milady dropped his voice and narrowed his eyes. 'I tell you all this, Hester Jones, not because I expect my sorry life to interest you, but because it seems to me *this* man will have a not dissimilar history. He, also, came back to Knibden. But unlike me, he has not lived to tell his story. That will be for *you*.'

'Me?'

The crowd around us nodded vigorously. 'Yes, you!'

'What *man* are you talking about?' I asked. 'What *story*? Has he *died*?' Only now did I notice that, apart from the fellow with bushy ginger moustaches wearing a brown baggy suit, everyone else in the room was dressed in black. As if for a funeral. And so, as it happened, was I.

'You are to stay at the Gallimore Hotel, Miss Jones. That was his last Will and Testament . . .'

'Drinks all round,' Mr Matchett put in. 'That's what the guest said. And very generous too . . .'

'A guest?' I queried.

'The guest at the Gallimore. We have just come from his funeral . . .'

'A tragic affair . . .'

'Sweet wine for Miss Jones!'

'It was his last wish.'

'Sweets for the sweet!'

My glass was filled again. Someone was sobbing loudly from the emotion of it all. What did these people want from me, I wondered, almost moved to tears myself. *Who* were they talking about, *who* had just been buried?

'I do not see what any of this has to do with *me*,' I protested hurriedly. 'I never met the dead man, your guest. We did not even get as far as Knibden that time, and it was so long ago I cannot remember why we even thought of coming. My poor mother probably fancied a break. Knibden just happened to be a place *en route*. The expedition was not a success. Doomed at the outset, my father said. Like me . . .'

'Things that are barely remembered,' someone across the room intoned gravely, as if reading set lines. '*Things that ought to have been forgotten, but cannot be. That have become forgotten, when they should not be.* That's what *he* wrote – the stranger who died in our midst.'

'Talk, talk, talk – where's it getting us? Don't you see –' a man with a thin foxy face pushed forward, jabbing his forefinger urgently in my face ' – whoever the girl is, she's perfect!'

There were cries of 'Yes, yes!' and, 'She'll do!'

'Not so fast.' Michael Milady solemnly held up his hand. 'Miss Jones has not yet passed the audition. There may be other, more attractive, propositions still waiting in the wings.'

'Better qualified too . . .'

'Can someone explain?' I asked. No one had ever called me 'perfect' before. Naturally I was intrigued. 'Are you getting up some show? A new Aladdin for next Christmas? Am I to play Mistress Freely, or the Princess Macaree?'

'Steady now, Miss!'

'The Knibden Alhambra closed down years ago.'

'*Explain!* It's for *you* to explain, dear. That will be your job.'

'We'll pay!'

'We can afford to – there are thousands . . .'

'Millions!'

'How I loved the old Alhambra . . .'

'We are not now speaking of any show!' Michael Milady interrupted above the chatter. 'There is no script. And not, necessarily, a happy ending to send us back out into the long cold night. A desperate man came to Knibden last week, Miss Jones, and booked himself into the Gallimore Hotel . . .'

'He must have been desperate to want to stay there!' someone butted in. A burst of laughter was followed by indignant cries of 'Hush, don't put her off!'

When the excitement died down, Mr Milady continued, 'Like my poor mother all those years ago, this guest died. But unlike my mother, *he* must have known he was dying, since he came prepared. In a letter found on his person, it was discovered that the man had, at some point or other in the past, become the owner of the Gallimore. A fine hotel in the centre of town that has been practically empty for years, run very diligently by a Mr and Mrs Mason who have only ever dealt with the wealthy owner through his bank. The Masons never met him. They managed his hotel but it was a condition of their employment that they never even knew his name. The dead man willed that he was to be buried with due care and solemnity, a wake to be held with free drinks all round, the costs to be borne by whomsoever it pleased but reimbursed to them *ten-fold* out of his estate when the rest of his terms are complied with. Which is where you come in . . .'

'Me?'

Milady nodded. The whole room nodded. 'Now that we have buried our stranger with all the care and solemnity anyone could wish, the rest of his terms *must* be complied with if we are ever to see our money back. Let alone reimbursed to us, ten times over. It was his wish, he wrote, that *someone who had nothing to do with him, or the town, be appointed – someone who, by being thus appointed, will forego for ever any chance of benefiting under his Will when the terms of that Will eventually become known, whatever those terms turn out to be.* Finding that someone-who-is-not-someone has not been easy. Yet, until this "someone" has been appointed, and has carried out the task set down for them by the stranger, nothing can be done to distribute the vast sum of money left by him on deposit in the bank. Or to reimburse those of us whom it has pleased to incur the expenses . . .'

'To be repaid ten-fold.'

'How very peculiar!' I exclaimed, for I had never heard of such a thing. My own parents had left me to pay a pair of burly men in a van with red and gold lettering on the side, to take away everything they'd owned. 'Wouldn't it be easier, since the man is now dead and buried, to simply disregard . . .'

'Now look here, Miss . . .'

'Can't be done!'

'Expectations have been raised, Miss Jones!' Michael Milady waved his arms about impatiently. 'All Knibden is alight with dreams and desires. Everyone hopes to be the one to benefit. And hope, like a great slumbering dog once awakened, will not lie down again easily. It barks and snaps the more ferociously for having been asleep. For the first time in years people have something to live for. Anyone present in this room today – apart from yourself that is – might inherit this great fortune. Who knows which of us may soon be richer, and by how much? Look around you! Take Neville Tagg over there – froth gathers like drifting snow upon his moustaches as he sips free beer and pictures himself behind the wheel of a brand-new Ford *Fiesta*, selling his insurance policies in comfort and at high speed . . .'

The young man with the ginger moustaches near the door raised his glass and grinned across at me sheepishly. I saw now the bicycle clips on his baggy brown trousers, and the large notebook jutting out of his jacket pocket. 'You should get yourself insured, Miss!' Neville Tagg called out. 'One of our All Risks policies, I reckon you'll need. This may well prove a dangerous task.'

There was a chorus of amiable objection. 'Nonsense, Neville! Don't listen to him, Miss! The lad gets a nice fat bonus for every Knibden Municipal Insurance Company policy he sells.'

'There isn't an insurance policy in the world that could begin to cover this,' Michael Milady told the room sternly. He turned back to me. 'We were at our wits' end e'er now, Miss Jones. The someone-who-is-not-someone to investigate the Will, must be found straightaway. On the day of the burial. It was one of the dead man's stipulations. But no one in the town would accept the job. Why forego the chance of a great inheritance when there is no way of calculating what that chance might be? We were drowning our sorrows, and even on the point of giving up, when we spotted you, a silhouette against the evening sky stumbling along the railway embankment towards us, the SITUATIONS VACANT column of a newspaper clutched tightly in your hand. As the skies darkened and the rain started to pour we watched you, of your own free will, turn from the path and come down to meet us. A day of destiny if ever there was one, Miss Jones.'

I glanced in surprise at the soggy newspaper I was still holding. The red ink markings had run – as if I'd cut myself, and been bleeding. 'Have you advertised the job?' I asked faintly.

'How could we?' Mr Milady retorted. 'As we have already told you, Knibden no longer has its *Bugle*, *Gazette* or *Daily Bystander*. To advertise nationally would merely draw in outsiders, fortune hunters wanting easy pickings. Or nosy people only after a story.'

There were murmurs of eager agreement.

'Or insurance salesmen hoping for brand-new Ford *Fiestas*?' I suggested.

'Neville Tagg is not the only one with his hopes riding high,' Mr Milady rebuked me firmly. 'If you want to criticize any of us, Miss Jones, you must criticize us all. There is no one in Knibden who isn't busy making plans. Plans of what to do with the money if and when it becomes ours. Plans that will doubtless be devised and revised many times over before your task is complete. How can we help ourselves? Observe Beryl Laffety who only discovered after she'd been tragically widowed the true nature of her tragedy.'

The large woman in the bright orange dress who had been arguing earlier with Mr Matchett, turned her bulk towards me and smiled a broad smile as Milady continued, 'Mrs Laffety's tragedy was to discover her tragedy not truly her own. It turned out the late Mr Laffety had three other families in three other towns, three other Mrs Laffetys with their own little Laffetys all mourning the exact same husband. Three others doing battle

25

with Mr Tagg over a Knibden Municipal Company Life Insurance policy that is almost certainly invalid. If you insure the same life several times over, you have not insured that life at all. A legacy now from the generous stranger would make all the difference, eh Beryl?'

'It would that!' Mrs Laffety slurped from her glass. 'I don't want it for myself, mind,' she said, leaning into my face as if examining her big features close up in a mirror. 'But there's the children to think of. You name it, Miss Jones, they want it! And why not, I say. Just because they're Laffetys – we are the Knibden Laffetys, after all! And while you're about it, we could do with a bigger house. It's *only* money we're talking about – only it's *money* I haven't got. And if the rich guest is dead, I don't see as it makes much difference to 'im now *who* 'as 'is fortune – a Laffety or no. Another rum and ginger, if you please!'

Milady silenced Mrs Laffety with a nod. 'Then, take Victor Matchett, of Buckworth & Matchett's – printers that have seen better days. Mr Matchett will be a man with a lot of scores to settle, and settling scores is always a pricey business. Furthermore, Hester Jones: note Messrs Follifoot, Treadgold and Macready.' Three men lolling together, who had taken off their jackets and rolled up their sleeves, waved to me cheerily and clinked their tankards together. 'These three have always done very well for themselves. Why should they not scoop the jackpot now?'

'Hear, hear!' The three men nudged one another.

'Then allow me to introduce our bookish Miss Willow, and dear good Miss Quinn!' Two trim ladies standing side by side sipping sherry raised their tiny glasses to me and murmured, 'Miss Jones!' 'Already Verity and Belle dream of setting their unhappy pasts to rights. Belle most likely requires funds for good works, and who knows what dear Miss Willow intends. But they are not the only ones in the town with visions of what life could be – and visions, we all know, cost money. There are others out there, of course, others whom you will meet who for reasons of their own could not come to the Swan this evening, but they'll all be busy speculating on their chances. And deciding how to spend the fortune if it becomes theirs. Meanwhile the Reverend Sibson, here, who officiated so efficiently this afternoon. Doubtless he hopes for a little bequest for his church – and your friendship with this Reverend Philip Peebles may well make you sympathetic to his claims . . .'

'Oh, I wouldn't say . . .'

A stooping, rather wizened man in a dog collar bowed to me stiffly. 'St Redegule's needs a new roof, Miss Jones. And a new spire. Damp is rising up through the floors. The old rectory has no form of heating. I can't help thinking that if our dear departed brother, whoever he was, had known . . .'

'While I,' Michael Milady went on quickly, 'even *I* am not exempt. I, too, have my hopes. In *my* mind's eye, the lights of Montague Cayke's greatest triumphs blaze again over Knibden's boarded-up Alhambra. Miss Rose Meldrew and Mr Chas Fonteyne will star once more at the top of the bill, and another small boy can trail behind Aladdin and pull the tail of the pantomime cat. My scattered companions could be fetched from their places of retirement across the Seven Seas for one last glorious curtain call before the lights of the Imperial Players are extinguished, for ever. Even Montague Cayke's prancing dogs . . .'

'The famous dogs!' someone shrieked. 'What I wouldn't give to see Harry, the Astonishing Prancing Dog again!'

'He wore a little silk jacket and cap . . .'

'And smoked a clay pipe . . .'

'He cocked his leg against the leading lady . . .'

'Miss Rose Meldrew.'

'This task you mention, what exactly is it?' I unwound the towel from round my neck and shook out my hair which was now almost dry. I wondered if I shouldn't just thank these good people for their hospitality, pick up my suitcase and be on my way. Leave them to sort themselves out.

'Ah yes, Miss Jones!' Mr Milady moved towards me as if he read my thoughts, and wished to block my path. 'Why would Harry, the Astonishing Prancing Dog in a little silk jacket and cap, interest a sensible girl like you! How right you are to recall us to our task. Whoever the dead stranger was, poor man – and let me say quickly he was by no means "poor", there is goodness knows how much money lodged in the bank . . .'

'Thousands . . .'

'Millions!'

'We have the bank manager's assurances . . .'

'Though he is sworn to secrecy, under the terms of the Will, the sums and the man's identity not to be disclosed. It is a fair supposition that the guest at the Gallimore came back to Knibden specially. Not like you, Miss Jones, who didn't make it thus far the first time, and who came today – if you are to be believed – only by chance, and the vagaries of the railway system. Nor like me, who returned home to Knibden at the end of a long itinerant career, having nowhere better to call home. *This* man, the dead guest, came back to Knibden with the deliberate intention of leaving a Will that would expose something that has been lying here in the town all these years, undetected. Some dark secret it will be your job to uncover . . .'

'*Things barely remembered, that ought to be forgotten but can't be* . . .' a woman chanted with a meaningful nod. 'That's what the dead guest wrote.'

'Who was he? Someone must have known him,' I said.

'And is afraid to speak out? Perhaps.'

'They'll confide in you, Miss Jones! You have the face of one to whom people will tell confidences.'

'Whoever the man was, he clearly intended to reward in large measure,' Mr Matchett observed.

'It would be punishment, now, to be left out.'

'An odd way of going about things . . .'

'Not in the ordinary line of human behaviour, certainly . . .'

It was arranged, then, that I should go straightway to the Gallimore – the main hotel in the centre of the town where the man had come to die. I was to sit down at once and write an account of myself – *tell us who you are, and how you came to be here, Miss Jones* – and then, if Mr Williams, the dead guest's executor who was overseeing the Will on behalf of the bank, and Mr Milady, who had become the town's spokesman in this matter, were both satisfied with my story, it would be my job then to proceed.

I was too tipsy and tired to do other than consent to this dead stranger's plans for me. Late at night in the deathly hush of the lounge of the Gallimore Hotel, broken only by the loud ticking of a black marble clock on the mantelpiece, having been furnished with pen and paper and left to begin this account, I started to write. I expected to finish in the morning. Finding it morning as I got to this point.

'Well, Miss Goody-goody Jones! You are certainly someone-who-is-not-someone.'

I looked up. 'Mr Milady?'

The man nodded. 'We are in your hands.'

I glanced involuntarily at my hands, observing only that they were badly in need of a wash. Gradually the events of the previous twenty-four hours came back to me. My head swam. My back ached. I had fallen asleep across the desk. A pool of ink had gathered like tears beneath my pen.

Michael Milady held the papers he had prised from beneath me. 'We will pay for your board and keep while you complete your task, Miss Jones, and then it seems likely to me that whoever gains most from the stranger's Will will want to give you a little consideration. To see you on your way. To Penzance, if you still have a mind to go there. Or perhaps you will fall in love, and live happily ever after here in Knibden! Who knows? That will be up to you. These though are our terms which you are free to accept or reject, as you wish.'

I rubbed my eyes. Mr Milady, a frail, rather shabby figure, not at all the dramatic presence he had seemed the night before, stood before me thumbing through my hastily written account of myself. It was an enormous dark room we were in, the lounge of the Gallimore Hotel, full of old sofas, little unlit lamps, tables and chairs. 'I hope you can read my writing,' I said. 'I hope *you* haven't mistaken any Susans for Swans.'

'It seems clear enough, Miss Jones – what little there is. You have not, shall we say, led the most exciting life.' Michael Milady glanced at me almost mockingly. 'But that makes you perfect for our purposes. We can hardly expect someone-who-isn't-someone to have a great deal to say for themselves. Besides, it is our lives that are of interest now, not yours, so I expect you will do very nicely.'

'But what exactly am I meant to do?' I asked. The task I'd been set did not seem nearly as simple and straightforward as it had done the night before.

Mr Milady sighed and gazed beyond me out of the window. 'My dear, if only we knew!' Not even the great Montague Cayke's Imperial Players had ever played anything like it. I had, it seemed, been appointed to discover the unknown terms of a wealthy stranger's Will, for only when his intentions had been uncovered could they be put into practice. A vast fortune apparently to be disposed of, here in Knibden: *Appoint someone on the day of my burial*, the man had written, in the letter subsequently found on his person, *to ruthlessly seek out the Truth, and when that Truth is known, so shall my will be. This is my last Will and Testament.* He had not signed the letter but referred to instructions already lodged with the bank. These had, on examination, borne out his peculiar missive.

'There is no doubt about it, Hester Jones, *you* must be that someone.' Michael Milady smiled at me. 'I am sure you are capable of being totally ruthless . . .'

3

Dickie Paisley and his Band

As Michael Milady and I now lapsed into a tired, thoughtful silence, eager voices could be heard outside the room. The door was thrown open and two women came in but they did not advance far enough beyond the doorway to see us. 'You'll never believe this,' one of them was saying. 'They *did* manage to find someone – a Miss Hester Jones!'

'Well, I never! You *do* surprise me.'

'There'll be a lot more surprises before this business is over. Not all pleasant ones, I'll be bound.'

'Oh, I don't know – *someone*'ll come out of it nicely. *Very* nicely . . .'

'Who, though?'

'That's the question – and that's *her* job now. Dripping wet she was, all over the carpet.'

'The swan that came into the Swan, eh!'

'More of an ugly duckling by the sound of it. I'd left by the time she arrived. No one knows the girl.'

'They wouldn't, would they? Not with her being someone-who-isn't-someone.'

'She's staying here at the Gallimore.'

'Nothing but the best for our Miss Jones.'

'I was hoping to catch a glimpse.'

'Maybe they'll buck up a bit round here. Just look at the state of this room! When you think what the Gallimore used to be like.'

'What must the owner have thought when he saw?'

'No wonder it killed him!'

The pair roared with laughter. 'Better not let Mr Mason hear you – you know the pride he takes. He'll have us both thrown out.'

'Hmm! Mr Mason didn't even get the dead guest to sign in the Gallimore's register.'

'They'd given up keeping proper records. With so few people staying these days.'

'That's no excuse! Think what bother would have been saved if we knew *who* the man was – even if we don't yet know who he's left his money to.'

'Or why. It's all very odd.'

'The dead guest was obviously keen to hide his identity. I reckon if Mr Mason *had* asked the stranger his name, he'd only have made one up. As it is, at least we *know* we *don't know*. There won't be any false trails.'

'If you ask me, our guest had the whole thing carefully worked out. He was a clever man.'

'He's certainly got us guessing.'

'Which is what he wanted.'

'But, *who* could he have been? The Masons say they'd never seen him before, but how can they possibly remember everyone who's ever stayed here?'

'If the Masons had kept a proper register, like in any respectable hotel . . .'

'They are now – it begins with Hester Jones!'

'Talk of closing the stable door!'

'The Gallimore has been a great deal busier since the man died. Mainly with people coming in to have a nosy.'

'Like us, you mean. I hear they've had to quickly take on new staff to cope. And now this Jones woman is staying here . . .'

'Perhaps it will regain something of its former glory!' The speakers sniggered. Then one of them said, 'They used to do wonderful tea-dances at the Gallimore, do you remember? Up in the old ballroom. With Dickie Paisley and his Band!'

'Of course I remember! Of course I remember Dickie.'

'Maybe they will again now – in honour of the dead guest.'

'Maybe this Hester Jones will organize them.'

'I *do* hope so! I wonder what happened to dear old Dickie. We all loved him.'

'There were some that loved him more than others – know what I mean?'

'I do, indeed!' The women nudged one another companionably and then drifted from the room, banging the door shut at last behind them. Michael Milady turned to me, curiously triumphant.

'You see!' he said. 'Everyone is *so* excited. We are all relying on you, Miss Jones.'

'Who were those two?' I asked.

Michael Milady shook his head. 'I haven't a clue! But there isn't anyone in Knibden not taking an interest.'

'And this Dickie Paisley?'

'What of him?'

'Could *he* have been the dead guest? Returning to the site of his band's former triumphs. Dying here, for old times' sake.'

'Maybe.' Milady shrugged. 'How should I know? You'll have to ask around, Miss Jones. Add him to your list of possibilities. But don't forget, I have spent most of my life away from Knibden, there are others who will be far more help to you than I. You must follow up every lead. But first, I suggest you get some rest. You had a long day yesterday and not much sleep last night. You will need your wits about you when you meet the committee.'

'Committee?'

'This afternoon. At three.'

I glanced at my watch. It was already late morning. 'Why the urgency?' I asked.

'Everyone is very keen to get on with things,' Milady said. 'And Mr Williams, the executor, will not stand for any further delay . . .'

I now understood, only my arrival had been left to chance. Within hours of the guest's death, a committee had been formed to superintend his burial and the execution of his peculiar Will. The committee was made up of those who had contributed towards the costs of carrying out the dead stranger's wishes, costs to be reimbursed to them ten times over when the matter was eventually resolved. The people of Knibden had competed to be allowed to take part – the ten-fold return on their stakes had seen to that – so there was plenty of money in the kitty to fund an investigation. 'He was a shrewd man, our guest,' Mr Milady observed.

'And did *you* put any money into this "kitty"?' I asked.

'Me?' Milady laughed. 'Very little – an Imperial Player's pension is not a grand affair. Like you, I have enough to live on so long as I am not extravagant. Besides, a committee needs a chairman who will remain impartial – my stake is so small I am hardly likely to get carried away. But don't forget, although I will not benefit much from the ten-fold return, I could still be a beneficiary under the terms of the Will.'

'Do you think you might be?'

'I can hope, along with everyone else. My mother, after all, came from these parts. Someone might have remembered the wrong done to poor Melinda Milady and sought all these years on, to redress . . . But there will be time to go into that later. You will have to examine everyone's claim. I think you will agree, Miss Jones, that *we* have gone about this whole business in a sensible fashion. Especially when you consider there is no precedent for this kind of thing. No code of conduct to make it easy. We have had to work the procedure out for ourselves.'

'Yes,' I agreed. 'Your arrangements certainly sound sensible enough. And who is on this committee?'

'You met many of them in the Swan last night. At the guest's official wake. They accompanied you back here to the Gallimore after . . .'

'Why wasn't the wake held here at the hotel?' I glanced round the heavily furnished lounge that was so large and dark the morning light flooding in through the tall narrow windows did nothing to brighten its furthest corners. 'If the man died *here*, and you tell me he *owned* the place, wouldn't it have been more . . .'

'Come now, Miss Jones!' Mr Milady chided. 'I thought you told us extravagance was not in your nature. The Gallimore is the grandest establishment hereabouts. A big party here would have cost a pretty penny. It is my job to keep costs down – I can see I'm going to have to keep my eye on you!' He laughed and then bent towards me and, although there was no one else in the enormous room, spoke low. 'The fact is, the Gallimore's manager, Mr Mason, is not at all happy. As you will discover. Mrs Mason too is nervous. They are both greatly upset. A man dying in their charge. The peculiar Will in his pocket. Discovering afterwards that the dead guest had owned the hotel and was their absent employer. It is enough to upset anyone . . .'

'Yes, I suppose it is.'

'It would have been rubbing salt, vinegar, and every other condiment in the Gallimore's dining room, into the wound if we had held the party here. Celebrating our good luck under the

Masons' noses, and obliging them to do all the work! Besides which, the landlord of the Swan, Mr Calderon, is on the committee and offered a good price and a decent discount for the privilege. We are keeping strict accounts of everything we spend. Obviously we expect to incur further expenses before your task is complete. It is only fair everything is added together and the total, multiplied ten-fold, eventually deducted from the estate. The party in the Swan was a necessary formality – free drinks all round, the stranger wrote. Since the occasion resulted in our discovering you, against the odds, it was money well spent. A sound investment. Then there will also be the cost of your keep. No one will expect you to live frugally, Miss Jones. We only ask that you solve this matter for us as speedily as possible.'

'I'll do my best.'

'I'm sure you will.' Milady smiled. 'You are a godsend, my dear!' He took my right hand and raised it elaborately to his lips. 'We might have waited for ever for one such as Hester Jones to walk in through the door . . .'

For a moment I suspected the man was making fun of me. But then, I reflected, you probably could not spend your life as one of Montague Cayke's Imperial Players without some lasting effect. Perhaps I was merely tired, and anything at all – let along Michael Milady – would have seemed exaggerated and strange.

'And now, my dear Hester, I must leave you to rest. The Masons will take you to your rooms. You are to have a suite on the first floor from which you will be able to watch the town. The most expensive, alas, but much the best for the job. Mr and Mrs Mason have been instructed to see to your every need. The committee are agreed, no point penny pinching at this stage.' Michael Milady rang a bell beside the mantelpiece.

Almost at once, a small woman came scurrying in, tying an apron about her waist and apologizing profusely. I was introduced to Mrs Eileen Mason, manageress of the Gallimore Hotel. She looked at me anxiously and, when Michael Milady had gone, she beckoned me to follow her up the wide central staircase of the hotel to the first floor. Along a corridor she produced keys and unlocked an enormous dark oak door. Pushing it open, she stood back and waited politely for me to enter. The first thing I saw was my own cardboard suitcase sitting on top of the wardrobe, looking as if it had always been there. Its few contents were already arranged round the room. 'Let me know if there is anything further you require, Miss Jones,' Mrs Mason whispered breathlessly. 'Perhaps you would care for some breakfast? Or maybe a light lunch, later? You are not now required, I understand, until the committee meets downstairs at three o'clock.'

I thanked her and said that a light lunch just before three would suit me well.

As soon as Mrs Mason had hurried away, I locked the door behind her. I drew the heavy curtains across the windows and flung myself down fully clothed on the bed. Before I fell into the deep, much-needed sleep that I knew must come, I lay for a while in the shadowy darkness, wondering what Hester Jones had gone and let herself in for now.

4

A Pair of Bright Blue Eyes

'May I join you since we are apparently the only diners?'

I glanced up, straight into a handsome pair of bright blue eyes. 'Yes, do!' I said, trying to sound casual. Trying to sound as if Hester Jones dined *à deux* every day of the week. How often my mother and I had watched lone females being joined by men they did not know in tea-rooms and on buses, my mother nudging me rather vulgarly and saying that dining *à deux* would happen to me if she were not there. Implying that I wished she were *not* there so that strange men would come up and start conversations that would lead on, over the jam sponge and custard, I knew not where. 'Talk of sponge and custard,' she would laugh. 'Your face!'

'I have only just arrived,' the owner of the bright blue eyes explained as he seated himself at my table and shook out a napkin which he spread neatly across his lap. 'I did not expect them still to be serving lunch.' He folded his arms and looked at me. He was older than he had first appeared, with an easy, attractive manner as if he took it for granted the whole world would fall in love with him. I, of course, had no intention of doing any such thing. He waited for me to speak and when I did not do that either, he said, 'I like to come to Knibden at this time of year. I always stay at the Gallimore Hotel.'

'Do you? What for?'

He laughed. 'A holiday. To walk, fish, visit my mother. Oh, I beg your pardon. The name's Roger. Roger Ambrose.' He stretched a firm confident hand across the table. I shook it with a confidence I did not entirely feel.

'I'm Hester Jones,' I said. I was sitting in the dining room waiting for the late light lunch Mrs Mason had offered. 'I'm a stranger here,' I explained. 'I arrived yesterday evening. Quite by chance . . .'

Roger Ambrose smiled pleasantly. 'Well, *I* was brought up in Knibden. I know the town inside out!'

'So you're not another stranger then, Mr Ambrose?'

'I should say not! My mother lives just round the corner. At the schoolhouse – she is the headmaster's wife.'

'Then why stay in a hotel?'

The bright blue eyes played momentarily on my face. If he thought my question impertinent, he answered it nevertheless: 'As a small boy I always wanted to stay at the Gallimore. I often used to stand out in the Market Square eating penny chews and gazing in at all the lights and lovely furniture. I thought it a fairy-tale palace and dreamed of staying here one day. Now I can afford to, I come whenever I can. I relive something that never . . . I often think we spend our adult lives doing the things we wanted to do as children.'

'When *I* was younger, I wanted to be an arithmetic teacher. Now look at me!' I giggled.

'Yes, look at you!' my companion said, with somewhat excessive appreciation.

Another woman in my place might have blushed. She'd lean across the table and tap the handsome wrist. 'Flattery gets you everywhere, Mr Ambrose!' she would lisp rather silkily while my mother tut-tutted and I stared studiously in the opposite direction. And yet, as I spread butter thickly on my bread roll, I could not help thinking how nice it might have been if I could have included someone like Roger Ambrose in the account I'd given of myself. I had deliberately glossed over Philip Peebles's unprepossessing looks and manner. The dandruff on his collar, the smell of milk in the stuffy parsonage that had combined unpleasantly with the oily sweat about his person. His podgy hands and simpering smile, not to mention the apologetic way he lived under his bossy older sister's thumb. What a contrast to my present self-assured companion! I allowed myself to gaze across the table into Roger Ambrose's beautiful blue eyes. Wasn't I employed to investigate *everyone*? Delve into their darkest secrets, discover the precise nature of their interest in the dead guest!

The waitress who brought in my lunch just then was gratifyingly surprised to find Mr Ambrose seated at my table. She glanced at me as she handed him a menu. Without looking at it, he waved his hand and ordered the same light lunch I was eating.

'Our tastes coincide,' I remarked when the girl had gone.

'So it would seem.' Roger Ambrose looked over at me, and paused. 'It's very strange, you know . . .'

'What is?'

'That girl.' He pointed towards the door. 'There never were *girls* at the Gallimore before. Only Mr and Mrs Mason – and there was never enough to do to keep *them* busy. Yet today, they hadn't got a room ready when I arrived – they said they were rushed off their feet. Mostly when I've stayed here, I have been the only guest.'

'Really? But how can an empty hotel afford to stay open?' Why hadn't the Gallimore gone out of business long ago?

Mr Ambrose shrugged. 'The Gallimore Hotel has always been one of life's mysteries.' He laughed loudly. A little too loudly. Then he changed the subject. 'And you, Hester Jones? Are you in Knibden on holiday? With friends? Passing through, maybe?' I shook my head to each of these suggestions. 'Then you are on your way somewhere exciting? You certainly look as if you might be.'

'No. I *was* on my way to Penzance, but that was just a name on a railway destination board. I now have work to do here in Knibden.' Then, as I chomped my lettuce, egg, tomato and radish salad I told Roger Ambrose all about the mysterious guest at the Gallimore who had recently died, whose Will I was to endeavour to determine.

'How very extraordinary!' he said when I had finished. 'A bit like a game of Cluedo.'

'I suppose it is.'

'What a splendid pursuit – how I envy you. No wonder the town seems different. I sensed the excitement the moment I arrived. Guess the Guest! or is it – Hunt the Heir to the Millionaire!'

'It could be an heiress,' I pointed out. 'The dead man might have left all his money to a woman.'

'Of course he might.' Roger Ambrose smiled at me.

'Not *me* though,' I said quickly. 'That is the point about me, Mr Ambrose. I am someone-who-is-not-someone.'

'Well you look like "someone" jolly important to me, Miss Jones. I'll tell you what. While I am here on my holiday, I could help you play your game. What fun we shall have – it'll be something to do when it's raining. Better than tramping about the countryside getting mud on my boots, or sitting beside the canal with my rod, getting soaked through.'

'I wouldn't want to keep you from your fishing,' I said.

'This will only be another kind of fish, Miss Jones. And who knows what we may catch!'

'And your mother? Aren't you in Knibden to spend time with *her*?'

'I can't be under my dear mamma's feet *every* hour of the day.'

'I suppose, since your mother lives in the town, she – or you yourself even, Mr Ambrose – could be beneficiaries? *You* might inherit the dead guest's fortune.'

'How splendid that would be!' Roger Ambrose's face lit up as if someone had flicked a switch. 'Highly unlikely though, I fear. I never was a lucky fellow – except for meeting you here like this today.' He laughed, delighted at his own gallantry. 'But who could possibly die and leave me, or my poor mamma, a load of money? Still, it is an exciting thought. And something to think about. This has given me quite an appetite, Miss Jones – Hester, if I may . . .'

'Of course, you may!'

'And you must call me "Roger", since we are now a team.' At this point the waitress returned with Mr Ambrose's lunch. He and I paused like two conspirators until she had left the room. Then, despite his avowed appetite, Roger Ambrose chased the lettuce, egg, tomato and radish idly round the plate with his fork. 'Suppose I tell you, Hester, that my mother worked at one time here in the hotel – when I was a baby. When the Gallimores were still in charge.'

'Really? The Gallimores were people, then?'

'Most certainly. You see that picture . . .' Roger Ambrose pointed with his fork over my shoulder and I turned to look at an enormous oil painting hanging at the far end of the dining room behind me. Five beautiful young women with long golden tresses wearing magnificent ball gowns stood clustered round a seated gentleman. '*Those* are the Gallimores. Painted in their prime – on New Year's Day, 1900. Right at the beginning of this century. The Gallimores were by far the most illustrious family in these parts. That old man with the spectacles and whiskers is Sir Mayhew

Gallimore, MP for Knibden. He was an author too, as famed in his day as Disraeli or Dickens. That's why he's got a book in his lap.'

'Which is his wife?'

'Oh no – those are *all* his daughters – the Five Beautiful Gallimores, they were known as. They were famous for miles around. Their mother, the first Lady Gallimore, died giving birth to a sixth daughter – she was so mortified at not coming up with the heir Sir Mayhew needed, both she and the baby girl did the decent thing. They were buried together and Sir Mayhew went off to London leaving the Five Beautiful Gallimores to grow up, and live it up, here on their own in Knibden with only servants to look after them. The Five were wild and wayward in their youth. The painter of that picture was in love with the eldest, Sarah, the girl on the left in pink – but although she loved him, she refused to marry him. He was an artist covered in paint, and she was the heiress to Sir Mayhew's fortune.'

'They all look pretty disdainful.'

'They got paid out in the end. Shortly after that picture was painted, Sir Mayhew married again, fathered a son and snuffed it. His whole estate went to the baby boy and the Five Beautiful Gallimores were suddenly destitute. Their suitors slunk away. What made it worse was that the boy's mother, their step-mother, the second Lady Gallimore, was slightly younger than them. A music hall artiste Sir Mayhew had taken a fancy to in London. Anyhow, the second Lady Gallimore rapidly became the talk of Knibden for her step-daughters' suitors all slunk back, this time to pay court to *her*. But the rich widow wasn't having any of them. And when the Gallimore money was spent she turned the house, Gallimore Hall as it was then, into a hotel and set the Five Beautiful Gallimore girls to earn their keep by running it. Lady Gallimore and her spoilt son, Gurney – Sir Mayhew's son and heir – and her two other younger daughters, who were probably not Sir Mayhew's but no one ever said, worked the five sisters to the bone.'

'Gracious!'

'You must ask my mother. She will tell you about them. They were still here when she first came to the town. She had a job for a short time working in the Gallimore's kitchens. But perhaps you

41

have met my mother already? And my step-father – the head-master, Edmund Veitch.'

'I may have met them last night in the Swan. There were so many people, and Mr Milady . . .'

'Edmund Veitch and Michael Milady do not like each other.'

'And you, Mr Ambrose? Do *you* dislike your step-father, Edmund Veitch? Is that why you are staying here and not with him and your mother at the schoolhouse?'

'How quick you are, Miss Jones! I can see we will all have to watch out!' Roger Ambrose laughed loudly, and popped a radish into his mouth. When he had finished crunching it, he said, 'But no, in this instance you are wrong. Just because I prefer to stay here at the Gallimore you must not think there is any animosity between us. Quite the contrary. My own poor pater died when I was a few months old – which is why, I suppose, Gurney Galli-more inheriting a fortune from a father *he* never met has always interested me. Not that *I* inherited anything – my mother was left penniless. Luckily Edmund Veitch came to our rescue. Why don't you come with me now, I'm sure they'd both like to see you.'

'But I am meeting the committee at three o'clock.'

'Committee! What committee?' Roger Ambrose was as sur-prised as I had been.

'They are to superintend my work. Michael Milady is the chair-man. Maybe Mr Veitch is coming.'

'I'm sure he will be. Edmund Veitch wouldn't miss a committee – exactly the kind of thing he would enjoy.' Roger Ambrose laughed again, good-naturedly. 'Besides, he'll want to keep an eye on Michael Milady.'

'You know Mr Milady?'

'Of course. Not that anyone knows much about him. He re-appeared in Knibden some years back, having been away all his life round the world. There are those who can remember him acting here as a small boy, at the Knibden Alhambra . . .'

'As Aladdin's younger brother,' I joined in. 'With Miss Rose Meldrew and Harry, the Astonishing Prancing Dog. Mr Milady came back to Knibden after a lifetime away, rather like the man who has died. He pointed this similarity out himself.'

'Did he now! How delightfully curious it all is. I suppose

Milady hopes as much as anyone to inherit the dead stranger's fortune?'

'He wants the bright lights of Montague Cayke's Imperial Players to shine again over Knibden's Alhambra. He wants his former companions fetched from their places of retirement across the Seven Seas.'

'But the old theatre has been boarded up for as long as I can remember. It would need completely rebuilding.'

'Maybe it *will* be rebuilt. Now there is the money.'

Roger Ambrose stared at me. Perhaps he thought me star struck and pictured me queuing for hours in the rain outside the stage door, hoping to catch a glimpse of Mr Fonteyne swaggering away from the Alhambra after a performance. My companion narrowed his eyes. 'It is as if Michael Milady came back to the town despite all those years away, knowing this might happen. Don't you think so, Hester?'

'I hardly . . .'

'It might be as well if we keep *my* part in your investigations secret. I can probably be more help to you snooping about on the quiet.'

'And do *you* have hopes, Mr Ambrose?' I inquired lightly.

'I don't know what you mean!' he replied.

'The Gallimore Hotel is part of the inheritance. It belonged to the dead guest. If *you* were to inherit – and you have made a point of telling me that your mother worked here when you were a baby – why, the fairy-tale palace you loved so much as a child would all be *yours*. You could come *inside* to eat your penny chews.'

Roger Ambrose rose abruptly from the table. 'I must go!' he said. 'My mother will be expecting me.'

I finished the rest of my lunch and by the time the waitress returned to clear the plates, it was a few minutes to three. 'He's gone, then?' she asked unnecessarily. My fellow diner's lettuce, egg, tomato and radish salad lay largely uneaten.

'He can't have been hungry,' I said.

'Nice looking, don't you think?'

'I really wouldn't know!'

The girl bent her head so I could not see her face.

'Have you been working here long?' I asked.

'I was taken on this morning,' she mumbled.

'Now then, Doris!' Mrs Mason had come noiselessly into the room. The girl retrieved the last of the plates and hurried away. 'You'll have to forgive us – she's only new, I haven't got her trained up yet. But she really shouldn't be chatting to the guests.'

'That's all right. I think I am meant to talk to everyone, delve into their secrets, divine their innermost thoughts. Perhaps young Doris will be the one to inherit the fortune!'

Mrs Mason's face remained impassive although her eyes watched me warily.

'Where is Mr Mason?' I asked. 'I have not yet met the manager of the Gallimore Hotel.'

'He's keeping himself occupied, Miss. He's not at all happy about this business, but I expect he will talk to you in good time. We can neither of us throw much light on the matter. We are strangers ourselves. We came to Knibden about ten years ago, having answered an advertisement in a newspaper. We have loved the Gallimore, like a child. The rest of them are only interested in inheriting a fortune, while we . . .'

'You?'

'Well, there's uncertainty now. The fate of the hotel we have worked so hard for all these years is in the balance. Who knows what may happen next? Daniel Mason is a worried man.'

'I'm sorry,' I said, although it was hardly for *me* to apologize. It was impossible not to feel sympathy, she looked so anxious. 'It must be awkward,' I said soothingly.

5

Those to Whom Much is Given

'Take a seat, Miss Jones. Let me introduce everyone. Many of us you have already met.'

A long table had been placed down the centre of the room. Faces I vaguely recognized from the night before were ranged along one side and opposite them stood an empty chair on which Mr Milady indicated I should sit. He, meanwhile, took up his position in the middle of the row of committee members as if presiding over a formal feast. He pointed his finger up and down the table mentioning names: Mr Matchett of Buckworth & Matchett's, the printers, was there; Mr Calderon – the landlord of the Swan, a large hearty man who had been busy the night before handing out drinks from behind his bar; the two ladies, Verity Willow and Belle Quinn I remembered, and others too, too many smiling faces to take in at once. There was a rather floridly dressed, short plump woman with silver hair called Norah Bird. And the three men, the builder, Follifoot, Treadgold, the doctor, and the jeweller, Macready, who had sat together the previous night and were sitting together again now. Edmund Veitch, the headmaster, was introduced. He sat down at the far end of the table nearest the door, a pad of paper ready in front of him and a fountain pen poised. They were all smartly dressed. Mr Veitch even had a flower pinned neatly in his button hole. This was clearly an important occasion, the first official meeting of their committee.

Mr Veitch coughed and announced that he would be taking the minutes. There were no apologies for absence, everyone being present – except Mr Williams from the bank who was expected to come later when the bank had closed. William Williams was not, strictly speaking, *on* the committee but, as the dead guest's executor, he would officially need to approve the appointment of Hester Jones. They foresaw no difficulty in this regard, there being no other candidates. Meanwhile, it was his job, nay his

45

pleasure, Veitch said, as committee secretary on this delightful occasion, to welcome Miss Jones.

'It is *our* job this afternoon,' Mr Milady immediately countered, 'to first agree on the workings of this committee. Then tell Hester Jones exactly what we require of her. She cannot be expected to carry out her task unless we give her clear instructions on how to proceed.'

There were murmurs of agreement. I was informed that some members of the committee had put up larger amounts of money than others, but when it came to making decisions, all were to have an equal say. The amount of money to be repaid finally, being ten times the various sums invested, meant that the final share out would be far from equal. Those who had contributed most had the most to gain from a resolution of the dead guest's affairs, whatever that solution turned out to be.

'And, of course,' Mr Matchett added excitedly, 'one of us, at least, stands to benefit substantially. *Someone* has got to inherit . . .'

'At the moment there is no telling who.'

'May I point out,' the elaborately dressed lady, Miss Norah Bird, interrupted shrilly, 'that it is tea time.'

'But we've only just got started, Norah!'

'Miss Bird is right – it *is* tea time . . .'

'No one doubts that.'

'Could we not run to a cup of tea? Out of the kitty.'

'The kitty!' There was considerable indignation at the suggestion, but Michael Milady looked inquiringly up and down the table.

'Well?' he asked.

'Well, what?' barked Veitch.

'The question is, are we to fund refreshments for ourselves? Out of the kitty.'

'Necessary expenses, we said. I, for one, do not regard *tea* as necessary.'

'Here, here!' Matchett agreed with Veitch. He folded his arms across his chest and sat back.

'Miss Jones has only just had her lunch – a Gallimore Hotel lunch!'

'Paid for by us!'

46

'Yes, but don't forget, the committee can put *all* necessary expenses in the ledger,' Norah Bird persisted. 'Repayable, ten-fold.'

'Nothing's repayable until the case is solved. At this rate, it never will be.'

'A cup of tea each will scarcely delay matters.'

'Why not sandwiches, also?' Follifoot put in. 'And coffee. Some will prefer coffee to tea. Let's have a choice.'

'Yeh, why not cakes, and scones with jam?'

'What do you say, Miss Jones?' Milady asked. 'Are you not a little partial to cake?'

'This has nothing at all to do with her – she's not the one paying!' exclaimed Veitch.

'Talk, talk, talk! Refreshments, indeed! What is there to refresh? We haven't *done* anything yet. What about the matter in hand?' Mr Matchett, the printer, was beside himself. 'We are wasting time.'

'It is already ten past three!'

'Am I to write all this into the minutes?' Edmund Veitch asked despairingly.

'No one asked you to take minutes anyway! You took it on yourself . . .'

'Minutes should contain *everything*,' Dr Treadgold pointed out. 'Minute by minute.'

'And *everything* must be done properly. All completely above-board.' His friend Follifoot agreed with a smirk.

'Yes,' said Belle Quinn earnestly. 'It is important we not only *act* fairly in regard to the dead stranger, but are *seen* to do so. By the whole town.'

'Hear, hear!'

'I can't write this fast.' Veitch mopped his brow.

'If only one of us could do shorthand!'

'We should employ a proper secretary.'

'There's no cause to go running up the costs. I dread to think what the final bill came to last night in the Swan!'

'With the incredibly good discount I promised, and all the services of the establishment thrown in for free, the total was just over six hundred pounds,' put in Mr Calderon. 'Very reasonable when you consider . . .'

'Well, that was a nice bit of business for you!' Matchett rounded on the landlord of the Swan, but the affable Mr Calderon only smiled.

'Drinks all round, the guest said. And it was his wake!'

'But *we* were paying . . .'

'Don't you see?' Norah Bird interrupted their quarrel. 'Everything we spend, we'll recoup *ten-fold*. That six hundred pounds automatically becomes six thousand. The more we spend, the more we'll all get back. When this business is concluded. When the Will is proved. The Swan got a nice profit, but so will we! As shareholders in this remarkable venture.'

'But only at the expense of the inheritance.'

'The inheritance is *enormous* – whoever gets it can hardly object . . .'

'If that person were me – and there is no reason at this juncture to suppose it might not . . .'

'And no reason, Mr Veitch, unless you know something the rest of us don't, to suppose that it might!'

Edmund Veitch ignored this. His eyes blazed. 'I should be furious at having to pay out ten-fold for secretaries, not to mention teas taken *by other people*.' He glared at Norah Bird.

'Obviously we must keep the costs down,' Mr Milady said soothingly, 'but modest refreshments when people have given up the afternoon to come to a meeting – a sandwich and a cup of tea, or coffee – I cannot believe whoever inherits the dead guest's fortune will begrudge the rest of us that. *I* certainly wouldn't. Not when we will have been instrumental in seeing that they get what is theirs.'

It was generally agreed, then, that such expenditure was justified.

'We are all of us putting in time, apart from the money,' Norah Bird said. 'And for those of us in business – I run a boutique just across the way, select ladies' fashions, Miss Jones, you should look in, and welcome! – time and money are much the same thing. It is a big sacrifice to close my shop like this for the afternoon – who knows how many customers will arrive only to find Miss Bird's shut and go away grumbling at the inconvenience and never come back.'

Mrs Mason was rung for and the order for refreshments given.

She glanced nervously in my direction for she had probably heard the raised voices from outside the door.

'Don't forget,' Mr Milady pointed out as soon as Eileen Mason had gone, 'the hotel benefits from the extra business, and since the Gallimore will be part of the inheritance . . .'

'That's true! The more business we put the Gallimore's way, the better for whoever inherits.'

'The better for us all, since we will recoup any outlay ten-fold.'

'Let's get spending!' yelled Mr Follifoot.

'What do you say, Miss Jones?'

'It doesn't seem unreasonable,' I replied, more amused than anything.

'Hester Jones takes a lofty view,' Michael Milady observed. 'And that is what we employ her for. She is not one to take sides on little matters, nor will she be swayed by all the petty considerations that must influence the rest of us. We pay her to stand firm in her judgements, and judge Knibden as she sees fit.'

'I reckon Miss Jones is precisely what the dead guest had in mind.'

The committee looked across at me now with new approval. I sat up straight and uncrossed my legs. Milady said, 'While we are waiting for our refreshments, we may as well proceed . . .'

'About time!' This was Mr Matchett.

Milady smiled. 'As I said earlier, it is up to us this afternoon to tell Miss Jones what we expect. Do we, for instance, require her to report back to us regularly, or only when she has finished? Do we ask her to systematically interview the whole town?'

'She is not a police sergeant.'

'She is whatever we make of her.'

'How shall we instruct the girl?'

'Leave it to her. Miss Jones must have her own methods, and so long as she gets on with the job, what does it matter?'

'Quite!'

'Onerous as our task is – getting at the truth must ever be a heavy assignment – I see no reason why we shouldn't make the most of the situation.' Everyone turned in astonishment to the rather refined lady who had not said much until now. Belle Quinn adjusted the little felt hat on her head and gazed round the room with an air of wonderment. 'We should all have a little

49

enjoyment. It is obviously what the dead guest wanted, and it is up to this committee to make sure no one in Knibden feels excluded. We have a duty to keep others, not so fortunate as ourselves, informed of developments. Involve them in the fun, make sure they too . . .'

'We are not public benefactors, Miss Quinn!'

'Oh, but I think we should see ourselves in that light,' Belle Quinn insisted. 'Chance has placed those of us here in this room today in a unique position. We are to witness at first hand the unfolding of this remarkable tale. The dead guest's legacy. And, from those to whom much is given, much must be expected. I believe we *owe* it to the dead guest, to the Gallimore, and to the town, to do all we can to ensure this wonderful Will brightens the lives of our fellow citizens as was surely intended . . .'

'Here, here!' Someone banged on the table.

'Anything *I* can do to assist in this matter, Missie Quinn, regardless of personal gain . . .' Follifoot began.

'Well *I* propose to furnish Hester Jones with a history of Knibden. I will begin by instructing her in the history of the Gallimore Hotel,' Veitch said grandly. 'Gallimore Hall, as it was once. The hotel is obviously at the centre of the whole business.'

'I don't know how you make that out!'

'Some of us should be present. To listen . . .'

'To check . . .'

'Are you suggesting I . . .' The schoolmaster turned red with indignation. 'Facts are facts!' he yelled down the table, note-taking forgotten.

'Facts can be made to alter their faces. To suit the occasion. We all know your wife used to work at the Gallimore. In the old days . . .' This was Follifoot.

'That was a long time ago . . .'

'You obviously expect . . .' Treadgold joined in.

'Please, gentlemen!' Milady intervened. 'This kind of quarrelling gets us nowhere. Besides, there is nothing at this stage to quarrel over – whatever must our poor Miss Jones think! And what if Mr Williams from the bank were to hear? The executor has yet to sanction her appointment and goodness knows what we will do if he doesn't. I do not need to remind you all that, should the unusual Will now be declared null and void, not one of us stands a chance of inheriting the fortune, let alone recouping . . .'

'It won't come to that!'

'If Miss Jones systematically trawls through the town's past, she is bound to find the answer.'

'I am not so sure,' Matchett said. 'The past is gone . . .'

'The past is private! Miss Jones is a stranger . . .'

'The solution has to be *here*. In the *present*. Staring us all in the face.'

'If anyone has any ideas they should speak to Hester Jones.'

'We should *all* speak to Hester Jones. In strictest confidence, of course. Whatever we say to her . . .'

'So long as it isn't well-meaning mumbo-jumbo!' Follifoot snorted at Belle Quinn.

'Miss Willow wishes to speak now,' Mr Milady said. 'She has been trying to get a word in for the last half hour. Verity Willow is our librarian, Miss Jones. She will doubtless assist you if there are any library books you require.'

'Library books! Miss Jones hasn't time to read *library* books!' shouted Matchett.

A pale, soft-spoken woman of middle years, with fine white hair neatly clipped back on both sides of her head like a young girl, spoke up now. 'Actually, Miss Jones, I am only the *assistant* librarian. If there is anything you need from the library, you should speak to George Allendale, our chief librarian. I am sure he would be very pleased to help you.' She hesitated. 'I, I just wanted to say . . .' Her cheeks had turned an unbecoming scarlet.

'Yes, Miss Willow?' Mr Milady prompted gently.

'It's like this: the more I think about the dead guest, the more it seems to me this is like a whodunnit. Only better. We have all the excitement, and mystery, of a corpse . . .'

'Oh I say!'

'Let Verity continue!'

'But instead of looking for a *murderer* in the town, we are seeking someone to benefit. No one is slinking around, dreading being caught by Miss Jones. No culprit is out there busily covering over his tracks. Not one of us need *fear* the conclusion of our investigator's investigations. On the contrary – we are all of us *hoping* to be the one picked out in her identity parade. I mean, oh dear, I'm not saying this very well!' Miss Willow clasped her hands together. The blood had drained from her cheeks. Her clear pale eyes had become uncannily bright, and her voice was reduced to a strangled whisper. 'When there's been a *murder*, people want the crime solved as fast as possible. To prevent the murderer striking again. But this is different. Although it needs to be solved quickly, this is *one off* – we should enjoy every minute. There will never be anything like it, ever again.'

'You don't know that! It might create a vogue – it could become fashionable to write Wills in this way. Miss Jones may find herself much in demand for this kind of work.'

'I think it's a brilliant scheme,' Mr Follifoot shouted out. 'I'm seriously considering writing a new Will and doing much the same thing myself!'

'Yes,' agreed his friend Macready. 'We are all of us in with a chance. Not just the next of kin going in the moment someone dies, and grabbing what they can.'

'Selling it off to burly men in vans . . .'

'*Any one of us* could be the person the guest chose, the one he thought most deserving.'

'But we do not know who the dead man was! How can we possibly find out who he thought deserving? It's absurd.'

'It's mad.'

'It's up to Miss Jones.'

'Come now, it is obvious that there must be one amongst us who treated this guest so well in his lifetime that he wanted to leave them everything . . .'

'Or someone *he* treated so badly he felt it incumbent on him to make amends in this way.'

'Why didn't he just do so then? Why all this bother? Why include Miss Jones? Why involve us all?'

'He has created more of a splash.'

'A sensation!'

'*He* obviously didn't think it would be difficult to discover the answer. No offence Miss Jones, I'm sure you're very competent, and all that, but if someone unconnected with the town can be expected to solve our little mystery, then the truth cannot lie very far below the surface.'

'The truth never does.'

I nodded. 'This must refer to something fairly drastic,' I remarked. 'Something that will readily become apparent.'

'Well said, Miss Jones!'

'She's sharp.'

'The difficulty will be knowing where to start.'

'We must all give Miss Jones every assistance.'

'She must be instructed to write her findings down.'

'She should begin by writing up this meeting. You have gone far too fast for me.' Poor Mr Veitch mopped his brow. He screwed the top back on his fountain pen and clipped it into his breast pocket. 'Like the cavaliers at Knibden Bridge in 1641, I hang up my pikestaff, and admit defeat!'

'Miss Jones, too, has a tendency to overdramatize – have you read her account of herself? *The night I was born a violent thunderstorm rent the sky!* Why on earth would any of us want to know that?'

'I am not at all sure Hester Jones is the person for the job. We need someone level-headed.'

'Down to earth.'

'With a lot more experience of the world.'

'No one level-headed or more experienced would ever have accepted an assignment such as this.'

'It is done now.'

'Who else was there?'

'No point crying over spilt milk.'

'Perhaps we were a bit hasty. Taking the first person who came along.'

'She was the *only* person who came along!'

'The important thing yesterday was to get on with the business. The investigator had to be found on the day of the burial – and we had delayed the burial long enough . . .'

'Shhh!'

'Well, it's true! We waited over a week hoping Miss Jones would come along. But bodies begin to corrupt. Worms start to crawl . . .'

'Oh, please!' Belle Quinn held a handkerchief to her mouth.

'It is all very well criticizing now but at least Miss Jones turned up when we needed her. Unconnected with Knibden. Unconnected with anyone. Someone-who-is-not-someone.'

'So far as we know.'

'What are you saying?'

'Come now – she is the perfect choice,' Belle Quinn smiled at me appeasingly. 'I think *we* should all be very grateful.'

'They are taking their time with our tea,' Norah Bird said.

'The hotel is understaffed – there's a new girl, Doris . . .'

Belle Quinn pushed back her chair and rose to her feet, her face lit by the afternoon sun that streamed at her across the heavily polished table. Lit too by the burning coals of her own inner fire. 'I feel,' she said tremulously as she gazed out of the window into the distance, 'that I am part of something nobler and greater, at last. Something that has gone on all around us. Unknown to anyone, but which will reach out shortly and embrace us all. I cannot now imagine life without this new interest. It seems impossible to me that we could have gone on as we have been all these years. That only last week . . .'

'It is as if we have been waiting for this to happen,' Mr Matchett remarked, picking up on her mood. 'I, too, have felt it.'

'And I.'

Belle Quinn smiled kindly at the speakers. She continued, 'Something new and wonderful has come amongst us . . .'

'Yeh – Hester Jones!' I don't know which of the three said it, Follifoot, Macready, or Treadgold, but the spell was broken. There was a snigger. Miss Quinn faltered, appeared to recollect herself, and sat down.

'Oh I say, this is all a bit . . . Well, with great respect, Miss Quinn, this whole business is *only* about *money*,' Mr Calderon, the landlord of the Swan said. 'One or other of us is going to become very rich. That's all.'

'What do you mean – *that's all*? Isn't that enough?' Norah Bird asked.

We all laughed, all except Belle Quinn. And Verity Willow, who now said dreamily, 'This has *already* made *me* feel rich.'

'You, Miss Willow! Rich?'

Knibden's assistant librarian nodded firmly. 'Yes. It is as though I have inherited something from the guest already. Nothing in my life can ever be the same. Nor would I want it to be.'

There was an awkward silence, then several people murmured, 'I know what you mean!'

Emboldened, Miss Willow went on, 'I feel such possibilities stretching before me. So many things I may be able to do at last. Great changes I would like to make to my life . . .'

'Well, that's true of any of us round this table,' Matchett said. 'We'd all *like* to make changes . . .'

'Changes cost money.'

'There *is* money. Thousands!'

'Millions!'

'But what about all the people in Knibden not actually on your committee?' I asked. 'And not here today. Surely just because they didn't put up some cash to help with the investigation, it doesn't mean they're any less likely to inherit the fortune.'

That sobered everyone up a bit. 'Yes, of course,' Mr Veitch said tersely. 'It could be anyone in the town. *Anyone* at all. And not always the most obvious choice. It could even be one of the children at school, or Beryl Laffety, or Mr Parris . . .'

'Bill Parris!'

'You should speak to William Parris, Miss Jones,' someone said. 'He skulks around the municipal gardens. Digging the flower beds.'

'He dug the dead guest's grave.'

'Only because Sibson asked him to. The man's a wastrel . . .'

'Always into some dodge or other.'

'Oh, I don't think that's fair!'

'These things never are. It is usually the least deserving who get the most. When my grandfather died . . .'

'It could be General Bensusann, then. The old man's loaded already – that great house of his. It would be typical if he . . .'

'Those to whom much is given have a lot already, eh?'

The conversation tailed off as several trolleys laden with sandwiches, cakes, tea and coffee were wheeled into the room, and fallen upon with great eagerness. When the meeting resumed at last, tempers were markedly better.

'I think we are all agreed Hester Jones must be given a free hand,' Michael Milady said. 'She should go about her task unhindered and consult us only as she sees fit. We have appointed her – we must respect her methods.'

'Hear, hear!'

'No point keeping a dog and barking yourself.' This was Veitch.

'I think there should be a tea-dance,' I said, not at all sure why I said it. The words were out before I could check them. 'With Dickie Paisley and his Band.'

'Good gracious!'

'Why on earth?'

'It might reawaken people's memories,' I said. 'It might help . . .'

'The girl's right . . .'

'Dickie Paisley passed on years ago.'

'Dickie Paisley caused no end of trouble . . .'

'There's no way *he* could be the dead guest!'

'But what a splendid idea!' Belle Quinn clapped her hands in girlish excitement. 'If none of you object, and if Miss Jones approves, *I* would be happy to start organizing a tea-dance, right away. In honour of the dead guest.'

'You do that, Miss Quinn,' Milady urged. 'It must be held here at the Gallimore, of course.'

'Up in the old ballroom, like in the old days . . .'

'It should be held here on Saturday.'

'But that's only the day after tomorrow!' Miss Quinn objected.

'A tea-dance on Saturday evening would be just the thing.'

'How can I possibly organize everything in just two days? Music, dancing, flowers, food . . .'

'I'm sure you will manage.'

'We must all give Miss Quinn every assistance.'

'But what about the cost?' This was Matchett.

Just then, though, a tremendous roar came from the road outside. We all turned to the window. Six or seven motorbikes could be seen careering round and round Knibden's War Memorial in the main Square. 'Disgraceful!' cried Veitch. 'They should be stopped.'

'The one in front is the eldest of the Laffety boys.'

'Best ignored,' Milady remarked.

'It's intimidation!'

'They're only young,' breathed Miss Willow.

'How sad they have nothing better to do!' said Miss Quinn.

56

'They'll be able to come to your tea-dance!' Matchett put in sarcastically.

'It's like before,' Norah Bird said in a firm distinct voice. 'Everything is happening just like before.'

'It's nothing like before,' someone contradicted her.

'Before? This has happened before?' I questioned Norah Bird above the din of the bikes outside.

'Oh yes,' Norah Bird adjusted the frilly collar of her dress. 'You, Miss Jones, have been sent here to us. There's no doubt about it. There comes a time in everyone's life, when outside agents are at work, righting the evil man cannot correct by himself. This is a town founded on folly . . .'

'Hester Jones does not need to know this!'

'Yes, she does. Of course she does. Knibden was famous once for its lottery, Miss Jones. You have heard of the Great Knibden Lottery?'

I shook my head.

'Why bring that up?'

'It's the history of Knibden's lottery Mr Veitch should tell Miss Jones. All the ills in this town go back to the lottery . . .'

'Life is a lottery . . .'

'When I was small,' Norah Bird went determinedly on, 'when the Alhambra was still open, when Daddy . . . The Great Knibden Lottery was still held here in the town. All the men bought tickets – only men were allowed to buy tickets – and the tickets all had one of three pictures on, a trumpet, a dragon or a naked woman. This is just like having one of those tickets in your pocket again, knowing you might win a fortune. This time next week, if you are lucky enough to have the right number and the right picture on your ticket, the whole of your life could be transformed, out of all recognition, for ever. There'd be nothing to hold you back then. Nothing to keep you in Knibden. Nothing in the world you could not do – just knowing this might happen was enough to keep you going. It's the same again. All things seem possible – the dead guest has seen to it. He has *deliberately* resurrected the Great Knibden Lottery.'

Norah Bird's words had electrified the room. 'When did these lotteries stop?' I asked.

'The last one was nearly forty years ago.'

'They didn't stop – they *were* stopped,' someone put in.

'They'd been going for hundreds of years,' Veitch said. 'Ever since the Civil War when Knebbeden, or Knibdenne, lost its castle in defence of the King but later gained the right to hold a lottery, by way of compensation.'

'Knibden was famous for its lottery.'

'Knibden was *built* on its lottery.'

'In the end it got out of hand. People used to pour into the town from all over the country, just to take part. Men came to buy tickets, women came to keep an eye on their menfolk, or to take advantage of such a large congregation of men with money in their pockets. There was mayhem . . .'

'A good time was had by all!'

'Knibden became notorious. The lottery raised lots of money for the town but caused more trouble than it was worth.'

'It was worth a great deal.'

'There was a riot.'

'A man was killed.'

'My uncle nearly won the last prize.'

'It destroyed him.'

'It destroyed more than him.'

'I refused to take part.' This was Veitch.

'The Reverend Sibson succumbed to temptation. He bought a . . .'

'And has never been allowed to forget it. It ruined his career.'

'It bankrupted his soul . . .'

'I don't know why the Great Knibden Lottery had to stop – it was such fun!' Norah Bird enthused. 'But now we have *this* instead – this Will. It really is like before, only now the naked women, trumpets and dragons are all rolled into one. We *all* of us have a ticket to win – and this time, Miss Jones, *you* are in charge! Nothing can go wrong. What fun we will have.'

'Oh, hardly!'

'I shall have to be getting along.' Belle Quinn stood up and began hurriedly buttoning her coat. 'I have an appointment at the hairdressers. I am already late.'

'Is that the time?'

'If no one has any more . . .' The meeting began to break up.

'We will all come to you, Miss Jones.' Belle Quinn took me

reverently by the hand. 'And those that do not come of their own accord – you must go to them. We are depending on you, and I know you will not let us down. Meanwhile, *I* will begin preparations for the tea-dance – if you can solve this mystery at short notice, I can certainly organize a few waltzes! You are truly an *inspiration* to us all.'

'A most satisfactory meeting,' others murmured politely as they left.

'Good luck, Miss Jones! Take care of yourself! Goodnight . . .'

'Well done, well done!' Michael Milady said when at last everyone else had gone. 'We are all very satisfied . . .'

'This Great Knibden Lottery,' I began.

Mr Milady chuckled. 'The naked woman, the trumpet and the dragon, all rolled into one! Norah Bird is right enough there. How Montague Cayke loved the Great Knibden Lottery! He always timed the visits of his Imperial Players to the town to coincide with the draw. Cayke's timing, all right! And time enough for that later, Miss Jones. Now to more immediate matters. Mr Williams, the executor, will come from the bank as soon as he is able. He will fill you in on any terms and technicalities. Meanwhile, this room had better become your office. The Gallimore will have to be paid a fee for the use thereof. Out of the kitty, of course. Mr Mason is a stickler – the absent owner, whoever he was, could not have hoped for a more fastidious manager . . .' As Michael Milady was speaking a rather gaunt but impeccably dressed man had come into the room. He smiled a grim thin smile when he heard these last words. Then he coughed.

'The autumn is not a busy time for us here at the Gallimore,' he remarked. 'From late September onwards we can expect little trade. I have been thinking, if this had to happen in the hotel, now is as good a time of year as any. It was almost thoughtful of the unknown guest to have died when he did.'

Milady swung round. 'Mr Mason,' he said. 'Allow me to introduce Miss Hester Jones.'

59

6

Stolen Tranquillity

'We meet at last,' I remarked.

'A place like this takes a lot of running,' Mr Mason protested as soon as Michael Milady had gone. 'This business has given us a great deal of extra work.'

'I can see that,' I said.

'My wife and I are professionals. We have managed hotels all our working lives. This stranger's death is the first on premises run by ourselves.'

'Hotels must probably expect to lose the occasional guest,' I answered him chattily.

'But *not* hotels where *we* are concerned. Our assiduity in such matters is renowned.'

'I'm sure it is. You cannot surely be blaming yourselves?'

'Ah well!' the aggrieved Mr Mason now conceded, 'it *is* a fairly regular occurrence, death.' He eyed me strangely. 'You want to watch yourself,' he said after a pause.

'What do you mean?' For a moment I wondered if Daniel Mason, manager of the Gallimore Hotel in Knibden, was threatening me.

'Only what I say. It's a strange place, Knibden. You're not from round here are you?'

'No. I fell asleep on a train . . .'

'Even so . . .' Mr Mason contemplated me dourly. He shook out his wrists and straightened his cuffs. Evidently he took the man's death personally. By his reckoning, any guest at the Gallimore should always leave the place alive. 'I knew there was something odd about the man from the moment he arrived.' Mason narrowed his dark watchful eyes. 'Just as I know there is something very odd about *you*.'

'Me? Well, *I* have no intention of dropping dead with a letter in my pocket!' I assured him with a quick smile.

Mr Mason shook his head at my flippancy. 'No good can come

of this,' he mumbled accusingly. 'And if any harm should befall my hotel, I will hold *you* personally responsible.'

'I didn't create this absurd situation!' I felt rather angry at being blamed for the notions of a dead man I had never met.

'You are upholding the scheme by going along with it, Miss Jones,' Mason said. 'Someone-who-is-not-someone, indeed! You will be the *someone* responsible for any outcome . . .'

'What "outcome" can there be?'

Daniel Mason shrugged. 'Time will tell! But, as I say, you want to watch yourself. We're strangers too, don't forget. My wife and I only came to Knibden ten years ago – it's an odd, unstraightforward . . .'

At this point, Mrs Mason put her head round the door. 'You are wanted on the telephone, dear,' she told her husband. 'More inquiries!' she sighed, pausing in the doorway as she waited for him to go. When we heard a door slamming in the distance, she came nimbly into the room and sat down. 'Don't take any notice of Daniel, Miss Jones,' she whispered, tapping her small neat fingers nervously on the table. 'He's bound to be upset. The Gallimore means so much to him, it's more than a hotel. It has all been such a shock. He blames himself.'

'What for?'

'For one thing, we have only ever dealt with the bank. Now, of course, we wonder why we never insisted on meeting the owners. Or on knowing, at least, *who* they were. It would not have been unreasonable to ask who our employers were. But the truth is, it suited us. We have both been content all these years not to see them. They never came near the place and we were able to more or less forget they existed. The Gallimore was as good as our own for all the interference. And now: this! It's like a punishment.'

'Does Mr Mason have hopes?' I asked bluntly.

Mrs Mason sighed. 'I wish he had! Until this business Daniel Mason was a contented man. If he hoped for anything, it was only what all hotel managers hope for – that each day should run at least as smoothly as the last.'

'And you, Mrs Mason, do you have hopes?'

Eileen Mason smiled a private smile. 'I have,' she confided, 'but they are not hopes Daniel Mason might share. They are not

61

hopes anyone in Knibden can know about. They date back to long before we ever had anything to do with the town. Or the Gallimore. They can have nothing at all to do with the dead guest.'

And then she told me. Eileen Mason had been Eileen Mahoney when she'd come to England following the advice of an older sister who'd been kind enough to give her money for the fare. A girl is unusually susceptible to an older sister's counsel and money from her purse at such times, but the seventeen-year-old Eileen had not done what her sister had told her to do next. Instead, she had taken a job at a pleasant seaside hotel where it happened Daniel Mason had been the manager. She'd impressed him by working hard all through a particularly busy summer. Guests had commented to him, even, on her helpfulness, picking her out from among his other staff so that, although he was busy and she was quiet, Mason had noticed young Eileen Mahoney going diligently about her duties.

Every night during that long summer, Miss Mahoney had lain in her bed in the little room at the top of the hotel, listening to the warm sea lapping the shore far below, and feeling the first stirrings of the life growing within her. When at last this interlude of stolen tranquillity ended – for her condition was no longer concealable – Mr Mason had called Eileen into his glass-partitioned office and handed her her wages. He'd added a little on top on account of how hard she had worked and the regret he felt at the necessity.

The desperate girl had broken down then, and wept; Daniel Mason gave her his handkerchief. That would normally have been an end to it – but, as Eileen Mahoney dried her eyes, she had begun in a soft lilting voice like the buttery honey served in silver-plated dishes at breakfast in the hotel's dining room, to tell the manager Mason a lie. She mentioned one of the early-season guests, a married man who had stayed two weeks with his wife and five noisy children early on that summer, taking advantage of the cheap early-season rates. Taking advantage also of Miss Mahoney. One morning while his wife and noisy children were braving the early-season breezes that blew off the sea, riding reluctant donkeys still fat from the winter months along the sands, the man had returned to the hotel on some pretext and come upon Eileen fetching fresh linen out of a cupboard at the top of the back stairs. He had shoved the girl roughly forward on top of the folded sheets. Stifling her protests with some of the starched linen to hand, he'd ripped open the ribbons that held her aprons.

Mason stared at the sobbing chambermaid and struggled to recall that early-season guest. He recollected the particularly generous tip the man had left at the end of his cheap-rate stay. 'An unusually accommodating hotel,' the guest had enthused producing several handfuls of coins from his pocket as an assortment of suitcases, shrimp nets, tin buckets and spades was being packed into a waiting taxi. His wife stood at his side, smiling and nodding, while their five noisy children clambered on top of each other like shrimps in a bucket, smearing greasy fingerprints all over his glass partitions. 'Your staff, and particularly the young Irish chambermaid, have given great satisfaction,' the man had said. At the time, Mason had merely regarded the big tip as a good omen for the summer to come but now, as he watched the girl weeping into a handkerchief that had itself been starched and pressed, and housed in the offending linen cupboard, Daniel Mason sighed. You could manage a hotel and hire your staff with all the care in the world, but what control did you have over guests who came and went, and did as they pleased, simply because they had the means to pay?

Mason had stood at his window and watched Eileen Mahoney leave. All through the rough winter that followed, when the rooms of the empty hotel were being repainted and blistering winds howled along the deserted beaches, Daniel Mason had been unable to forget his last sight of her. For the first time in his professional career, he found himself wondering where a girl he'd dismissed so summarily could have gone. When, the following spring, Miss Mahoney turned up in his glass-partitioned office, without the burden of a full womb, or carrycot, he had handed her a fresh set of aprons and told her how all the rooms had been repainted in her absence. He did not ask what had happened about the baby. Nor had she ever told him.

The Masons' wedding had been executed one day that summer in the short gap hotels enjoy after breakfast, when all the beds have been made but preparations do not need to start yet for lunch. It was celebrated during the afternoon with the cutting of an iced cake in the hotel lounge. Slices were handed round to all the guests present who were delighted by a whiff of romance in the hotel in which they happened to be staying. 'You'll never guess what!' they would write on their postcards home.

The young Mrs Mason did not tell her new husband how the moment he'd left the room, the old man who'd spent the week in the corner gazing grumpily out at the rain, had informed the other guests that the hotel manager probably got married *every week* in order to provide diversion for bored guests. The women had protested vociferously, but the man held firm, adding that Mason would be under instructions from the owners to go through such a charade whenever the weather was bad. If they came back next week, and if the clouds did not lift, they would find another iced cake being cut and the man embarking on yet another lifetime of bliss with yet another of the sweet pale girls.

'Gracious!' the women said then, and began calling rather unpleasantly to Eileen for further slices of free cake. 'You learn something new every day . . .' they would scribble to their loved ones, on those postcards home.

Over the years, the Masons had worked their way up, successfully managing lesser hotels where the state of the linen was kept second to none, until ten years ago they had been appointed to take charge of the Gallimore. They had answered an advertisement in the hoteliers' press and been interviewed in Knibden by a Mr Fechnie from the bank. The Masons had expected to go on running the Gallimore for the rest of their working lives, retiring most likely in the town, in due course. Nowadays Mrs Mason, who was considerably younger than her husband, did most of the work while the elderly Mr Mason sat behind the wooden desk in the entrance hall keeping his practised eye on things. And all the while Eileen Mason ran up and down stairs, and washed and starched the Gallimore's sheets and aprons, she recalled the face and feel of the baby boy she had handed over all those years ago, ten minutes after he'd been born. She had named the boy 'Donald' as she kissed him 'goodbye', but this Mr Mason had never known.

'He must be out there *somewhere* in the world!' she said wistfully now. 'If only you would find him for me, Miss Jones.' Whenever young men checked into the Gallimore, wanting somewhere out of the way for their honeymoons or young men's gallivantings, she would look at them carefully, calculating their ages, hoping to detect signs in them of her long-lost baby. Donald would have been called something else, of course, by whoever had taken charge of him, taking him away from the room beyond the room in the whitewashed home run by whitewashed nuns where she had gone to give birth.

Mrs Mason's habit of letting herself into guestrooms, pretending to close curtains or rearrange flowers, had been largely responsible for the Masons' reputation for assiduousness. The reputation that had helped them get taken on at the Gallimore. Many a fanciful girl had woken in the dark to find the hotel manager's wife peering down at the man beside her. These maidens sensibly shut their eyes again tight and pretended to be asleep until the peculiar old woman went away. No girl had ever mentioned the incident in the morning, not liking to make a fuss, nor able to deny absolutely that she might have been dreaming.

'The man, the guest who died, Mrs Mason. Are you telling me that *he* could have been your . . .'

Mrs Mason shook her head firmly. There was no way the dead guest had been her Donald. 'Yet . . .' She paused.

Mr and Mrs Mason were among the few in Knibden to have actually met the anonymous guest, and later seen his corpse before it was sealed into its coffin. He had arrived inconveniently late on Saturday night. Daniel had shown him up to his room. The guest had asked to be allowed to lie in. Eileen Mason had not let him lie in. She had gone to his room at first light on Sunday and, something in the angle of his head on the pillows reminding her of baby Donald, she had impulsively tried to rouse him from his slumbers. But the man was not asleep, and did not respond. Mrs Mason had no idea of course that this guest had been the owner of the Gallimore, staying with them incognito, or she might have been more circumspect about creeping round his room. In any case, when she opened the curtains to let the dawn light into the room, she had seen the dead man was far too old and did not in any way resemble Donald. Or anyone else she had ever known. Neither the early-season guest with five children who had left a big tip – but never laid a finger on her. Nor the fellow back in Ireland who had walked the young Eileen home from a fiddle-dance, taking hold of her hand in the moonlight and leading her into the clover patch behind his pig sheds.

'I shook him, Miss Jones,' Mrs Mason confessed in a whisper. She had shaken a corpse – which had shaken her.

'The father of your child,' I asked, 'what became of him?'

Mrs Mason laughed. 'Why, Miss Jones, can't you guess? He married my older sister – that was why she was so keen to get me out of the way, she gave me the fare to England. He died many years back but she still writes occasionally to remind me how she once lent me money when I was desperate. I send her little sums when I can. She does not know I did not follow the second part of her advice: I never went to the house in the back streets of Liverpool, near where the ferries come in. I got work in a seaside hotel. I met Daniel Mason. He married me out of pity, which is as good a reason as any, and together we have ascended the ladder of our profession. Until we ended up here, in charge of the Gallimore . . .'

'And what about you and Mr Mason? If baby Donald ever does come back, will there be half brothers or sisters for him to discover?'

'Daniel and I never had children – they would not be good for a hotel. We are professionals. The welfare of the establishments we have managed has always come first. It must be so. And now you can understand the calamity this has been. No guest ever died in our care before . . .' She began to weep.

Mr Mason returned. He looked in amazement from his weeping wife to me. 'There's a Mr William Williams from the bank to see you, Miss Jones,' he said stiffly, placing a hand on his wife's small hunched shoulders. 'The dead guest's executor . . .'

7

The Executor

'I am, in actual fact, a newcomer to this town, like yourself.' William Williams eyed me warily, weighing me up as if Hester Jones were some tamed creature he didn't quite trust. 'My predecessor at the bank, Mr Fechnie, apparently agreed to the arrangements a long time back,' he explained as he sat down. Mr Williams looked tired and uncomfortable. He blew his nose and loosened his collar. Then he sniffed indignantly. 'I don't mind telling you, Miss Jones, this whole business has given me great cause for concern. Even before the guest died, I was having sleepless nights, worrying . . .' He broke off.

'You knew about the dead guest's Will *in advance*, then? This has not all come as a big surprise, the way it has to everyone else.'

William Williams nodded glumly. 'I knew all right,' he said, shuffling his feet and taking a handkerchief from his pocket to mop his brow. 'When I arrived in Knibden, just over a year ago, I found I had inherited confidential files. Files not known about by head office. Files I was charged, in a handwritten confidential memo from the late Mr Fechnie, not to mention to anyone. Not even to my superiors. Peculiar documents, in short, that should never have been written, which have sat in the drawer of my desk, like a time bomb ticking away under me.' Williams cracked his hands together. 'A time bomb that has now *gone off*! Theodore Fechnie, I soon discovered, had been a law unto himself. It was my misfortune to step into his shoes. What was I to do? Break a bank manager's code of honour, and betray my predecessor? Or let down the bank?'

'What did you do?'

'As most men do – I simply hoped I would not have to *do* anything. When the bank honoured me by giving me a branch of my own, and sent me and my wife to Knibden, I naturally wanted everything to run as smoothly as possible. I was determined not to show any weakness by referring back for instructions, or asking for help or advice. At first, all went well – very well indeed. Then the guest died and I suddenly had the choice of seeming surprised and going along with something preposterous. Or putting my foot down and upsetting everyone. I never really had that choice. By the time I, as a newcomer in the town, found out what had happened at the Gallimore, it was already too late. The business had found favour. Everyone was excited, and talking about what they would do if the enormous fortune came to them. A committee had been formed, with Michael Milady – for some reason – in charge. I, alone, had misgivings . . .'

'I don't see why, Mr Williams, since you evidently disapprove of the odd arrangements, you don't just say so. Put an end to the whole thing right away. As the dead guest's executor, I'm sure you have the authority . . .'

'Oh yes, I have the *authority*! Simply scratch "Refer to Drawer" across the business and send it back, you say?' Mr Williams twisted in his chair and struggled to remain polite. 'If the dead guest's Will were *now* to be declared null and void, on account of any intervention by *me*, the chances are the whole of his estate would be forfeited. No one in Knibden would benefit. Then where would that leave the bank? If I disappoint the whole town by depriving everyone of the chance to inherit, imagine the damage it would do. I would be remembered for the rest of time as the bank manager who deliberately went about sabotaging his customers' chances of becoming rich! Surely you can see I cannot take that risk. My hands have been tied from the outset.' William Williams frowned. 'But you, Miss Jones . . .'

'Me?'

'You turned up here of your own accord, and agreed to take on the job, *voluntarily*! I cannot think why.' Clearly Hester Jones now represented all the irregularity and disruption this man disliked about the dead guest's eccentric Will.

'I . . . I was persuaded into it,' I mumbled. 'I had nothing better . . .'

Mr Williams and I contemplated one another. I saw him soften a little. 'You needed employment, I suppose,' he said pityingly. 'In that respect, you are not so different from me. But *I* was *sent* here. From the city branch. It was meant to be promotion.' William Williams remembered rather grimly how he and his wife had once looked forward to coming to Knibden. 'I was an assistant manager at the city branch, but I never assisted in anything like this. There are no head office guidelines or directives applicable, I am left entirely to follow my own judgement. Even Mrs Williams, who supports me always in all things, thinks I have made a mistake. She is annoyed, as I am, that I have been put in this intolerable position. And yet, what troubles me most about this whole business is the knowledge that if *I* had been the first on the scene, and had found the dead guest's letter and could have foreseen all the bother it would cause, I might easily have been tempted to overlook a client's instructions, this once . . .' William Williams shuddered. 'By the time I received Mason's phone call too many people in the town had got their hopes up. A committee had been formed. A death certificate obtained. Signed very helpfully by Dr Treadgold. Cause of death, in case you're wondering: cardiac arrest. No suspicious circumstances. It might have been easier for me if there were! Arrangements had already been made for the dead guest to be buried in hallowed ground. The Reverend Sibson, vicar of St Redegule's, apparently considered this the least he could do for a man who chose to die within earshot of his bells. The only problem was the someone-who-was-not-someone who needed to be found on the day of the burial. They had delayed the burial long enough. And then, just when I hoped there would be an end to the matter, without my having to raise a finger, you showed up, in the nick of time.' He grimaced.

'Mr Williams,' I asked, 'do you really have no idea who the dead man was, or why he acted as he did?'

'That is *your* job. You cannot seriously expect me to breach the bank's confidentiality. Even if I knew. Which I don't.' William Williams eyed me critically. 'I hope you will get on with your task as quickly as possible, Miss Jones. I know it is pleasant for you here, a nice hotel, afternoon teas, late light lunches and so on, but do not try my patience too far. I anticipate closing the files on this strange case as soon as I can.'

'Well, yes,' I said. 'I, too, am not anxious to extend matters unnecessarily. Besides, I don't believe whatever there is to be discovered cannot be found out pretty quick. I would not be the least surprised if someone did not know the answer already.'

'Let us hope so!' Mr Williams sighed. 'I understand there is to be a tea-dance. Here at the Gallimore?'

'Yes, up in the old ballroom. On Saturday evening. Belle Quinn is to organize it.'

'Excellent, excellent! How very convenient.'

'Convenient? It is very short notice.'

William Williams nodded. 'The dead guest stipulates that the contents of his Will *must* be discovered by the someone-who-is-not-someone *within three days* of his burial.'

'Three days!'

'One of those days has already nearly passed. You now therefore have *two days* left in which to complete your task. Miss Quinn's tea-dance on Saturday evening will mark the conclusion of your allotted time. I shall expect you to announce the result of your investigations during a break in the dancing.'

My jaw had dropped. 'You must be joking!' I said in a low voice.

'Miss Jones, I do not joke. I am not aware that William Williams has ever joked in his entire life.'

I stared at the dead guest's executor. 'The committee didn't say anything to *me* about three days! Mr Milady did not mention . . .'

'I expect they didn't want to alarm you.'

'I am alarmed! It's . . . it's not possible.'

'How can you tell what's possible, or not possible, Miss Jones?' William Williams scoffed. 'The dead guest obviously thought it *was* possible – and *he* should know! Besides, there are always rules to contracts of this kind, strictures that must be strictly adhered to. Otherwise, think of the chaos! I may not particularly like the arrangements, but I cannot deny that if our dead guest had to settle his affairs in this manner, at least he had the good sense to impose a sensible time limit on the disruption. And a sensible time limit on your stay. It makes me think there is hope for us yet.'

'And do you have hopes, Mr Williams?'

'Indeed I do! I hope that by the close of business on Saturday, three days after the dead guest was consigned to his grave, the cheque – so to speak – will be cleared. This whole business will be satisfactorily concluded, and you will be off on your travels again, to Penzance. I suggest you make every effort to find that train ticket you "lost", Miss Jones. You may well need it after the tea-dance.'

I promised Mr Williams that I would do my best to recover my lost property.

'I'm glad to hear it! I hate to see anyone "lose" anything so valuable,' the man who had charge over the dead guest's fortune, and the town's money, told me. I said I appreciated his concern, and added that it was probably possible to find the solution to the mystery within the prescribed time. As he himself had said, the dead guest must have thought it possible – and hadn't I managed to paint the whole of my parents' house in three days and three nights? I can be quite efficient when I get going.

Mr Williams shook his head. 'If only one could be sure! This whole business is all so unpredictable, unprescribed.' He looked unhappy. He was obviously a man who preferred situations you could control, forms you could fill in neatly, plots you could map out in advance. I told him how I had once wanted to be an arithmetic teacher. In those days I had liked sums that added up neatly and saw myself standing in front of a class wearing a long blue skirt, chalking countless numbers up on a blackboard. Not . . .

'Yes, yes, I read your account of yourself!' The bank manager waved a hand impatiently in the air. 'We are wasting precious time, Miss Jones. The first of your three days is already nearly over. You have only tomorrow, Friday, and then Saturday up till the tea-dance, to complete your task. There is no point sitting about chatting like this to me. Whatever happened in Knibden, happened just as much before my time as yours. I had never even heard of the town until I got sent here – why, but for my position at the bank, I too could have been the someone-who-was-not-someone!' William Williams gave a little squawk of amusement. The two of us looked at each other now with no little astonishment, for it was *incredible* to discover this man and I should have anything in common.

'The Masons see themselves as newcomers also,' I remarked. 'They came to the Gallimore a decade ago, having looked after hotels all their working lives. They are professionals. This stranger's death is the first on premises managed by themselves . . .'

William Williams nodded. 'It will be hard for them now,' he said soberly. 'There must be uncertainty over what will happen to the hotel. The Gallimore was one of the stranger's assets and for the time being, the Masons must go on running the place on behalf of the bank. Then, who knows? Hopefully there will soon be a new owner, of your choosing Miss Jones, things will settle down again and this whole strange business will be forgotten.'

'Not exactly of my *choosing*, Mr Williams. More my *discovering* – presumably the truth is out there, waiting to be revealed.'

'As you say, as you say!' Williams sighed wearily. 'In the meantime I will tell Mr Milady that I approve your appointment. On behalf of the bank. I am uneasy, but not especially with you. You cannot help yourself, and I dare say the someone-who-is-not-someone may as well be you, as anyone.' He almost smiled.

'Thank you,' I said, for this was certainly intended as a compliment.

'May I inquire where you intend to begin?' Mr Williams, despite his exhaustion, looked genuinely curious. 'I wouldn't have a clue how to start myself. In fact, I do rather admire you for agreeing to take this on . . .'

'The whole business is obviously connected to the hotel in some way,' I said.

'That would appear to be a fair assumption.'

'But in what way? Who does know? Am I really to be left totally in the dark? I mean, surely you must have *some* idea, Mr Williams, even if you are not allowed to tell me?'

William Williams shook his head.

'What about the Great Knibden Lottery?' I ventured.

'I understand the lotteries were stopped in the town many years ago. When my predecessor, Fechnie, was a young man. I cannot see what bearing . . .'

'How will you, Mr Williams, or anyone else, know if I get it right?'

'At the end of the three days, I am required to produce sealed documents. If, on inspection, those papers prove that your findings are correct, I shall then distribute the dead guest's estate accordingly. One thing I will say, Miss Jones: you must be careful how you proceed. The *process* of the investigation is of utmost importance.'

'Oh?'

'Our guest obviously wanted someone such as yourself *actively* burrowing into the town's hidden past. That much I am vouchsafed to tell you. And since everyone in Knibden hopes to gain, I dare say most people will assist you. But, get on with your work, Miss Jones, and *be seen to do so*. This is a fine hotel, make the most of your stay. Enjoy yourself while you are here – I am sure that is what the dead guest intended. The committee seem happy to meet your expenses . . .'

'They *are* very organized,' I remarked.

'And so should you be! But my advice is to take advantage while you can. Get everyone to tell you their stories as soon as possible. Their co-operation may not last. I know the time left to you isn't long, but it's longer than you think. These things have a habit of quickly turning nasty.' Mr Williams sighed. 'And now, if you will excuse me, Mrs Williams must be wondering where I have got to. My poor wife will have my dinner waiting on the table and my slippers warming by the fire. It has been another long day. A quiet town, we were told, a quiet country-town branch. I have never seen a bank as busy as we have been of late. People keep coming in on any old pretext, pretending to query some financial transaction but only really wanting to know how we are getting on. Hoping for clues. From now on, though, I shall refer them all to you, Miss Jones. Frankly, I wish to hear nothing more of the matter until it is resolved.' He stood up. 'I will see you at Miss Quinn's tea-dance. But before you make your announcement, Miss Jones, perhaps you will do me the honour of partnering me in the polka?'

I laughed (although the man did not speak in jest), and we shook hands.

As William Williams was leaving the room, Roger Ambrose entered, full of excitement and flushed from his walk. The bank manager looked hard at Mr Ambrose observing, if not the incredible bright blue eyes, at least the green trousers, red waistcoat and long curly blond hair. Mr Williams glanced doubtfully back at me (perhaps wondering if I might not prefer to perform the polka with this partner instead), then he nodded politely, and departed.

Roger Ambrose pulled out a chair and sat down. 'Who was *he*, then?' he asked. 'Your gentleman friend?'

73

'That was Mr Williams from the bank.'

'Ah ha – the guardian of the dead stranger's millions! We had all better be on our best behaviour with your Mr Williams.' Roger Ambrose made a long face and put his feet up on the table. He offered me a cigarette which I declined, then he lit one for himself. 'And how did you get on with the committee, Hester Jones? My step-father informs me you made a good impression – and not many people impress Edmund Veitch!'

I smiled non-committally. Outside, the motorcyclists were still revving their engines. The fatherless Laffety boy at their head. There was a timid knock on the door and the young waitress, Doris, entered. 'I am to ask you both if you will be dining tonight,' she said, with the boldness of a shy person.

Mr Ambrose immediately told her we would.

'I'm afraid I can't,' I objected quickly. 'It turns out I only have three days to complete my task – and since one of those days is nearly over, I had better start my investigations right away. Perhaps you would be kind enough to bring me something in my room later.'

The girl stared. 'Yer not frightened?' she asked.

'Frightened?' I laughed. The time-scale was daunting, but did not scare me.

Roger Ambrose blew a long dense puff of smoke, and turned to face me square on.

'I thought, mebbe . . .' The young Doris spluttered. Her eyes opened wide. 'I mean, Miss Jones! How can you *sleep* in the very same room – in the very same bed where the stranger died? No one could pay me enough!' She shivered theatrically and clutched her sides.

Roger Ambrose watched us closely through the smoke that writhed in the air about him. 'Hester Jones won't be frightened of ghosts!' he said. 'Why, the ghosts of Knibden are far more likely to be terrified of *her*.'

I left the pair giggling, and making whooping ghost noises, as I hurried away upstairs. In the seclusion of my own room again, I admit, I looked about me with fresh eyes. With the eyes of the last guest who had been shown in here. A man whose history we do not know yet, who entered this room and saw what I see, knowing he was unlikely to leave again, alive. Knowing, also,

74

that his carefully planned wishes, written neatly and lodged at that moment in his pocket, would bring untold disruption to the town sleeping peacefully beyond the window. And would bring *me* here – not Hester Jones especially, but someone-who-was-not-someone – to investigate.

I looked slowly round the room, observing its faded grandeur, the peeling paint, the high ornately plastered ceilings, the cracked grey marble wash basin in one corner and the old dark wardrobe on which my cardboard suitcase reposed. I sat down rather tentatively on the great lumpy bed. Then I went across to the window and pulled aside one of the heavy, velvet curtains. Outside, the lamplit streets were nearly empty, the Laffety gang had given up circling the main Square on their bikes and gone home. The last of the shops were closing. What was it, I wondered, out there in the darkness of this small quiet town that the former occupant of this room wanted exposed? *Things barely remembered,* he had written, *things forgotten that ought not to be, things that ought to be forgotten but cannot be . . .*

The Gallimore Hotel had been locked and bolted for the night when the guest arrived so that the manager, Mason, grumbling at being roused from his slumbers by prolonged ringing, took little notice of the weary traveller beyond showing him up to this room and then asking him (a little perfunctorily) whether he required anything further. When the man shook his head, Mason had muttered, 'Then, Sir, I bid you goodnight – what *little* is left of it!'

The guest, swathed in a greatcoat that entirely obscured his person, had turned away from Daniel Mason who now fancied he'd caught a slight smile tremble on those thin blue lips – for the guest had been no guest at all! He was Mason's employer. And had been for the last ten years. He'd *owned* the Gallimore Hotel. Furthermore, the fellow obviously *did* have a very good idea how 'little' was 'left', since he had in his pocket precisely the right amount of money to pay for his one night's stay. Not a penny more, nor less. He'd also had with him only the clothes he was wearing. Clothes in which – after their labels and laundry marks yielded no clues to his identity – the people of Knibden had seen fit to bury him. Consigning their mysterious stranger to spend all eternity shrouded in garments as anonymous as himself. Then commissioning me, another stranger, who had arrived quite by

75

chance on the day of the burial and could not be connected in any way with the mystery, to live here in the dead guest's room. And sleep here in the dead guest's lumpy bed. And spend three days discovering what it was the man had not been able to narrate for himself.

I am his instrument, I said out loud. Already the first of those three days had gone and I had spent it without knowing how precious it had been. I am the someone-who-isn't-someone, the third person, the dead guest's representative in the Land of the Living. My eyes fixed on the clock on the wall – its gentle ticking had kept the stranger company as he'd breathed his last, and would now mark the passing time for me as I went about my task.

My thoughts were interrupted just then by Daniel Mason. 'You have visitors, Miss Jones!' I jumped. I had left the door open and not heard the manager of the Gallimore Hotel enter the room behind me. 'They say it is urgent and you will not mind being disturbed when you hear what they have to tell you. I have asked them to wait downstairs.'

I thanked him. 'I will be down directly,' I said, suppressing a sigh.

'No peace for the wicked, eh?' Mason quipped mirthlessly.

'No,' I agreed. 'It seems not.'

PART TWO

Trumpets, Dragons and Naked Women

1

The Colossus of Knibden

'So, Miss Willow, what is it to be?' George Allendale demanded the moment his assistant returned. 'Unrequited love?'

Verity stared. 'I beg your pardon?' she said blankly.

'The eternal triangle?' George went on. 'Or perhaps you favour a particularly exquisite revenge tragedy!'

Verity Willow turned her back on the jovial young man, and busied herself hanging up her grey coat. She tucked her straw basket neatly away under the library counter. 'I'm sorry it all took so long, if that's what you mean.' She climbed precariously on to her stool and drew a handkerchief from the sleeve of her cardigan. She blew her nose, then seized up some unfiled cards, dropping one nervily so that it skidded across the floor. 'They talked and talked . . .'

'Committees do – I did warn you!' George bent down and retrieved the fallen card. '*Madame Bovary*!' he remarked dispassionately as he handed it back to Miss Willow. She did not thank him for his trouble.

'They talked about everything, almost, except the matter in hand.' Verity thumped the cards on the desk. 'You'd have thought we had all the time in the world . . .' Absent-mindedly she patted Madame Bovary back into shape. 'When we only have three days . . .' The routine filing was her job but ever since this business over the dead guest started, Miss Willow had been unable to concentrate. The piles of unfiled cards had piled up. So too, the heaps of returned books that needed shelving. 'And the first of those days is now nearly over.' She looked about her in despair.

I am letting things slip! Verity told herself gleefully. If *I* had a guilty conscience, I would certainly have betrayed myself by now. Miss Willow glanced furtively up into the painted eyes of Arthur Dawes Dobson, founder and chief benefactor of Knibden's public library who sat watching with keen interest from his place on the wall. 'They would *not* listen to me,' she told the man.

'There was more discussion about whether the committee should pay for a *tea* for itself than . . .'

'My dear Miss Willow,' Allendale interrupted. 'When two or more people are gathered together, nothing – not even the death of a loved one – assumes greater importance than the procurement of tea!' He chuckled mischievously. 'I was about to suggest a cup now.'

Verity clutched the edge of her desk. ' "The death of a loved one",' she repeated in a strained voice. Yes, *he* had been loved all right. But *dead*? No – never! *He* had not been a man to simply *die*. The notion was so absurd she felt like laughing. It was against the rules, of course, to laugh in the library.

'I'll put the kettle on,' Allendale said, but made no move to do so. He folded his arms. The dead guest must have been loved by someone, he supposed. Why not Miss Verity Willow? 'Anyhow,' he went on with a boyish grin, 'I haven't missed you one little bit this afternoon. No one's been in – except Mother who came to show me some frightful new wool for my winter jumper. You missed a treat!'

Verity looked over her shoulder, and visibly registered George's presence for the first time since she had returned. 'I'm sorry?' she said.

Knibden's chief librarian needed no further encouragement. 'Miss Willow will put her foot down, I told her. My assistant is a sensible woman. She will refuse to work alongside a man wearing lime green. There will be trouble in this library, Mother, if you persist with this abomination. In the interests of good industrial relations, you must go straight back to the wool shop and change the stuff!' George paused. Clearly his wit was lost on his assistant this afternoon. He changed tack. 'Even my mother remarked on how *quiet* it was.'

'Oh?'

' "The town is dead, George," she said. "As dead as the buried stranger." '

Verity stared at George, her mouth wide open.

In fact, what George's mother had remarked on as soon as she'd bustled into the library that afternoon was Miss Willow's absence. Mrs Allendale also spotted the piles of unfiled cards and unshelved books, and she'd asked George rather sharply if the silly creature he worked with had got herself caught up in this ridiculous business over the guest at the Gallimore?

George was not to know that his mother had also seriously considered getting involved – for the sake of her son – but by the time she had made up her mind to do so, sufficient funds had already been raised. The committee had already been formed. 'Plans for the guest's burial and wake are well in hand,' Michael Milady explained, shaking his head and turning away her money. 'You and your son are most welcome to attend the funeral at St Redegule's, though, and then accompany us all back afterwards to the Swan. Everyone will be there,' Milady had told her proudly. 'The guest left instructions, free drinks all round.'

Edina Allendale was so astounded at having her beneficence thrown back in her face that only when she regained her composure had she been able to inform Mr Milady that 'everyone' would *not* be there. She and her son were by no means in the habit of frequenting the Swan! Nor was it fitting for George in his position, or for his mother for that matter, to accept 'free drinks'. Especially not at some unknown stranger's expense. 'The dead guest could have been *anyone*,' she'd jibed. 'And, for all any of you know, this great fortune of his could have come from *anywhere*!'

Michael Milady bowed his head.

'Criminal activity even,' Mrs Allendale drove home her point. There was something decidedly underhand about dying in this fashion – and as for leaving such an unstraightforward Will . . . 'You'll find your committee is laying itself open to serious charges. Being accessories after the fact. Aiding and abetting, handling stolen . . .'

Mrs Allendale was not altogether sure of her ground. Privately, she considered things might have been different if she had been *on* the committee, and able to influence events. Then she'd have seen it as her bounden duty to be at the Swan making sure no one abused the dead guest's generosity. The dead man would never now know what a stalwart champion he could have enjoyed in Edina Allendale. Oh yes, she would have been assiduous in defence of the dead stranger's interests, for there are always those ready to take advantage of the foolish whims of others. Especially if those 'others' are rich, and dead, and have no easy means of

81

protecting themselves. People appointed to safeguard the affairs of the deceased were often, in her experience, the very ones from whom they had most to fear.

In her disappointment, and hurt pride, Mrs Allendale said none of this. Instead she glared at Michael Milady and asked the funny little man with the unsightly gap between the top of his socks and the hem of his trousers, why the dead guest's wake was being held in a back-street public house, and not at the smart hotel where he had actually passed away? Was there not something distinctly underhand in this also? Michael Milady either did not, or would not, understand her question. They were on the look out for someone-who-was-not-someone, he told her. If Mrs Allendale came across such a person, would she kindly let him know.

How fast and freely flows the drink that flows elsewhere at someone else's expense! What a long, fretful night the night before had been. While the whole of Knibden caroused in the brightly lit Swan of Edina Allendale's imagination, she and her son had been obliged to while away the hours, as usual, sitting either side of the coal-effect electric fire in their living room. He, absorbed in his book; she, cracking boiled sweets, clacking her knitting needles and making desultory attempts at conversation.

At last poor George could stand it no longer. He flung down his thick volume on the final days of the Roman Empire. 'You *were* invited, Mother!' he cried out in his exasperation. 'You *should* have gone!'

Mrs Allendale pretended not to know what he was talking about. 'I hope you don't treat the books in your library in that violent manner!' she remarked.

'Well, *I* wouldn't have minded going,' George said. 'It might have been a bit of fun for a change!'

'Fun!' Mrs Allendale shrieked. 'It was a *funeral*, George!'

'The dead man could have been *anyone*, Mother.'

'That's what *I* told Michael Milady.'

'So we should have been there, to pay our respects. In case the poor chap turns out to be someone we knew. Besides, I'd quite like to have gone to the party afterwards in the pub. We don't often get to go to parties . . .'

Mrs Allendale breathed in sharply. 'It wasn't a party, it was a wake! And if you think I'd dream of setting foot in that . . . That den of iniquity!'

'The Swan? Come now, Mother! I believe the establishment is fairly respectable. It must be if Verity Willow and Belle Quinn are going . . .' George retrieved his book from the floor and found his place among the crumpled pages. He suspected he had gone too far. His suspicions were quickly confirmed. Mrs Allendale swallowed the boiled sweet in her mouth and stilled her knitting needles. After a chapter or two stubbornly following Calperius' last stand and the ignominious retreat of his beleaguered forces from the Northern Provinces of Vintniorum, George could bear the preternatural silence in the room no longer. He asked his mother outright what was wrong, and she immediately accused her son, outright, of having his eye on Janice.

'Janice?' George had no idea whom his mother was talking about. Calperius' principal women had been called Zoë and Hyena – while the busty barmaid at the Swan had never once ventured into Knibden's public library. 'It's late,' he said, stretching and yawning ostentatiously. 'I think I'll go on up.'

When Edina Allendale heard that a someone-who-wasn't-someone had come forward, and that the committee's first meeting was to take place that very afternoon, there'd been no time to lose. She hastened to the library, pausing only to purchase the lime-green wool *en route*. The colour had been the nearest to hand in the shop so she was not surprised the dear boy did not like it. She *had* been surprised, though, to share the revolving doors on her way *in* to the library, with Verity Willow on her way *out*. Mrs Allendale just managed to position herself by the great window at the front of the library – the vantage point she'd been planning for the afternoon – in time to see the girl dashing madly across the far side of the Square, and *up the steps of the Gallimore*!

'I'd have credited Miss Willow with more sense,' George's mother said tartly. She popped a large lemon sweet into her mouth and sucked hard. Why had she herself hesitated? *If only* she had made up her mind to invest some of her savings at once, she too could have been over there in the Gallimore, instructing this someone-who-was-not-someone who had miraculously been found. Doubtless tea would be taken during the course of the afternoon. A nice hotel tea, free of charge – patty cakes, watercress sandwiches trimmed of their crusts, fruit scones with purchased jam and plentiful dollopings of rich double cream.

Mrs Allendale heaved hard and sighed long. The truth, she admitted silently to herself as she ran her tongue over the bitter lemon sweet, was that she'd never expected the scheme to get off the ground. Michael Milady was not a man to organize anything. Hadn't the great Montague Cayke's World Famous Imperial Players been disbanded, and all the Astonishing Prancing Dogs put down, once they'd been left in his care? As for finding a 'someone-who-was-not-someone' prepared to take on the task of determining the stranger's strange Will: she had considered this impossible. No one in their right mind would voluntarily give up their own chance of inheriting the fortune. What's more, the dead guest must have known this. The wretched man had set out to tease the whole town, dangling a large sum of money in front of their eyes only to snatch it away again because the impossible terms he'd imposed could not be complied with. It was a cruel, clever joke, one she grudgingly admired – but it was a joke that had also backfired. Now that this someone-who-wasn't-someone had come forward, the fortune would very likely be distributed. In less than three days' time! And serve the dead prankster right, whoever he had been. It was only a shame the man was safely tucked in his grave, and could never now be made to know the folly of his ways.

Mrs Allendale vehemently cast on lime-green stitches. She crunched sweet after sweet. Every so often she paused to gaze across the empty Square at the tantalizingly closed doors of the Gallimore Hotel. Was the whole thing *legal*? Weren't there laws to prevent people deliberately engineering things so that after they were dead the lives of the living could be disrupted in this fashion? If there weren't such laws, there should be. Hadn't the formalities following the guest's death been glossed over rather hastily? Hadn't everyone been rather too keen to collude in the dead man's plans for them? Just because of the large sum of money on offer. If she had the time, she'd write to someone in authority – but there was no time! By Saturday evening the whole business would be over. Some undeserving wretch in the town

84

would have become very rich. But, as yet, there was no knowing who.

How strange, though, that no one else had seen fit to question the *legitimacy* of such a peculiar Will. Mr Williams at the bank, the townspeople, even the dried-up vicar of St Redegule's, Gilbert Duncie Sibson, who had happily laid the guest to rest within the sound of his bells. The foul-mouthed builder, Follifoot, and his two cronies, Dr Treadgold, who'd been happy to sign the death certificate on a rich man she was pretty certain he'd never seen before, and the jeweller, Macready. Belle Quinn also! And now this person they had somehow found, this Hester Jones – they had *all* gone along with it. As for Verity Willow....

'That woman grows more preposterous all the time!' Mrs Allendale declared.

'Am I to presume you are referring to my colleague, the inestimable Miss Willow?'

'She'll have gambled her *life*'s savings on this man's *death*.'

'Oh?'

'You want to watch yourself, George! There's no knowing what a woman like that may do next.'

'Verity's harmless enough.'

'I wouldn't be so sure! People change completely when large sums of money are involved. They come out from inside – like slimy shellfish, or scaly tortoises – and they reveal themselves for what they really are. As for this "committee" that's been got up – why, *not one* of them, over there...' she jabbed her free knitting needle in the direction of the Gallimore, 'is any wiser than the rest of us. For all they know, the dead guest could have left his whole fortune to you.'

'*Me*, Mother!' George too now glanced across the Square at the tantalizingly closed doors of the Gallimore Hotel. 'Why *me*?'

'Why not? Or me, for that matter. It's just like the Great Knibden Lottery all over again. Anyone in the town could win. We are *all* of us in with a chance – not just the busybodies over there this afternoon, sitting about importantly, scoffing free teas.' Mrs Allendale clicked her tongue, and knitted two rigid rows of rib stitch.

'I can't imagine Miss Willow sitting about importantly,' George objected.

85

'But I can imagine the silly girl losing the whole of her investment in this ridiculous venture! Then where will she be, your precious Miss Willow? It's not as if she has a son to fall back on in her old age.'

'I dare say she'll end up in the Knibden workhouse,' George laughed. 'Languishing at public expense. Just think – we'll be able to visit Verity there, and take bread and water. You'll enjoy that, Mother.'

Mrs Allendale sniffed, and pointed out that it was against the rules, even for a chief librarian, to laugh in the public library.

'Very quiet,' George told Verity now. 'I reckon everyone's far too excited about your mystery to want any books.'

'It is hardly *my* mystery,' Verity blushed.

'You are too modest,' George smiled. 'Of course, poor Mother is terribly jealous.' Indeed, Edina Allendale had hurried off home the moment the Gallimore's doors showed signs of opening. She had chosen to brave the Laffety gang circling the Square on their motorbikes rather than face a triumphant Miss Willow just then. 'I reckon you and I might as well take a holiday.'

'A holiday, George?'

'Close the library down – who'll want to read books when they have the real thing? We'll be *completely empty* now with everyone too busy wondering if they are going to inherit the dead guest's fortune, and deciding how to spend it when they do. I doubt we'll see *Madame Bovary* in here again! Meanwhile, everyone'll forget to return books they've already taken out, and they'll run up huge fines they won't be able to pay – unless they *are* lucky and do inherit. But in any case, *our* fortunes are assured. You and I will be able to retire very comfortably, Miss Willow, on the vast amount of fines we'll collect. All thanks to your dead guest.'

Verity smiled indulgently as the young man prattled on. 'Yes,' she said when he had finished. 'It *is* rather exciting.'

'That's better! You were a bit het up.'

'You'd be het up if you'd had to listen to Norah Bird. She hardly put any money into the kitty and yet, there she was . . .'

'While you, Miss Willow? I suppose you have donated your life's savings?'

Verity shrugged. It was not his business, nor could an investment, repayable ten-fold, be described as a 'donation'. 'I thought you said you were going to make tea.'

Verity followed George to the doorway of the small kitchen and watched him fill the kettle. She liked the boy, even though he had a clever tongue, an overbearing mother and had been appointed over her. She noticed the bald patch on the back of his head. He is young to be so old, she thought pityingly. He had always reminded her of the august Arthur Dawes Dobson, the founder of Knibden's library and museum who looked down on them from his wide gilt frame while they worked. The likeness had struck her the very first day George had come to take charge of the library. With the passing of the years the similarity between the two men had increased and would, Verity supposed, go on increasing. It amused her to think that in another thirty years, and if George grew a beard, George Barrington Allendale and Arthur Dawes Dobson would be quite indistinguishable.

'So, you hardly got a word in, Miss Willow?' George prompted.

'They did *not* listen to me.' Verity leant against the door frame and watched George fuss about with mugs and tea bags. She was a tall, overly thin woman with long hands and awkward feet. Her pale girlish complexion and very fine fair hair that had turned imperceptibly silver over the years defied anyone to guess her age. 'I *know* I am right,' she protested softly. 'This *is* a whodunnit, but one with a difference. I'm not at all sure the girl they've found is up to the job – they need Hercule Poirot. Or Jane Marple. Or even a Randolphe Shyne. Whereas this Hester Jones – she did not strike me . . .' Verity broke off abruptly.

'What did she strike you as?' George Allendale sighed inwardly. You'd expect Miss Willow to keep cats or small dogs, but she kept neither. She did not knit or do *petit point*. It was impossible to say what gave her such a perpetually preoccupied air. His mother had no time for his assistant but this, George supposed, was to be expected since he spent his days cooped up with the woman. Heaven help a *wife* – if he ever had one – with whom, presumably, he'd spend his nights! George pictured his mother and Miss Willow ganging up, reducing the poor girl to tears. He saw himself standing over the weeping female, looking helplessly from one to the other as Miss Willow told him her version, his mother roundly contradicted her, and the girl's wretched sobs drowned out them both. The kettle started to boil. George Allendale switched it off.

'Miss Jones didn't really strike me as anything,' Verity said thoughtfully. 'That was what was so odd. All the time I sat there at the meeting I couldn't help wondering what *you* would make of our someone-who-isn't-someone. In the end I invited Hester Jones to visit the library. I told her she should consult you.'

'Me!' George laughed. 'Why, Miss Willow, what can *I* possibly tell your sleuth that you wouldn't be able to yourself?'

As he spoke, George noticed a strange expression flit momentarily across his assistant's clear blue eyes. As if he'd suggested Verity possessed some dark secret she ought, indeed, to tell Hester Jones. Could his mother be right this once? The old girl was taking the whole affair much too seriously. Fancy risking her life's savings when no one had any real idea who the dead guest at the Gallimore had been. *Someone*, though, would inherit the great fortune – why should that someone not be Verity Willow? She would come to him and hand in her notice. 'You'll never guess what . . .' she would say.

'We must all help Hester Jones since she has kindly consented to assist us,' Miss Willow was now saying primly.

'So!' George smiled. 'What do you intend doing with all the money?'

Miss Willow did not hesitate. 'It's not the *money* that interests me,' she declared.

George smirked. 'Everyone always says "it's not the money". No one likes to look greedy.'

'No,' Verity shook her head firmly. 'It is *not* the money. What *is* important is that someone chose to leave their worldly goods to you. You meant more to them than anyone else they were leaving behind. You were the only one they felt they could trust in the end.' It was the ultimate avowal of love, the final reckoning up of their earthly account after they had gone. When all the books were returned, and the last library fines on this earth paid. The drawing of the line under the mess they'd left behind.

'So,' George struggled to sound bright and breezy. 'Who do *you* mean more to than anyone else in the world? Who was he, Miss Willow, own up!'

Verity eyed the young man measuring milk from a cardboard

88

carton into two of the library's cracked mugs. She gripped her thin arms tightly above the elbow. George was right, of course. It would be a big responsibility, a large sum like that. Everyone should probably have a plan ready for if it came to them. Raymond Bast would certainly have had a plan! Oh yes – *he* would have known what to do if a big sum of money came *his* way.

Oh dear! thought George, glancing sideways at Verity. His mother's words rang in his ears: *People change completely when large sums of money are involved – they come out from inside, and they reveal themselves for what they really are. You want to watch yourself, George!* He remarked, in casual conversational tones, 'I must say, Miss Willow, I *am* rather looking forward to meeting your Hester Jones.'

'Oh?' Raymond Bast would have known what to do with Hester Jones, also! 'Yes, yes, she seems . . .' Verity received her tea and followed George Allendale back to the library's main desk. 'She'll be very busy. She's already used up the first of her three days – I doubt very much if she will find time to visit us here.' Verity sighed. 'Hester Jones is to do as she pleases,' she told George in between sips. 'She is insisting on an elaborate setting for her denouement.'

'Pardon?'

'Instead of just gathering us together in the hotel lounge, the way Poirot or Miss Marple or Randolphe Shyne would have done, Miss Jones demanded we hold a tea-dance, up in the old ballroom like in the old days.'

'A tea-dance!'

'With Dickie Paisley and his Band. She wants the whole town invited. You, and your mother, included . . .'

'Whatever for?'

'So that she can announce the recipient of the dead guest's fortune in style, I suppose. Everyone agreed at once. Miss Quinn, in her goodness, consented to organize it – though with only two days to go, poor Belle will have her work cut out. Meanwhile, Mr Veitch offered Miss Jones history lessons – and quite why he thinks the royalist cavaliers, hanging up their pikestaffs after the siege of Knibden Castle in 1641, will help Hester Jones's investigation, I can't imagine!'

'Neither can I!'

'They say, though, that she has her methods. And she does seem to have made a good start. She's already been lunching with Veitch's step-son, Roger Ambrose, who's come back to Knibden specially. Miss Jones probably thinks she can catch a suspect off his guard over an egg, tomato, lettuce and radish salad! And Neville Tagg chatted openly to Miss Jones in the Swan last night . . .' The fellow had been nudging the girl, and winking encouragement. Even Belle Quinn had commented on it. The men would flock to help Hester Jones the way years ago they had flooded into the town to try their luck at the Great Knibden Lottery. Trumpets, dragons and naked women. George Allendale, for all his cleverness, would find himself drawn in – Verity wondered what Mrs Allendale would think of *that*. Perhaps the lime-green winter jumper was a clever maternal ploy to put Miss Jones off. The girl may not be Poirot, Miss Marple or Randolphe Shyne, Verity decided, she may only be a someone-who-was-not-someone, but Hester Jones was not likely to be put off quite so easily.

It was George Allendale who now glanced up at Arthur Dawes Dobson. There was a man! he thought. Secretary of Knibden's Antiquarian Society, founder of the library and museum. Archaeologist, palaeontologist, speleologist, Egyptologist – not that you'd think much Egyptology could be done around Knibden, yet Arthur Dawes Dobson had managed it. He would certainly have been able to manage this Hester Jones. He'd have had her stuffed, and exhibited in a glass case with a carefully written label pinned underneath! 'If *I* inherited the fortune,' George said, 'I would revive Dawes Dobson's museum.'

Verity spluttered and nearly spilt her tea. When she recovered herself, she said, 'What a splendid idea!' Then she added, 'I have never told you this before, George, but I've always thought of you as another Arthur Dawes Dobson.'

'He was a crook!' George Allendale protested. The man had brought shame and scandal to Knibden.

Verity could see that George was pleased though. 'He was an enthusiast,' she corrected him. 'Archaeologist, palaeontologist, speleologist, Egyptologist . . .'

'He was a man who knew how to enjoy himself,' George said with undisguised feeling. 'And whatever else he did, or didn't do, he left Knibden with this library. And the museum too must have been quite something in its day.'

'Well, yes. I believe it was.' Verity was taken aback.

George Allendale went on, 'I have often thought it would be rather fun to open that room up again, dust off the exhibits, re-write the labels, rearrange everything. If *I* were to inherit the dead guest's fortune I could build a splendid new edifice to house it all. Just behind the library where the old museum used to be, exactly as it was in Dawes Dobson's day. No expense spared. I'll write a guidebook. I can see it all now – rows of beautiful rosewood and glass cabinets with ivory and brass inlay . . .'

What was left of Knibden's once famous museum was today crammed into a locked store room at the back of the kitchen. When George had first come to work at the library, he had insisted they unlock the door to have a look. It was the most depressing treasure house you ever saw. Crushed boxes cram-med with dusty objects piled to the ceiling. Stuffed animals that had come off their pedestals and birds with dusty feathers and broken wings jammed in on top of each other. George turned over a few boxes and unearthed a collection of what looked like rusty Roman spearheads but could equally well be the tops sawn off cast-iron railings. Verity Willow had been astonished. 'I never wondered what was in here,' she'd said. 'I never thought to unlock the door and look.'

'There could have been *anything* hidden away!' the eager young George had laughed. 'Dead bodies, even . . .'

They had found the painting, and decided to reinstate it above the library's main desk. It had hung there watching them while they worked, ever since.

After Arthur Dawes Dobson's disgrace, and death, his portrait had been taken down and stored. The splendid glass-domed rooms that had once adjoined the library and housed the famous museum, had been left to deteriorate until eventually, a long time ago, it had been flooded during a particularly bad storm one night. That part of the building had had to be pulled down. Anything salvaged from the wreckage had been stashed away in the tiny store room. Concrete was later smoothed over the site to form a convenient car park at the back of the building and this was used these days, despite the sign George had put up saying FOR LIBRARY USERS ONLY, BY ORDER OF THE CHIEF LIBRARIAN by people driving into Knibden from nearby villages to visit the shops. Only last week Allendale had actually watched a woman get out of her car and trot openly along the pavement to Miss Bird's boutique. A while later she had returned, climbed into her car and driven away. No pretence, even, at coming into the library to browse. Or ask a question. If the museum were rebuilt on the site of the car park, Miss Bird's customers would have to park elsewhere. George Allendale said now, with considerable restraint, 'I can't help wondering if the guest at the Gallimore is connected somehow. To Arthur Dawes Dobson, and all that business.'

Verity opened her mouth, but closed it again without responding. She had been thinking only of Raymond Bast. It hardly seemed likely, she thought, Dawes Dobson died such a long time back. But to humour George, Miss Willow now gave a little light laugh and said, 'Well, who knows? They *say* it is to do with something that has been lying here in Knibden all this time, and that museum stuff has certainly been locked away longer than I can remember.' She glanced at the young man reappraisingly. 'I never knew *you* were interested in Arthur Dawes Dobson. You never said anything before.'

'I walked up to Knibden Crags a week ago on Sunday,' George Allendale told Verity then. 'Mother had been out of sorts the whole of Saturday, so when I woke early that Sunday morning, I got up and went straight out. No one else was around. It was a wonderful climb but when I reached the top the mist was so thick I couldn't see further than the end of my nose. I clambered on to the highest boulder and stood there, master of all I surveyed. I might have been the only person alive in the whole wide world. And, since there wasn't the view to look at, I found myself thinking about Arthur Dawes Dobson and those expeditions of eminent men he took up to the Crags all those years ago, showing off the entrances to the caves and then bringing them back down to the town. And in here, to inspect his finds.'

'And take their money off them! The man was a rogue.'

George ignored this. 'While you were at the committee meeting this afternoon,' he said quietly, 'and Mother was sitting at that window chattering on, it occurred to me that I must have been up there, thinking about Arthur Dawes Dobson, at *exactly the time* the guest at the Gallimore died.'

Verity gave a little gasp.

'It's funny,' George went on. 'But if instead of taking the path up to Knibden Crags, I had gone into the Gallimore. On a whim. And ordered breakfast. Who knows – I might have seen him . . .'

'Who?'

'The guest. It never occurred to me to do so, but *if* I had . . .'

'It never occurred to any of us,' Verity Willow murmured. 'He died in his sleep – the poor man did not get any breakfast.' She too had been up early that bright cold morning, a week ago last Sunday. It was only a short walk from her cottage to the Gallimore. She could so easily have been there with him, if she had known. So near, yet further off than ever! She blew her nose. I must pull myself together, she thought. If I carry on like this I shall be of no help to him at all. I shall betray . . .

George sighed. Arthur Dawes Dobson, bestriding the world like the Colossus of Knibden, had been a man who had done as he pleased. And good luck to him. Sooner or later, we all end up dead and buried, like the guest at the Gallimore. Dawes Dobson had not had a mother trailing round after him with lime-green wool. Nor had he eked out his days drinking luke-warm tea in cracked mugs with Miss Willow. *His* car parking signs would never have been treated with contempt by women motoring into town to buy frilly frocks from Norah Bird. He had sold bogus artefacts at vast profits to the British Museum, and museums all over the world. He had single-handedly caused what had been termed 'a diplomatic incident' as nations threatened to go to war, their national museums made fools of. After Dawes Dobson's exposure, Sir Mayhew Gallimore had stood up and made a long, much reported speech in the House. The general public had learnt the meaning of the word *chicanery* and people who had no interest in museums flocked to Knibden to see for themselves the place where deception on such a scale had taken place. Arthur Dawes Dobson became a local hero. Knibden had cocked a snook at the rest of the world. Only the girl who had loved him wept. His wife returned to her mother in high-minded disgust. His sons, Wilfrid and Johnny Dawes Dobson, both held their heads as high as they could until both had been mercifully gunned down, somewhere in Northern France during the Great War. Their names carved for all time on the War Memorial in Knibden's main Square, Missing in Action. Presumed Dead.

What, a century hence, would anyone ever say of George Barrington Allendale? There was little enough to say, now. Unless, of course . . . George took a deep breath. If *I* inherit the fortune, he thought. If, in three days' time, *I* suddenly have all that money at *my* disposal . . . Might he not conquer Vintniorum and – how he would like to see his mother's face! – take his pick from among the beautiful maidens for which its Northern Provinces, *urbi et orbi*, were famed? 'Mother,' he would say, introducing a scantily clad damsel closely resembling Hyena. 'My *affianced* refuses to kiss a man wearing lime-green. You must return that stuff to the wool shop, this instant!'

It was Verity's turn to note a strange wild look in the chief librarian's eyes. She glanced from George Barrington Allendale up at Dawes Dobson, and back again to George. For the first time she noticed that the rather old-fashioned, pernickety young man she worked with had started to grow a beard. 'You had better speak to Hester Jones, George,' Verity Willow said urgently. 'Really you must!'

George Allendale nodded solemnly. 'I look forward to the pleasure,' he said.

2

Miss Bird's of Knibden

Norah Bird paused on the steps of the boarded-up Alhambra to retie the crimplene lavender scarf about her head. It was nonsense, of course, talk of opening up the theatre again. It had been derelict for years. There was not much left behind the rotting hoardings; a couple of dilapidated walls and a few pillars with peeling plaster held upright by rusted scaffolding. Norah watched Verity Willow scurrying like a hungry grey squirrel back across the far side of the Square, past the Laffety gang on their bikes, and into the stuffy safety of her library. How odd to carry a straw basket about town, as if she were out blackberrying! How odd too, the way Miss Willow had spent the whole afternoon carrying on about whodunnits, and murder.

What if it were *not* nonsense? Or, if the *talk* had been nonsense, but a miracle could be made to happen, nevertheless. Miracles do occur, that was the nature of miracles – look at the way Hester Jones had materialized out of nowhere, just when they'd needed her. So, why should the lights of the Alhambra *not* blaze again, exactly as Michael Milady had described last night in the Swan? If the money were to be distributed in three days' time – why, by this time next week the rebuilding could be underway! A new Alhambra would rise like a phoenix from the ashes. Miss Rose Meldrew and Mr Chas Fonteyne would be fetched from their places of retirement across the seven seas. Even the astonishing prancing dogs . . .

Norah Bird felt a thrill of excitement. The world was changing under their feet – they had *all* become players upon an Imperial stage. She waved exuberantly to Miss Quinn who was entering the hairdresser's just then, and did not notice. Belle Quinn was a valuable customer. Not that she ever bought anything from Miss Bird's of Knibden but, with her taste for fine linens and the best woollen weaves, Norah Bird liked to keep in with her. Was Miss Quinn really going to organize a tea-dance like in the old days, with Dickie Paisley and his Band? Norah made a mental note to get in some suitable stock as soon as possible. The women of Knibden were bound to want new for the occasion – a range of fresh floral prints in select winter fabrics would probably be the thing. Miss Bird's of Knibden would not let them down.

Norah lingered a moment longer trying to picture the Alhambra's entrance as it used to be, as it soon would be again. The white stucco pillars covered in brightly printed posters that advertised forthcoming shows. She had been lingering here, in exactly this spot, studying those posters the day Jack . . .

Norah refused to think about Jack. Instead she remembered the time long before Jack came to Knibden when she and her best friend Amy Tagg, Amy Pasco then, young Neville Tagg's mother, had sat together in the middle of the front row. They'd been taken to a matinée performance by one of the nice old men from Norah's father's works – Mr Nye or Mr Sharps. The man would have been given the afternoon off for the purpose, she supposed. Her father'd have summoned whichever of them it was into his office and handed over the tickets. 'Take Norah and her little friend,' Daddy would have told Mr Nye or Mr Sharps and they'd have been delighted, preferring an afternoon of unexpected idleness in the luxury of the Alhambra to the rigours of supervising recalcitrant men in Mr Bird's tannery.

The two little girls had sat together shrieking encouragement at Aladdin's younger brother who was up to all kinds of tricks that had seemed pretty hilarious at the time. They'd opened their mouths as wide as they could, hugging each other and bouncing about in their seats, joining in with the other children ranged about them in the darkness, shouting for all they were worth. Shouting till it hurt.

What a nice afternoon this had been also. Well worth closing the shop for. My contribution to the committee's funds may only have been small, Norah thought happily, but I have worked hard for what I have. I am not wealthy like Belle Quinn, or well read like Verity Willow, yet I, Norah Bird, have an equal say in this business. For once, I am in with an equal chance.

She would do her bit to help matters along. Oh yes! She would invite Hester Jones to Miss Bird's of Knibden. The girl could do with smartening up. Besides, the committee should provide their investigator with some decent new clothes, in deference to the man who had died. Who had he been? It was odd the way no one else had mentioned the lottery to Hester Jones. Yet there were few in the town, even these days, long after the fiasco of the last lottery, who ever thought of much else. Norah grinned. *Things that ought to be forgotten but cannot be . . .* As if the dead guest's words might refer to anything other than the last Great Knibden Lottery, and all the bother it had caused!

'*I* have never forgotten,' she murmured. Not even for one instant.

There'd been loud music, bright coloured lights, a small box of Cadbury's theatre chocolates to share, and men in tight tights that had made her and Amy giggle and dig each other helplessly in the ribs. Then Aladdin's younger brother had stomped round the stage, chasing the pantomime cat. The boy looked real enough. Too real – as if he had just stepped in from the outside world, and might provide some link that would include them all in the magical events unfolding before their eyes. Norah Bird shuddered at the horror of that moment when the orange cat had yelped and spat, waving its great cardboard claws in the air and clutching its injured backside. The roar of the other children had drowned out her own wild panic. Norah had started to cry. Beside her, Amy, eyes ablaze and mouth wide open, full of chocolate and missing milk teeth, sat howling like a wolf in the moonlight, oblivious as the rest. I knew then how it would all turn out, Norah thought. I sat there on my own in the darkness, and I *knew*.

Mr Nye or Mr Sharps from the tannery had leant over and put an arm round Norah. Slowly, after she'd shaken him off, she had seen that the marmalade cat was not hurt. The tail could be fixed back on, but something in Norah Bird was not so easily mended. She'd started choking on the chocolate in her mouth, and had had to be taken outside. Out – to here, where she was standing now. Only now there was nowhere to flee to. No Mr Nye or Mr Sharps to take her home. No Mummy or Daddy waiting there for her. This is all there is, Norah thought as she contemplated the peeling plaster pillars of the derelict Alhambra. We are not phoenixes. We only get one go, and this has been mine. She turned her head back bravely in the direction of the Gallimore. I have always made the best of everything, and I will go on doing so. It is what the dead guest would want. Over the next few days, Hester Jones

97

would come to see this also. Then she would stand up at the tea-dance and, before announcing the lucky winner of the stranger's fortune, Miss Jones would tell the town that Norah Bird too should be rewarded, for her brave efforts. She should be invited to Buckingham Palace and made a fuss of.

'Dreaming?' Neville Tagg sounded his bicycle bell. He'd intended flying past his mother's old schoolfriend, making the high-spirited bird noises and flapping his hands that he usually did whenever he saw funny plump little Norah Bird. Then he remembered the committee meeting that had just taken place; Miss Bird was *on* the committee overseeing the great fortune. Neville Tagg applied such violent pressure to his breaks, his note-book nearly fell out of his pocket.

'How did you get on?' he asked as he got his breath back. He was already late for his meeting with Aubrey Wilkes Tooley. Too bad! Give the old man something to grumble about. The pro-prietor of the Knibden Municipal Insurance Company, in pursuit of whose interests Neville spent his days pedalling round town, would only grumble at him anyway.

Neville's mother, Amy Tagg *née* Pasco, and Norah Bird had been at school together. They'd often swapped clothes the way little girls do. Norah had told him this once so that every time Neville looked at Norah Bird he couldn't help recalling it. Every time he cycled past her shop and saw the ugly mannequins with their painted pointed eyebrows staring haughtily down at him from her windows, it seemed to Neville a disgusting thing to have done. It was probably what had killed his mother. Some-thing had. Mrs Tagg, *née* Pasco, had died when Neville was young – too young to remember much about her. All that he knew of his mother, he had learned from her friend, Norah Bird. 'The dead guest,' he prompted Norah now. 'I bet *you* know . . .'

Norah, her face neatly framed in lavender crimplene, smiled sharply at Neville. One thing I *do* know, she thought, it was lingering here, on this very spot, that I first met Jack! Jack Tagg who had married her best friend Amy and fathered Neville.

Amy Pasco had been in the same class as Norah, their desks side by side on the first day in the Infants'. 'You will be my friend,' the six-year-old Norah had told the six-year-old Amy, unzipping her brand-new pencil case and bestowing on the girl the sharpest of the gleaming new pencils Daddy had given her the night before. Amy had taken the pencil and held it up to the light, examining its point and glancing suspiciously at Norah. Then, with a flick of her thick blonde plaits, quick as a snake in the grass, the pretty Amy had added the pencil to her own assortment of writing things that she kept in a battered tobacco tin held together with an elastic band. The girls had been friends ever since.

Neville knew that Mr Pasco, Amy's father (his own maternal grandfather), had worked for Mr Bird who owned the old tannery. Amy's brothers had all worked there also. A stinky place, it had been. With two nasty foremen, Sharps and Nye. No one had been sorry, except Mr Bird, and possibly Sharps and Nye, when Mr Bird had gone out of business. People didn't wear leather gloves all the time the way they once had, Mr Bird had explained to Norah. Foreign imports of leather goods were so much cheaper and, in any case, new plastics were gradually replacing leather for most things. The market had steadily dwindled until, eventually, Mr Bird had given up the struggle to keep the tannery open and the factory had been bought up, flattened, the site turned into cheap housing. The Tills lived at Tannery Row. Neville glanced at Norah and wondered what his dead mother's friend would say if she knew about him and Susie Till!

Susie did Norah Bird's hair at the Silver Scissors Salon where she worked. The salon was straight over the road from Miss Bird's dress shop and once a week Norah Bird locked her shop and went across to have her hair done. Neville hated to think of his girl handling the stuff that grew on Norah Bird's head, twisting the strands of coarse wire between her little fingers, snipping the old tough ends and then spraying it into shape with the hairspray Susie smelled of when he held her in his arms, holding her big soft body down on the narrow bed in the house he shared with his father's widow. Telling Susie to be quiet when she wriggled beneath him, covering her mouth with his own body in case his step-mother heard. Hoping, perhaps, that one day his step-mother might hear, and be outraged. 'I want you out of the house,' the second Mrs Tagg would say. 'You, and that hairdresser!'

If *he* inherited under the Will, Neville Tagg supposed he'd find himself marrying Susie and buying a house of his own to keep her in. But no – if the dead stranger's fortune was suddenly his, surely he'd be free to do as he pleased. Even the sky high above would not be the limit! Neville tugged at his ginger moustaches and gazed up into the darkening skies beyond which he intended to soar. Why, if there was that kind of money, he could buy out old Wilkes-Tooley! Neville nearly fell off his bike, despite the fact that he was stationary and stood with both feet flat on the ground. He steadied himself and started whistling. That's what he'd do! He'd run the Knibden Municipal Insurance Company himself and show Aubrey Wilkes-Tooley how the business could have prospered all these years. He'd throw away the antique ledgers and compendiums, all those tables of life expectancy that were beyond him, making a bonfire of the lot in the middle of the yard where he rested his bike whenever he went to see the wheezy old man. Wilkes-Tooley was always telling him how grand the Knibden Municipal Insurance Company had once been – well, under Neville Tagg and his new-found millions, the Knibden Municipal Insurance Company could *motor* again!

'Oh dear, Mr Tagg, only three new policies this month!' Wilkes-Tooley would wag his finger. 'Hardly pays for the bell on your bicycle, Mr Tagg.' Cough, splutter, croak. While old Wilkes-Tooley recovered from his idea of a joke, Neville would hang his head and gaze fixedly through his thick eyebrows out of the window. Soon the lecture recommenced. 'Once there were *teams* of young men like yourself, bicycling away . . .' The way the old man talked, you'd have thought it was Neville's fault the company was so run down. Three new policies a month was a remarkable achievement when you consider what a struggle it was to sell each one. He'd even tried to interest Hester Jones in an All Risks policy last night at the Swan. Everyone had laughed – but they'd all soon see. It was obvious someone employed to do what Miss Jones was doing ought to be insured.

'If I had a car,' Neville often tried to tell Mr Wilkes-Tooley. The Knibden Municipal Insurance Company image was all wrong. Bicycle clips and pocket notebooks meant people laughed in pubs. Bigger national companies could afford to offer more and better to customers for less. They had glossy glass offices and their representatives got about in fleets of shiny matching vehicles. A Ford *Fiesta* – Michael Milady had been spot on! Neville himself had never dared go so far as to actually specify the make and model. Even the slightest suggestion of any expenditure – a new notebook or refill for his biro – was always greeted with a lengthy guffaw that endangered the dust on the company ledgers. Well, the dead guest had seen to it at last – things were about to change!

Neville Tagg stroked his ginger moustaches as he envisaged, now, teams of young men like himself. All working under him. All properly respectful, of course, as he had never been of Aubrey Wilkes-Tooley with his over-friendly wife and three unfriendly daughters. He pictured these eager young men hurtling round town – and other towns too, why not? why not expand? why not take over the world? – on their bicycles, chasing the business of what would then be *his* insurance company. Neville would raise the bonuses he paid out on all new Knibden Municipal Insurance Company policies, and he'd offer brand new Ford *Fiestas* as rewards and incentives. From time to time, the police would call at his office, propping their black bicycles in the yard.

'Pardon me, Sir, for intruding . . .'

'Well, Officer?' Neville would not even look up. The most eager of the lads had been caught speeding, such was his desire to impress Mr Tagg and sign up more policies per month for the company than anyone else. 'Is that all?'

'*All*, Sir?' The policeman would shuffle out muttering. 'This will have to be settled in Court.'

Neville thought fondly of that particular eager young man, a young man in truth not at all unlike himself. He saw the fellow being let off with a stern warning by an indulgent judge, and possibly even a hefty fine which Tagg would generously pay for him – 100 m.p.h. in the High Street! He had given the Laffety gang on their motorbikes a run for their money – and *that* could be regarded as a public service. The jaunty young man of Neville's imaginings would leave the Court, leaping down the steps two at a time, and fall straight into the arms of one of Wilkes-Tooley's disdainful daughters whom he would marry right under Aubrey Wilkes-Tooley's own nose, and set up home with her. The middle daughter, perhaps, the beautiful lofty Lalla.

Just think, Lalla Wilkes-Tooley, the wife of one of Neville's employees, a bloke who looked just like himself! Now *there* would be a turnabout. And all brought about by the dead stranger's Will . . .

Miss Bird had said something Neville didn't catch. 'Beg pardon?' he asked. Then he smirked. What would Norah Bird say if she knew that while she had been twittering on, he'd been contemplating the difficulties of containing the large flowing limbs and statuesque bosom of Miss Lalla Wilkes-Tooley in the single bed on which he nightly impaled the hairdresser, Susie. Neville thought Norah Bird might have spoken to him of his mother which was something she frequently did for she lived, he considered, rather peculiarly in the past. It was only because Miss Bird often mentioned her that Neville ever thought about his mother at all. Norah Bird had never allowed her schoolfriend Amy Tagg, *née* Pasco, to die. Hair grew, Susie had told him, having read it over a customer's shoulder in a glossy magazine, even after you were dead. You buried people but as their flesh decayed, their hair went on growing, filling the coffin like an overstuffed cushion on which the hard earth must sit to keep it all from spilling out.

When Norah Bird repeated what she had said, Neville heard the woman talking *not* about his late mother, Amy Tagg, *née* Pasco, but about a marmalade cat that had met with an unfortunate accident which had somehow been partly her fault.

'You should have been insured!' Neville laughed carelessly, touching Norah on the arm so that she could feel his touch long after he had rung his bell and, with a cry of 'Must go – urgent business!' careered off down the street. It was not a touch Norah Bird cared for. That the fair elfin Amy and handsome Jack Tagg could have produced such a great gawky son! Norah could not help wondering if Neville meant she should have been insured against the cat, or against the little girl who had sat beside her in the darkness, egging on Aladdin's younger brother up there on the Alhambra stage.

Norah Bird shut her eyes. Buy your tickets here, buy your tickets here! came the cry of the vendor who had positioned himself rather cheekily outside the entrance to the Alhambra hoping to entice playgoers to purchase lottery tickets with their money instead of theatre seats.

'What shall I go for?' Jack had asked.

'I beg your pardon?' Norah Bird was eating a water ice. Men did not often accost Miss Bird in the street. The citizens of Knibden tended, on the whole, to be extremely deferential towards Mr Bird's daughter. The one the Pasco girl had cleverly managed to befriend. You never knew when you or someone in your family might want work at the tannery. But Jack had only just arrived in the town. He had no idea that Miss Bird was *the* Miss Bird. A job at a stinky tannery was the last thing he had in mind.

'You help me choose,' Jack said to Norah. 'Then I'll have *you* to thank if I win, and *you* to blame if I don't. Either way, I get a kiss!'

Norah laughed. Jack had a way of making you laugh but Norah did not know this then. Nor did she know whether he was serious about the kiss but it occurred to her that here might be an adventure of her own to recount that evening. It was usually Amy's alarums and excursions the friends discussed as they sat together in the Birds' front sitting room, trimming new collars on their coats, speculating about their future husbands and making plans for the coming weekend. Norah glanced at Jack, taking in as much as she could so that she'd be able to describe him accurately to Amy later. Then she obediently leaned over the ticket vendor's tray and examined the piles of naked women, trumpets and dragons. She did not want to seem shy so she said, 'I think you should buy one of the women. They haven't won for years and people reckon they might this time.' She had heard a couple of the tanners saying this. She had also heard her father telling Sharps that he must crack down on lottery gossip in the works. Production per man-hour was significantly down and this was not something, in the present state of things, he could afford.

'Right,' Jack said to the vendor. 'You heard the lady – I'll have two of your best women, please!'

Just then Messrs Follifoot, Treadgold and Macready came round the corner, deep in conversation. 'Afternoon, Miss Bird!' one of them called out when they were almost on top of her. Norah moved away quickly. As she did so she could hear the three men behind her examining what was left of the old Alhambra – just as she had done.

'It would cost a bloody *fortune*!' Follifoot was saying.

'But there *is* a bloody fortune,' Treadgold and Macready both replied. 'Work could get started in three days' time – we must form a consortium and tender for it right away. No time to lose.'

It's not all talk, then! Norah thought. She had tried to tell her parents what had happened in the crimson velvet seats of the front row but it had been difficult to explain. She had been frightened. Of Amy. She had looked at her friend and seen a wolf. Mr Bird had taken his pipe from his mouth, and patted his daughter on the head. He'd called her his 'little Norah-bird' in the way that for years after he'd died she'd lain in bed at night, trying to imagine him doing again. 'My little Norah-bird,' she had whispered. 'My little Norah-bird,' she whispered again to herself now.

But Norah, even when she was 'small' had never been 'little'. In fact she'd been quite podgy and on one occasion, her form teacher Miss Pringle had called her out of the dinner queue because the buttons on her regulation overall were unfastened. When Miss Pringle saw that it was useless trying to do them up she had clapped her hands for silence and told Norah, in front of all the other children, that if she ever wanted clothes to fit her, she'd have to cut down on the chocs! It was Miss Pringle's idea of a joke. The other children, including Amy, had dutifully tittered but when Norah recounted the incident at home, her father had not been amused. His little Norah-bird could eat as much chocolate as she liked. As for finding clothes to fit, he would buy her her very own dress shop! His little girl was exactly as he would wish her, and she was never, ever, to listen to anyone who told his little Norah-bird otherwise.

The following day Mr Bird sent Mr Nye to have a quiet word with Miss Pringle who was herself as skinny as a rake. There'd been no meat on the woman, Nye reported back at the tannery but this, and the other things he said about her, could not have worried Bird's foreman unduly because at the end of the school year, to the astonishment of everyone, including the couple themselves, Miss Pringle left the school to marry Mr Nye. Norah, who'd been instrumental in bringing the happy couple together, was bridesmaid.

Miss Pringle – or rather 'Mrs Nye' as she'd just become – took the ten-year-old Norah to one side during the celebrations that were held, at Mr Bird's expense, in the Gallimore Hotel. She had stood close to Norah in a corner heavily hung with coats and wraps so that Norah Bird had been unable to back away. The bride laughed and smiled, and anyone glancing in their direction would assume a jolly exchange was taking place between a teacher and her favourite pupil. In fact, the new Mrs Nye was telling Norah that she dared say Norah and her well-to-do family expected her and Mr Nye to be grateful for the generosity shown to them. Norah Bird, foolish in flouncy satin, stared up at the woman and shuffled her feet. The bride then said it was only right that Mr Bird should finance an expensive wedding party at the Gallimore. He was stinking rich, and Mr Nye had worked for him faithfully in his stinking tannery all these years with very little by way of reward, or thanks. There'd been occasions Miss Pringle had heard about, when poor Mr Nye had been obliged to drop everything at a moment's notice and escort his employer's spoilt daughter to the Knibden Alhambra so that she and her friends could sit through matinée performances, stuffing their faces with violet creams and shouting at him. Besides which – here Miss Pringle raised her pointed chin – the marriage today would never have come about if Norah had not been a sneaky child, reporting at home a teacher's carelessly truthful remarks at school. The former Miss Pringle handed Norah the bridal bouquet of yellow flowers that her own parents had paid for, looking at Norah with the same defiance she turned on unruly classes at school. Norah Bird understood then that Miss Pringle had been so desperate to marry and leave teaching, that even her own father's foreman with the piggy eyes, Mr Nye, had done. And Miss Pringle saw no reason why her bridesmaid should not know it.

A child had been born to the Nyes. It had its father's piggy eyes and only lived ten years, a great lump of a child that had always needed a pram and had never managed to do up its own buttons or eat its own chocolate and had died at exactly the age Norah had been when Miss Pringle made her unkind remarks. The town had looked on in amazement at the way the ex-school-teacher doted selflessly on the hapless infant. Its death was worse for the woman than if it had never lived. She had taken to her bed, resolutely staying there until she could join her beloved offspring in its grave. Mr Nye only survived his wife by a day or two for, on his way to her funeral, he had stepped out on to a busy road, directly into the path of a passing Noddy van.

It is dangerous to cross me, thought Norah Bird whenever she considered the fates of Mr and Mrs Nye. And their infant. And Jack. And even Amy – Amy Tagg, *née* Pasco, Neville's mother who had died when he'd been little more than a baby.

'It is dangerous to cross me,' she would tell Hester Jones. And it occurred to her now – as she unlocked the door of Miss Bird's and turned the cardboard CLOSED sign round to OPEN, although it was late in the day and she could hardly expect any customers – that young Neville Tagg had left her outside the derelict Alhambra, just then, in rather a hurry. 'Must go, urgent business!' the boy had cried when it was no secret the Knibden Municipal Insurance Company hardly did any business these days. Come to think of it, Neville did not usually slam on his breaks to pass the time of day with his late mother's friend in the street. Ever since he'd been tiny it had amused Amy's son to fly past her at full speed on his bicycle, making high-spirited bird noises and flapping his hands in the air as if he had wings and hoped somehow to take off and glide up into the sky. The whole town was in a state of excitement about the dead stranger – but how could young Master Tagg possibly imagine *he* might have anything to be excited about? *The dead guest*, he'd prompted her, shoving his great ginger moustaches close into her face, *I bet you know* . . . Norah Bird shuddered. She remembered now the eagerness with which Neville Tagg had greeted Hester Jones on her arrival, the night before, in the Swan.

I must keep my eye on that boy over the next few days, Norah Bird decided. If for no other reason – and here she cackled out loud as she removed the lavender crimplene from about her head – than for the sake of his dear, departed mother, Amy Tagg that had been Amy Pasco when the two little girls had been friends, and swapped clothes together, all those years ago at school. Before Jack Tagg came to Knibden and Norah had foolishly encouraged him to select two naked women in the lottery.

3

The Silver Scissors

Susie Till snipped and clipped. Belle Quinn said, 'Don't overdo it, dear, I'm not a privet hedge!'

Susie laughed loudly. 'Millions!' she said, describing a great stash of money in the air with her comb. 'Who do you think will get it all, Miss Quinn?'

Why not Neville? Then they could get married and set up home right away. The day after tomorrow, when the dead guest's money was handed out, she would become Mrs Tagg! They ought to get engaged at once. Susie had seen the solitaire of her dreams in the window of Macready's, that morning. She'd be able to have her own salon, and not take orders any more. Just till the babies came along. She'd have all the latest in tilting hair-driers and swivel tinted mirrors. There'd be the dead guest's money, of course – no expense need be spared. Susie's Salon could open up next week and soon put the rotten Silver Scissors itself out of business! Or maybe not. Maybe Susie'd give up doing hair altogether. Mrs Tagg could stay at home all day with her feet up. Feet that didn't half ache right now – these boots were a mistake. For work, anyway. And they wouldn't be right for shopping in neither. She'd make sure she walked past here laden with carrier bags and boxes for everyone to see and, sometimes even – why not? – come in and have her own hair done! Take the weight off her feet – actually *sit* in these chairs, have highlights and all to remind herself how far she had made it along that golden path that stretched so immeasurably between Miss Susan Till and that new posher self of three days' time, Mrs Neville Tagg. Susie sighed! And envisaged now that glossy, lucky creature sitting alongside Belle Quinn. Both glancing through magazines and commenting loudly on items of interest and advertisements for nice things to buy. 'I'll have *two* of those,' Mrs Tagg would say. 'Just in case . . .' And then, when at last they were released from the driers, preened and ready to venture back into the outside world, they would pick up their handbags and agree to go together to the Gallimore, and take afternoon tea. 'What a splendid suggestion, Mrs Tagg!' Miss Quinn would say. 'I'm very partial to a scone, with jam.'

'Well, *who* do you think, Miss Quinn?' Susie cried.

Belle Quinn glanced in the mirror at Susie's flushed and painted face. The girl really ought to wear a bra! And a stronger deodorant. And as for the knee-high, shiny black boots – there was a time, not so long ago, when such items were the mark of a certain sort of woman. A woman with a good deal more experience of the world than this child – or Belle Quinn herself, for that matter – possessed. Belle found herself thinking of the naked woman that had been printed on the Great Knibden Lottery tickets. No wonder there had been so much trouble in the town. A large voluptuous creature crudely carved on a printer's block at the time of the first lottery centuries back and used ever since, she supposed. No one quite having the power to prevent it. A private joke from the past, passed down. 'It could be anyone in Knibden,' Miss Quinn said lightly. 'It might even be *you*, Susie dear!' And, perhaps because this seemed so pitifully unlikely, and also because the good Miss Quinn felt a little guilty at her uncharitable thoughts about Susie Till's boots, she heard herself mentioning the one name the poor child wanted to hear. 'Or Neville Tagg, maybe.'

'Do you really think so, Miss Quinn?' Susie squealed. 'Why, *you* are on the committee, *you* should know . . .'

'I am as much in the dark as anybody,' Belle Quinn shook her head, causing Susie to snip perilously close to the scalp.

By one of those strange coincidences that happen – but are, most likely, not really coincidences at all – Miss Quinn had had an appointment at three o'clock that afternoon. Booked weeks ago, long before the committee meeting had been arranged for today at exactly that time, long before the mysterious stranger had died in their midst, disrupting everything. Belle telephoned the Silver Scissors first thing that morning to ask if her appointment could be brought forward. 'I was hoping you could fit me in earlier. I know it's terribly short notice,' she'd apologized. 'But with only three days to solve this mystery, the committee is very keen to get on with things. And I would *so* like to look my best. In deference to the guest who died. In deference also to Hester Jones.'

But it had been impossible. 'You know I would if I could,' Susie's boss had said, but the whole town suddenly wanted to smarten itself up. People who hadn't been to a hairdresser in years were pouring in to the Silver Scissors to have their hair trimmed, and enjoy a bit of a gossip. 'The dead guest has certainly done his bit for business!' the salon owner laughed (rather coarsely, Miss Quinn felt). Apart from which, if Belle Quinn were to have her hair done *after* the committee meeting, the Silver Scissors would be able to hear what had taken place behind the closed doors of the Gallimore, straight from the horse's mouth.

'Well, *you* must have a better idea who's going to get it all,' Susie persisted. She thought the horse's mouth a bit unforthcoming.

'Maybe I have, dear, maybe I have,' Belle Quinn murmured kindly, not wanting to disappoint. Aware that Susie had been told to stay till the committee meeting was over and Miss Quinn came, however long it took. 'There's someone in charge now. A girl has been officially appointed, you know. Miss Hester Jones. You should speak to her. Everyone must speak to her. Perhaps Miss Jones will make her way to the Silver Scissors – her hair certainly looks as if it needs seeing to.'

At the mention of Hester Jones, Susie's nipples hardened visibly beneath the soft tight fabric of her jersey. She had heard about Hester Jones! How she had wandered into the Swan, bold as brass, and gone right up to her Neville at the party Susie herself had been unable to attend on account of the numerous little Tills who needed putting to bed. Mrs Till being a widow and having to work nights to support them all. What sort of woman wanders into a public house in a strange town, dripping wet and with only a small cardboard suitcase, looking for work and accosting another girl's bloke, Susie Till wanted to know. Privately she was of the opinion the free drink and the dead guest's fortune were to blame. Miss Jones would have heard what was on offer and turned up to grab her share of what was going.

'Did yer fancy her?' she had asked Neville who had groaned and turned over, but Susie had been quick to notice he'd not actually *denied* wanting to have his way with Hester Jones. She pictured Nev's step-mother finding him in bed with the Jones girl, and not minding much because she'd think Miss Jones able to swing things for them. Mrs Tagg would probably start getting up early and taking the couple cups of tea in bed every morning, with slices of toast, thinly buttered. Susie saw the woman seating herself on Nev's old satin eiderdown and nattering on about the dead guest with Hester Jones while Neville blushed crimson and dropped breadcrumbs everywhere as he tried to hide his freckled nakedness with the sheets. Susie liked Neville needing her at night – but she had no illusions: this Hester Jones would do just as well. All women were much the same to a man in the dark. There'd be wedding bells peeling before long, Susie thought miserably, but unless she acted promptly to defend her interests, they would not be ringing for her.

Susie Till knew there was no point hoping for anything for herself from the dead guest, directly. No one who died at the Gallimore could possibly have even heard of the Tills, let alone left them anything. But Nev – Nev had class. Everyone knew his dead mother had been best friends with Norah Bird in the days when the Birds owned the whole of the land on which the Tannery Estate was built. Stinking rich they had been till Mr Bird lost it all, and the houses went up, and Norah was left with only her dress shop when once she'd thought to inherit half of Knibden. Nev must surely be in with a chance – and Susie intended to share that chance with him. If Neville Tagg ever got the Ford *Fiesta* Michael Milady had promised him last night in the Swan, she was determined to be the one in the passenger seat at his side, wearing the solitaire she had seen in Macready's window that morning. Not this Jones woman. She'd murder her first! Susie Till now imagined Neville's step-mother encouraging Hester Jones to move out of the Gallimore Hotel and into the Tagg house, permanently. Using Hester Jones, indeed, as a means of getting rid of Susie Till which was something Susie instinctively felt Neville's step-mother (who did not yet know of her existence), was bound to want to do.

'She's got quite a position of power, hasn't she?' Susie sounded out Miss Quinn.

'Power?'

'Hester Jones.'

'Not at all. The girl's only employed to find out the truth, dear.

After that, I dare say she'll be on her way. Not the sort to settle, I shouldn't think. Not in a quiet place like Knibden.'

Susie Till was glad to hear it. She glanced out of the salon window and saw Norah Bird deep in conversation with her Nev. Norah Bird was also on the committee. Norah Bird, whose best friend long ago had been Nev's dead mum, was bound to do something for him. As Susie watched, she saw her intended suddenly leap on his bicycle, wave his legs in the air and then pedal exuberantly away. He knows something! she thought.

Her scissors snipped. Neville would need smartening up, of course. He could hardly expect a woman like Mrs Neville Tagg to put up with those baggy brown trousers! Fortunately, Susie knew exactly how this smartening up might be accomplished. Her days spent reading magazines over people's shoulders had not been in vain. Nor had Susie been slow to notice that articles telling you 'How to Transform Your Man on the Cheap' cost an awful lot of money to implement. When they gave you '20 Tips on Turning Your Frog into a Handsome Prince' they invariably assumed you had the wherewithal to do so. Now there was likely to be that wherewithal, it seemed to Susie as she watched Norah Bird disappearing into her shop the other side of the road, that all the cares she had in the world would soon be dissolved by the dead stranger willing things her way. She sighed. How she longed to fling her arms round the dead man, kiss him even, if that would show her gratitude. Since the stranger wasn't there just then for her to do so, Susie turned her attention to the task in hand. She examined the back of Miss Quinn's head.

Neville Tagg, meanwhile, speeding along on his bicycle felt himself already transformed. Life would never be the same again! It was so blindingly obvious he couldn't think why he hadn't seen it before. Neville decided to put off going to see old Wilkes-Tooley till he'd worked out a plan of campaign. The solution had come to him while he'd been talking to Norah Bird: the dusty compendiums he had so long despised, all the Knibden Municipal Insurance Company's ledgers that went back to the year dot and lined the walls of Wilkes-Tooley's office, were bound to contain the answer. *Things forgotten when they should not be* . . . Somewhere in those thick dusty volumes must lie the truth, as buried as the buried stranger! If the dead guest had been connected to Knibden back in the heady days when everyone in Knibden had business with the company, when teams of young men like Neville were cycling round town pushing policies, then the dead guest's affairs must be recorded somewhere in those tomes. It was merely a question of discovering where. It was merely a question, also, of getting old Wilkes-Tooley out of his office while he, Neville Tagg, set to and discovered the answer. Neville stretched his brown baggy-trousered legs high in the air. Why, he could even have hugged old Norah Bird at that moment! Then, thinking of hugging, he thought of the haughty Miss Lalla Wilkes-Tooley whom no man would dare to embrace. And he thought, poor little Susie! He'd be leaving her behind. He would move on now to bigger and better things – and it seemed to Neville as he pedalled furiously along Knibden's streets that he had already done so.

Luckily Susie did not know this. Her attention had in fact just been diverted from the horror of Miss Quinn's closely cropped hair to something new she had spotted through the salon window. Two sprightly old ladies were making their way down the steep path that led directly from the rectory attached to St Redegule's into the centre of the town. 'Old Gilbert Sibson has had visitors, I see!' Susie remarked.

Belle Quinn swivelled in her chair so violently that if Susie Till had still been wielding scissors a nasty accident might have resulted. As it was, Belle gasped and turned pale. 'Good gracious!' she said.

Susie almost felt sorry for her – everyone knew Miss Quinn had once been sweet on old Gibsey. Not that you'd guess it to look at either of them these days.

The old ladies could now be seen purposefully mounting the steps of the Gallimore and, as Belle and Susie watched, they disappeared from view.

'Who were *they* when they're at home, then?' Susie demanded, unwinding the damp towel that had lain rather tight round Belle Quinn's neck.

'They are not at home. That is the point,' Miss Quinn said faintly. Her hair looked dreadful but she could hardly blame Susie. Neither she nor the girl had been concentrating. 'They have come back to Knibden to make trouble. Those two have done nothing but make trouble all their lives.' It was no surprise that the pair had turned up in Knibden now. They would delight in deliberately encouraging Hester Jones down all kinds of blind alleys, regardless of the fact that she only had a couple of days to complete her task. The two were sure to be at the tea-dance she herself had been persuaded to organize, egging on the proceedings, flirting shamelessly with the bandsmen . . .

'Fancy!' said Susie, losing interest. What concerned her right now was the size of tip Miss Quinn might leave as she left. But Belle Quinn paid her bill in the exact amount and hurried off home, too distracted to slip Susie anything.

Susie shrugged and began locking up the Silver Scissors for the night. Mrs Neville Tagg probably wouldn't leave the girls in here anything either – especially if they made her hair look like a blown dry privet hedge!

'I never was much good at anything,' Susie reflected cheerfully as she took up a broom and, pivoting on the heels of her black shiny boots, carelessly swept Miss Quinn's cuttings into an untidy heap. She thought she might walk past the jeweller's on her way back to Tannery Row, and check if her solitaire had been left on display in the window overnight.

Veitch met his step-son on the doorstep. 'Oh yes, very impressive,' he said in reply to Roger's inquiry about Hester Jones. 'You keep your eye on her.'

'I intend to,' Roger Ambrose laughed. 'And I'm not the only one! The whole of Knibden will be watching Miss Jones.'

'Good lad, good lad.'

Veitch entered the schoolhouse and found Louisa sitting on her own in the dark. 'How did it go?' her voice called to him softly. 'Your committee meeting.'

'I took the minutes,' Veitch proudly told his wife. '*And* I informed Miss Jones how you used to work at the Gallimore. In the old days.'

'Oh?' Louisa felt cold all over. Why had he told the investigator that?

'She would only find out anyway,' Veitch went on. 'If there's anything you can tell her yourself, Louisa, any help you can give . . .' His wife was sitting hunched with her back to him. 'Roger has tired you,' he said solicitously.

'My head,' Louisa replied softly. 'I think I'll have an early night.' She rose to go upstairs. 'I've left you some food in the pantry. Under a cloth.'

'Thank you, my dear – but tea was provided. A very nice hotel tea.' As Louisa passed close to him, Veitch thought to take her in his arms but did not do so. When she had gone, he went over to the chair she'd vacated and sat for a while in the darkness trying to catch a faint trace of the lightly scented warmth she had left behind.

This is how it would be, he thought, if Louisa were to die. The woman would slip from him with as little drama as if she were going upstairs for the night. Dear Roger, of course, might visit from time to time and the two men take long awkward walks together, covering great distances along the highways and byways round Knibden with their hands behind their backs and talking about everything, almost, except the one subject most dear to them both. And then, tired and silenced by their exertions they would tacitly agree to postpone the return to the empty schoolhouse and stop off at the Gallimore for tea. Veitch saw himself being lead by the younger man into the hotel dining room. The two of them sitting down without thinking at a table for three, and finding comfort at last over cakes and sandwiches in the presence of that third, unoccupied chair.

Edmund Veitch clicked his tongue impatiently and rose to switch on the light – what nonsense was this? Life without Louisa was unthinkable. He blamed the dead guest for bringing on such morbid thoughts. He poured himself a large stiff whisky and, after marching restlessly round the room with the stubby glass in his hand, caught sight of his face in a mirror. Veitch smiled sternly at himself and removed the flower he had placed in his button hole on the way to the committee meeting that afternoon. Then he resumed his seat.

Hester Jones would doubtless find out the truth, he supposed. It could hardly be wondered at if poor Louisa was suffering an even worse headache than usual. And no wonder, either, that dear Roger had hurried back to Knibden to offer the comfort and support only a loving son can give his mamma at such a time.

Edmund Veitch sighed contentedly. Over the next three days, and until Hester Jones made her announcement at Miss Quinn's tea-dance, Louisa and the lad he had raised as his own would be in need of his firm steady guidance as never before. The whole town would be in need of leadership . . .

Veitch pictured the young man *he* had once been stepping down on to the platform of Knibden station. Surrounded by packing cases and confusion. The ticket vendors shouting noisily about trumpets, dragons and naked women and swarming round him as they did round every newcomer, so that his first wife had had to come to his rescue, diving in with her umbrella and chasing the men and their tickets away. She and her husband had arrived in Knibden with considerably nobler intentions than the purchasing of trumpets, dragons and unclad women, the first Mrs Veitch had informed everyone on the platform. She'd pointed to the stacks of books held together in long leather straps that were being lifted down from the train, as if rapping on the blackboard with her ruler, and triumphantly revealing to a class of dunderheads her *quod*, her *erat* and her *demonstrandum*!

Eventually, under Harriet Delilah Veitch's expert supervision, a porter had been induced to convey the Veitches' effects in a handcart to the schoolhouse – only to find that the place had not been made ready to receive them. The school authorities apologized. All normal activities in the town were unavoidably delayed, they'd said, on account of the chaos and excitement in the run up to the lottery. It was a bad time to arrive – and, in any case, they had not expected the new headmaster until a day or two before the start of the autumn term. Harriet Veitch had had a word or two to say about that! In the end, a cramped, inexpensive room had been found for the weary travellers at the back of an upper floor in the Gallimore Hotel. It was hardly the welcome the couple had anticipated and when at last the boxes and books were delivered to their room late that night, the first Mrs Veitch tearful in curlers and face-pack coldly refused the station porter his tip.

The Veitches had stayed a week or so at the Gallimore while the schoolhouse was being prepared. And it was there in the hotel, while his first wife rushed round the town seeing about furniture and linen, that Edmund Veitch had first encountered the beautiful young Louisa Ambrose.

Louisa, who had *also* been married at the time. To Roger's father, a man with unforgettable bright blue eyes.

4

The Last of the Gallimores

'We have returned,' one of the ladies said.

'To be of assistance,' the other added, by way of explanation.

They stood side by side clutching little embroidered handbags and smiling graciously at Hester Jones who looked from one to the other, and waited. When neither spoke, she said, 'I have had a long day.' Miss Jones had been about to fall into bed when the manager of the Gallimore Hotel, Mr Daniel Mason, informed her that she had visitors. On urgent business.

'We should have been sent for, Miss Jones,' one of the old ladies said smartly. 'But we have come anyway.'

'To help in the investigation.'

'To give you every assistance. It is our duty.'

'We have always done our duty.'

'Oh, I wouldn't say that, Tilda. There have been times . . .'

'Tilda' giggled. There had indeed. Good times and bad.

'Well, who are you?' Hester Jones asked, sounding ruder in her astonishment than she intended. The old ladies were now look-ing at Miss Jones with no little astonishment themselves.

'We are the Gallimore sisters!' they chorused.

'I see,' said Hester Jones.

'I don't think you do, dear!'

'You can't possibly when we hardly understand the whole thing ourselves. It is clear, though, that we are connected, in some way.'

'It is probably what we have been waiting for.'

'We have certainly been waiting for something. And now . . .'

'Here we are! We have returned at last. I am Bessie, and this is Tilda. Surname: Gallimore! Our time has come.'

'Our time has been a long time coming – that is the nature of time.'

Hester Jones quietly sighed and suggested they all sat down. The elderly sisters did so eagerly. Their tiny handbags propped on their knees, they resembled two pampered lap-dogs greedily anticipating something sweet to eat. Or young children expecting a bedtime story. 'So you think you are connected to the man, the guest who died here?'

'Without a doubt.'

'Who was he then?'

'It *could* have been Gurney. Our brother.'

'Gurney Gallimore.'

'Except that he, poor fellow, is dead already. He died way back.'

'In Paris. Or was it Berlin? He did not, in any case, die in Knibden.'

'Dear Gurney was dead to us long before he actually died, Miss Jones. That's families for you.'

'No, your guest cannot possibly be our poor dear Gurney. But, if a man passed away with such purpose in *this* hotel . . .'

'In our hotel.'

'Our home.'

'The hotel is *yours*?'

'*Was* ours. Well, no, it never was *ours*. But we lived here. We lived here all our young lives. It was Gurney's, until he sold it. To pay for his women.'

'We were chansonettistes. I played the piano.'

'I sang.'

'We were the Gallimore Girls.'

'Ask Michael Milady.'

'He could have engaged us . . .'

'Not any more, I cannot reach the notes.'

'My fingers do not play.'

'You are thinking we are a pathetic spectacle, Miss Jones, with our reconstructed faces and carefully tinted hair. You are thinking the dead guest could never have been interested in such creatures as us. Yet, once we could have *starred* at the top of Cayke's bills. Imperial players on an Imperial stage.'

'We could have ousted the dazzling Miss Meldrew.'

'She never had a touch of our talent. Montague Cayke was one of our keenest admirers. He was famous across the world for his timing . . .'

'But *we* never gave him the time of day. We were young. We were beautiful.'

'It was a fairy story, people said. Like in a book, only no prettily printed covers could contain it.'

'It is a story we dwell on.'

'We like to discuss it. Sometimes we tell it.'

'We could tell it to you, Hester Jones. If you are to solve this mystery, in three days flat, you should apprise yourself as soon as possible of all the facts.'

'That is why we are here.'

'We came as soon as we could. Listen to that clock ticking away on the mantelpiece. The dusty old thing has ticked away all our lives, ticking our lives away. Now those lives are nearly over, the clock will tick in earnest. *Things that ought to have been forgotten, but cannot be. That have become forgotten when they should not be* – as if that could refer to anything other than *our* story!'

'In a way, it is our story. And in another way it has nothing at all to do with us.'

'Except that we ourselves no longer have a story. And this one is big enough . . .'

'Even for you, Hester Jones! We have a duty to tell it. We are guardians of the truth.'

'We were witnesses. We saw it all!'

'Not all, Tildie, dear. No need to exaggerate. We were lucky enough to observe a fleeting part of the whole – which is more than most people can hope to in their lives. Our mother married Sir Mayhew Gallimore, late in his life, early in hers, and she became the second Lady Gallimore. The first Lady Gallimore, a pallid peevish creature, had died long before. Her five grown daughters were our step-sisters: Sarah, Caro, Charlotte, Elizabeth and Anne. But Tildie and I were Gallimores too.'

'Though I doubt we should've been!' Tilda put in. The pair giggled.

'Mother had been Miss Florence Farr. Florrie Farr on the stage. Not that *she* ever acted at the Knibden Alhambra. Or any other Alhambra. When Sir Mayhew married her, she only had one pair of gloves.'

'And they were red.'

'She made no secret.'

'Neither did he. That's what our step-sisters couldn't stand. The public humiliation of suddenly finding themselves with a step-mother their own age who had less of a pedigree than their old deerhound Guss. Then Gurney arrived, pushing them all aside as Sir Mayhew's only son, and heir to the Gallimore fortune. And, if that weren't bad enough, Bessie and I then came along, frilly little things, doted on by one and all. When Sir Mayhew died, the five sisters were left destitute. They were completely dependent on their young step-mother who put them to work so that they spent the rest of their lives fetching and carrying for her three spoilt children – perhaps you know all this, already, Miss Jones?'

'We are boring you?'

'Well,' Miss Jones hesitated. 'I have seen the old painting in the hotel dining room. Of the Gallimore family. I suppose you must both be on it?'

'That picture!' Bessie Gallimore clicked her teeth. 'We have lived with that picture all our lives, Miss Jones. It has – in some senses – been hanging over our heads!' The two screeched with laughter. Then Bessie continued, 'The Five Beautiful Gallimores, they were known as. At first it was a description, later it became a joke. A mockery. They were our *half* sisters – they were very much older than us. The painting was done before ever Sir Mayhew met our mother. It was partly *because* of that painting that he did meet our mother. It was commissioned for a ball, you see. A fantastic affair, held here in this house, to celebrate the start of the new century. Sir Mayhew hoped his daughters would use the occasion to pair off and marry. And save him the bother and expense of five separate weddings. But the Five Beautiful Gallimores were too proud to do anything so convenient. They enjoyed the Turn of the Century Ball but reckoned their suitors were only after their father's money. They were proved right. The moment their step-brother Gurney was born, no one was interested in them any more. Even the dog transferred his affections.'

'Old Guss spent the last years of his life wandering round Gallimore Hall behind Gurney who teased him mercilessly with a stick and hung from his ears. The creature liked standing over us too, drooling into our pram.'

'I think that broke their hearts – more than the rest of it – Guss betraying them. When he died, and Mamma ordered his moth-eaten corpse to be thrown into the incinerator, they did nothing to stop her.'

'After Sarah died, poor old stick, I found his worn leather collar in the bottom of her tin box. So she must have forgiven the old traitor to some extent.'

'You never told me that before!' Bessie said to her sister.

'I'm telling you now,' Tilda sniffed. 'I put the collar in her coffin with her. I strapped it round her ankle.'

'My God, Tildie!'

'Anyhow, Sir Mayhew Gallimore was furious with his daughters. When he'd been widowed and they'd been orphaned he had employed a whole army of domestics to take care of the five growing girls back in Knibden while he took himself off to London, and the Houses of Parliament and all his literary activities. He was an old man at the time of the ball. It was a splendid affair – and naturally reported in all the papers. The *Knibden Gazette* and the *Knibden Bugle* devoted themselves to the occasion. But one national paper obtained the right to print a gravure of the painting and, carried away by this scoop, some clerk in the office embellished the story. No ball worth its salt is complete without news of an engagement, and no newspaper worth *its* can neglect to purvey a whiff of romance to its readers. The portrait's painter, an up-and-coming young academician, Francis Dale, was declared to be enamoured of the eldest Miss Gallimore. Dale, after all, was known to have been present at the ball – Sir Mayhew had foolishly invited the fellow to stay on after the canvas was completed and join in the fun. An imaginative scribbler in the newspaper's offices declared, in the caption beneath the picture, that a happy announcement concerning its talented painter, Mr Dale, and the beautiful heiress, Sarah Gallimore, was expected shortly. You only had to look into her eyes to see it might be true. Sarah, Caro, Charlotte, Elizabeth and Anne read this fiction aloud to each other over their breakfasts. They kicked slender slippered feet in the air and laughed uproariously. By chance, however, the same paper fell into the hands of a pretty petticoated thing who had for years been Dale's mistress and frequently acted as his model. *She* did not laugh uproariously. Francis Dale had not been back to the lodgings they shared and her purse was practically empty. There was nothing for it.

Investing her last few shillings, she travelled to London to put her case before Sir Mayhew Gallimore, MP for Knibden.

'Day and night the young Florrie Farr waited outside the House of Commons. And then, almost as she was expiring from exhaustion and hunger, her patience was rewarded. She spotted Sir Mayhew Gallimore MP, recognizing the man from the gravure of her lover's painting that had appeared in the paper. "Your proud, beautiful daughters have everything, Sir Mayhew. While I, I have nothing. If Francis Dale marries Miss Sarah, I shall be destitute." The scene vaguely resembled something from Dickens. Certainly there were no encounters of this kind in Sir Mayhew's own novels where he took great pains rich and poor were never obliged to meet face to face. The novelty of the situation, not to mention the daintiness of the red glove resting on his sleeve, appealed somewhat to Sir Mayhew. He was struck too by the contrast between this dejected desperate creature before him and the plump disdain of his carefree daughters. That very day – or shortly afterwards – he took Miss Florence Farr to his bed. That was not that surprising. What did surprise was that sometime before his next trip home to Knibden, Sir Mayhew Gallimore MP married her. He brought his bride back to Gallimore Hall and introduced her to his staff and daughters. Florence stood meekly before the astonished household in her cheap clothes, blushing, her engorged womb barely concealed. While the Five Beautiful Gallimores gaped and the line of servants sniggered, the elderly Sir Mayhew took his new young wife by the hand and, laughing aloud, he led her past his po-faced daughters up to the top of the Gallimore table. He would laugh again when the daubster, Mr Francis Dale, came to the house to see Sarah – and encountered Miss Florrie Farr, installed now as the second Lady Gallimore! "Now *that* was a picture worth beholding!" Sir Mayhew had remarked of the portraitist's boggling face. When Sir Mayhew's new wife gave birth to the son he'd never had, he instructed his lawyers accordingly so that when the old man passed on, shortly afterwards, everything he owned was left in trust for the child, the control of the Gallimore fortune in the boy's mother's hands. Sarah, Caro, Charlotte, Elizabeth and Anne Gallimore sat about then. As beautiful as ever but destitute. Their marriage prospects gone for ever.'

'Snooty bitches,' Tilda picked up the story. 'They hated her. They despised her. Nothing that happened to them afterwards ever altered that. When to make ends meet, Gallimore Hall had to become an hotel, they blamed her. They blamed Gurney, they blamed us. They did right, poor things. Mamma was extravagant by nature. Under her guardianship, the Gallimore fortune slipped through her fingers. She filled the house all year round with fresh flowers, and young men. A rich young widow, she had more sense than to remarry, but this did not stop her having a good time. The Five Beautiful Gallimores had no choice but to stand by and watch her. Silently critical, they were too proud to say anything. The suitors who had once paid court to them kept on coming to the house but now they came to see the young Lady Gallimore. Sarah could only look on as Francis Dale took up again with his former mistress. On her terms this time, not his. No wonder the Five became bitter – we only ever knew them as crabby old women. The handsome picture painted at the turn of the century, when they were in their prime, was hung on the dining-room wall as punishment . . .'

'Now they are all dead.'

'And Gurney, and Mother too. All gone. Like shadows on a sunless day. We are the last of the Gallimores. Not that we were ever really Gallimores. Sir Mayhew was a thing of the past long before we were born. We are telling you this so there can be no misunderstandings later, Miss Jones. When *we* are dead, there will be no more Gallimores.'

'Only the hotel.'

'And I dare say that will change hands and alter its name. Gurney never had any children.'

'Poor Gurney. He never had much luck with women.'

'He never had much luck. In the end he sold the hotel.'

'Who to?'

'Ah, there you have us! We don't know. But he sold it. Complete with the five old ladies who earned their keep running the place. Gurney had no choice – he was bankrupted the way Knibden men traditionally went bankrupt. He'd spent the last of his money on a lottery ticket at the time of the last Great Knibden Lottery. He bought a woman, but dragons won. Typical Gurney!

He never had much luck with women!' The two old ladies tee-heed.

Then Tilda said mischievously, 'He might have gone for *you* though, Hester Jones!'

'Me?'

'Gurney's taste in skirt was unpredictable.'

'Just think, Miss Jones: if our poor dear brother *had* taken up with you, a son of *yours* might have been the heir to the Gallimore! Not that there would be anything left to inherit by now. The wheel had swung full circle. The first Gallimore arrived in the town way back without a penny, and made his fortune in the Great Knibden Lottery. Poor Gurney lost all that was left the same way.'

'Now *that* was really the start of the fairy tale – the arrival of Monsieur Henri Gallimore in Knibden. No one who saw the miserable band of prisoners shuffling into the town that was little more than a village at the time, could have guessed what was about to begin. These sorry veterans of Waterloo, chained together by their hands and feet, jeered at and pelted with rotten eggs and over-ripe tomatoes, had been lent for service to the company that was building the new canal. Herded into small wooden shacks by night, worked from dawn to dusk digging and breaking stones, the Frenchmen must have wished they had perished alongside their compatriots on the bloodwashed battle-field. It was a wretched existence. Hated by the starving Irish whose jobs they had taken, and by the English whose sons had been lost against Bonaparte, the men's lives were valued only for as long as they could work. The canal company fed them enough to keep them on their feet and whipped them mercilessly at the first sign of slacking. Meanwhile, they were set upon by dogs for sport and had pistols fired at their chained feet to make them dance.

'The new canal wasn't popular in Knibden. An absentee land-owner had persuaded the canal company to take their waterway across his land. By the time tardier local gentry cottoned on to the profitable possibilities of such a venture, the route had been fixed and surveying completed. The people of Knibden could only watch as the canal was hacked along its northern boundary, making the town an important stopping-off point between the industrial cities. Although the Great Knibden Lottery had not yet become famous or grown to the scale it later attained, it happened that as the canal was being worked near the town, a lottery was about to take place. People pouring in from the nearby countryside to purchase trumpets, dragons and naked women, gathered in clusters on the banks of the canal to watch the earthworks. Nothing like it, in those days before the railways, had been seen before. The feat of engineering appealed to men of a technical disposition, while the uncouth and the ladies delighted in the sport afforded them by the Frenchies. They took bets on which prisoner would drop dead next, then pelted their favourite in a bid to ensure their bet won.

'Thus it happened that a fair young lady, the daughter of one of the local bigwigs who was miffed at having missed out on such a big investment opportunity, took to giving her governess the slip every afternoon and going down to the cuttings with her brother and sisters, soiling pretty kid gloves throwing orange peel and tomatoes at the toiling prisoners. While thus engaged, the girl's eye fell on one of the men. The filthy sackcloth, still encrusted with dried blood from a shot wound in his side, could not hide the handsomeness and strength of his physique. Though no one was betting *he* would sag, the girl took careful aim. Her ripe tomato hit the fellow full in the eye. She squealed with maidenly delight but the proud, brave face the handsome foreigner raised wiped out her pleasure. Their eyes met. They fell in love. From that moment the poor girl could think of nothing but setting the man free.

'One morning, at first light, she rose early and dressed herself with care. She let herself out of the house and made her way to where the Frenchies were being whipped from their hut. When she saw her love and heard the overseer bellowing: Prisoner Number 286, she stepped smartly forward and announced to the startled canal company employee that she had come from the barracks with orders for Prisoner 286's immediate release. She waved papers (her laundry bill) in the man's face and he, distracted by the tremble on her rose-red lips and the delicate quiver of her smooth white bosom, at once ordered Prisoner 286's chains to be unlocked while he proceeded to yell for 287 and 288 to come forth and face the day.

'Henri Gallimore staggered towards his fair saviour. His legs so light without the irons he felt he was flying into her arms. And indeed, she intended to saddle her mare and let the man take flight before anyone realized what had happened. Unfortunately by the time she had taken him the back way to her father's stables word had got out that one of the prisoners had been falsely released. The hunt was on. There were plenty of red coats in the town at that moment for the lottery and a Frenchie on the loose promised the perfect *divertissement*. When the girl and her charge arrived at the stable, her father's hands were all clustered round a vendor of lottery tickets who was doing his last round, hoping to get rid of his final women, dragons and trumpets before the lottery got underway and unsold tickets were rendered worthless.

'The girl immediately offered to buy up all the remaining tickets and distribute them amongst the stable hands in return for their co-operation. The vendor who had expected to be stuck with the tickets, and take a terrible loss, suddenly found himself with gold in his pockets. And the hands who had hoped at best to club together and buy one ticket between them, were now in possession of *several* women, dragons and trumpets, *each*! They all felt as if they had won the lottery already, and promised the girl every help. One ticket she held back. A naked woman. This she gave Henri in token of herself. The hands said it would not be safe for the fellow to take the mare and ride off just then but they agreed to hide him for a day or two and help him slip away during the furore following the climax of the lottery.

'Soon redcoats arrived at the house. The girl was questioned in front of her parents. She dissembled as best she could, but was no actress. It did not take long for the stable where her mare was housed to be searched. The man was taken from his hide-out in the straw, stripped naked and marched into Knibden's main Square for a public thrashing. One of the side-shows laid on while people waited for the draw. The girl's punishment that she must stand beside him and watch. Every lash across his handsome body made her flinch. If the soldiers held back at all it was out of pity for her suffering. The people of Knibden scarcely attended to the spectacle, being far more concerned to find out if they had won the lottery than see a Frenchie thrashed to death before their eyes. As the great barrels of lottery tickets were finally rolled into the Square, Henri Gallimore slumped forward and died in the poor girl's arms. Without further ado, and to hold the crowd's interest, the winning number was pulled. Only tickets with women on were now eligible as this motif had been chosen in the initial draw the day before. Silence fell. Silence reigned. A murmur went round as every man turned to his neighbour. The murmur rose. No one stepped jubilantly forward. Then the trembling girl freed herself from her dead lover's arms.

' "Here!" she cried in her agony. "Are you all satisfied?" She held in her blood-bespattered hand Henri Gallimore's lottery ticket. It bore the winning motif and the winning number. People stepped back in shame, shielding their eyes from the sight of the vanquished victor lying in his own blood, and the woman wailing for a love that could never be again. "And here," – she pointed to her womb. No one dared gainsay the right of the unborn child to its father's prize.

'Rich now and able to do as she pleased, she took her beloved's name and built a great house on the site where Monsieur Henri was slain. She invested the rest of her winnings heavily in the canal he had helped to dig. The canal company prospered and the value of her shares multiplied many times over, even before the baby was born. And there you have it, Hester Jones. The story of how the Gallimores became rich and established themselves in Knibden.' Bessie Gallimore sat back. Tilda patted her hand.

'That *is* a fairy story!' Hester Jones remarked.

'And now, you must excuse us, dear. It is late, we are old and tired. It is past our bedtime. The Reverend Sibson will be wondering where we have got to.'

'We are staying with Gilbert Duncie Sibson at the rectory attached to St Redegule's. Such a kind young man! We have known him since the day he arrived in Knibden. It was the same day Edmund Veitch came to take up his post as the new headmaster. They stepped down from the very same train, only Gilbert Sibson did not have a wife with the strength of purpose of the first Mrs Veitch. Unlike Mr Veitch, *he* made the calamitous mistake of purchasing a lottery ticket . . .'

'He was not to know.'

'Ignorance is no defence. In this world, or the next.'

'It proved his undoing. You must visit us at the rectory whenever you please. You must ask us . . .'

'Anything you like. We have nothing to hide.'

'And nowhere to hide it if we had!' So saying, Tilda and Bessie Gallimore stood up and, bidding Hester Jones 'goodnight', they tripped out of the Gallimore Hotel, swinging their tiny broidered handbags as they went.

'How did we do, dear?'

'Very well. We have set the girl on the right path.'

'I wish someone had set *us* on the right path . . .'

'No, dear. The wrong paths are much more exciting. Now we had better hurry, young Gilbert will be waiting up for us.'

'In his nightgown.'

'And cap! Poor fellow, we must *do* something for him before we leave.'

'We certainly must – that is the good thing about having led an exciting life oneself. One does not begrudge a little excitement to others.'

'On the contrary, one cannot bear to see wasted opportunities.'

'We will do what we can for the present incumbent of St Redegule's.'

'We will make sure he has plenty of partners at Belle Quinn's tea-dance.'

'But not Belle Quinn!'

They laughed, then Bessie said soberly, 'The Reverend Gilbert Duncie Sibson buried the dead guest. He said the last rites.'

'And will do the same for us, when the time comes . . .'

'Meanwhile, Tildie, who knows what may happen! *We* may be about to inherit this dead stranger's fortune. The day after tomorrow, when Hester Jones stands up before the people of Knibden, she may point her finger in *our* direction.'

'The dead guest *did* die in the Gallimore!'

'On the site where Monsieur Henri . . .'

'He obviously returned to return what was once ours!' The sisters laughed together. 'And even if he didn't . . .'

'We will enjoy the story. We are witnesses once more . . .'

'A pair of silly old ladies, more like! Hoping for a last little bit of harmless fun.'

'The dead guest would never begrudge us that, Tildie. Men have never begrudged the two of us anything!'

Bessie took Tilda by the hand. The path back up to the rectory ran alongside the graveyard where the unknown stranger rested in his freshly dug, unmarked grave. It was a steep, treacherous climb in the dark but if either sister should slip, the last of the Gallimores were resolved to fall together.

Gilbert Duncie Sibson stood in the darkness of his bedroom watching the old ladies make their way inexorably up the hill towards him. He had left the door open downstairs but turned out the lights so the pair would think he was asleep. Tomorrow Sibson intended to rise early and spend the day on his knees praying to the blessed St Redegule for guidance. Only *that* Lady in her most bountiful mercy could help him, and Knibden, now.

5

Watchers in the Night

George Allendale worked through the night. There was no time to lose. Nor any time to sleep. He let himself into the library and crept about with his torch. He opened boxes and made lists. He avoided shining the beam up at Arthur Dawes Dobson but all the while he worked he was aware of the painted presence willing him on from the darkness behind.

George thought, I have never felt so wide awake in all my life. Why wait for Hester Jones's pronouncement? He would borrow the money at once to restart the museum. His mother had savings she did not need. These could now be spent. In the morning he would approach the builder, Follifoot, for an estimate to rebuild the great glass dome on the back of the library exactly where Dawes Dobson's famous museum once stood. Archaeology, palaeontology, speleology, Egyptology – George felt like sitting down immediately to start work, by torchlight if necessary, on his guidebook.

Calperius rose early the morning he and his men left Britain, the cold windswept land his forefathers had made their own, for ever. Valiantly had the Conqueror of Vintniorum ascended Knibden Crags and, with sorrow weighing heavily on his heart, stood astride the highest boulder in the morning fog, surveying the beautiful villa below that would now be left for the Barbarian hoards, and the barbaric elements, to pillage and smash. This was the end of the world as he knew it. The cataclysm long postponed. These few pebbles all that remain of the great mosaic floors Zoë and Hyena would have walked across when they went to give the Great Calperius his pleasure. This black pebble, a blink in the eye of an owl – these pale stones, part of the terrified mouse clutched tight in its beak. Knibden's Romans were superstitious people – they had cause to be, in view of what came after – so the semi-clad Zoë and Hyena would have been careful to side-step this creature of the night, and we can be pretty sure these particular pebbles (case A, exhibits 10–16) would never actually have been trodden on *by the bare, pretty feet of Calperius' women . . .*

Somewhere in the shadowy darkness behind the industrious George, the painted eye of that other dread creature of the night, Arthur Dawes Dobson, blinked.

Edina Allendale, meanwhile, sat up in bed in her hairnet and bed-jacket. She had heard George go out and at once taken up her lime-green wool to while away the sleepless hours. Eventually, at four in the morning, still knitting one, pearling two, slipping three, she resolved to be brave. As she had been brave when Mr Allendale went off, leaving her to rear their small son on her own. 'You can keep everything,' he had said.

'And George?'

'You can keep him too! I only want my freedom back.'

A few years later, a letter had come informing Mrs Allendale of the man's death. It seemed that on leaving her the wretch had remarried, almost at once. He'd only wanted his freedom back from her to give it up immediately to another. She had borne the slight well, even writing a gracious letter of condolence to that other, newer, more enticing Mrs Allendale. She had good cause to quarrel, she had written to that lady, but it was pointless doing so over a dead man. Especially a dead man like George's father. It then transpired – after a funeral she neglected to attend – that the infuriatingly fair Mr Allendale had left his ex-wife a sizeable sum of money enabling her and George to live very comfortably on the boy's paltry librarian's salary. It was typical of her ex-husband, she'd always felt, that by behaving so reasonably, even from beyond the grave, he had cruelly deprived her of the pleasures of righteous indignation.

Now, as she sat bolt upright in bed, she saw that her husband had managed to deprive her and George of something even more worthwhile. By dying in such an open, far from underhand, fashion the man had ensured that his first wife and child knew for certain the great fortune the rest of the town was so happily speculating about *could not possibly be theirs*! Had they *not* been apprised of Mr Allendale's fate, and the exact extent of his generosity, she and George could now both be wondering if the dead guest had been his father. What fun they might have had in the evenings, sitting either side of the coal-effect electric fire in their living room, hoping the millions in the bank would soon be theirs. And deciding how to spend it when it was. Edina Allendale pictured herself mounting the steps of the Gallimore, sitting Hester Jones down and telling the girl her version of events. She would have been able to rehearse her husband's many shortcomings and receive due sympathy at last for what she had endured. She dug her needle fiercely into the back of the knitting to retrieve an errant lime-green stitch. What a cruel hateful prig Mr Allendale had been! 'I will stand by you,' he had said. 'I will do the decent thing.' How she wished she had never met the man. How she despised the decent thing!

Mrs Allendale had left the library before Verity Willow returned from the committee meeting but when George came home later that evening, he'd been agitated and pensive, almost furtive – when she asked him what Miss Willow had had to say for herself, he was as annoyingly unforthcoming as ever his father had been.

So! Was there something Edina Allendale did not know? Something Hester Jones had told Miss Willow, that Miss Willow had reported back to George which she could not guess at but which put her son in the running, after all, for the enormous bequest? Mrs Allendale laid her knitting aside. She remembered how George had expressed interest in the party at the Swan. He, whose head was always deep in a book, had openly regretted not keeping Janice, the barmaid, company! Edina Allendale shuddered. The time had come to intervene. If George were about to inherit a vast sum of money, she would not sit by clacking her knitting needles only to see him share his good fortune with some busty trollop from the Swan. No, indeed! Miss Jones would be the first to know of her son's good fortune. Miss Jones would undoubtedly be interested in becoming the chief librarian of Knibden's bride. George's mother resolved to rise and go to the Gallimore first thing in the morning. She would introduce herself and explain to Hester Jones how, shortly after four o'clock that morning, she had sat up in bed and bravely told herself, You will not be losing a son, Edina, but gaining a someone-who-is-not-someone for a daughter-in-law. She would make it clear from the outset in her dealings with the girl that she would not stand in the way of George's happiness. For *his* sake she had been prepared to cash in part of her savings. The boy came first – and if he came first with Hester Jones also, the two women in George Barrington Allendale's life would very likely get along fine.

Bill Parris sat in his hut crouched over his stove. The eldest Laffety had been again, snooping about. There were tyre marks on the grass. Parris had stood at a distance watching the funeral. Earth to earth, ashes to ashes – who could they have been burying in that unmarked grave? No one so far as he knew had been ailing. No house stood empty. He had noted no difference in the milk bottles left on the doorsteps in the mornings so no milk orders had been cancelled, or cut down. Parris prodded the primus. Bill Parris. Odd job man. Municipal gardener. Shifter and dogsbody. Do anything for a few pence in his pocket would Bill Parris. He who remembered everything but communicated nothing. Secrets were as safe as the grave with William Parris. Safer! Why, he had even seen the stranger arriving late at night at the Gallimore – he'd have carried the man's bags for him if he'd been asked. He had watched the light go on and the curtains being drawn in the rooms on the first floor that were given over now to another stranger, Miss Hester Jones.

The dead guest had not looked like a man about to die, but looks, Bill Parris knew, could be deceiving. Veitch's first wife, Harriet Delilah, had not looked ill and yet she had suddenly keeled over. One minute she'd been pressing a sixpence on him and the next, Edmund Veitch was kneeling at her graveside sobbing fit to burst. Then, before the well of tears could possibly have dried up, the schoolmaster had remarried. A pretty young widow, Mrs Louisa Ambrose, mother of Roger Ambrose. The young man who'd recently returned. And shared an egg, tomato, lettuce and radish luncheon with Hester Jones.

I am the someone-who-is-not-someone who should be investigating, Parris thought. No one knows what I know – not even me! No one could be less someone. Parris took another swig from his bottle. A few more swigs, another bottle maybe, and as the night wore on, William Parris would become even less someone than he had ever been.

Ray Laffety loomed in the doorway.

'You clear orf!'

Ray Laffety put his hands in his pockets. He stood silently for a while and then sauntered away.

The lights were still blazing in the bar of the Swan. Calderon and his sister were having a row. It was the middle of the night but they had waited until after closing time because rows were bad for business. The Swan had benefited hugely from the death of the guest at the Gallimore. Calderon getting on the committee, and offering to hold the wake at the Swan, had been a stroke of genius. But was this good enough for Barbara? No. Calderon was having it off with the barmaid. One gets it where one can. Not in my front parlour you don't. Parlour, indeed – this is a public house, not the Gallimore Hotel! Don't I know it, and haven't you always made sure I've known it.

'Pipe down,' Calderon said. The barmaid was upstairs waiting for him.

'You're pathetic,' Barbara said.

'I am,' Calderon admitted. He was putty in their hands, these girls with their tapering scarlet nails and tight sweaters. They had only to swing their hips at him, even with his sister watching and, great lumbering fellow though he was, the landlord of the Swan would skip like a new-born lamb to their tune.

Usually a girl Calderon took up with couldn't stand the atmosphere after a while. By the time she'd had enough of the brother and sister quarrelling, he would most likely have had his fill of her. He'd have looked sorrowful at her departure, but really he'd be relieved. After a few weeks he and Barbara would start speaking to each other again. This had been the pattern of their lives. Long silences, whispered threats, brooding looks, tearful departures. This time, however, things weren't going according to the usual pattern. The barmaid in question, the fair Janice Oakes, had developed a keen interest in this business at the Gallimore. She had seen Hester Jones arrive. Janice had not put herself forward as someone-who-was-not-someone – although she might have done, for what possible connection could there have been between a pouting barmaid and some aged millionaire who'd snuffed it in the town's posh hotel? It would have been folly, though, for the sake of a temporary job to forgo whatever there was to forgo – and there was obviously a lot of money, one way or another, to be had. Janice wondered at the Jones woman going along with it all. She must either be simple, or there was more to her than met the eye. Best stick about. Calderon, after all, was on the famous committee and, as for his sister . . . Janice wore her sweaters tighter and added a little more swing to her hips – if there was to be a tearful departure from the Swan shortly, it would not be the barmaid weeping.

Victor Matchett had left the Swan at closing time. 'Go steady now,' Barbara Calderon said for the printer had a tricky walk home, back along the murky canal towpath to Buckworth & Matchett's in the dark. The man wasn't in a fit state to walk anywhere. Follifoot had been plying him with drink. Matchett was celebrating. The old firm of Buckworth & Matchett's was back in business. The town needed its own newspaper to keep people informed of events, Dick Follifoot had said. Now that there were events. The dead guest dying, the tea-dance being organized by Belle Quinn. 'Over the next couple of days you could make a bloody fortune,' Follifoot said. People would want to keep *abreast* of the latest developments. They'd buy every edition, however many editions, as they rolled off the presses. You couldn't print enough to supply the demand. Follifoot ordered another bottle. Never mind the dead guest's fortune – by the tea-dance on Saturday evening, Matchett could easily be the richest man in Knibden. The women would be queuing up to show him their wares. 'You'll be fighting 'em off, mate!'

The men drank the good health of Buckworth & Matchett's. Then Dick Follifoot suggested dropping the 'Buckworth' since there hadn't been a Buckworth in the business for years, but Matchett raised his glass and pointed out that the name was there for anyone to see, cut in big steel letters across the top of the old factory gates. Besides, he'd added, avoiding Dick Follifoot's eye and gazing at the rich dark liquid in his glass, he had been fond of old Henry Buckworth. 'Mr Buckworth was very good to me. And to my poor father.' Victor Matchett slurred his words. He had found himself slurring a lot over the past in recent days.

'Streuth!' thought Follifoot, who knew better than to mix sentiment with business. Or sentiment with anything, come to that. He thought it a crying shame too that sprawl of buildings beside the canal standing empty for no reason he could see, other than the indolence of their present proprietor. The site had

135

development possibilities and if Matchett were foolish enough to overextend himself, reviving a newspaper for a town that did not need one he, Richard Follifoot, sole trader, builder of Knibden, would step in swiftly, and develop some of those possibilities.

When Follifoot excused himself and went to join Treadgold and Macready waiting for him at another table, Matchett sat on alone, pondering. He wondered whether he mightn't employ one of those Laffety lads the way Henry Buckworth had once employed his father, making him a partner in the firm, commissioning elaborate new gates with both their names on and eventually, because his own brother, Godfrey, had been so useless, giving Buckworth & Matchett's entirely into Matchett's father's care. Victor Matchett remembered as a small boy watching the old man sitting in his chair while his father ran round doing all the work. In the Swan this evening, Matchett pictured himself sitting in *his* chair, Ray Laffety running round. Girl typesetters would come tripping along the canal towpath once more. The buildings would echo again with the sound of their giggles.

'I'll get going at once,' Matchett said aloud.

'You do that!' Barbara Calderon urged.

First thing in the morning, Matchett would walk across the yard and open up the old shed to see what state the machinery was in. He could not think why he had let it lie idle so long. A dab of oil here, ease a gunged-up ink wheel there – how pleased Henry Buckworth would have been to see newspapers rolling off Buckworth & Matchett's presses again. And might not a new, revised *Knibden Bugle* atone a little, perhaps?

'I'm sure it would,' Barbara said.

Who could the guest at the Gallimore have been, Matchett wondered as he cradled his glass in a corner of the Swan, and Calderon called 'Time!' and Follifoot concluded his animated whisperings with Treadgold and Macready, that even though dead, and buried in the graveyard of St Redegule's, he had the power to reach a clutter of run-down buildings way out of Knibden along the old canal?

'Go steady now,' Barbara Calderon said, for everyone knew how one dark night, at the time of the last Great Knibden Lottery, not long after the death of his elder brother, Henry, when the old firm of printers Buckworth & Matchett's had been left in Victor Matchett's care, Godfrey Buckworth had slipped on the muddy towpath and been discovered next morning by a startled fisherman, bloated, face down.

6

In the Darkness before Dawn

In the darkness before dawn while the rest of the town recovered from its sleepless night, Dora Williams stood at the stove in the kitchen of the flat above the bank, cooking her husband's breakfast. Blood ran from the slippery chunks of raw liver, encrusting itself like lace trimming along the edges of the bacon rashers. Dora shivered and drew the cords of her dark pink winceyette dressing-gown tightly about her. The dead guest's executor's wife stared in horror at the food gurgling in the pan. 'I am Madame Bovary,' she told herself as she prodded the spitting meat with a stainless steel fork. 'It is I who am to blame. I wanted so much for something to happen that now it has. I have wilfully drawn poor William, and the whole of Knibden, into something incalculable.'

Yesterday, while the town held its breath as the first meeting of the committee was taking place at the Gallimore Hotel, Mrs Williams tried to pass the afternoon sitting calmly on her sofa. After half an hour she had sought to distract herself with a library book. Scarcely concentrating at first, she began turning the pages of *Madame Bovary*. They spat at her, fierce as the blood from the meat in the pan. When the farmer's daughter, Emma, marries the widower Bovary and almost at once discovers the boredom of the married state, Dora Williams laid the volume aside. She intended returning it at the earliest opportunity to Knibden's public library. Whatever appalling tragedy lay in store for Mrs Bovary, poor Mrs Williams did not want to find out. 'I have problems enough of my own!' she thought and in spite of her earlier resolve not to do so, she wandered over to the window and drew aside the net curtain. When at last she could tear her eyes away from the tantalizingly closed doors of the Gallimore Hotel, Dora stalked round the flat for a further half hour before sinking back down on the sofa once more, and resuming *Madame Bovary*.

When William Williams returned home late and, to please his

wife, mentioned that Belle Quinn was to organize a tea-dance, like in the old days with Dickie Paisley and his Band, Dora stared at her husband. 'How nice, dear!' she said with a brief bright smile. Inwardly she felt mocked. She had just read the chapter where Mr and Mrs Bovary were invited to a ball by their betters and the young wife had been taught to waltz by a viscount. Dreams of waltzing round Paris on the unknown viscount's arm would thereafter cast a shadow of dissatisfaction across the simple routines of Emma Bovary's existence. And no wonder! Dora Williams knew it would be fatal to dance at the tea-dance. She inquired of her husband why Miss Quinn should have taken it on herself to organize such a thing? William Williams shrugged his shoulders and said he believed the idea had come from Hester Jones. 'They say she is a dab hand at the polka!'

Vehemently then did Mrs Williams brush down her husband's coat. Wasn't it bad enough that their lives were suddenly subject to the whims of an unknown dead man? She unlaced Mr Williams's shoes and placed on his feet the slippers she'd been warming. When she could trust herself to speak again, she said, 'I'd have thought the town in enough turmoil without this dab hand, this Hester Jones, coming along and stirring things up further!'

William Williams did not reply. His wife disliked him ever mentioning other women and, from what he knew of other men's goings on, he could hardly blame her. Dora now inquired, rather quietly, if her husband had decided to go along with Hester Jones's appointment. The dead guest's executor mumbled that really he had no choice. The girl was not ideal, but the general feeling of the committee and of the town appeared to be that she would do. 'If the dead guest had intended me to be in any way particular,' William Williams observed, 'he'd scarcely have settled matters in the way that he did.'

Dora nodded. 'Whatever decision you make is bound to be the right one, William. You can only be expected to do your best and, whatever happens, I'm sure no one will blame *you*.'

'I blame Fechnie,' her husband replied at once. 'I know it isn't done to speak ill of the dead, but what can my predecessor have been thinking of, permitting this to happen? And what can the

bank have been thinking of, employing a man who could sanc-
tion such nonsense?'

Dora nodded vigorously again. She had wondered the same
thing herself, she said. Theodore Fechnie had a lot to answer for.
It was a shame he was dead and could not be brought to account.
As her husband ate the supper she had prepared, Dora glanced
round the tidy flat, the home she kept spotless, whose roof must
protect the couple from the wind and rain, and whatever else
might come beating down now on their heads . . .

For thirteen years Dora had been hopelessly in love, so she'd
thought at the time, with the manager of the city branch of the
bank where she was working as a clerk. For thirteen years
the manager had visited Dora every evening at her lodgings on
his way home. Home to a crippled wife who could apparently
give no satisfaction either as a woman or as a wife. When William
Williams arrived at the city branch to become this same man-
ager's new assistant, it happened by an unfortunate chance – that
now seemed to Dora no chance at all – he had taken rooms at the
very same lodgings as Dora. When the manager used this as an
excuse to terminate his after-work visits, Dora had naturally
turned her ministrations on Mr Williams. Soon she was con-
vinced her love for the manager all those thirteen years had been
a mistake. As some sort of penance she'd insisted that they invite
him, and his crippled wife, to the wedding. Not that you could
see what was wrong with the woman who had walked without
aid of a chair or stick though she'd clung on the manager's arm
all day, smiling vaguely at Dora and barely uttering a single
word.

Dora had thrown herself into the role of wife with a zest
anyone less deserving than William Williams might have found
alarming. She immediately gave up going out to work herself
and, from the first morning of their matrimonial bliss, had risen
early to lay out her husband's clothes and cook him his breakfast.
The rest of her day, while he was at the bank, she devoted entirely
to preparations for his every need. Each piece of liver and each
rasher of bacon sizzling in the pan beneath her fork had been
carefully handpicked at the butcher's. In her quest for the best
and freshest produce to set before her husband, Mrs Williams
was famously oblivious to the long queues that formed behind

her in shops. Since their arrival in Knibden she had made no friends. Other than occasional visits to the public library, Dora had had no time to spare for outside interests. She watched over her husband's interests, though, with an unremitting determination that she hoped would blot out the sins of her past.

In the darkness before the dawn, this morning, as she timed the eggs and laid the table, she found herself dwelling on an earlier past: those far-off days of her childhood. Her frail mother sending her off hungry to school from the tiny, sparsely furnished room they had shared. Then one day, without warning, her mother marrying a jovial man she had apparently met on the bus. There had been a lot of laughter at the wedding, and laughter afterwards so that Dora had found it difficult to take her mother's marriage seriously. Her new step-father had sent her to learn shorthand typing, promising her a job with his firm when she'd completed the course. Which she never did. Her mother had died – as suddenly as she had married – and Dora had gone to work at the bank, losing touch with her step-father because she'd felt unable to introduce him to her lover, he and the manager being much the same age. The jovial man had in any case, shortly afterwards, married yet again. Another woman he had met, amid gales of laughter, on yet another bus. If there were gaps in Dora's life, they had sealed over tightly behind her.

Dora smiled to herself as she pulled back her husband's chair. Luckily *my* past will be of no interest to Miss Hester Jones! *I* am merely the wife of the executor. We had never heard of Knibden till the bank sent us here. Till the manager at the city branch wanted his assistant, who had married his former mistress, a female clerk rather past her best, out of the way. My role in these proceedings to rise early and send the dead guest's executor down the stairs to his office on a full stomach, ready to face the day. And all the days that lay ahead until this business was resolved, the tea-dance was over and Hester Jones would be on her way again, to Penzance. At least the three dread days stipulated by the guest were already reduced to two . . .

William Williams appeared in the kitchen in the immaculately pressed shirt and polished shoes Dora had left out ready for him the night before. He pecked his wife on the cheek, sat down at the table and waited patiently while she placed his plate in front of him. 'Excellent, excellent!' he said, in the manner he had unwittingly picked up from the manager he'd assisted in the city.

Dora bit her lip. She took her seat opposite her husband to watch as he ate. 'Salt, dear,' he reminded her with a slight sniff of annoyance and she rose flustered to fetch it from the dresser.

'My mind is elsewhere,' she confessed.

'Ah!' Williams sprinkled salt heavily on his plate. He could not imagine why Dora should be preoccupied, but to show he was not seriously aggrieved he remarked, 'I don't anticipate being late again tonight, dear. The bank should be a little quieter now that Hester Jones is investigating.'

Dora Williams nodded sleepily. All I can think of is the dead stranger, she thought. And how I willed something of this sort to happen. She wanted to weep. She wanted to throw herself on the floor at her husband's feet and claim the wrong-doing as her own. I am Madame Bovary, she would like to say. You must alter the tragedy of the ending before it is too late.

But William Williams was raising a fork full of cooked meat to his mouth. He held it mid-air. 'I dreamed about Fechnie again last night,' he told his wife.

'Oh?'

Williams chewed a juicy chunk of liver, swallowing all the pieces before he again spoke. 'I dreamed I went down to my office this morning, as usual, hung up my hat and coat and when I turned round, there he was, sitting calmly in my chair. Smoking a cigar. For a moment or two we contemplated one another in silence. Then he said, with a cheerfulness in his voice that made my blood run cold, "Well, old boy! And what does it feel like stepping into a dead man's shoes?"

'I looked down at my shoes and saw they were not my own, beautifully polished as always by your dear self, but large dusty things, several sizes too big.

' "The young inherit the earth," Fechnie went on. "And while someone in Knibden is set to inherit a fortune from the dead stranger, you, Mr Williams, have already taken all that was precious to me. You have charge of my bank," he said. "Every morning you hang your hat and your coat on my peg. You spend your days in my chair, at my desk. Even the blotter you use is still smeared with ink from my pen . . ." '

William Williams paused. Dora could see her husband deciding whether or not to go on. She held her breath and sat very still until he did so.

' "Make no mistake, Mr Williams!" Here Fechnie rapped on my desk like the very devil at hell's gate, and I couldn't help wondering what the clerks behind the door would make of all the noise. Then I remembered there were no clerks outside the door. And I thought it as well I always start the day much earlier than they do. I could faintly make out the cleaner banging about with her mop and for once I was glad Mrs Parbold makes such a racket while she works. "I am watching over you, Williams," Theodore Fechnie said. "Even more diligently than your Dora does!" '

'He mentioned *me*!' Mrs Williams frowned at the effrontery.

William Williams finished his egg, put down his spoon and wiped his lips neatly with a napkin. 'He seemed to know all about you, dear.'

'*All*?'

Williams nodded. 'My predecessor was going to tell me something,' he said wistfully. 'Something he felt I should know.'

Dora gaped at her husband. Of course the late Mr Theodore Fechnie would have been aware what went on at other branches! Managers talk among themselves. It would have been common knowledge in the higher reaches of the bank that, for thirteen years Mr Parker, the manager of the city branch, visited one of his female clerks in her lodgings every evening on his way home. To Mrs Parker, who was no more crippled than any other wife who, without need for a stick or a chair, might cling on her husband's arm all day, and barely utter a single word.

Sometimes Mr Parker had arrived and sat himself down at the little table in the corner of Dora's bed-sitting room to eat the dainties she'd bought for him in a brown paper bag in her lunch hour. On other occasions, he'd ignore her preparations and proceed straight to the truckle bed, apologizing that he didn't have an excess of time. 'Excellent, excellent!' Mr Parker would say when the lovemaking was finished and he pulled his socks back up, snapping them on to the funny little garters he wore around his calves. In the bank, 'Excellent, excellent!' signified that columns of figures tallied, but in Dora's bed-sitting room it had been the signal to rise, put on her dressing-gown and be ready to present him at the door with his briefcase and umbrella. Word got around: dark pink, lace-trimmed winceyette, the colour of uncooked bacon before it was thrown into the pan and encrusted with blood. Theodore Fechnie, far away in Knibden, would have heard how the new assistant at the city had taken rooms two floors directly above the girl and when Parker used this as an excuse to terminate a routine of thirteen years that had become tedious to him, the front desk clerk swiftly and successfully transferred her account, marrying the new assistant right under her former lover's nose. Fechnie would have laughed that such a thing had happened to Mr Parker. He'd have slyly drawn head office's attention to it by suggesting that when the time came, they might alleviate the awkward situation that had arisen in the city by sending William Williams and his second-hand goods to Knibden. There'd have been a note on some file to that effect – she knew right enough, she had written many such notes and memoranda herself, on behalf of Mr Parker who had made love to her every weekday evening, except on Bank holidays, for thirteen years. When Theodore Fechnie went away on holiday shortly before his retirement and suddenly dropped down dead, the bank felt honour bound to act on advice he had left. Williams had been summoned. They'd have told him it was promotion, not feeling the exact circumstances, the colour of his wife's dressing-gown, or her activities outside normal banking hours, needed to be gone into.

'About the dead guest,' William Williams was saying. 'I feel *certain* Fechnie was on the point of disclosing who the dead guest was. And who in the town is set to inherit the fortune. It was on the tip of his tongue to tell me.'

'Why didn't he then?' Dora asked bitterly.

'The alarm clock sounded. I could hear you banging about in the kitchen. I woke up.'

Dora Williams averted her eyes from her husband.

Long after he had descended the cast-iron aerial steps that linked the Williams's flat with the world below, Dora sat on at the breakfast table, staring at the traces of egg on her husband's napkin.

It was an outrage, she thought, that every time anyone started reading *Madame Bovary*, the terrible conclusion loomed into sight, yet there was nothing anyone could do to prevent it. No one could take the foolish farmer's daughter by the shoulder and shake some sense into the girl, any more than poor Dora could head off a catastrophe now. Mrs Williams cupped her head in her hands. There was no point fighting. Her own fate was as mapped out ahead of her as Madame Bovary's was in the library book. How much better then to surrender and even enjoy the inevitable. Dora Williams rose at last from her chair and strode bravely to the window.

'I am to stand at William Williams's side and watch whatever it is I have brought down on this town. Nothing I can do, as the dead guest's executor's wife, will alter anything. I am to blame. It is only right I should be punished.' She flung open the curtains to let in the early morning sun. 'I *shall* go to Belle Quinn's tea-dance!' she declared. 'And I will sit on the sidelines and make conversation as unwiltingly as any other wallflower. I will even look on, without comment, when my William stands up in public with Hester Jones. But I myself will not dance. No, not even if a hundred unknown viscounts take me by the arm and attempt, there and then in the ballroom of the Gallimore Hotel, to the music of the late Dickie Paisley and his Band, to sweep me off my feet!'

William Williams had ascribed Dora's pensive mood that morning to his interest in Hester Jones. How could he help but be interested – he'd be failing in his duties to the dead guest if he did not make it his business to interest himself in the girl. But that, he supposed, was the problem. At least *he* had his responsibilities as the dead guest's executor. Hester Jones, that other newcomer to the town, was busily employed as the investigator. Even the Masons had the Gallimore to run. Poor Dora, alone in the whole of Knibden, was completely excluded. She had neither a task to perform nor the excitement of hoping for something from the dead stranger's Will. He felt sorry for her, but the moment he set foot inside the bank, William Williams dismissed the unhappy woman from his thoughts.

'Mrs Parbold!' The cleaner was early today. She was usually late.

'I couldn't sleep,' Mrs Parbold said. 'I and the rest of the town. There's been lights burning everywhere all through the night.

You'd think the electric was given away free of a sudden! No one can sleep. We're all like kids before Christmas. I thought I might as well get up and get over here, and get my floors done with.'

'I see!' Papers on his desk had been moved. Some of the keys he left lying about as a test for his staff had been touched. William Williams smiled at Hilda May Parbold.

'I'd best get on,' she said, shuffling about a bit and swishing at the floor with her mop. 'I'm wanted up at the Bensusanns' later.'

'Give my regards to the old General.' It was General Bertram Bensusanns' file that Mrs Parbold had been holding when he'd entered the room.

'I will that! Though why I keep going up to that rambling old house, a woman at my time of life, is a mystery to me!' She rubbed her thighs as if her limbs already ached from the climb. The Bensusanns' stood on a crest just below Knibden Crags. It was a long walk round by the roads but Mrs Parbold had been making the steep climb up the rhododendron-clad hill for a good many years now. And she looked set to tell the dead guest's executor all about those years.

Before she could begin, William Williams shunted Mrs Parbold and her mop out of his office, and shut the door. If she had any information, he said as she went, she should convey it with all speed to Hester Jones. She'd find her breakfasting at the Gallimore. Meanwhile, following his terrible dream, the dead guest's executor was resolved to brave the haphazard filing system he had inherited and make a proper search, at last, of all the late Mr Theodore Fechnie's papers.

7

In the Garden of the Bensusanns'

General Bensusann was up early. He sat in a deck-chair in his garden and sniffed the chill morning air in anticipation of all that was to come. I am an old man, he thought excitedly. Though I doze beneath the unwashed windows of the room in which I was born, I'm still as dangerous a beast as any out-of-season stalker, sizing up his prey. I am ready for anything. I am certainly ready for Hester Jones. He opened one eye and watched Desmond Chase who was perched rather nervously a few rungs up a ladder, running a dirty cloth over a window pane, whistling 'The Last Rose of Summer' while he worked.

There were one hundred and eighty-seven windows at the Bensusanns'. The General had told Chase this when he'd first come to work here. The General had once had them properly counted. 'For insurance purposes,' he'd said. 'Your predecessor, Mr Lethbridge, did the counting.'

Chase wished now he had acknowledged his mistake there and then. He should have picked up his kit-bag and gone straight back down into Knibden and caught the first bus out. He could not think how he, Desmond Chase, ever imagined he might take over where Mr Lethbridge had left off. He knew now he should never have tried.

As the General watched the incompetent Chase slopping about, making the windows even more of a mess than they were before, he thought how Mr Lethbridge would never have whistled while he worked. *The last rose of summer*, indeed – *left a-bloomin' alone*! All the roses in the garden of the Bensusanns' had been choked in their beds long since. 'You've two more floors to do when you've finished that one,' the General called out, for he liked to keep his batman, Chase, on the ball.

Desmond Chase felt dizzy. He put this down, as much as anything, to lack of sleep. He was under instructions to check that figure, one hundred and eighty-seven, but every time he endeavoured to count he always found himself distracted, usually by getting drawn into conversation with the General.

'So what's happening about this Will, then?' the General called up now. Chase pretended not to hear. 'Thirty-two,' he said, wringing out the cloth and dipping it with a flurry in the bucket that hung from his ladder. 'Thirty-three.' He flicked away the excess water and tried to whistle louder. *No flow'r of her kindred, No rosebud is nigh, To reflect her blushes, Or give sigh for sigh.*

General Bensusann repeated his question, barking up at him now as if issuing orders to a platoon.

'They've got a girl in, Sir,' Chase yelled back. He polished a circle on one of the panes so that he could watch his employer in the reflection. Thirty-four.

'What's that?'

'A *girl*, Sir. I told you. Appeared at the Swan out of nowhere. If you'd come along, like I wanted you to, you'd 've seen her. The whole town turned out. There was much weeping and wailing for the dead man – the Reverend Sibson excelled himself at the service . . .'

'That parson fellow wants his head examining. So do the rest of them! As for Fechnie at the bank – I'm surprised at *him* going along with it. Makes me wonder if we should be entrusting our money to a man who can countenance such nonsense.'

Chase, in his turn, wondered what money, exactly, the General thought he was entrusting to the bank. He said surlily, 'You know perfectly well, Sir, Mr Fechnie's dead. It's a Mr Williams now. William Williams. Sent from the city branch. You should have gone . . .'

The General grunted. 'I can't be expected to attend funerals and wakes when I don't know who's being buried. Never heard anything so absurd in all my life.'

'What about the Tomb of the Unknown Warrior?'

'What about it?'

'They put Tombs of Unknown Warriors all over the place after the war. No one ever bothered whose body went in *them*. That was the point. The warrior was unknown. It is probably the point now.' The wiry Chase clung to the ladder and watched the General's angry face in the polished pane. He had stopped any pretence of window cleaning and suspected he had lost count. Thirty-six – or was it -seven?

'Unknown warriors was war,' the General snapped. 'This is Knibden. In *peace*.'

'Not much peace, though, is there? The whole town's in turmoil. Mrs Parbold was up here early, and that's never been known before. She said there were lights blazing in all the houses right through the night. The electric is being given away free – in honour of the dead guest, I suppose. I, myself, haven't slept in days . . .'

'You, Chase? I don't see any cause for *you* to lose sleep over this business. Some stranger dying at the Gallimore Hotel can't possibly have anything to do with *you*!' The old man laughed, a hard hammering laugh like a burst of rapid gunfire. 'How dare some upstart arrive in the town and die, just like that! Manoeuvring everyone with his Will like a jumped-up brigadier, when we none of us know the scoundrel's name and rank, or how much he had stuffed in his billet box! You wait till I write *my* Will, Chase. Then we'll see . . .'

See what? Desmond Chase wondered bitterly. He did not trust himself to speak. The General had held his unwritten Will over him long enough. It was what kept him here, and had kept Chase in Knibden these last twenty years. So much so that if he inherited anything from Bensusann in the end, he reckoned he'd have earned it, the hard way. 'You *might* have met the dead man,' he argued with his employer for the sake of arguing. 'He could have been a friend of yours, some old comrade you saved in battle, coming back here to leave you his fortune.'

'Hrmmph!' scoffed the General.

'Well, he *might* be, for all you know. For all anyone knows.' This was one of many private theories Chase had given some thought to during the long wakeful hours. Old Bensusann had no family. He never had visitors except nosy people from the town who occasionally ventured up here on some pretext when they were probably only after something in his Will. The well-meaning interfering Belle Quinn for instance, wanting good money for good works. And that flimsy virginal creature, Verity Willow, who had once or twice escorted the General back from the library when he'd gone there for his afternoon nap. Who knew what *she* needed money for! Chase shuddered. For all the quietness of the life he led now, General Bensusann must have been acquainted with a good many illustrious and wealthy people in his day. It was likely this strange business was connected with something in the man's colourful past. Chase imagined the husband of some woman Bensusann himself had long ago forgotten. The General had saved a man's life in the heat of battle and later been invited to visit his grateful family. They'd have treated him like a hero, his parents, his brothers. His doting sisters would have been all over him hoping to claim him for themselves but the man's wife, a cherry-cheeked eager thing, had shown her gratitude to her husband's saviour in the way women did. Her husband would have known what was going on, but said nothing in view of his great debt. When it came to writing his Will, however, he had avenged himself on his wife by leaving everything to his saviour, her lover. He'd have pictured his wife's cherry cheeks glowing even brighter when the Will was read out. Not that it mattered much to Chase *what* the General had done to acquire the legacy, but if the Bensusann coffers were to be swollen shortly by the dead guest, that could only mean money for the old General to pass on when *he* died. Someone had apparently said something to that effect at the committee meeting yesterday for General Bensusann's name had been cited. Macready, the jeweller, had said as much to Chase over a pint. 'They reckon those to whom much is to be given in three days' time, have a lot already. Your employer was mentioned in this connection . . .' No wonder Desmond Chase had been too excited to sleep. 'Anyhow,' he called down to the General now, 'you should have come to the party in the Swan. The booze was free. You'd have seen Miss Jones . . .'

'Nothing's ever free! Goodness knows, Chase, *you* ought to know that by now! Someone, somewhere, has to pay.'

'But not *us*. They've organized a committee who put up the cash. The place was awash. Yer should have come. The girl's perfect – I said so at the time!'

'What are you on about, you fool?' The General eyed Chase darkly. 'You've been helping yourself to free booze from me for years. Don't think I don't know. Sherry in the dining room, whisky in the kitchen. Brandy in the . . . Why go chasing into the town? It's the girl, isn't it, what's her name? You're after a nice bit of . . .'

'Thirty-eight!' Chase said aloud. One thing was certain – if, by some unlikely miracle, *he* Desmond Chase inherited the dead stranger's fortune, he wouldn't wait around any longer to see if the General left him anything. No, Sir! The old man could count and clean his own dirty windows then. 'She's been told to question everyone,' Chase said.

'She'll be coming up here then,' Bensusann nodded with satisfaction. He looked about his garden, as alert and fearless as ever in his prime. He'd be waiting for Miss Jones.

'Only if someone tells her to.'

'Who is she anyhow?' Know your enemy, thought the General. The first rule of engagement.

'She's called Hester Jones,' Chase told the General what he knew already. Then he took up his rag cloth again and made an elaborate show of rubbing at a small area of encrusted dirt.

'Plain?' the General asked.

'As a pancake! Flat-chested too.'

'Haa!' General Bertram Bensusann adjusted the brim of his hat. He had a horror of flat-chested women. Mrs Parbold who was anything but flat-chested had rushed up to the house to tell them the news the day the guest had been found dead at the Gallimore. General Bensusann had a horror of her too. She was to be heard in the distance just now, banging about with her mop. As if a mere mop could make any difference to the state of the Bensusanns'! 'Do you think there *is* a lot of money at stake, eh?'

'It *could* be as stated. Things sometimes are.' Desmond Chase had given this a lot of thought also.

'They're all after it, of course. Everyone in Knibden?'

'Reckon so.'

'Even the flowery Quinn woman, and that sweet Miss Willow?'

'Them two more than anyone. They're both on the committee. Miss Quinn is organizing a big tea-dance, when Miss Jones will read the Will. Everyone will be there – tomorrow evening. You'll have to go.'

General Bensusann closed his eyes. He pretended to be asleep. He did not *have* to do anything.

Desmond Chase resumed his whistling. *I'll not leave thee, thou lone one! To pine on the stem, Since the lovely are sleeping, Go sleep thou with them . . .*

The gardens of the Bensusanns' had once been famous. Nowadays the public rarely got past the gates which were locked with lost keys and the locks rusted up. It was debatable, in any case, whether you could still call the grounds of the Bensusanns' 'gardens', they were so overgrown. Yet the Bensusann garden had once been celebrated throughout the land, created by the General's mother, a brilliant beautiful woman with a mania for horticulture. The birth of her one and only child had got in the way of her grand passion. She had lost nine months while she bore him, and a further three while she recovered from the exertions of his birth. Ottilie Vigo Bensusann never forgave her son the harm his coming into the world had done. If she needed to spend all her time tending the trees and shrubs she loved, it was young Bertram's fault. Gardens never recover from neglect, she'd told him. Plants never forget damage done to them before they are fully grown.

Despite this setback, the garden of the Bensusanns' had been spectacular and often featured in horticultural magazines because before Ottilie Vigo had married the distinguished essayist, Sidney Mastermain Bensusann, and buried herself in Knibden, she had been a leading light in glittering social circles and had known everyone you needed to know to place articles about yourself in the illustrated monthly journals. She had met and fallen in love with the celebrated essayist on one of his rare jaunts to London. He, scarcely daring to think she would come, had invited the beautiful Miss Vigo to visit his family seat. She, enchanted by the quaintness of the house and the funny little town of Knibden, rather whimsically imagined herself dwelling for the rest of her life in this delightful backwater, floating romantically away from the cut and thrust of the busy world.

' "Of Trumpets, Dragons and Naked Women"!' she had laughed, curling up in a window seat after lunch one afternoon with a copy of her fiancé's famous essay on the Great Knibden Lottery.

'I shall buy a ticket at the next lottery,' Benny had said. Then he had coughed, and added a trifle daringly, 'I shall buy a naked woman in your honour, Miss Vigo. You will bring me luck, I feel sure – just think what we can do with the money if we win!'

'We don't need *money*!' Tilly had laughed.

'We could restore this old place to its former glory.' Even at that time, when the Bensusanns' was still a family home, lived in by generations of Bensusanns, the rambling old house was in need of a fortune being spent on it. 'We could replace the broken windows and put in bathrooms . . .'

'I shan't let you!' Tilly Vigo shrieked. What need had they for nasty modern conveniences when the pair had their love to transform the place? It was the very lack of electric light, hot running water and fresh paint that gave the Bensusanns' its charm. 'It's all so perfectly perfect as it is, Benny darling! Why, it's pretty much as it must have been when William Shakespeare could have stayed here.'

'Queen Elizabeth did.'

'Did what?'

'Stay here. She slept in your bed.'

'You're joking!'

Benny darling was not joking. Good Queen Bess had once passed through Knibden. So it was said, whispered down through the generations of Bensusanns. Tilly Vigo shivered deliciously. She loved a touch of history. 'Now go away!' she ordered her lover. 'Leave me to read this masterpiece in peace!'

Sidney Mastermain Bensusann did not go away. Nor did the lovely Tilly Vigo force him to. The essayist sat himself down on the floor beside the exquisite pair of feet that belonged to the woman he loved, and watched as she turned the pages of one of his most celebrated essays. No writer fears the dart of the critic the way he trembles to impress the woman he worships. Bensusann resolved to compose an essay 'On the Perilous Laws of Literature and Love' the following week. While he contemplated those perilous laws, Miss Vigo read:

The 1880 Municipal Guidebook to Knibden mentions a wonderful new camera obscura, the very latest in camera obscura technology, erected by Public Subscription and housed in an ornate wooden tower in Knibden's municipal gardens. The Guide remarks particularly on the naked woman, carved in curiously antique style, over the entrance to the tower where, for a small fee of threepence farthing you could climb five twisting flights of stairs to the darkened room at the top where a great polished bowl was set in the floor. By revolving a handle attached to a crystal lens in the roof you might watch, unseen, for as long as you wished, a moving technicoloured picture of the people of the town strolling in the parklands below. Then, if any particular sight especially took your fancy, you could pull the handle downwards to focus in sharply on that part of the picture.

The 1890 edition of the same guidebook makes no mention of any camera obscura. For this, many blame the naked woman. How fairly they do so you may judge for yourself.

The camera obscura was funded, like most things in Knibden, from the takings of the Great Knibden Lottery. These lotteries are held regularly at irregular intervals in the town under an Ancient and Special Dispensation that goes right back to the heady days of Charles II. The young King, restored to his rightful throne, freely handed out favours that cost him nothing to reward towns that had rallied at great expense to themselves to his poor pater's cause. Though Knibden had had its Castle razed to the ground and most of its sons put to the sword – or rather the pikestaff – after the Royalist defeat in 1641, it was lucky enough during the Restoration to gain the right to hold its own Lottery. A lucrative right this proved too.

Once lotteries were a widespread and popular means of raising revenue, but they have generally fallen out of favour. They cause a lot of trouble and are regarded perhaps with suspicion. Wealth, after all, should be won by honest toil and prayer. The part played by LUCK in the business of getting rich being something people prefer to downplay. For politeness's sake, if nothing else, a man must ascribe any fortune he makes to good fortune, whereas any truly fortunate gain should always be explained away by some tale of hard work and accomplishment. Winning a lottery is too unequivocally lucky. There can be no pretending you have done anything more than your fellow human beings to deserve your luck. Most towns have done away with their lotteries but Knibden has thrived for centuries on its, untroubled by the niggling of conscience or the niceties of killjoys. So far.

My purpose here is probably to warn. Knibden is a small happy town. I should like to see it remain as such. Who knows what the Century unfolding before us will bring, and who knows what trouble might be *saved for this place if the Ancient and Special Dispensation it has so long enjoyed could be revoked now.*

The way the Great Knibden Lottery works, and it certainly does work, is that half the sum raised from the sale of tickets is spent on some municipal project. The other half being put up as the prize. Early on, only fairly modest items were procured for the town in this fashion. A wedding present in silver for some Gentleman's daughter, an apprenticeship in a useful trade for an orphan, a dowry for a foolish servant girl who needed marrying off in a hurry. One year the large family of a man who'd been struck by lightning received £46 — though this was to prove unexpectedly controversial as the rich widow subsequently found herself courted by many of Knibden's menfolk, in some cases men with wives and sweethearts of their own already. Such hiccups aside, the scale of Knibden's Lottery has grown steadily in size over the years and, as it has done so, the town has become known in certain, not altogether desirable, quarters as the place to be whenever a Lottery is on. Every footloose chancer in the land makes his way to the town, along with many a respectable fellow hoping to better his lot — and why not? A very commendable and natural ambition to be sure. The town benefits hugely from the extra trade which means that everyone in Knibden shares in the bonanza. No local taxes are necessary, employment is plentiful, a lot of fun is had and the town's people are effortlessly prosperous. It is a happy state of affairs. The winners are always happy too for, while the number of tickets on offer doubles each time to meet the ever increasing demand for tickets, the prize money also doubles. This prize is awarded, by tradition, as one enormous lump sum. A man may become as rich as Croesus, the poorest pauper overnight a prince. It is the stuff of fairy tales. There is surely no other lawful way in this world of gaining wealth so instantly with so little effort or risk. All you need do is to purchase a ticket and have Lady Luck smile on you — and the fact is, each time a Lottery is held, Lady Luck DOES smile on someone. What if that someone were YOU?

An astonishing law applies to the sale of Great Knibden Lottery tickets: no matter how many are printed, there are never enough to go round. The more tickets are sold, the greater the prize money. As the sum of the prize money grows, the more people are attracted to the town to buy tickets which in turn means that next time the prize will be even greater and even more people will want tickets. Meanwhile, as the takings grow so too does the scale of the municipal project possible as a result. Never has a more magical money-making machine ever been contrived. The Great Knibden Lottery, and the fortunes of the town, are set to spiral unstoppably.

Or are they? To answer this question, allow me to explain the workings of this Lottery.

An elected Committee of the town's Worthies oversees the arrangements, both of the Lottery itself and spending the money raised afterwards. Over the years Knibden has acquired all kinds of civic amenities the provision of which in other places must depend on the whim of some local philanthropist. Knibden does not need grimy industries whose generous owners might take it into their heads to build blocks of almshouses or provide a new steeple or stained glass for the church. The Committee of Worthies decides what is currently required and can always be relied on to reflect the mood of the times. Occasionally more frivolous projects have been favoured. The camera obscura, for instance. Or the famous Alhambra, a vaster greater theatre than the size of Knibden could ever warrant, but the town is a cheerful fun-loving place, ready to grow and keen to rival any other town you might care to mention.

Almost as soon as the building scheme from the last Lottery is completed the Committee sets the process of the next Great Lottery in motion. The first thing to do is decide the number of tickets to be offered and though they double the number each time, and fear so many tickets can never sell, there is always a mad scramble towards the end with people frantic not to be left out. When all the tickets have been officially sold, they immediately begin to change hands on the street at double or treble their original price. Each ticket bears a number and one of three pictures: a trumpet, a dragon or a naked woman – great crude woodcuts dating back to a time before the delicate hand of Mr Thomas Bewick transformed the art.

At sunrise, on Day One of the Lottery, one of the three designs is drawn. The holders of tickets bearing the winning motif – the trumpet, the dragon or the naked woman, whichever – then charge jubilantly through the streets waving their little pieces of paper in the air and whooping for joy. They alone are now in with a chance of the prize. By tomorrow evening half of all the great mass of money collected by the Lottery could be theirs, and theirs alone. Tickets bearing the other motifs are all now worthless and soon discarded, trampled underfoot as the disappointed hordes chase through the streets after the lucky ones, des-

156

perate to get back in with a chance. There is no time to pause. Some tickets are extracted by force, others change hands at alarming rates, prices see-saw up and down as their owners calculate the odds of winning the final prize against the certainty of a quick big profit. Fights break out. No one gets any sleep on the night of Day One. Activity on the streets is frenzied, the ale houses do good trade while sensible folk bar their windows, bolt their doors and try to keep their dogs and daughters in. Friends who purchased tickets together fall out over who paid for which design. New friendships are forged as people band together in hastily formed syndicates to raise the sums demanded by those lucky enough to possess tickets of the winning design. Enmities and alliances of thirty-six hours reach fever pitch towards sundown on Day Two when the winning number of the winning design is chosen and all the other bits of paper, on which such high hopes have rested, become suddenly worthless.

To hold a ticket at all gives you hope. To find that your ticket bears the favoured design means that from sunrise on Day One to sunset on Day Two, you live through a paradise of expectation in which all things are possible. You soar, and swoop, then soar again. This flight must be followed, admittedly, for everyone but the one lucky winner, by a sinking into a slough of despair, all the worse always for the closeness you may have come to winning. Those lucky enough to possess the right design but a number close to the winner suffer most, of course. The numbers on either side of the winner inflict unbearable agony. Yet, those with the wrong design altogether but whose ticket had had a number of the right order of magnitude often experience a curious afterglow as they fretfully rejoice at what so nearly might have been. The fortune that might have been theirs 'if only'. The magical life they might have led, thereafter.

Things eventually drift back to normal. Surprisingly quickly too. Life must go on as before, even if it never quite does. For thirty-six hours you have flown, and once you have known flight, as Monsieur Bleirot or Samuel Willcocks Smith will tell you, nothing can ever be the same again. Walking the dull earth, one foot in front of the other, feels intolerably tedious.

Often the Lottery winners are mere chancers – young men who come to Knibden solely to try their luck at the Lottery. They spend lavishly while they are here, wining and dining the women of the town. They believe in their expectations and allow themselves to feel rich. Such men tend to take away their winnings, if they win, and are never seen or heard from again. Often they take, too, a train of young women, Knibden girls who until they had found themselves on the arms of the winner on his winning night had seemed steady enough creatures. Even if the winner is an inhabitant of the town, he rarely stays on in Knibden. With the means to fly now, away he will go. And who can blame him? I say 'he' because – and perhaps I should have made this clear earlier – although the weaker sex may serve on the Committee of Worthies that oversees the Lottery and spends the half of the takings that is put aside for Public Works, they are sensibly precluded from buying tickets. Why put unnecessary temptation in their way? They might spend the house-keeping money or barter their babies. Besides, the crudely cut naked woman on a third of the tickets makes the enterprise unsuitable. I dare say Mrs Pankhurst may take issue with me. I dare say she and her fair followers will one day arrive in Knibden and valiantly chain themselves to the town's railings that were, by the way, paid for from Lottery money a hundred years ago. Knibden had iron railings long before any other town. It has not been recorded how many of Knibden's wives and sweet-hearts have been abandoned by men who have won the Lottery, upped sticks and left. Or by men whom the excitement of the Lottery has rendered permanently discontented. Knibden does not hold enough for them afterwards. They want a bigger horizon in which all things might again be possible. In which all your life you hold a ticket in your pocket that might win. For those sorry females left behind in this way, there is always the consolation of the new Public Work to look forward to. Once Mrs Pankhurst has won the Franchise for her sex, I fancy she might turn her attention on the Knibden Lottery. It is my belief that either women should be allowed to buy tickets also, and have their lives ruined on a par with men's, or the Lottery should be banned altogether for the sake of future harmony between the sexes.

As I have told you, following the Lottery of 1875, the Lottery Com-mittee erected a camera obscura. Think how good it will look in our guidebook, they said. The 1880 edition will need printing 'ere long. How pleasant it would be to include it amongst our attractions.

The camera obscura idea had won out over other projects including a clever super-trough for horses, insulated and regulated so that the water never froze in winter or dried up in summer. There was also a periscope that could swing high overhead and by means of powerful optics permit Knibden's inhabitants to see the sea far away to the East and also to the

West. This periscope had been invented by a remarkable Dutch woman, Miss Millicenta Vantickel, whose name had told against her when it was discovered that the patent required the periscopes to be known in perpetuity as Vantickels. After long and anguished deliberation the Committee felt an item with such an appellage inappropriate to a Public Work. How could you boast a 'Vantickel' in your municipal guidebook! Apart from which, one Cardigan Cardew had argued, if the lower orders were to see the sea simply by paying a penny to look through a periscope, they might get it into their heads that this was their due and expect regular holidays to traipse off to the seaside in future. Knibden's parlourmaids would soon think of nothing but flaunting their ankles on the sands, and Board School children would cease to concentrate on their sums. Who needs to look at the sea a long way away when, by revolving a handle attached to a crystal lens in the roof, you could watch in full moving technicolour, what was going on immediately around you. When news reached everyone's ears that the periscope had been decided against, the youth of Knibden who had never seen the sea and had hoped to do so by means of the Vantickel's powerful optics, staged a protest in the town Square that threatened to get nasty until Cardigan Cardew had the soldiers summoned from the nearest barracks. As the cavalry rode into Knibden, the Vantickel and the sea far away to the East and the West were quickly forgotten. The remarkable camera obscura had been erected instead.

Sir Mayhew Gallimore M.P. and his wife (the first Lady Gallimore) came specially from London for the grand opening. The band had played, the sun had shone. Even Queen Victoria sent a gracious message, tied with a tartan ribbon, direct from Balmoral. The only blemish on the proceedings had very nearly been the delicate matter of the naked woman.

By long custom the winning emblem was always prominently displayed on the Public Work. If only the trumpet or the dragon had been drawn! By now, though, the ornate wooden tower in Knibden's municipal gardens was built, a wood carver had been commissioned and his carving set prominently in the arch above the entrance to the tower, a faultless relief copy of the woodcut which had graced one third of the tickets since the Lottery started way back in 1688. There had been so much else to concern themselves with that it was only the day before Sir Mayhew was due to draw aside the little red piece of velvet covering the carving, that the Committee met in an emergency to address what was now perceived to be a difficulty. Was it seemly, the indomitable Cardigan Cardew asked his fellow Worthies, banging his fist on the table, for the wives and servants of Knibden to see, for Queen Victoria's own wishes to be read out beneath, and for Sir Mayhew Gallimore and the frail first Lady Gallimore . . .

Why couldn't you have brought this up before? someone asked but was quickly hushed. The last time the naked woman had been drawn, half a century back, a certain Mrs Burrel was known to have abandoned her responsibilities as wife and mother and taken up a life of drunken debauchery in the arms of the Lottery's winner. The series of milestones subsequently erected on the roads around Knibden are still to this day known as Burrels. Each Burrel bore a crude version of the woman depicted on the winning ticket and, though the women and the mileages had long since eroded, in their youth, the older men on the Committee could remember blacking in parts of the incised design, rubbing soot to make certain parts that stood out, stand out further. No wonder they intended to deny the same pastime to the youth of 1875. Who knew but when Sir Mayhew pulled the golden cord to draw back the little red velvet rag, what some impudent urchin might have effected?

The thought of such depravity made the Lottery Committee shudder. Naturally the ladies had not considered this hazard and the gentlemen had, until now, kept what reservations they'd entertained to themselves. It was a crisis. The Grand Opening of the Camera Obscura was all set for the morrow. The band was ordered, the weather forecast was fine. The tartan ribbon was even then being tied by royal fingers up at Balmoral. How then to insure against the impertinences of youth? There could be no question of hastily smoothing down the carving, thereby breaking with a tradition that went back to Charles II, just because of something some lad who ought to be whipped might or might not do. It was Cardigan Cardew who came up with the solution to the problem: twenty-four hour surveillance must be mounted immediately. There would be no problem by day, the ticket seller at the turnstile could keep a watchful eye. But at night, the worthy citizens of Knibden must take it in turns to watch and ensure that their naked woman went undefiled. A rota was drawn up. People volunteered their servants to undertake three- or four-hour shifts. Two servants to be in attendance at any one time, and forbidden on the pain of instant dismissal, regardless of previous character, to speak to each other. This to obviate any collusion. It was a stroke of genius.

160

Naturally Cardigan Cardew was chosen to present Sir Mayhew to the town. Pleasant smiles attended the day. Eyes were delicately averted from the naked woman whose contours were in any case camouflaged since she had been carved out of her own warm wood. All boded well. And yet . . .

The child conceived that night at Gallimore Hall, by the first Lady Gallimore, was a girl. Sir Mayhew wanted a boy. Worse was to follow.

About nine months later, about the time of the birth of the Gallimores' eldest daughter, Cardigan Cardew paid his threepence farthing and mounted the three flights of stairs to look down unseen, as had become his wont, on all the milkmaids and parlourmaids strolling in and out of the rhododendrons in Knibden's Municipal Gardens with their beaux. There, in glorious technicolour among the dark-green leaves and lush purple flowers, Mr Cardew espied his own wife's unmistakable unclad form, entangled with . . . It is not known if Cardew recognized the bare male buttocks as he pulled the handle of the camera obscura sharply downwards, to focus in.

Nor is it clear how the camera obscura burned to the ground. Perhaps in his astonishment Cardigan Cardew let slip his lighted pipe. There was so much wood the timber blazed for hours and afterwards. As the smoke died away, it was generally agreed that the edifice had been a mistake. The twenty-four hour surveillance necessary to preserve the decency of the naked woman, carved in curiously antique style over the entrance, had cost Knibden folk dear and, in any case, encouraging people to watch each other closely and unseen for threepence farthing was bound to cause problems in a small town. No one blamed poor Cardigan Cardew, the chief advocate of the project, since he alas had perished in the conflagration. Since it was highly likely he was not the only man who had spied his wife in this way, there was no real proof that he had taken his own life or deliberately destroyed the camera obscura. It was just his bad luck to have been at the top of the tower at the time.

Mrs Cardigan Cardew was in luck though. She came into a tidy sum from her husband's Knibden Municipal Insurance Company Life Assurance Policy. And that Company was in luck also for, although they had had to pay out handsomely in this case, much lucrative business ensued. The pay-out to Mrs Cardew reminded people of the benefits of such policies and soon the bereaved widow Cardew was paid further big sums to hold back her tears and appear in leaflets smilingly urging people to take out policies with the Company: look what happened to me, *she was quoted as saying.* Wives of Empire, Consider the worst but prepare for the best. Yes, you and your children could be left destitute tomorrow, a widow with orphans, penniless in your prime. Fortunately my Dear Departed had the foresight to provide against this eventuality by taking out a Knibden Municipal Insurance Company policy insuring me against his death. Since he was young enough, and certifiably in the best of health, the policy cost him little. It has paid me dear. Indeed, I have been better off since poor dear Cardigan's death than I ever could have been with him alive! All thanks to the Knibden Municipal Insurance Company. Wives, I urge you! Make your husband prove his love for you – at once – by providing for you and your children in this way. In the event of the unthinkable, let there at least be compensations, and cash. Take out a Knibden Municipal Insurance Company policy *today* on his behalf – do it yourself, if need be. And don't forget – you don't need to be married to benefit in this way. Why not take out a policy on other women's husbands too. My unmarried friends did. See how they benefited!

There followed a testimony from a certain Miss Angelica Hook, Spinster of the nearby parish of Knibden Brook – long since swallowed up by the town – an old schoolfriend of the widow Cardew, testifying that she had had premonitions concerning her friend Mrs Cardew's husband. In the best of health maybe, an upstanding member of the community undoubtedly – on the Committee of the Lottery no less – and yet Miss Hook had put money down against Cardigan Cardew's dying. A small policy that would now provide for her amply in her old age. The idea had caught on. The Knibden Municipal Insurance Company had flourished.

In time Mrs Cardigan Cardew, the wealthy widow, had married again. A little while later her new husband had come to grief in a riding accident, his horse skidding perilously on the ice, and the Knibden Municipal Insurance Company had found itself again paying out heftily. And again, but this time as a Mrs Percival Vestey, the same grieving widow was to be seen in Knibden Municipal Insurance Company brochures, smilingly urging people to take out policies. In time, again, Mrs Vestey remarried. Of course she did: she was a rich woman and had plenty of offers. The new husband was a respectable fellow called Mr Jenks. It happened that a friend of Mr Jenks was a pharmacist who grew somewhat concerned about the large quantities of poisons the new Mrs

Jenks began buying. The pharmacist, and others, could not resist putting down a lot of money against Mr Jenks's early demise but fortunately for Mr Jenks, his friend the pharmacist was a chatterbox. After a singularly large measure of ale in the Swan, he informed his friend of his wife's unusual shopping habits. Naturally Jenks became nervous. Without going home, he hurried straight to the local magistrate. This gentleman was inclined at first to do nothing. Albert Jenks had liquor on his breath while Mrs Cardew/Vestey/Jenks was something of a celebrity. Her bravely smiling picture adorning Knibden Municipal Insurance Company literature, was disseminated nationally. She was quite an advertisement for the town. The death of a husband can be like winning the Great Knibden Lottery, she declared to the world at large. After some judicial consideration of the case, the magistrate decided it probably wouldn't be a bad idea to take out a Knibden Municipal Insurance Company policy himself on Mr Jenks's life. When, sure enough, Albert Jenks, despite having been amply warned, died a nasty quick death a week or so later, the local constabulary were reluctant to move in. Too many people in the town stood to do very nicely from insurance claims. In the end, though, post mortem tests were done on Mr Jenks, the results of which led to the exhumation of the late Percival Vestey. There was so much arsenic in that man, the Coroner told the Knibden Bystander, it was less surprising Mr Vestey had fallen from his horse than that he ever succeeded in mounting the animal in the first place!

In due course, Mrs Jenks/Vestey/Cardew was hanged, but the real loser was the Knibden Municipal Insurance Company which was forced, by public pressure from frightened husbands, to stop allowing policies to be taken out on lives willy-nilly. Only those closely related might now do so. Supposedly on the grounds that – despite the evidence of Mrs Jenks/Vestey/Cardew – wives and husbands were unlikely to bump each other off just for the money. If Knibden's male inhabitants breathed a sigh of relief at the threat that had been removed to their mortality, there were one or two matrons left angry at the way Mrs Jenks had carried on. She had gone too far. If the woman could have been content merely to collect advantageously from the death of one husband, or even two, and had not accepted money to widely advertise the fact that she had done so, others among them, given time and a little careful plotting, might also have enjoyed a little of her good fortune.

It was, of course, just like the Lottery. One person collected every-

thing. And not always the most deserving. She may have been hanged in old sackcloth but in her day, Mrs Jenks/Vestey/Cardew had worn shot silk, which was more than most of these other disgruntled matrons ever would.

By the time the guidebook to Knibden had been reprinted in 1890, and the reference to the camera obscura erased, the naked woman of the tickets had become indelibly associated in the minds of the good people of Knibden with the three-fold identity of Mrs Jenks/Vestey/Cardew who had benefited by chance, and then greedily sought to repeat the exercise once too often by stealth. The eventual fate of Miss Angelica Hook, Spinster of Knibden Brook, is nowhere recorded though it may be generally assumed that after her little windfall she married advantageously, and moved away.

'Is it all true, Benny darling?' Tilly Vigo demanded. 'Or did you make it up?'

'It's all true,' the essayist replied.

'Extraordinary!' breathed Tilly, gazing rapturously out of the window in the direction of the town down the hill. 'How I long to know what happened to Angelica Hook!'

Who can blame Sidney Mastermain Bensusann for feeling gratified at having his work so openly admired by the woman he loved most in the world. Naturally the distinguished essayist looked forward to married life with Miss Ottilie Vigo as a paradise on earth that would last considerably longer than the thirty-six hours between sunrise on Day One and sunset on Day Two of the Great Knibden Lottery. He pictured himself writing his essays in his study every morning, and Tilly reading them in this same sunny window seat in the afternoons.

The wedding took place as soon as Tilly Vigo's relations recovered from the shock of her engagement, much to the amusement of those who marvelled at a shy middle-aged scribbler from the provinces carrying off their chiefest beauty from under their very noses.

Mr Lethbridge sat beneath the lions in Trafalgar Square and read an account of the Vigo-Bensusann wedding in the *Daily Mercury*. He also read an extract from the bridegroom's essay on the Great Knibden Lottery 'Of Trumpets, Dragons and Naked Women', and a description of the old house that was to be the

164

happy couple's home. The bit about Good Queen Bess's bed and how the young bride-to-be had already slept in it, interested him. The following day, being on the look-out for a suitable post just then, Mr Lethbridge looked up Knibden on a map and then sat down and penned a careful letter in an unflorid but capable hand to Mr and Mrs Bensusann, enclosing impeccable references and offering his services as butler at the Bensusanns'. 'I can come to Knibden at your earliest convenience,' Lethbridge wrote.

Creating a spectacular garden soon became Tilly Bensusann's revenge on her husband. Her friends, had they known, would not have been altogether surprised. Having married the fusty old essayist in foolish haste, she was not a woman to repent sensibly like other people at her leisure. Instead, she threw herself at the old Bensusann family soil with such fierce industry that the force of her fury raged visibly all round the outside of the house. The trailing, trained and rampant verdure spread and flashed like a green electric storm, while the vast avenues of trees and swathes of fiery herbaceous borders she planted with such frenzy could have been gashes gouged in anger across the poor man's flesh.

Sidney Mastermain Bensusann cowered in his library, unable any more to think of fresh *themas* for essays. He let his correspondence with editors of literary periodicals lapse. He did not know what he had done to offend the beautiful young woman he had married and this bewilderment undermined the confidence an essayist must have in making his assertions and arguing his case. Whenever the poor man glanced out of any of the hundred and eighty-seven windows of the Bensusanns' he could see his young wife digging and delving with terrifying passion. Meanwhile, Mr Lethbridge went between master and mistress, decorously serving them both with inscrutable and equal dedication. The infant, Bertram, was left to wander the house as freely as a pea in a rattle.

The miserable hush that hung in all the dark damp rooms of the Bensusanns' was made steadily worse by the luxuriant lively growth that could be seen through every window. One morning, as Bertram Bensusann wandered aimlessly from room to room he had come upon his father lying on the floor of his study, a pistol in one hand, his blown-out brains in the other. The child stepped calmly over the bloody mess on the rug, repositioned a chair to climb up and open a window, then he called down to his mother dibbing in the border below. Bertram Bensusann never forgot the look of impatience on her face as he told her what had taken place. She was still carrying her dibbing stick when she came indoors. She prodded his father with it to make sure the man was dead, then rang for Lethbridge and instructed him to do what needed doing. And to get the rug cleaned.

'Very good, Ma'am.' The butler bowed, and Mrs Bensusann immediately returned to her garden.

Lethbridge looked at the child. 'Chin up!' he said and reached in his pocket. 'Here, have these.' He handed Bertram a packet of brightly coloured postage stamps. They come from all over the world, he told the boy. The great world Master Bensusann would see one day when he grew up and could go away from Knibden and do as he pleased.

Timidly young Bertram took the stamps. They were all shapes and sizes and spoke to him of colourful places far away from the airless dark rooms in which he was then obliged to dwell.

'People collect them,' Lethbridge said. 'You could collect them if you wish. I will find you a special album to stick them in. Meanwhile, be a good chap and run along while I do what needs doing and get this rug cleaned.'

Ottilie Vigo Bensusann's gardening did not stop with the death of the man it had been aimed at. Quite the reverse. The mania had a hold on Bertram's mother the way the ivy now had its tendrils into the plasterwork all round the house. More articles and fresh photographs appeared in horticultural magazines and the public, curious after reading reports of the essayist's death at his own hand, flocked to view the garden of the Bensusanns'. Mrs Bensusann needed the money from entrance fees to purchase plants so she welcomed the trippers herself, guiding them tirelessly up and down the paths and borders, posing even for photographs. Teas were served by Mr Lethbridge on the terrace – for tuppence halfpenny discreetly placed in a tin – with Bertram required to be in attendance wearing the little suit of blue velvet with a lace collar his mother had had sent up from London for these occasions.

One day, about a year after his father's death, a man had come to the house. He was collecting together the works of Sidney

Mastermain Bensusann for an annotated edition, he had said. Ottilie had been in the garden. 'You are the son?' he'd asked reverentially.

Bertram had nodded. He'd been eight years old at the time. 'I collect stamps,' he had told the man. 'Would you like to see my album?'

The scholar had sat down on the floor beside him and, while Bertram turned the pages of his stamp collection, the man had spoken about his father, describing the essayist as a literary genius. When Ottilie Vigo Bensusann entered the room and heard the visitor talking about that bore, her late husband, in this flowery manner, she flew into a rage. She sent the scholar packing and, as soon afterwards as she could, she instructed Lethbridge to burn all that was left of Sidney Mastermain Bensusann's books and papers as if they had been roses with the black spot. She then dispatched her son to school.

His father's gory death had later stood the young heir to the Bensusanns' in excellent stead. While fellow recruits retched and faltered, he carried on, bayonet at the ready, towards wherever the Eleventh Knibdens had been heading when interrupted by enemy fire. Bravery came so naturally to the General he scarcely understood the word -though it had been used often enough over the years when people tried to record Bensusann's heroic deeds.

Ottilie Vigo Bensusann did not long outlive her husband. She had worked herself steadily into the earth. Every time Bertram came home from school she had seemed to her son a little closer to the ground she dug. Bertram could not remember her funeral – perhaps he had attended so many since, of people he'd been fonder of than he had ever been of his mother – and so it seemed to him that she had probably buried herself, digging and dibbing at her garden until she had ended up under the Bensusann soil. He had never done anything about keeping up the gardens in case someone should dig down and find her there, releasing the woman to come after him again, earth all over her hands. 'Bertram!' she would call before swooping and lunging. No enemy bayonet bearing down on him, glinting with fresh blood, ever held for General Bensusann the terror of his mother's dibbing stick caked in earth.

Occasionally, during the school holidays or on leave from the army, the young Bensusann had hacked his way through the undergrowth, trying to figure out where the celebrated avenues of limes and maples had stood. 'Best left,' Lethbridge once said and Bertram Bensusann readily agreed. He'd been happy to leave the whole place in Lethbridge's capable hands.

When true hearts lie wither'd, And fond ones are flown, Oh! who would in-habit, This bleak world a-lone. Oh, who . . . Desmond Chase glanced down at the old General and, confident his employer was really sleeping, he nipped down the ladder, wrung out his rag and went away into the outdoor scullery to make a brew of his strong tea. Eventually fragments of conversation drifted across the uncut lawn.

'. . . and she's only got two days left now to discover the truth!'

'Can't be done!'

'She'll do it all right! You saw her in the Swan – girl like that can do anything once she puts her mind to it.'

Mrs Parbold could now be heard asking Desmond Chase what *he* would do if all the money came to him.

'I'd chuck it in here,' Chase replied immediately. 'Go round the world on a cruise.'

'Give over. What'd you want to do that for?' There was a murmur. Then Mrs Parbold again: 'End your days in some nasty foreign place! Me, I'd buy a nice cosy cottage, roses round the door. I'd show the town I'm as good as any of 'em, even if Mr Parbold once . . .'

'If *you* inherit, Mrs P, you could buy the whole town, never mind a poxy cottage. And if its *roses* round the door you're after, buy the Bensusanns' off the old General. Then you'd have roses by the bucketful . . .'

'Here!' the Parbold screeched with mirth. 'What would *I* want with this tumbled-down ruin? I couldn't be doing with all that great garden, growing at me all the time. Gives me the creeps. And what about the old man . . .'

'I reckon he'd be pleased to sell. He could end his days in luxury. At the Gallimore Hotel. *I* might buy it off him, if I inherit.'

'You! I thought you said you'd be off round the world on a cruise. It's me what's cleaned this great place all these years. If anyone's goin' to get their mop on it . . .' Hilda Parbold and

Desmond Chase glared at one another. 'And what makes you think you're in with a chance?'

'Wouldn't you like to know?'

'Yes, I would. Because I . . .' Mrs Parbold's voice dropped. General Bensusann sat very still, inwardly straining every muscle to hear what was said next. They only ever talked freely, he supposed, when they thought he was asleep. And then it seemed to General Bertram Bensusann that he must *be* asleep because he heard now a voice very like the voice of Hilda May Parbold telling his batman, Desmond Chase, an extraordinary tale. A tale he did not need to hear, to know the details.

'So there!' said Mrs Parbold.

There was more indistinct murmuring.

'Give over!' This was Chase. Chase, howling with laughter. 'The old devil!'

Well! thought General Bensusann, if the truth were to emerge at last, so be it. But a lot can happen in two days. The whole course of world history can be changed. Bloody *wars* can be declared, and then lost . . .

General Bertram Bensusann, sole survivor of the Eleventh Knibdens, now disbanded, glanced perkily up at the bright autumnal sunshine reflected in the hundred and eighty-seven windows of the house in which he'd been born. He was ready for anything. He was certainly ready for Miss Hester Jones. If the dead guest's investigator did not make the steep climb up the rhododendron-flanked hill to see him, tomorrow evening he would advance on Knibden and attend the tea-dance. He would corner the girl in her quarters at the Gallimore Hotel and, to the music of Dickie Paisley and his Band, General Bertram Bensusann would supply his name, rank and number as required under international conventions governing such things. What happened next would be down to her.

8

The Summer of Raymond Bast

'It won't be me, of course,' Verity Willow murmured. She lay with her eyes closed tight against the morning light. For the first time she could remember, she wished she did not have to get up and go to the library. She would far rather lie here in her bed thinking about the guest at the Gallimore and the fortune he had left, than face the cherubic face of George Allendale with his merry quips and endless cups of tea. It came of living with his mother, the terrifying Edina, she supposed. No wonder the poor boy had had to get out of the house and make the steep climb up to the Crags in the fog, and then stay there half the day pretending to be Arthur Dawes Dobson! He'd been up on Knibden Crags at exactly the time the guest died – why go out of his way to tell her that? Why tell her anything? It was as if the boy were deliberately establishing an alibi for himself. So, where had George Barrington Allendale been, the morning the guest at the Gallimore had died? Verity sighed and turned over. No doubt Hester Jones – for all that she wasn't a Miss Marple, Hercule Poirot or Randolphe Shyne – would find out. Verity thought now of Hester Jones in her rooms on the first floor of the Gallimore. Was she sound asleep, or would her task be keeping her awake, also? Was the dead guest's investigator lying in the dead guest's bed even now, saying, Well, one thing's for certain – it can't be Verity Willow!

'It *could* be me,' Verity protested out loud. Of course it could! Hadn't Michael Milady told Hester Jones that the dead guest's heir could be *any* of them. In which case, wasn't there some man who'd been absent from her life, a man who might have come back specially to Knibden to die, and to leave her all his money? Singling Verity Willow out in this extravagant manner as if apologizing publicly, once and for all. Someone in the town was set to inherit a great fortune; why should that someone not be her?

Verity opened her eyes wide with astonishment. Then she sat up, horribly awake now. What *exactly* was she hoping for? This man, whoever he was, who had returned, was *dead*! Gone for ever

– as irrecoverable as time itself. That was the point about the guest at the Gallimore: *he was dead*! They had buried him the day before yesterday. The same day Hester Jones arrived in their midst to solve the mystery. Verity quickly slid down again inside the warm bed, pulling the blankets tightly about her. The death of the man who'd been absent so long from *her* life was definitely not something she craved. Tears sprang in her eyes. 'I loved him,' she whispered into the rough worn wool of the blankets. 'I still love him! Wherever he is, whatever he is doing, whatever he has done, I have always loved Raymond Bast. I always will.'

Thoroughly alarmed now, Knibden's assistant librarian pulled herself out of bed. She found a handkerchief and dabbed her nose. Then she lay down again on top of the bedclothes. She was completely exhausted but far too awake to go back to sleep. No, she must pull herself together – *he* could not have been the guest who'd died at the Gallimore! Raymond Bast had not been a man to simply die . . .

'My name,' he had said, standing on their front doorstep on a merry May morning that had grown merrier and more Mayish in the memory, 'is Raymond Bast.'

Verity had gazed at the visitor, looking past his tall dark shape at all the birds flittering happily about the front garden and the pretty pink blossom that hung from the cherry trees like clusters of tiny lanterns swaying in the breeze. 'Who is it, dear?' her mother called out from the back so that Verity, looking again at the tall dark stranger clutching his hat and smiling up at her, had wondered, indeed, who the man could be.

'I am Raymond Bast,' he'd prompted helpfully and she had then repeated this information loudly so that an echo of her voice calling out his name had seemed to reverberate through the house, ever since.

Later, shortly afterwards it must have been, sitting in their sitting room, stirring heaped teaspoons of expensive sugar into his tea, Mr Bast had said, 'I'm afraid I have a very sweet tooth. I am an author, you see. I have come to Knibden for peace and quiet. To write my next book.'

Verity gaped, but her mother replied at once, 'Why, I believe I have seen your works, Mr Bast. At newsagents' stands, and in the public library.'

171

'You frequent the public library, Mrs Willow?'

'Not often, I don't have the time. I never was much of a reader, but my late husband . . .' Helen Willow liked to speak of Verity's father, and did so always as if he were dead which at the time he had not been. 'Verity reads, though,' she smilingly offered up her daughter.

Raymond Bast turned to Verity. 'And do *you* go to the library, Miss Willow?' he'd asked very courteously.

'Sometimes,' Verity admitted. She often went there after school. Not to read books necessarily but as somewhere to go that was not home, where her mother's lodgers eyed her greedily over their evening meal. She was thirteen. During the last year the growing protuberances that would be her breasts drew the men's eyes on her as they talked together about how trade was doing, speculated on their chances in the next Great Knibden Lottery, and crammed sausages and folded slices of bread smeared thickly with margarine into their mouths. 'I usually do my home-work at the library.'

Raymond Bast did not seem particularly disappointed that nei-ther mother nor daughter had read his books, though he was clearly quite pleased they had heard of him. 'I write the Randol-phe Shyne mysteries,' he told them. His books were not really for women, his readers being chiefly men who travelled to work by railway. 'Fellows on the 8.07 into town who feel the need to transform the perfectly dreary gentleman sitting opposite, with a half-guinea balczite pipe hanging from his mouth, into a Balkan spy, smoking pungent Eastern tobacco while decoding messages in the Announcements column of the morning's *Times*.' Raymond Bast sighed.

'Why would they need to do that?' Verity asked, genuinely puzzled, but her mother told her to hush. Mr Bast had not come to Knibden to discuss his readers.

'He wants peace and quiet, dear. Not little girls asking questions.'

'Just so!' Raymond Bast smiled at Mrs Willow and drank his tea. But he'd smiled kindly across at Verity also so she had known he was being polite to her mother and did not in any way regard Verity as an inquisitive chatty child. He had then told them of the need to escape the perils of literary London in order to settle quietly and write his next book.

'Perils?' her mother had asked.

'Why, yes!' Bast made it sound worse than the Blitz. Writers, even well-known ones such as Bast himself, were obliged to get about and be seen by the arbiters of literary taste so that if you stayed too long in the capital, attending all-night literary parties and giving dramatic readings to gatherings of those literary arbiters, you ended up never writing a single word. 'That is certain death to an author,' he'd laughed. 'And can you imagine Raymond Bast *dead*? What would happen to Randolphe Shyne, and the love of his life, Miss Maisie Vollutu? What would happen to all the little men on the 8.07 if there was never another two-shilling Bast to keep them amused?'

'I suppose they'd all be bored,' said Verity picturing a railway carriage full of little men staring out the railway carriage windows, yawning.

'Just so,' Mr Bast said again. And maybe he had added, as so often after that he had done, 'Verity and I understand each other.' Her mother always smiled when he said this. Helen Willow had smiled a lot that summer.

Mr Bast did not have much luggage. Nor could he say precisely how long he wished to stay. He had chosen Knibden because it was out of the way. He'd arrived that morning and asked the stationmaster where he'd be likely to rent a quiet room. The stationmaster had scratched his head and then directed him to the widow, Mrs Willow. 'She takes in lodgers,' he'd said with a wink. The cottage at the end of the quiet lane immediately struck Bast as just such a place where inspiration for another masterpiece might strike. 'It is a while since I finished my last book,' Raymond Bast told them. 'Time to start a new one.'

'What's it called? What's it about?' Verity inquired eagerly, not knowing then that these are not questions writers like to be asked. Not knowing then how much Mr Bast disliked any form of questioning. Verity's mother had glanced at Mr Bast and said to hush. Helen Willow then told Mr Bast that she'd assumed he had come to Knibden for the Great Knibden Lottery that was due to take place again later that summer. She had taken him for an early arrival.

'The Great Knibden Lottery?' Bast asked as if he had never heard of it.

Verity and her mother then explained about the trumpets, dragons and naked women. And the large sum of money that would be the prize. Soon people would be pouring into the town from all over the country. There wouldn't be a bed to be had in the place. But, as it happened, Mrs Willow had recently made a decision to cut down on 'paying guests', as she liked to call them. She'd decided to give up opening her house to all and sundry although there were still a couple of the old regulars: the quiet, elderly Mr Harris who came once a month on Thursdays. He travelled in hats. And a Mr Storr who came every other Thursday, but not necessarily. It depended on his schedule. He travelled in Bibles. There had been quite a few others who'd stayed regularly in the past but she had recently put a stop to that. It had got quite out of hand with three or four different faces at the table every evening. Your home did not feel your own. Verity had taken to going to the public library after school.

Raymond Bast nodded understandingly. Verity could recall every feature of his fine angular face, the dark dancing eyes that rested on you thoughtfully. The long chiselled nose. Just remembering how he'd looked almost hurt. He had offered to pay her mother three months' rent in advance, but hoped Mrs Willow would be kind enough to accept money for just one, until he'd had a chance to have a word at the bank. 'Or until I win the lottery!' he'd quipped.

Mrs Willow smiled. 'Yes, of course, Mr Bast,' she said. 'And by the way, Mr Fechnie at the bank is always very helpful. You may mention my name . . .'

'That's good.'

'But where are all your books? Your papers? Your manuscripts?' Verity wanted to know. His small suitcase could not contain more than a few changes of clothes.

Raymond Bast laughed. 'I don't need books – all I need comes out of here.' He'd tapped the side of his handsome head. 'I *write* them, Verity, not *read* them.'

As for papers and manuscripts, there was a brand-new pad of blank paper in the fabric compartment inside the lid of his case on which he hoped soon to get started. 'I travel light,' he laughed.

He also said he'd be grateful if Verity and her mother would keep his identity, and also his profession, a secret. He knew what it was like in a small town – if people got to know Raymond Bast was temporarily residing in their midst, every female scribbler for miles around would be queuing on the doorstep with half-written novels under their arms, seeking words of advice and letters of introduction. 'You wouldn't want that now, would you?'

Mrs Willow laughed. 'Heaven forbid!' she said. 'Of course we will be discreet and do everything we can to make your stay here a quiet one.'

'But,' Verity had asked, 'can't I even tell the girls at school? Can't I tell my friend, Belle?'

'Most particularly you are not to tell the girls at school. And expecially not Belle. Not *Belle* of all people!'

Verity and her mother had laughed. It was as if Raymond Bast knew something about Belle Quinn that they themselves were unaware of.

There had followed then the long glorious summer that Verity thought of ever afterwards as *The Summer of Raymond Bast*. It was the biggest whodunnit of her life, one no prettily printed covers could contain . . . And now, Miss Hester Jones had summoned the whole town to a denouement at the Gallimore Hotel. Tomorrow night, during a break in the dancing, the dead guest's investigator would unveil the truth.

'We doted on him,' Verity whispered to the little pink roses on her bedroom wall. The wall that had once divided her room from his. 'How we doted!'

A day or two after he'd come, she had gone back to the public library. 'You're a stranger, Verity!' the then librarian, Lavinia Lobb, had said.

'It's not so busy at home,' Verity explained. 'I can do my homework there.'

'School nearly over for the summer?'

'In a couple of weeks.'

'That's good, dear. And it's the lottery again this year. The town is already getting busier.'

'Is it?'

'Oh yes – you notice standing here. As the town gets busier the library gets quieter – during the weeks in the run up to the draw, no one takes out any books, but no one brings back any either. People run up fines thinking they'll easily be able to pay if they win – they can none of them think of losing. Afterwards it's chaos . . .' Miss Lobb sighed. She had lived through previous lotteries and seen the disruption they caused. Her brother, Denis Lobb, had bought a trumpet when trumpets were drawn in 1916 but he'd not had the right number on his ticket and had marched away to battle. His number had come up then, all right. His name engraved for all time on the War Memorial outside in the Square: Denis Lobb, Private. Killed in Action.

Eventually Verity managed to slip away from Miss Lobb. It was sad about Denis Lobb – but people didn't want to hear about her dead brother every time they came into the library. Nor did they always want to hear the story of the last hockey match before the war when Lavinia Lobb had scored a goal and her dead brother, and all his dead friends, had cheered.

The Raymond Basts were plentiful, and well thumbed. None of them still had their paper covers on. 'So it's mysteries you want!' Lavinia Lobb had crept up behind her. 'There's always a waiting list for the latest Randolphe Shyne.'

'Randolphe Shyne?'

'Raymond Bast's detective. Like Agatha Christie's Hercule Poirot. Only Randolphe Shyne has a lady friend – the lovely Miss Maisie Vollutu. I am not sure Mr Poirot ever had a lady friend . . .'

'Oh! Well, it's not really my . . .' Verity had hurried away from the shelf and from Miss Lobb's sharp eyes, not wanting to betray her mother's new lodger by showing too much interest in Raymond Bast's works. She supposed now her interest in books generally, and whodunnits in particular, had dated from that moment. It had seemed only natural that when she left school she should go and work for Miss Lobb. Eventually Miss Lobb had retired and George Allendale had replaced her. Lavinia Lobb did not enjoy her retirement. For years after, Miss Lobb used to drop in to the library every day to talk about her brother and see how things were going on without her. She would remark rather peevishly on even the slightest changes that were made. And when I retire, Verity thought, I shall probably do the same. She imagined an elderly George Allendale, by then the spitting image

176

of Arthur Dawes Dobson, and herself even more decrepit. And the new young girl they would get in when the time came to replace her, laughing at her for being unable to keep away, laughing at George for putting up with the funny old thing. Lavinia Lobb had been outraged when George rescued Dawes Dobson's portrait from the store cupboard. 'The man was a crook,' she had cried, white faced and shaken. He brought disgrace to the town. And to his two sons, Johnny and Wilfred, who were friends of Denis's and had been there at the last hockey match and had thrown their caps into the air when she'd scored her goal. Their names were also engraved for all time on Knibden's War Memorial outside the library's main window: Missing in Action. Presumed Dead.

'I think I had better be *Harry* to you,' Raymond Bast said casually that merry May morning long ago when he'd denied all knowledge of the Great Knibden Lottery, and sat removing biscuit crumbs from his lap which he then put on the side of his saucer. He was always fastidious about his clothes, which was one of the things Verity liked to remember. She had spent hours in the kitchen rubbing blacking into his shoes with scrunched-up newspaper. She had lovingly mended a tear in his jacket, using a new darning technique she'd just been taught in Domestic Science at school. Wherever Raymond Bast had gone when he left them at the end of that summer, her schoolgirl's painstaking stitches had gone with him. There'd been comfort in that. 'Call me "Harry Best" while I am here. Then no one will suspect.'

'*Harry Best!*' Verity repeated incredulously, but her mother had readily gone along with the scheme.

'Yes, of course, Mr Bast – I mean Best.'

As far as Knibden had been concerned, then, the Willows's new lodger had been a pleasant polite fellow called Harry Best. When people asked her mother what Mr Best did, because he was obviously a cut above her usual travelling salesmen, she had replied that Mr Best was a gentleman of private means who had come for a short stay in a country town while his London flat was being redecorated. Prior to his forthcoming marriage. It got damaged in the Blitz. Mrs Willow was not keen on fibs, as a rule, but this got round the difficulty nicely. Nor was Mrs Willow sure how the story of the forthcoming marriage crept up on her. A little invention to smooth things along. The effect of living with a writer living in the house, she'd told herself. And indeed, Mr Best did spend a lot of time *in* the house. He stayed in his room a good deal – writing, Verity and her mother supposed. Every so often, though, he had made long expeditions, getting up before them and returning late at night, letting himself in with his key. It was from one of those expeditions he had returned with the little tear in his jacket.

Verity had been thirteen years old that summer. The summer of Raymond Bast, which was also, of course, the summer of the last Great Knibden Lottery. Verity's father had left them years before. He'd come back after the war and, just as she and her mother had got used to having him in the house, he had gone away again, giving no reason. 'He found Knibden a bit quiet after all the excitement,' her mother said at first but gradually she'd decided it would be easier if her husband had died and she could think of him, and speak of him, as some sort of hero. One of the few to whom so many owed so much, who needed no complicated explanation to explain their absence. Helen Willow, possessed of the dignified washed-out beauty of faded silk, had consulted Theodore Fechnie about how best to make ends meet and it was he who had sensibly suggested taking in lodgers. It was hard work and Mrs Willow managed valiantly but the zest for life had gone out of her. She rarely smiled or laughed for there was little in the grinding routine of her life to smile or laugh about – until that summer, and the appearance of Raymond Bast, or Harry Best as they had called him, on their doorstep.

Although money was always scarce, Mrs Willow had been kept well supplied with certain commodities by her salesmen. At the time of Mr Bast's arrival she'd had a plentiful array of last season's squashed hats from Mr Harris, and a whole set of Bibles from Mr Storr, the pages of which had got stuck together in the damp. If you had enough damaged Bibles you'd be sure to find the page you wanted legible in one of them, Mr Storr had claimed. When her mother died, Verity threw away all the unsaleable hats and mildewed Bibles the poor woman had hoarded. But what had Mr Bast given them? Nothing that could be put out with the dustbins. He had not even paid his rent after that first month – though it was only after he was gone that Mrs

Willow remembered this, and blamed herself entirely for forgetting to ask. 'He was so taken up with his new Randolphe Shyne mystery,' she told her daughter.

Verity stared hard at the little pink roses on the wall beside her and thought now about Herbert which was something she only did from time to time. Herbert Vale, like Mr Harris and Mr Storr before him, had lodged at the house one day a week since Knibden was a convenient place to stop part way on his round. He sold cardboard boxes – not that this tells you anything much about Herbert Vale. Verity had thought so at the time. And she thought so even more now he was dead. Few in Knibden these days ever remembered that Miss Willow, the assistant librarian, had been for a short time a long time ago, a Mrs Herbert Vale. Verity herself was astonished every time she recollected this. She wondered what she would say about Herbert to Hester Jones.

'You look sad,' he had said to her on their wedding night. Verity was sitting combing out her thin blonde hair in the mirror. When she heard him speak she raised her pale eyes and focused them on Herbert's mirror image walking up behind her and placing his hand on her shoulder. She was so amazed then to find herself in a seaside hotel bedroom, with a man wearing striped pyjamas whose short fat fingers reminded her of the stubby pork sausages her mother fried every evening for the paying guests' teas, Verity told Herbert Vale about the summer of Raymond Bast. 'I have never told anyone before,' she said when she had finished.

'I knew there was someone else,' Herbert said quietly. He had always known. It did not matter, he'd added rather humbly, taking her long slender hands in his short stocky ones and holding them kindly, so that later, when they climbed into bed and lay side by side not touching, like seasoned floorboards, Verity wondered if Herbert had heard a word of what she had been telling him about the events of that extraordinary summer. He did not touch her that night, or any night after, nor did he ever again refer to what she had told him but always kept a respectable distance as if acknowledging that his pale young wife's affections belonged, by some prior attachment, to another man.

When Herbert's sister had come up to her after the funeral, Verity told her of her decision to return to Knibden. 'I may as well,' she'd said. She had hoped so much for a child – a little boy she'd have called Raymond, and written stories for about mice and rats with human characteristics who lived in lighthouses and enjoyed adventures that always ended safely. Verity felt she had probably married Herbert to have that child, but little Raymond had not come about as she'd hoped. The sister, who had no children either, and was not married and didn't want them, narrowed her eyes.

'Isn't Knibden the place they have the famous lotteries?' she asked.

'Not any more. The last one took place when I was thirteen – the year dragons won. There was a riot.'

Herbert's sister pursed her lips. She looked like a dragon who might riot herself.

'Poor Herbert,' Verity whispered softly. She was uncertain what to say or what there was to be said to Herbert's sister, but felt an explanation was owed. 'It was a nasty crash.' The little van they had bought to help him sell his cardboard boxes had been crushed as if it were itself made of cardboard and the body they had pulled from the wreckage so corrugated it had been hard to recognize the features as Herbert's.

Herbert's sister also felt an explanation was called for. 'Herbert said there was someone else,' she hissed.

'There was,' Verity admitted quietly. It was raining steadily in the graveyard but she did not mind getting wet. It had not rained once the whole of that long glorious summer Raymond Bast had been with them.

'You knew?' The sister was surprised.

'I knew?' Verity felt confused. There was so much about Raymond Bast she had never known at all.

Then Herbert's sister had told Verity about Herbert Vale's other woman, the one he'd been keeping since long before he had ever known Verity.

'Why did he marry *me* then?' Verity blurted out.

'He probably felt sorry for you,' the spiteful Miss Vale replied. 'Living with your mother in that out-of-the-way place where even the famous lotteries are a thing of the past.'

Verity returned to Knibden, to her mother's house, and went back to work in the library. Miss Lobb had been pleased to have her. A brave young widow, she kept herself busy filing cards and replacing returned books in their shelves.

'You stole him from me!' It was a nightmare. It was a line from a Raymond Bast. Eventually Randolphe Shyne would step in and sort out the misunderstanding. The mistaken identity would no doubt solve some other mystery Shyne and Maisie Vollutu were working on elsewhere. Verity, meanwhile, tried to smile at the woman but the woman would not be smiled at. 'I've tracked you down!' she screamed.

'I did not know,' Verity said simply. Fortunately it was the lunch hour, Miss Lobb was out, and no one else was about to witness or report the encounter.

'His sister said you did. She said she told you about me at the funeral. The funeral I have only just found out about. I've been worrying myself sick wondering where Herbie had got to. There's bills to pay an' . . .'

The marriage to Verity had been a ghastly mistake. Herbert had been, in all but the law it seemed, practically married already. To someone else he'd lodged with on his cardboard-box rounds. There was a lump sum due to his widow from Herbert's Knibden Municipal Insurance Company life insurance policy, and this Verity hastily promised to the woman. To help pay the bills. 'His death was unexpected – the sum should be quite large.'

'I don't want your money!' Herbert's other woman had shrieked, grabbing a copy of *Middlemarch* from the returns stack and hurling it across the room. The book gashed Verity's face and ripped its spine as it bounced off Verity and fell to the floor. Verity straightened up as best she could, and limped to her stool.

'I should like you to have the money,' she said.

The woman glared at her, agreeing to accept the cash. For the sake of peace and for her children. Herbie's children. For Verity's sake too, the woman added. 'You'll feel far happier if you pay me off.'

'I'll send it,' Verity promised. 'As soon as it comes . . .'

'That won't be necessary. I'll call back,' the woman insisted.

Verity spent the rest of the afternoon putting the *Middle* back to *march* with sellotape while avoiding Miss Lobb's searching gaze. Herbert's other woman took to coming to Knibden whenever she had the time, wandering into the library with a child or two on each arm, demanding to know if the money had arrived yet, urging Verity to chivvy the Knibden Municipal Insurance Company. 'They're all crooks,' she had said, threatening to see about the business herself.

'Oh, don't do that!' Verity pleaded. The children, she was pleased to see, did not in any way resemble Herbert Vale. Or the little boy, Raymond, who had never been born. A pale quiet child who liked nothing better than adventure stories about brave whiskery creatures his mother wrote specially for his bedtime. Tell me the one about Matilda rat and the lighthouse, *again*! 'I'm sure Mr Wilkes-Tooley is processing the claim as fast as he can . . .'

Miss Lobb, who had to be told what was going on, had been very kind, considering. Both she and Verity were greatly relieved when the Knibden Municipal Insurance Company payment came at last. The next time Herbert's other woman turned up, Verity handed it over. The woman snatched the cheque from Verity's hands with as little ado as a dog seizing a bone. She bounded out of the library, never to be seen again.

'You'll never guess what!' Lavinia Lobb said one morning. She clicked her tongue and read out a piece in the paper.

We have all heard of the umbrella trick: the man of the house dies. The widow and children gather in mourning. There comes a knock on the door. The umbrella mender looks abashed. He apologizes for intruding at such a time, and says he will return later. The family assure him they welcome the distraction. It's just that the deceased left his umbrella to be mended. The bill is quite big. The umbrella was badly broken and now looks as good as new. Nobody quibbles. Nobody wants Dad's mended umbrella, so the canny mender goes on his way, money in his pocket and a 'mended' umbrella to take round to the next address on his list of bereaved families. Yes, we all know that one but now there's a new, superior scam: husband dies. Grieving widow is accosted by blowzy female claiming to be the other woman in the husband's life. The mother of his children. An unseemly public fracas is only averted by the widow quickly agreeing to give up her husband's life insurance policy when the money comes through. Cheque arrives, is eagerly snatched by indignant female and returned at once to insurance company in whose regular employ these professional 'other women' work.

'Well, well!' said Miss Lobb, arching her eyebrows. 'You learn something new every day.'

'Oh!' said Miss Willow. Or Mrs Vale as she had been then.

'You might have a word with Mr Wilkes-Tooley,' Lavinia Lobb suggested.

'I couldn't do that,' Verity decided. 'But I should like to be Miss Willow once more.' The insurance policy money had been handed over, and with it the benefits of having had a husband who had died. 'I am not a well-to-do widow,' Verity said. 'It is as if poor Herbert had never been.'

Her mother had not particularly approved the match – it puzzled her why Verity had married the cardboard-box man, but she never said anything. Her gentle kind mother did not say anything either when Verity returned home after Herbert's funeral to the bedroom with the little roses on the wall. Verity was her mother's sole paying guest then. The others, Mrs Willow felt, had been more trouble than they were worth. Except Harry Best, or Raymond Bast. What *fun* they had had that summer!

Verity Willow wondered whether she shouldn't go before Hester Jones straight away, and confess. But what could a girl like that, a someone-who-was-not-someone, know of a man like Raymond Bast? Should she warn her? Explain that there are men in this world who stop at nothing for their own amusement. That years after you thought the story was over, something could occur to alter all that has gone before. Loose ends you'd thought to have tied for good turn out to belong to some other, altogether more entangled, knot.

If *I* got the money, Verity Willow thought, I would not accept just the summer of Raymond Bast all those years ago. I would want to know about the autumn, the winter *and* the spring too. He must have been somewhere the rest of the year.

And then, from thinking about Mr Bast, or Harry Best – or whoever the man had really been – Verity thought about the guest who had died in the Gallimore Hotel. *If only* she had got it into her head last Sunday morning to pop down there! She might so easily have gone. There'd have been one other occupant in the dusty dark lounge, a man hiding behind *The Times*, smoking pungent Eastern tobacco and decoding messages. She'd have sat down by the window and ordered tea. And the waitress – or rather Mrs Mason herself, for there had been none of the new waitresses then – would have hurried off to fetch her order, leaving her alone with the unknown guest.

The man lowered his paper. 'It isn't Verity?' he'd said, adjusting his monocle and Verity would have looked at him across the empty tables as she looked back at him now over the empty years. The same handsome face. The same dark irrepressible eyes, undimmed.

'Raymond Bast!' she had cried in her joy. 'I don't believe it. It's a miracle!'

'Miracles happen, Verity. That's the nature of miracles. Only look at the way Hester Jones turned up when we needed her!'

And Verity wanted to rush over and bury her head in his arms, weeping for joy. Telling him all these years on that she had known all along he would come back to her. In the end she had been the only one he could trust. But, with a flick of his wrist, Raymond Bast beckoned her to show restraint. It was their game, remember. The last thing they wanted would be Hester Jones poking her nose in. Queuing up like every other female scribbler seeking words of advice and letters of introduction. 'Harry Best!' hissed Bast. 'When you speak to the investigator, Verity, I'm Harry Best, don't forget!'

Verity had not forgotten. She had never forgotten. She would have sat there then, in the lounge of the Gallimore Hotel, pretending to be Miss Willow, assistant librarian at Knibden's public library, and letting the warmth of her love wash over her, her cheeks aflame and her heart on fire. Just like Maisie Vollutu waiting for Randolphe Shyne at the aerodrome and, seeing him step from a VX Goose 921, she had looked away, not wanting to betray the man she loved to the agents of the enemy standing all around.

'Scones, Miss Willow. Jam? A nice slice of cake.' Eileen Mason, the manageress of the Gallimore, had returned with her tea. Eileen Mahoney, the chambermaid who had married Mason, the manager at the seaside hotel where Verity and Herbert Vale had stayed on their honeymoon. It was one of those rainy afternoons when entertainment is laid on to distract bored guests. An iced cake had been cut in the lounge during the course of the afternoon.

'The girl will be expecting,' one of the older women had whispered to Verity. 'A lot of that goes on among hotel staff – it's how they spend the short gap between making our beds and preparing the lunch. If you come back next year, there'll be a babbie here bawling its head off. Not very professional!' The woman began calling out rather nastily to the young bride for another slice of free cake.

'You'll never guess what,' Verity Willow had duly written, on her postcard home.

'No, no thank you, Mrs Mason. No cake.' Randolphe Shyne saw Maisie Vollutu look away. He thought how wonderful she was. After all this time apart, she still loved him. There had never been anyone else. Verity's brief marriage to a kindly man with stocky fingers who sold corrugated cardboard boxes for a living, had not altered her feelings in any way.

Verity sighed. She had *not* taken it into her head to go to the Gallimore Hotel last week any more than Raymond Bast, or Harry Best, or whoever he had been, was a man to simply *die*. But the guest at the Gallimore *had not* simply died – the way he'd chosen to depart from this earth, he could scarcely have created more of a splash.

'I must get up,' Verity said out loud. 'I will go to the library and resign my post. Tomorrow I will attend Belle's tea-dance. *That* much I owe the dead guest . . .'

9

A Blind Eye

Daniel Mason sighed. 'I knew there was something very odd about that guest,' he said wearily.

'Just as you knew there was something odd about me?' Hester Jones laughed.

'Yes, well!' The manager of the Gallimore Hotel shuffled his feet and almost smiled. 'I've been thinking, Miss Jones,' he began, but fell silent again.

'Is there something you'd like to tell me, Mr Mason?'

'I suppose there is.' The manager of the Gallimore glanced stiffly over his shoulder to check there was no one else about. Miss Jones was breakfasting early. None of the other guests or staff were down yet. You had to hand it to this investigator the town had appointed: she took her job seriously. She was up till all hours with the ancient Gallimore sisters, and then down again first thing this morning. The girl could have been successful in the hotel business. She should consider that line of work, he would tell her, when the time came. He would offer to put his experience and contacts in the trade at her disposal. So long as she left Knibden and took all this bother she had brought away with her.

'Is it something Mrs Mason doesn't know?' Hester Jones probed.

Daniel Mason nodded. Miss Jones was unnervingly quick on the uptake. He pitied anyone in Knibden with anything to hide. 'Eileen . . . Poor Eileen lives – she dreams. She always has. She used to tell me lies about the guests. She will tell you lies, Miss Jones. You mustn't mind her. This business has unsettled the woman. It has unsettled us all. It was Eileen who found the dead guest dead in his bed.'

'Yes, she told me. That, in any case, was not a lie?'

Mason acknowledged this. 'You see, I have been happy all these years not to think about any of it too much. Which seems ridiculous now, of course, and must certainly seem ridiculous to a sensible girl like you, Miss Jones.' Mason paused. Then he grew impassioned. 'Knibden never needed an Alhambra! No wonder the old theatre has been left derelict for years. The Gallimore Hotel was always the main scene of action. *Here* is where the dramas of the town have been acted out. I see this now. I also see that it always has been so. I have turned a blind eye to the truth and the truth is now staring me straight in the face, like a gaping death mask. Why!' He laughed bitterly, recoiling at the same time from that gaping death mask. 'We even have a corpse centre stage, just to draw in the numbers. You'll have noticed how the seats in the dining room are being snapped up. The Guest at the Gallimore is a box office success – and we have you to thank, Miss Hester Jones! A star attraction to provide fresh interest!'

'Really, Mr Mason!'

'You think I am overwrought. That I am going too far. If anything, I am not going far enough! When Eileen and I applied to come to the Gallimore it sounded like a job we could be happy in. The owner wanted nothing whatever to do with the place, I was told. We were to deal only with his bank. That suited me fine. It meant there would be no one looking over our heads all the time noticing Eileen's little oddities. Knibden seemed a pleasant enough out-of-the-way place with no great seasonal swings in trade, overworked one minute, overquiet the next like we were used to at the seaside. I looked forward to a gentle steady business we could cope with in old age. And where Eileen could live on after I have gone, for one must think about these things. I am a careful man. I married her to take care of her and I have done so ever since. The instructions we were given were simple and clear. We were to deal with the owner's bank; all decisions regarding the running of the hotel were to be left to us. It was a responsibility I thought I could shoulder. Mr Fechnie, the then bank manager, seemed satisfied that these arrangements were perfectly in order. He even implied that they were quite *common* – though in all my years in hotels I had never come across anything like it before. He told us we were ideally suited to the job. He named a salary far in excess of the remuneration we had enjoyed in our previous employment, and I don't mind telling you, Miss Jones, we felt we had landed on our feet. We moved here and started work straight away. Everything went very well at first. But then . . .'

'Yes?'

'We must have been here a few years when . . .' Daniel Mason went quiet.

'When what?'

'It began to disturb me. How peculiar it all was. The outgoings, even without the cost of our earnings, far outweighed the receipts. With so few guests, the Gallimore could only have been losing money heavily. Just keeping the lights on in a place this size . . . And yet – no one seemed to mind. Mr Fechnie, least of all. He always accepted my accounts which I took him on the first Monday of every month without question. He never commented or raised normal points of business. After a while it occurred to me that anyone less honest or scrupulous than myself could have got away with murder.'

'Murder!'

'So to speak. I began to get curious. I wanted to find out who the owners were. Why the place was as it was. I thought there might be some good reason that had to do with something I did not know, something about the Gallimore Hotel that suspended usual market forces.'

'Like what?'

'I don't know – but once I had begun to think about it, I could think of nothing else. I could not speak to Eileen though I felt that something of the kind was also troubling her. One day when I could stand the mystery no longer, I went to see Mr Fechnie. He was sitting behind his desk in the bank, twiddling his thumbs. Knibden is a quiet place, you will have observed, Miss Jones. I do not suppose a bank manager here finds a great deal to do. Anyhow, when I asked if I might make an appointment – I wanted to set the meeting on a formal footing – I was not too surprised when Fechnie said I did not need one. Why didn't I take a seat, then and there. Would I like a cup of coffee, and how could he help me? I stayed standing. I apologized and explained how there was only a short interval between when all the beds were made after breakfast before preparations needed to start for lunch so, if he didn't mind, I would state my business and get back to the Gallimore.

'Fechnie nodded approvingly. He folded his arms across his chest. "The Gallimore could not be in better hands," he said. "Everyone says so."

'For which I thanked him.

' "You have always kept to the terms of your appointment," he said.

' "Well, yes," I agreed. I had done that.

' "*And* you have never made life difficult by asking any of the questions you have been specifically excluded under the terms of your employment from asking," he went on as if he could perfectly read what was in my head, and on the tip of my tongue. "I appreciate that, Mr Mason. You have never been foolhardy enough to ask me to breach the confidentiality to which this bank is irrevocably sworn. We are entirely satisfied with you, Mason, and with your good wife also."

'I confess I stared at him. I wanted to ask who he meant by "we", but did not dare.

' "Now, Mr Mason," Fechnie continued, snipping the end off a cigar. He offered me one from his box but I shook my head. "Here I am!" He laughed. "Chattering on as if we had all the time in the world when you have only the short precious interval between breakfast and lunch. What was it you wanted to ask me?"

'What could I say? I shrugged my shoulders and simply muttered that I was glad everything was satisfactory.

'There was a pause. Theodore Fechnie scrutinized my face for a brief instant, and then stood up. The meeting was over. He walked with me outside and we shook hands in the doorway of the bank. Then, as I left him to hurry back to the Gallimore, something made me turn round. Fechnie was still standing there in the entrance to the bank, puffing on his cigar and smiling. It is hard to explain to you properly, Miss Jones, what a strange unearthly smile that was. Like teeth set in a skull, mocking. I have been unable since to forget that smile.'

'Why is that?' Hester asked.

'Fechnie *knew*. He knew it all. I see now, with the benefit of that most dearly bought commodity, hindsight, what I could not know then. How the man must have *marvelled* at our acceptance of our good fortune, and the ease with which he deflected any questions. He watched my willingness to accede to

189

the preposterous arrangements, knowing all the while that even more extraordinary plans had been laid. And that these too would find just as ready acceptance. Imagine how Theodore Fechnie's teeth would grin in his skull now! Eileen and I were like people in the past whose lives you read about, living happily from day to day without any knowledge of events to come. History renders them witless fools but at the time, even if they suspect what lies in store, there is little they can do. They may as well enjoy themselves . . .'

'Fechnie knew . . .'

'He knew all right. We know from Mr Williams that Fechnie allowed the dead guest to settle his affairs in the way that he did. For all we know, Theodore Fechnie advised the man. He might even have suggested the scheme to him. When I think how the former manager of the bank watched me enjoying my position as manager of the Gallimore Hotel, strutting importantly about town . . . Of course he could not help smiling! I feel a fool. Worse, I have drawn my dear Eileen into something foolish. My only consolation is that I am not the only one. Why, even you, Miss Jones, have become part of the dead stranger's plans.' Mason's voice tailed off as he thought about what he was saying. Then he began again, with greater passion. 'All these years we have been living comfortably in Knibden, taking care of the Gallimore, we were waiting for this. Only we could not know it. We lived as everyone lives, storing up for the morrow, completely oblivious that the morrow may not come. It must end in death. And it has ended. With the death of this guest, the anonymous stranger who owned the hotel. Who, aided and abetted by the late Mr Theodore Fechnie, was paying me handsomely to accept his absence and anonymity. And make an example of me. See, there goes Daniel Mason, people will say, pointing me out to their children. He was the manager of the Gallimore Hotel who accepted employment from a man he'd never met until he died in a bed in the hotel some ten years on. Why me, Miss Jones? What have I done to be singled out for mockery in this way? Where is the justice?'

'I do not know, Mr Mason. But the dead man must have had his reasons for acting as he did – reasons I hope to find out. Tell me, was that the one occasion on which you questioned the arrangements?'

'There was one other. More recently.' The manager of the Gallimore Hotel coughed. He and Miss Jones were no longer alone. He broke off and began fussily rearranging the dining-room furniture.

'I hope you don't mind,' Verity Willow said to George Allendale.

'Mind?' George was delighted. The last thing he needed was Miss Willow sitting about, pretending to file cards and return library books to their shelves. He would be grateful to have the place to himself. 'I am sure things will return to normal – when everyone loses interest in this mystery of yours. Till then, I appreciate, there isn't enough work for the two of us. *Madame Bovary* is still missing. I expect I can manage on my own.'

Verity had something she needed time for, she explained. Something that could not be done in a library.

'A rest would do you good,' George agreed.

Verity shrugged. It was not a rest she had in mind. 'Poor Miss Lobb!' she remarked.

'Miss Lobb?'

'Do you remember how she used to come in and get upset about any changes we made . . .' There were changes enough now. George Allendale appeared to have turned the whole place upside down.

As Verity Willow left the library she was surprised to share the revolving doors on her way out, with Richard Follifoot, sole trader and builder of Knibden, on his way in to give George an estimate of what it would cost to rebuild the great glass dome that had housed Arthur Dawes Dobson's museum.

Verity paused beside the War Memorial. Denis Lobb, Private, it said, one name among many. Lavinia had doted on her brother and spent her life's savings contributing to the cost of the memorial. The issue had split the town. There were those who considered it a scandal that lottery money should be spent erecting a memorial to Knibden's Dead. Anyone who preferred to pay themselves to have the names of their loved ones inscribed, had done so. Miss Lobb had done so. 'I loved them all,' she had said of Denis's friends who had cheered her goal at that last hockey match. Most of all she had loved Johnny Dawes Dobson. His name was on the memorial too. Missing in Action, Presumed Dead.

10

The Cold Sun

'We saw Dick Follifoot entering the library. Miss Willow resigned, and walked out!'

'Verity Willow and Dick Follifoot! That man has a finger in every pie.'

'I don't fancy Miss Willow's chances when Mrs Follifoot finds out.'

'She'll know already – not much gets past *that* woman.'

'*And* we saw Hester Jones chatting to Daniel Mason over breakfast.'

'Chatting! She hasn't time to chat.'

'She's got two days now.'

'Anything can happen in two days.'

'Not if she chats!'

'Who was he, do you think?'

'The dead guest?'

'Who else?'

'Who cares – I'm only interested in who gets his money.'

'They reckon Bill Parris. Or General Bensusann.'

'They can reckon away. Hester Jones will have to prove it.'

'She's to prove it at the tea-dance tomorrow night.'

'Not long to wait.'

'Feels like an eternity!'

'Will the dance be free, or are they sellin' tickets?'

'It had bloody better be free – or paid for . . .'

'By that do-gooder, Belle Quinn.'

'Miss Quinn after the fortune, then?'

'Who isn't?'

Belle Quinn, meanwhile, wrapped against the early morning chill in a woollen paisley shawl, sat calmly at the rosewood desk that had been her mother's and wrote to her sister in Penzance:

The Laurels,
Knibden.

Friday morning,
first thing.

It is a long time, I know. I have been remiss. I have been wondering how you are, Fleur – I should have written before but somehow, you know how it is, with so much to organize. First Daddy's death, now this tea-dance. A strange thing has happened in Knibden recently that has recalled you much to my mind. It may be a coincidence, the way you too went off to Penzance like that, but I find I cannot sleep until I have written. Naturally I want to know if there is anything you can tell me about Hester Jones. I am on the committee. I have a responsibility. To the town. To the dead guest – and to the great fortune he has left and which will very likely be distributed during a break in the dancing at my tea-dance tomorrow. It is probably absurd to seek to investigate our investigator, but it would be more absurd – since you are in Penzance and can probably throw light on it all – not to. Oh Fleur, we should never have quarrelled in the way that we did. And then let the quarrel go unpatched all these years . . .

As she was writing, Belle Quinn had no real intention of sending the letter. On several occasions in the past she had sat down and written to Fleur, letters that later, before they could be sent, she had torn up and put on the fire. Not all her correspondence had been conciliatory. Once or twice her despair at her younger sister's cruel treatment of their father had got the better of Belle's essential goodness:

Dear Fleur, Daddy died tonight. At five o'clock. I was with him to the end. He asked for you, of course, and I had to lie. Naturally I assured him you were on your way, Penzance is a fair distance and if he could only hang on, you would be with us soon. But I had been telling him the same thing for days, and in the end he must have known I lied – Penzance may be distant, but it is not so far for a loving daughter when death is near at hand.

Belle had wept and torn up that letter before the tears that coursed down her cheeks could splatter the neat ink. Of course, at the end, Daddy had not asked for Fleur! Although a couple of times during those dreadful final weeks he had suddenly mentioned her wayward younger sister. Fleur had been on his mind. Fleur who had absented herself all those years back had been more real to him than the daughter who had stayed so lovingly by his side.

'You must share all I have between you,' Harold Augustus Quinn had said one morning. 'You and Fleur.' This was his first reference to his other daughter in over twenty years. He'd started choking but when he could speak again, he added, 'There is plenty for both of you. When I am gone *you* must sort everything out, Belle.'

'Of course, Daddy,' Belle had said as soon as she'd got her own breath back. 'I will let Fleur, when she comes, have anything she wants.'

Harold Quinn leant over and patted her hand. 'You are a good girl,' he said wearily. 'You have always been a good daughter.' Belle had smiled bravely and smoothed down the tousled bed-clothes. A day or two later Daddy had brought the subject up again, 'There is more than enough money in the bank for you both. You and Fleur will be able to live very comfortably when I'm gone.'

'Let's not think of that now,' Belle said quickly, but Daddy had something further on his mind.

'All I ask is that you keep hold of my papers. Until such time as they are of interest to someone . . .' He had been weak, his dry lips had trembled. He was a defeated man.

Fighting back tears, Belle fervently seized her father's hand. 'I will publish your Works, Daddy,' she pledged, hoping to rally him. 'If there is money in the bank it must be spent on that. People should be able to read your ideas at last, and understand. It is my dearest wish.'

Quinn half closed his eyes as if even Belle's gentle grasp hurt him. He did not reply. In fact, he never spoke again.

The Cold Sun: an Inverted Universe, A Work in Twelve Parts fully described with accompanying diagrams, by Harold Augustus Quinn, Mathematician. This was a project Belle and her father had dis-cussed over the years. It seemed to Belle now that it had been their main, if not their only, topic of conversation. How many times Belle had taken up his tray and sat herself down beside the bed to enjoy a convivial conversation upon the subject. She knew exactly the size of each of the twelve volumes, the typeface Quinn thought suitable, the quality and thickness of the paper he preferred. Once or twice when her father seemed particularly low, Belle had tried to push the project a step nearer realization. One grey overcast morning she had gone in to her father and said brightly, 'I have been thinking, Daddy. Maybe we could entrust the printing to Mr Matchett. At Buckworth & Matchett's. I am told the firm is not very busy these days so I'm sure he'll be able to give your work all the attention it needs. And I could call there regularly, and keep a careful eye . . .'

Harold Quinn stared at his elder daughter. 'What are you talking about?' he demanded.

'*The Cold Sun: an Inverted Universe* – your life's work!' Belle gasped. What else did either of them ever talk about? 'It's such a nice walk out along the canal towpath to Buckworth & Matchett's. Why, I could go down there this afternoon . . .'

Quinn's grey fingers gripped the bedclothes. 'You have more than enough to see to . . .' he objected, seized by a sudden panic. That this should happen to him at his time of life! That Belle should think of abandoning him now the way little Fleur had abandoned him years ago. Victor Matchett was an unpleasant, hard little man, with all the unpleasantness and pushiness of hard little men. Had the fellow set his inky cap at Belle? The great old firm of Buckworth & Matchett's had declined over the years until nowadays most of the presses that used to thump away in old Henry Buckworth's day stood idle. The buildings Buckworth had built with such enthusiasm to house his presses in had been allowed to deteriorate. His ineffectual brother, Godfrey, whom the women and children of the town liked to chase, had drowned one dark night in the canal. Matchett had not been able to cope left on his own after the old man's death. Now, no doubt, he'd be looking about for a fresh source of revenue to see him through into old age. He'd have reckoned how Miss Quinn would shortly be inheriting from her elderly father and he saw himself installed in married luxury at the Laurels, waited on hand and foot by the endlessly accommodating Belle. But a man like Matchett would not stop there: when the time came, Belle's pushy little husband would scheme to deprive poor absent Fleur of her rightful half share of the inheritance. Harold Quinn sank back as far as he could into his pillows and eyed his daughter suspiciously. Matchett had probably already made his move. He'd have waylaid Belle in the town on some pretext or other. And now the foolish girl was using the publication of her own father's life's work as an excuse to go chasing after him. Doubtless she would take the twelve parts along the muddy towpath to her lover, one by one, and gradually the conferring over her father's complex mathematical data and diagrams would lead on quite naturally to hand-holding and other intimacies. Belle would put up a show of maidenly resistance, of course, but the girl would be flattered to receive a man's attentions at her time of life. No one had shown any interest in her since the Reverend Gilbert Sibson stopped calling at the Laurels all those years ago.

Belle, meanwhile, was smiling and prattling away. 'It's such a pleasant walk along the canal towpath to Buckworth & Matchett's, Daddy.' Belle envisaged herself, the loving devoted daughter, supervising the publication of the twelve instalments. She would rise early and deliver the text to Mr Matchett and call back again in the afternoons to check how the typesetting was coming along. She would bring the work home and sit up here with Daddy, painstakingly going through the page proofs, suggesting alterations and emendations that would show how much she understood, how much she, at least, of his daughters, cared.

But Daddy had been reluctant to see his life's work made public just yet. He'd shaken his head and slipped a little further down into the bed. 'Those pamphlets are only drafts at this stage,' he'd objected, and when she'd pressed him he had turned angry. 'I suppose you think I'm lying here doing nothing!' he yelled at her and later, when he'd calmed down, he explained that he was not sorry to be confined to his bed. It gave him the chance to work through some fresh, highly conflicting hypotheses that needed more thought before their extraordinary implications could be committed to paper.

Belle smiled understandingly. 'We'll wait till you're ready,' she had said.

Harold Quinn had been the most brilliant mathematician of his generation. So brilliant his ideas far outstripped those of his time. By complex calculations, only he understood, he had proved that the sun was cold. We lived, he maintained, in a negative universe.

Our perceptions were inside out. We felt ourselves to be freezing when we were in fact boiling hot. And vice versa. He had proved this conclusively, setting it out in the twelve papers, full of densely argued equations and abstractions, but – not surprisingly since he was a genius – his work had been beyond anyone else in an uninverted universe to understand. None of it had ever been taken seriously and Quinn had never received the recognition he and his elder daughter knew he deserved.

Harold Augustus Quinn had come to Knibden as an ambitious young man. Like most ambitious young men who made their way to Knibden he had come for the lottery – not, in *his* case, to take part. Nothing so mundane. The Great Knibden Lottery had seemed to Quinn the perfect mathematical machine on which to try out certain laws of probability applicable to random events that his Inverted Universe Theory had thrown up. A universe in reverse would mean that there was nothing entirely random about the workings of a lottery. Probability and inevitability were inextricably linked by a complex set of rules that underpin all matter. Since the interval between lotteries in Knibden tended to be about ten years – it took that long for the town to settle down, spend the vast sum of money raised on its municipal project and then get the energy and enthusiasm together again to start organizing the next lottery – this conveniently gave Quinn the ten years it took to examine his findings and modify his theories ready to test them out again on the next lottery.

So wrapped up had he become in this research, Quinn had gradually cut himself off from other mathematicians. The fellow students who'd accompanied him to Knibden for the lottery had been reluctant to leave the most brilliant of their number behind. They assumed he had become enamoured of one of the young maidens of the town and at first they had kept in constant touch, writing to him urging him to return and work alongside them – Bring the wench with you, if you can't bear to be parted! they had cajoled. Gradually, as Quinn's work became more esoteric – or to their lesser minds, downright eccentric – they were content to forget their nutty friend. He, for his part, had long since forgotten them. When a rich uncle he hadn't even known existed died, leaving him a pleasant sufficiency, Harold Augustus Quinn bought the beautiful old house in which Belle now lived, an elegant mansion on the edge of the town, surrounded by a laurel hedge and imaginatively named by some former owner the Laurels. The house exactly suited Quinn's purposes. He took on a housekeeper to take care of all domestic matters so that he could sit undisturbed for long hours at a stretch – often days at a time – in his study poring over his papers. It had been a happy life. The decades passed. The world changed. Life at the Laurels remained much the same, frozen in the silence of mathematical endeavour. The universe within these four walls, though not too obviously in reverse, had certainly not moved on. Sadly this was not true of Quinn's long-suffering housekeeper. One day that good woman had plucked up courage and knocked on the mathematician's door to ask permission to take on a girl to work under her. 'I'm not as young as I was,' she'd explained and to Quinn's gallant cry of 'Nonsense, you get younger every year!' she had said that that was as maybe but the house was becoming too much for her on her own. Quinn, buried deep in his papers, agreed to her request. A girl had come to the Laurels and there had followed then a time of much friction in the house which culminated eventually in the departure of the faithful housekeeper. Not long after, Quinn had married the maid – a sweet tenacious creature less than half his age who immediately bore him two daughters and died when Belle and Fleur were still small. Luckily Belle had inherited her mother's goodness, and tenacity. This stood her in good stead not only when dealing with the crotchety old housekeeper (who took the young Mrs Quinn's death as her cue to return to the Laurels), but also in dealing with the unruly Fleur. Even as a child Belle perceived the importance of their famous father's work and endeavoured to keep her younger sister in some sort of check so that he could work away undisturbed.

Why, Belle wondered now, as she sat at the little rosewood desk on which her long-dead mother had written her household accounts, had the wayward Fleur got it into her head to go to Penzance? Belle stared out of the window in the direction of the Gallimore Hotel. Was Penzance really just an arbitrary choice, the name furthest away on the railway destination board, as Miss Jones had suggested the other evening in the Swan? Or could there been some other more explicable reason Belle had not known, some other reason that, in the strange workings of a universe only dear Daddy had understood, linked those apparently random events: the death of a stranger in the Gallimore Hotel last week, the arrival of Hester Jones on the day of his funeral and the departure of her younger sister all those years ago. In short, was it *mere coincidence* the way Hester Jones had been deflected from her journey to Penzance, the same journey Fleur had apparently made for as little obvious reason years ago, or could Fleur and Hester Jones be linked in some way that Belle and the rest of Knibden did not yet know? Was the key to this mystery contained in those twelve papers, lovingly numbered and ordered, and sewn into sugar-paper covers, that comprised her father's life's work: *The Cold Sun*? They stood in his study on the shelf where he had left them, just as she had preserved all Daddy's things exactly as they had been the day he died. 'You must share all I have between you,' Daddy had said and Belle was not sorry Fleur had never returned to Knibden to claim what was hers.

She would come now, of course. She would hear of the great fortune that had been left to someone in the town and she would return to claim her share and there would be nothing Belle or anyone else could do to stop her. Belle had never been able to restrain her sister.

If *I* inherited the fortune from the dead stranger, Belle thought, I would publish Daddy's work at last. No more procrastination, and no expense spared. Belle sealed the letter firmly in its envelope and then, pulling the paisley shawl tightly about her, she wandered across the landing and into Daddy's bedroom.

'Is Fleur come?' the old man had asked.

'No.'

'Did you write?'

Belle nodded her head. She had written. 'I have written several times,' she said. She held up the envelope. 'See Daddy,' she told the empty room. 'I have written again.'

Belle opened the curtains and turned down the bed. 'Enough of this nonsense!' she exclaimed briskly. I have a tea-dance to organize. Knibden expects. The dead guest deserves. Music. Dancing. Flowers. Food. The list of things to see to was endless. Hadn't Follifoot told her the *Knibden Bugle* was to start again. He had suggested she call as soon as possible at Buckworth & Matchett's to place an advertisement for the tea-dance. Follifoot reminded her how she had told the committee it was important to make everyone in the town feel included in the search for the solution to the dead guest's Will. Now was her chance. She could announce the details of her tea-dance in the new, revised *Bugle*. Follifoot also mentioned that an old man had been in the Swan recently boasting that he had once stood in for the clarinettist in Dickie Paisley's band. Belle intended to ask the landlord, Mr Calderon, to help track the old man down. Then she would ask him to stand in again and organize a new band.

Knibden would have a tea-dance to remember, Belle thought joyously and, picturing the Reverend Gilbert Sibson clicking his fingers and kicking his heels to the music she had yet to organize, she smiled. Even with so little time to complete the preparations, Belle Quinn's tea-dance would be talked of in Knibden long after anyone who had been present was alive to remember it. Belle Quinn was never a woman to do things by halves, they would say. Hadn't she looked after dear Daddy with a devotion that had been *twice* what any one could hope for from a daughter? Hadn't she made up for Fleur's carelessness? What it was to be busy again! She caught sight of herself in Daddy's mirror, and stopped short. What *had* Miss Susan Till *done* to her hair? It was cropped short all over and made her look – Belle stared aghast – like *a common criminal*!

At that moment, for the morning was now late on, Susie Till was making her way at a not very fast pace towards the Silver Scissors Salon. Susie had worked late the evening before and in her simple, unmathematical way calculated that she was entitled to start late this morning to make up. She crossed over the road to pause in front of the jewellers. The solitaire was gone! As she stared at the cards of rings a man's hand came from behind the curtain and placed the jewel in the gap left in the middle of the biggest pad. Susie gazed at the sparkling solitaire, transfixed. She hesitated a moment longer and then, thinking how Mrs Neville Tagg would not hesitate when *she* was after something, Susie pushed open the door of Macready's and went boldly in.

'Yes?' Mr Macready glanced at the fat girl who had just entered his shop. It was the kid from the hairdressers. The tarty one who never wore a bra.

'I . . .' Susie wasn't sure how to ask for what she wanted.

'You have come to reserve a ring? Your young man is about to get down on bended knee to propose and you want to make sure that in the heat of the moment you get the jewel of your choice?'

Susie stared.

'Very sensible.' Macready eyed his customer; in particular he eyed her plump round breasts. He ran his fingertips over the smooth glass of his counter. 'I'd propose myself if I were the young man,' he said with a leer.

Susie flushed.

'Had you any particular bauble in mind?' Macready asked.

Wildly Susie pointed in the direction of the window. She heard herself saying that it was in the middle of the biggest pad of rings. She explained how she had seen it the day before on her way to work and its brilliance had played on her mind ever since. She *knew* it was meant for her.

Macready smiled and asked the girl her name. The Tills had a reputation – there were a lot of Till children. The man, Till, had had a tiny butchery business in one of the side streets and had passed on in rather unfortunate circumstances a while back. Mrs Till, meanwhile, was known to the shopkeepers of Knibden for being no better than she ought to be. It was said she traded favours for credit but this was not something the jeweller had ever had the opportunity of finding out for himself. Macready wondered whether he shouldn't tell the girl that Macready's was a reputable old family firm and she should take her own family's reputation, and custom, elsewhere. But he was reluctant to terminate the encounter just yet. 'Expensive tastes!' he said to tease her. 'I see only the biggest and best will do.'

Mrs Neville Tagg would not settle for less, Susie thought. She smiled at the jeweller.

Quickly positioning a swing mirror so that he could keep his eye on the girl while he turned his back, Macready reached into the window and fished out the solitaire from its place at the centre of the centre row of his card of rings. He was enjoying himself. The girl couldn't possibly earn enough in twenty years to buy herself such a ring and he doubted any bloke interested in her would have that sort of money to spend either. 'You expecting to inherit the dead guest's fortune?' he asked.

Instead of instantly denying this, Susie raised her large mascara-rimmed eyes and looked directly into his. She opened her mouth to tell him how Norah Bird, who was on the committee, had been Neville Tagg's mum's best friend at school but thought better of it. Susie's unfettered bosoms rippled and quivered. Well! Macready thought.

'I had a young lady in here yesterday after that same ring,' he said. 'She begged me to reserve it for her in case her fellow inherits from the guest who died at the Gallimore.' Macready was enjoying himself.

Susie stared at the jeweller. 'Not Hester Jones?' she blurted out before she could help herself. She pictured Neville coming in here with the girl who had accosted him in the Swan. He'd stand beside her gawkily, stroking his big bushy ginger moustaches while she slipped ring after ring on and off her finger until she pretended to choose this one, by chance, when all the while she had asked Mr Macready to put it by for her. Hester Jones had deliberately nipped in yesterday so that when she, Susie Till, the girl with whom Neville Tagg had spent most of his nights this past year, came this morning the best solitaire would already have been taken.

'I beg pardon, Madam?' Macready was saying.

'Hester Jones, the investigator . . .'

'I know very well who Hester Jones is, Miss Till.'

'Did she . . . Was *she* the one . . .' Was she the one who would shortly become Mrs Tagg?

'Are you asking me to breach professional confidentiality?' Macready fixed his stern penetrating gaze on Susie.

'Nnno . . .' In the moment of her discomfiture, Macready grabbed the girl's left hand and shoved the ring unceremoniously on to the third finger. It was tight. His action hurt her. The sparkling jewel looked ridiculous on her lumpy work-stained hand. How different these fingers, with their chewed-down nails, from the elegant manicured ones with which Mrs Neville Tagg would languidly turn the pages of magazines. A tear glistened in Susie Till's eye.

'That looks beautiful on you, Miss,' Macready said, still gripping her wrist. 'It could have been made for you.'

Women had flooded into the jeweller's in his father's time, in those heady weeks leading up to the lottery. They had stood in clusters examining items in the window, picking out pieces they liked so that when it began to seem impossible their menfolk would *not* win the lottery, they had been unable to resist entering the shop and asking to try on the goods. 'A small fee to reserve the piece, Madam,' Macready senior always said discreetly so that he had taken a fortune in unreturnable deposits against jewellery the females didn't have a cat in hell's chance of ever paying for. Outright sales had been good, also, as the lottery made men feel rich and they spent freely buying their women expensive tokens of regard. Jewels to gain access to their jewels, as it were.

Into Macready's had Miss Pringle once come on the arm of Mr Nye, the foreman down at Mr Bird's tannery, to purchase the ring that had gone with the ex-schoolteacher to her grave. The same woman had entered the shop on another occasion also, this time pushing a great pram and purchasing a little silver necklace for her unfortunate infant. Thin pretty links that had stretched around the child's blubbery neck like a wire of dew decorating a tree stump on an autumn morning. Macready had marvelled how the woman cooed to the creature, holding up the necklace for it to admire as if for all the world it understood a word of what she was saying. Miss Pringle's ring and the child's silver necklace lay together now, not in a velvet-lined box with Macready's, Knibden stamped in gold on the underside of the lid, but beneath hard clods of soil in the graveyard of St Redegule's, not a dozen yards from where the dead stranger also lay. What would one day be written on *his* tombstone, the present-day Macready wondered. What was it that Hester Jones would find out?

Before Macready's window also, Jack Tagg and Norah Bird had paused, on their way from the Alhambra to take a drink at the Swan. 'It's my lunch hour, I really ought to get back,' the seventeen-year-old Norah had told him as she finished her water ice. 'I work in a boutique . . .'

'You?' The gems in the jeweller's window reflected a thousand times over the astonishment in Jack's dark eyes. 'A shop assistant!'

Norah pointed proudly to Mrs Cooper's over the road. Mrs Cooper's was not any old shop. Nor was Norah a 'shop assistant', exactly. 'The *boutique* will be mine one day, when Mrs Cooper retires. Daddy is going to buy it for me.'

Jack took Norah by the arm then and said that the least he could do was buy her a drink seeing how she had given him such valuable inside information concerning the Great Knibden Lottery! He patted his breast pocket where two naked women reposed and touched the side of his nose and winked merrily to indicate Norah Bird's complicity. Plain Norah Bird was not accustomed to such attention. Intent on having an adventure of her own to relate to Amy Pasco in her parents' sitting room that evening, she had let Jack persuade her to go with him to the Swan. She didn't think much harm could be done. The elderly Mrs Cooper, who was schooling Norah in the tricks of the fashion trade, probably wouldn't mind if she stayed out a little longer than usual. Just this once. After all, there was a lottery on!

Perched on a tall stool in the Swan, unaccustomed to liquor at lunch time, Norah nursed a gin fizz – the drink Jack said was all the rage – and told him about Mrs Cooper's. As she did so she looked around her, carefully storing up details to tell Amy later. She observed Jack's clothes, his nice hands, the silvered cigarette case he'd extended to her, the way he took her hand in his as he gave her a light. His amusement when she'd choked on the Woodbine. And she noticed his shoes, the tie he wore, the chunky gold ring on his pinky finger and the way he winked across the room at a group of men with whom he had apparently made friends already. Jack made friends easily.

'The day it is mine Daddy's signwriter will come from the tannery and paint out Mrs Cooper's and put up Miss Bird's instead,' Norah boasted. 'I have already chosen the style and colour. It will be my trademark.' She had gone on, still taking little sips at the gin fizz, to tell Jack her dream of opening a whole chain of boutiques across the country, all with Miss Bird's of Knibden painted in sky-blue on white, Gill sans serif, over the door. Jack seemed interested, very interested, his knees touching hers, his arm about her waist. He had been easy to talk to and Norah enjoyed herself. She also told him how she intended to employ her best friend, the pretty Amy Pasco, as her assistant.

'Your young man,' Macready leant across the counter towards Susie. 'Do you, and he . . .'

Susie wrenched the solitaire from her finger, flung it down on the polished glass counter and ran from the shop.

11

Three Sisters

'I feel,' said Chickie Wilkes-Tooley portentously, 'as if this is what we have been waiting for.'

Lalla laughed. 'I'll say!' she said.

Bea, the eldest, smiled.

The three sisters lay back on the sofa linking arms and nodding to each other ostentatiously. After a while, Chickie went on rather wistfully, 'I wonder if we should have joined that committee. We could so easily have invested a little . . .'

'Oh, I do wish we had!' Bea cried. '*And* we'd have got our money back, ten-fold.' Hadn't she said so all along? Hadn't she . . .

'Joined their committee – I wonder at you both!' Lalla sniffed with haughty good humour. '*I* wouldn't want to sit down with Norah Bird. And then be told when to speak by Michael Milady. It was bad enough going to the funeral.'

'A dreary affair *that* turned out to be – even though we did get the front pew . . .'

'But if we were *on* the committee,' Chickie persisted. 'At least we'd know what was going on.'

'*We* are *our own* committee!' Lalla gasped impatiently. '*We* are what is "going on".'

The sisters laughed heartily – but, as soon as the laughter died, Bea muttered, 'I still think we might have gone to the Swan with everyone else afterwards. There were free drinks all round, like the dead guest ordered. Even Gilbert Sibson went.'

'And we all know about *you* and the Reverend Gilbert Duncie Sibson!' Lalla dug her sister playfully, and painfully, in the flesh about her ribs.

Beatrice Wilkes-Tooley blushed crimson and squirmed in her seat. 'Well, no . . .' There was nothing to know – but then, *that* was precisely Lalla's point. All through the dead guest's funeral, the man hadn't once glanced down into the front pew.

The imminent arrival of an heir to the dead guest at the

Gallimore's millions was a matter of considerable interest, of course, to these three unmarried Wilkes-Tooley sisters. Not that there was to be any *arrival*, as such: no deliciously eligible Mr Bingley coming in and buying up some Knibden Netherfield Hall. Far more excitingly – whoever inherited the vast sum of money, lodged so anonymously and tantalizingly in the town's bank, lived most likely in Knibden *already*. And must, therefore, be someone *already* known to them! Here, at last then, was an object worthy of their attention. No wonder the three girls sat together looking down from the window of the Wilkes-Tooley sitting room over the roofs of the town, casting three beautiful pairs of eyes with new interest at this view that had lain before them all their lives. To think that the heir was down there, right now, roaming at large! All they had to do was find out who he was and secure him for themselves, in advance. By anticipating the outcome of the investigation into the dead stranger's Will, and positioning themselves accordingly, the longed-for rich husband who'd assure them of the longed-for triumph over the other two, might be theirs shortly. Might be theirs, in fact, tomorrow evening, during the tea-dance! But, *who* could he be, this unknown heir? And who, for that matter, had the dead guest at the Gallimore been? It was obvious by the way a detective had been called in from outside, that if you knew who the dead stranger was, you'd find out his heir straightaway.

After a long, thoughtful silence, Lalla said calmly and with complete decision, 'It is important we go down into the town and befriend this Hester Jones.'

Her two sisters nodded their beautiful heads. 'We must give the girl every assistance,' Bea added.

'We'll assist her, all right!' Chickie bellowed. Again they all three laughed. It was a terrifying sound – and Mary Wilkes-Tooley, sitting quietly in a corner of the room turning up a peach-coloured dress for Lalla, remembered others her daughters had in the past thought fit to befriend, and she shuddered for this Hester Jones's sake.

'I don't think she's particularly *qualified* in any way,' Chickie observed.

'She more or less wandered in off the street. They took pity on her for some reason, and gave her the job.'

'Extraordinary!'

'Any one of us could have done equally well.'

'A damn sight better!'

'Except that *we* wouldn't want to spoil our chances . . .' Bea hesitated. And was lost. Quick as a flash her sisters turned on her.

'Our chances?' they chorused.

Beatrice Wilkes-Tooley, sitting disquietingly in the middle, bit her lip. 'I mean, well – there *must* be an outside chance . . .' She felt warm. Cold perspiration trickled from her armpits as she now blurted out what was uppermost in all their minds, 'Supposing *we* were to inherit the money? Ourselves. Directly.'

'Us?' Lalla laughed coldly. Chickie stared aghast.

'One of us, then. And not some *man* we'd have to marry in order to benefit. They say it could be *anyone* here in Knibden. So, *we* are *all three of us* in with a chance.'

'Good gracious!' Lalla's eyes opened extremely wide.

'Well, wouldn't that be wonderful!' Chickie sighed very volubly as if this same thought had not occurred to her also. As if their first thought, each of them, on hearing of the dead stranger's strange Will had not been: Let it be *me*! And if not me, then please, please, please, don't let either of the other two . . .

'If *I* was suddenly rich,' Lalla did her best not to sound too serious, 'I'd stop sitting about like this waiting for a wealthy husband to turn up. If tomorrow evening at the tea-dance, Miss Hester Jones stands up and points her finger at me, I'd . . . I'd get out into the world at last.'

'So'd I!'

'And me!'

And do what, exactly? their mother wondered, stabbing her finger and quickly sucking away the blood for fear of despoiling the lovely peach silk.

'Who wants a *husband* anyway?' Chickie scoffed.

We all do! each girl thought, letting her eyes again sweep the town below as though the heir himself might carelessly stray into her sights. *Especially* a husband who'd come into the vast fortune that even now sat waiting for him in the bank. *Any* man, even pimply Neville Tagg with his bushy ginger moustaches and notebook jutting out of his pocket, would be just about tolerable then. Lalla pictured her father's ungainly employee propping his bicycle outside the front door and shuffling in. 'Take off your bicycle clips!' she would cry as she set about his baggy brown suit with a wifely bristle-brush.

'My husband and I' the girls each heard themselves saying with great magnanimity to the other two. Yes, if they didn't inherit the fortune themselves directly – and none of the three knew any real reason why they should – then putting up with some man who'd been lucky enough to do so would have to be the next best thing. Chickie, Lalla and Bea smiled graciously, and suspiciously, at one another. What presents they intended to bestow at Christmas! How generous they'd be with cast-off clothing. I've always thought *puce* suited you so much better than me. Do take the dress, dear! I've dozens just like it – such a bore finding cupboard space to hang them all . . .

What unspeakable torture, though, if one of the others should get to the dead stranger's heir *first* and acquire, not merely a husband, but a rich one at that! If she should *lose* but one of her sisters *win* – oh the unbearableness, even of the thought! It would be like all those terrible tales of the Great Knibden Lottery they used to be told as children. Holding the number on either side of the winner had driven strong men mad. Owning the right number, but having the wrong picture on your ticket, the woman, trumpet or dragon, ruined all peace of mind for ever. So near and yet so far, there'd be no escaping thoughts of what might have been. Visions of those unrealized dreams would return to haunt you all your life as if, in a silly fit of temper, you'd slammed the door in your fairy godmother's face, catching her magic wand in the door jamb and snapping it clean in two.

'Are you *still* on Lall's dress?' Bea called over crossly to her mother. 'I'm sure I asked you to do mine *first*.'

'And *my* buttons need shifting,' Chickie joined in. Why did their mother have to sew in here, in the best room in the house? That corner was far too dark to see the job properly, and you couldn't put a stitch wrong with silk. The Wilkes-Tooley girls didn't have so many dresses, as yet, that they could afford to let any get ruined. Besides, they needed their costumes for the tea-dance tomorrow and, although it was very short notice, they would *none of them* stand for a rushed job. The Wilkes-Tooley outfits may not be 'new', and may have been let out, or taken in, on many occasions over the years, but the garments were certainly a cut above the rather vulgar fresh floral prints in select winter fabrics, purchasable off the peg from Miss Norah Bird. A large consignment of which had already been rushed to her shop in good time for tomorrow's tea-dance.

'I must have the order at once, or not at all!' Miss Bird had telephoned the manufacturers in Manchester at close of business last night and, in imperious tones even Buckingham Palace might tremble at, told a Mr Singh about the dead guest at the Gallimore, and the tea-dance that was to be held up in the old ballroom that weekend and how, even though it was very short notice, the women of Knibden were bound to want new for the occasion. She informed Mr Singh that Hester Jones, herself, was due to visit Miss Bird's even though the girl had only two days left now to solve the mystery. The committee were determined to pay for a whole new wardrobe for Miss Jones, in deference to the man who had died. Mr Singh – who'd apparently taken over the firm and changed its name since she'd last telephoned with an order – had been pleasingly quick to grasp the urgency of the situation. Since Miss Bird's of Knibden had never in its history let the women of Knibden down, and if Miss Norah would care to double the size of her order, *and* pay express carriage, the enormous consignment of fresh floral prints in select winter fabrics could be dispatched overnight. Mr Singh promised to send his best van personally, and instruct the driver to make haste with all speed as fast as possible.

'I'm doing my best, dear,' Mrs Wilkes-Tooley said. The slippery peach reminded her of the infant Lalla, refusing always to keep still in her hands. She sighed imperceptibly and shook her head. It never ceased to amaze her that those three little girls she'd once nurtured could have grown into the great ruthless women sitting across the room with their backs to her now.

Lalla nudged her sisters. 'We'll be needing our party frocks – and I don't just mean for this tea-dance that's being got up in a hurry at the Gallimore!' There would be balls and parties galore in Knibden after the dead guest's fortune was distributed, and the three Wilkes-Tooley girls intended to take their rightful place at them all, to the fore. Their photograph adorning the front page of every edition of the new revised *Bugle*.

Chickie, Lalla and Bea, their mother supposed as she plied her needle, must remember hearing about the Great Lottery that used to be held in the town. And yet, even though they were all getting on a bit now – why, the youngest, little Chickie, would be thirty-five in May! – the girls weren't old enough to have actually lived through the upheavals the lottery had caused. Brother had been set against brother, friend against friend, father against son. People had got into debt and ruined their lives in their desperation to buy tickets. The prospect of obtaining a vast sum of money with so little effort unsettled the steadiest of people. All over the town households had been wrecked, children and babies deprived of food. Wives and sweethearts routinely found themselves abandoned at a moment's notice while divisions that had lain dormant in families for years bubbled to the surface, causing ruptures that never again healed. Mary bit her thread and glanced surreptitiously across the room at the daunting profiles of her three fine daughters. The Great Knibden Lottery had been stopped for good after the last one. You'd have thought the town had learnt its lesson – but now there was this strange Will and a vast fortune again, up for grabs. Mary sighed. Each generation, she thought sadly, must be allowed to make its own mistakes. She had certainly made hers. And perhaps the dead guest too . . . He was probably avenging himself for some reason on the town that had held the lotteries.

'Blood!' shrieked Lalla. 'You've gone and got *blood* all over my bodice!'

Mary looked up from her sewing, white faced as if she had encountered a ghost. 'The dead guest!' she stammered, trembling violently. Her three grown daughters half rose from the sofa and turned to stare, as Mrs Mary Wilkes-Tooley, wife of the proprietor of the Knibden Municipal Insurance Company, let the lightly spattered peach silk slip from her fingers and lie in a crumpled, shimmering heap on the floor. 'Oh, your poor father!' she cried, her words barely audible through her sobs.

'Daddy?' the girls gasped in amazement. Their mother did not usually give them any kind of trouble.

Mary nodded and jabbered blindly. 'I take all the blame! I should have . . . If only I'd . . .'

Aubrey Wilkes-Tooley had come to Knibden entirely by chance

212

at the time of the last lottery. His father had recently died and, too proud to work for his dissolute older brother who'd inherited the Wilkes-Tooley estates and was now set to dissipate them, Aubrey had packed a small knapsack, kissed his elderly mother 'goodbye' and set out, as young men used to, to seek his fortune. Almost at once he had fallen in with a band of fellows travelling to Knibden to try their luck at the lottery. Aubrey decided to go along with them, and lay out a small portion of the little his late father had bequeathed him to purchase a lottery ticket. Disregarding the naked woman, and the trumpet, he'd plumped for a dragon – and what luck that fire-breathing animal had brought him! Within a month of coming to Knibden he'd wooed and wed the attractive Miss Mary Bridgewater. And when *her* father died, not long after, Aubrey Wilkes-Tooley had taken over the Knibden Municipal Insurance Company, a grand old family firm, which he had run as best he could ever since.

Among those jaunty young men Aubrey had encountered on his way to Knibden had been Jack – the same laughable, likeable, jolly Jack Tagg who had scarcely been in the town ten minutes before he'd taken up with a local rich girl who'd accosted him outside the entrance to the Alhambra, eating a water ice. The train they'd arrived on had been packed with young men like themselves, all eager to try their luck at the lottery. No wonder Edmund Veitch, the headmaster, and Gilbert Sibson, the parson, felt out of it. These two men had watched the excitement and high spirits of their fellow passengers with a mixture of bafflement and alarm. As they neared Knibden station and their heads positively rang with trumpets, dragons and naked women, they naturally wondered what kind of a town they were coming to? Poor Mrs Veitch, as the only woman in the cramped compartment, had been forced to spend the whole miserable journey staring doggedly out of the window, or counting and recounting her items of luggage. She eyed the nervous young fellow in the dog-collar and thought that he, at least, should know better.

Gilbert Duncie Sibson, travelling to Knibden to take up his first post as the new curate at St Redegule's, also suspected that he should know better. He sat uncomfortably amid the carefree revellers, now and then recalling that he'd intended taking advantage of the journey time to prepare his words of introduction to his new employer – the Reverend Jerabius Hartley, was it? He tried to dig the letter out of his inside pocket but it was impossible to move, so crowded about was he on all sides. *'My sister and I will be happy to accommodate you, my dear Sir, until an abode suitable to your estate may be procured here in Knibden.'* Gilbert had answered the letter at once, thanking the Reverend Hartley and his sister for their hospitality. He assured them that he would not trespass overlong on their kindness, and he had named the day of his arrival. Named the day! Gilbert thought ruefully. Could this Jerabius Hartley really be expecting him to woo his sister? Wasn't that why young curates were usually invited to share the same roof? Something of this sort had been whispered among the students at the seminary Gilbert had until lately attended. The best way to avoid such undesirable entanglements, the students informed each other after lights out in the darkness of the dormitory, was to introduce a measure of uncertainty about your affections by quickly involving a third party. In other words, some other female in the vicinity. Anyone would do. Gilbert was just recalling this useful advice when Jack produced a pack of cards and commenced a round of railway poker.

The men repositioned themselves as best they could to join in. Gilbert Sibson, wedged between Jack and Aubrey Wilkes-Tooley, took up his cards, aware of the woman's eyes on him. He felt her disapproval keenly. Edmund Veitch, of course, did not dare play poker, and with his wife sitting so bolt upright beside him, no one pressed him to.

Mrs Veitch felt she could hardly breathe. She tried to glance at her wrist-watch to ascertain how much longer she must endure this terrible journey but without her spectacles which were stowed away in the bottom of her travelling bag, she could not make out the tiny hands. She sighed. Her short-sightedness got worse as she grew older, and she was certainly feeling very ancient just then. The moment she'd entered the overcrowded train, she knew her husband's acceptance of the post in Knibden had been a mistake. And indeed, poor Harriet Delilah Veitch's forebodings were to prove well founded: within the year, she herself would be dead and buried, and another, younger, more beautiful creature installed in her place. Although it was entirely by chance both Edmund Veitch and the young curate, Sibson, were arriving in Knibden in time for the last Great Lottery, both men would find themselves caught up in the havoc as surely as if they had journeyed there, like all these other hapless individuals, solely intent on acquiring tickets.

Mary shook her head as she thought of those waves of fresh hopeful faces that had surged into the town from the railway station all those years ago. Some guardian angel should have stood on the platform at Knibden station holding the train doors shut, preventing those doomed young men from descending. Go back or go on, for their own sakes they should have been told – but no one would have listened. Any more than her three head-strong daughters would listen now if she tried to warn them about getting mixed up in this business over the dead stranger's Will.

She wondered whether she herself should not speak to Hester Jones. Tell her the truth, beg her to spare them all.

Gilbert Sibson had purchased a naked woman. Aubrey Wilkes-Tooley, a dragon. But Jack Tagg, impatient to find what the town had to offer, said he'd see them both later for a drink. One of the ticket vendors helpfully told them the Swan was the place, down between the canal and the railway. The barmaids were accommodating, and they'd find rooms there too if they were lucky.

Sibson said he was already fixed up and mentioned Jerabius Hartley's invitation. The vendors nudged him knowingly. He'd find Miss Hartley very accommodating, also, they'd said.

Mrs Veitch, meanwhile, struggled valiantly to ensure all her boxes and cases were off the train. The porters who found it more profitable to sell lottery tickets than to fetch and carry for travellers were impossible to enlist. Taking advantage of the right their employment gave them to be on the station platforms, they pushed round the new arrivals pressing tickets. Harriet Delilah Veitch they totally ignored. Edmund, to his credit, refused to buy a ticket. 'No,' he said with a vehemence that surprised even his wife, 'I do *not* want one!'

'Are you aware who you are talking to?' Harriet Veitch screeched as the vendors tried to jostle her husband. The straps holding one of the piles of books gave way. A lesser woman might have wept. Not the first Mrs Veitch. 'The new headmaster requires immediate assistance,' she shrieked. 'You are to convey his effects to the schoolhouse, without delay!'

Eventually, after much grumbling, the Veitches' possessions had been loaded on to a station handcart. Sibson and Wilkes-Tooley shook Veitch by the hand. 'Good luck,' the men said vaguely to one another. Jack, of course, had not hung about. He was already in the luck – he was already talking to Norah Bird outside the entrance to the Alhambra. Shortly he would accompany her past Macready's, the jewellers, to partake of refreshment with him at the Swan.

'An heiress,' he whispered to Aubrey Wilkes-Tooley as he stood at the bar purchasing gin fizzes with money he'd won playing railway poker. 'I found her out on the street.'

The streets of Knibden gleamed so bright just then with the dreams and desires of men that they seemed to Jack Tagg, Aubrey Wilkes-Tooley and the other recent arrivals, to be *paved* with gold. How rich they all felt. How full of joyous expectation.

'Good God! said Lalla.

'I can't see clearly.' Bea perched her spectacles on her nose.

'Him!' Chickie scoffed.

They none of them budged. If one moved, they all could – but it was as important to keep an eye on each other as it was to watch what was going on down in Knibden.

'How about we take a stroll into town?' Chickie asked. 'See about befriending that Hester Jones.'

With one accord the sisters rose and, as they brushed their hair and put on their coats, not one of them glanced in the direction of their mother who sat sobbing quietly in the corner. It was to be the most remarkable walk of the Wilkes-Tooley girls' lives. At the end of the lane they split up. They each pretended they had their own line of inquiry to pursue, and did not want the others to know where they were going.

The Evil Day

Neville Tagg propped his bicycle in Wilkes-Tooley's yard and raced up the steep stone steps to rap loudly on the door of the Knibden Municipal Insurance Company's head offices. They were the company's only offices, but this did not worry Neville as he pulled off his bicycle clips and scraped his fingers quickly through his tousled hair. How good to be alive – but what heaven to be young, this morning, with such prospects in the air!

Aubrey Wilkes-Tooley, who was no longer young and did not share Neville's sentiments at that moment, did not at once reply. Ever since a man had died at the Gallimore Hotel his days had been spent crouched over Knibden Municipal Insurance Company volumes that he had not opened in years, lost in complex unhappy calculations. After a wait that seemed interminable, Tagg pushed open the door and entered the room. He knew better than to interrupt the old man so he sat himself down and tapped his fingers impatiently on his brown corduroy trousers. He eyed the rows of tantalizingly closed books that lined the office. At last Wilkes-Tooley shut the ledger he had been examining, and sighed. For years he had put off the evil day – now, he concluded, that day had arrived. Perhaps it would be no bad thing. If the worst had to happen, let it happen at once. Let it happen when Hester Jones made her pronouncement at the tea-dance in the Gallimore. The world will end, Wilkes-Tooley thought, sometime tomorrow evening.

Neville Tagg coughed. 'Excuse me, Sir.'

The proprietor of the Knibden Municipal Insurance Company looked up and was surprised to see the young man with unkempt ginger hair sitting there. It took him a second or two to realize who it was. 'Tagg! Was I expecting you?'

'No, Sir, I don't think so, Sir. I'm sorry if I missed our meeting yesterday, sir. Fact is, I had a cold. The chain fell off my bicycle. Then I had to go right the far side of town about a policy. Wild goose chase it was, Sir. Added to which . . .' Neville stopped abruptly.

'There is more, Mr Tagg? More wild geese?' Aubrey Wilkes-Tooley felt weary. It occurred to him to sack the boy then and there. If the world were to end tomorrow, it might be a kindness to release this goose, Neville Tagg, back into the wild without further ado.

Neville coughed. 'You know the business about the guest at the Gallimore?'

'Eh?'

'The man who died.'

Wilkes-Tooley grunted.

'Can it be connected in any way with *our* business, Sir? I mean . . .' Neville felt flustered. He fidgeted in his chair. What did he mean? It had been clear enough in his head as he cycled along.

Aubrey Wilkes-Tooley stared coldly over the rim of his spectacles at Jack Tagg's son perched before him, pulling nervously at his bushy moustaches. You'd never have thought the lad had it in him! Aubrey rested his elbows on the desk, cradling his chin in his hands. Ever since he had heard of this peculiar business, he had felt old. He'd lain awake at night, and spent his days in the office going over and over the company books like an animal in a cage frantically pacing the same worn ground. He was certain the inheritance must comprise some life insurance policy his company had foolishly issued long ago and would now be obliged to pay out. Wilkes-Tooley was a worried man. Of course he was. An enormous sum of money, it was said, lodged in the bank. That was a cruel joke. At his expense – for the money lodged in the bank would most likely be Knibden Municipal Insurance Company money. Only the Knibden Municipal Insurance Company did not have enough money in the bank to meet a fraction of its obligations, let alone some inordinate claim. Even Neville Tagg had arrived at the same conclusion.

'I doubt if the dead guest has anything to do with us,' Aubrey Wilkes-Tooley said as airily as he could. Confidence in the company was all that kept it going – if anyone should get wind of young Tagg's suspicions, the old firm that had been in Mary's family for generations would be sunk. He, his wife and their three daughters would all be out on the streets. Notice of a creditors' meeting would appear in the new revised *Bugle*. There would be those who would rejoice at his downfall. Mrs Laffety and all those other disappointed widows whose life insurance claims had been found invalid for one reason or another over the years.

'I just thought . . .'

'You thought what, Tagg?'

'It stands to reason, Sir. If a man came back to Knibden deliberately to die here – as everyone says he did – very likely he already had dealings in the town. Very likely he had a policy with us. Which makes it simple.'

'Simple?'

'All *we* need do is look back through the books, find names of people we've lost track of, and before you know it, we'll have solved the problem. No need for that girl.'

'Girl?'

'Hester Jones. The one they've got in to investigate.'

'Ah.' Aubrey Wilkes-Tooley contemplated the young man. 'I see what you mean,' he said to buy time. After a long pause he added, 'She's good, is she?'

'They say she has her methods.'

Wilkes-Tooley nodded and started humming. He had heard how Neville Tagg had made it his business to attend the dead guest's wake and befriend Hester Jones at the Swan. The young man was clearly two steps ahead of him, at least. There was another long pause after which Aubrey Wilkes-Tooley said, 'Of course I will need to give this some thought.' He tried to beam at the lad amiably although he felt anything but amiable. He wished he was at home tucked up in his bed, fast asleep. He would like to stay asleep until the whole blessed business was over, and wake up only when the long painful tumble down the ladder of respectability was over and he could grovel about in the grime and the dust. As he probably deserved. 'I'm glad you have drawn the matter to my attention,' he said miserably.

'Well, yes . . .'

'I need to consider . . .'

'If you don't mind my saying so, Sir, time is not on our side.'

'No?' Wilkes-Tooley feared as much. More than anything he

219

feared the tea-dance tomorrow, when Hester Jones would make her pronouncement.

'The whole town is terribly excited, Sir. I reckon we need to get to the bottom of this before anyone else does. In the interests of the company. Frankly, if you think about it, Sir, *we* should have taken on Hester Jones to investigate. Now it may be too late. They say she's working on the case night and day. Any influence we might have had in the eventual outcome will soon be lost . . .' Neville glanced again at the great leatherbound volumes that sat so infuriatingly closed on the shelves. *If only* he could be let loose in here, who knew but that he, Neville Tagg, might discover the heir to the fortune *before anyone else*! Then he could whip round to see them on his bike, and do a deal. He would offer to work for the man – or woman – in future rather than for old Wilkes-Tooley. They'd be so grateful they were sure to supply him with the car of his choice. That Ford *Fiesta* Mr Milady had offered him in the pub the other night. Or, maybe – and here Neville Tagg smirked aloud – it might be possible to alter the evidence when he found it to make it look as if *he* were the heir. And if he did contrive to inherit the dead guest's fortune, he'd ask Miss Lalla Wilkes-Tooley herself to marry him!

Lalla's father noted the flash of wild excitement in the young man's eyes, he heard the smirk, and he nodded. It was surprising how events like this could show a man, even an uncouth youth like Neville Tagg, in a completely new light. Dishevelled, disorganized, Tagg was not the sort of bloke the company would ever have employed out of choice. Mr Bridgewater, Mary's father, had always been very discriminating about whom he took on. He had refused to employ Mary's childhood sweetheart, Peter, so that Peter Goodfellow had had no work and without any prospects he'd been unable to marry Mary. Peter's one hope of gaining her hand had been to win the last Great Knibden Lottery! But things were different these days. The Knibden Municipal Insurance Company had not been in such decline then and Mr Bridgewater had been able to pick and choose. He would never have chosen Neville Tagg! Looking at the eager young Tagg sitting opposite, Wilkes-Tooley was reminded again of the bright brash lads into whose company he had fallen. Cheerful fellows out for nothing more than a good time and easy money. 'We're off to Knibden,' they had said.

'Knibden?' he'd asked, dimly recollecting hearing about the fabulous lottery where a man could become a millionaire overnight. At first, Aubrey had said he didn't fancy his chances. It was a mathematical improbability. Tens of thousands of tickets would be sold; it was a waste of time trying. But then, when he considered he had no other plans just then he had changed his mind and gone along for the company. He marvelled at the merriment of his new companions, one of whom had been a jovial carefree chancer, Jack. Jack Tagg who'd cheerfully cheated at poker and then lost all his winnings buying tickets and taking up with girls in the town. Wilkes-Tooley sighed. He stared at Jack Tagg's son. 'Why don't you come to dinner?' he said.

'Dinner?' Neville Tagg was not accustomed to being invited out to dine.

'We can discuss this business further then.'

Neville gawped. He was meant to be seeing Susie that evening.

'We'll expect you about eight. Mary will be pleased – she doesn't get a lot of visitors.'

'Will your daughters be there?' Neville stammered. The imperious lofty Lalla? What could he wear – he only had his brown baggy suit.

Wilkes-Tooley shrugged. What a curious question – where else would they be, Chickie, Lalla and Bea? 'They'll be delighted to see you, Mr Tagg, a handsome young fellow like yourself!' Wilkes-Tooley chuckled. 'I dare say they'll all wait on you hand and foot – and fight ferociously over which of them you will escort to the tea-dance!'

'Tea-dance?'

'Tomorrow, at the Gallimore Hotel. In honour of the dead guest.'

Neville stared at his employer. First – dinner tonight! Then – the tea-dance tomorrow. To the music of the late Dickie Paisley and his Band, he Neville Tagg whose mother had been best friends at school with Norah Bird and had swapped clothes with her and died as a consequence, would step across the ballroom floor in the arms of Miss Lalla Wilkes-Tooley. All thanks to the dead guest!

'I know who it is,' Mary said quietly to her husband the moment he returned. She was not surprised to see him home so early. All over town the routines of decades had been abandoned overnight. Why, her own daughters had spent all morning sitting in near harmony gaping out of the window together in case one of them should spot something down in the town neither of the others could afford to miss.

Aubrey Wilkes-Tooley stared at his wife. Mary nodded. Peter Goodfellow, the fellow her father had not considered good enough for her to marry, had returned, she said.

'Surely not?'

'The girls were talking – and it suddenly came to me. Best not say anything, no one need know yet.'

'He has been to see you?'

'No – no . . . Don't you see? The guest at the Gallimore they're all going on about. The one who has died leaving a fortune. It's Peter, I'm sure it is. I always knew he would come back.'

Wilkes-Tooley looked at his wife in astonishment. She had been crying. He wanted to take her in his arms but did not dare. He saw now what he had refused to see all along. Mary did not belong to him. She had belonged all this time, by prior arrangement, to another man. The dead guest. The whole of the life he and she had shared together, even their three grown daughters, formed a mere parenthesis in her dealings with Peter. 'You think he has left you all his money, Mary?' Aubrey asked calmly.

Mary nodded. 'You too. He'll have included you, I'm sure. After all . . .' If it hadn't been for Aubrey she wanted to say, but she stopped. It did not matter in any case what she did or did not say, her husband hardly heard her. He had his own confession to make.

'I haven't told you this before, dear,' he rasped. 'There didn't seem much point when there was nothing we could do. The business is in desperate trouble – it has been for years. Without a substantial injection of money, the Knibden Municipal Insurance Company will be sunk . . .'

'I know,' Mary said quietly.

'You knew?'

'Yes. I always knew. But I couldn't help hoping for a miracle. Miracles happen, I often said to myself. That is the nature of miracles. And now *this* has happened. Oh Aubrey, if Peter *has* returned and left me – I mean *us* – his money, we'll be able to save the company. And the girls . . .'

No one need know the straits they'd been in. There would be no disgrace. Chickie, Lalla and Bea could get married at last. They would all live happily ever after. Aubrey Wilkes-Tooley felt exhausted. He sat down. 'It's not what I intended,' he mumbled. 'I had such high hopes when I started. Your father entrusted . . .'

'Never mind that now, dear. We always felt we ought to stay here in Knibden when perhaps we should have moved on. Maybe you should have let one of the bigger firms buy you up when they offered.'

'And lose the name?'

'Not necessarily. The Knibden might have been kept as a local subsidiary. Anyhow, if we get the money, you will soon be able to buy *them* up. They can become subsidiaries of *yours* – there is nothing I should like more.'

'And how *I* should like to restore the firm to what it was in your father's day.'

'It was lurching about dangerously even then. The assets never quite covered the liabilities. The Knibden Municipal Insurance Company was a liability when you took it – and me – on. You must not blame yourself. You were not to know. Anyway, if this all works out, maybe we will be able to do something at last for the girls. It can't be right the way the three hang about at home all the time . . .'

'They ought to get married.'

'That's easier said than done. Nothing much happens in Knibden. No eligible Mr Bingleys coming in and buying up any Netherfield Halls . . .'

'There's plenty happening now. I have invited Neville Tagg to dinner.'

'Neville Tagg!' Mary repeated. 'Dinner?' Then Mary laughed as a delightful vision came to her of the Tagg boy sitting down to dine with her three elegant daughters like some ungainly great bear crashing in on a doll's tea party.

'He has hidden depths,' Aubrey said gravely. 'There is more to Mr Neville Tagg than I would ever have credited.'

He was a start, Mary supposed. If after the tea-dance tomorrow there was to be a lot of money, thanks to Peter, the girls would be able to take that rightful place in the world they often spoke about. Their picture would frequently appear on the front page of the new revised *Bugle*. Mary Wilkes-Tooley sighed a mother's wishful sigh. Until then, though, Knibden's Mrs Bennet had the consolation that at least one of her unmarried daughters would be partnered at Belle Quinn's tea-dance, albeit by Mr Tagg. An act that would be looked on by the town as a kindness to their father's employee.

'I'm sorry, Susie,' Neville's voice sounded muffled down the phone.

Why had he rung? He didn't sound the least bit sorry. Couldn't he face her with his excuses? Susie wanted to cry. Instead she said, 'That's OK, Nev. I've spent all day doing other people's hair – I wouldn't mind a night in, doing my own. See you tomorrow, p'raps. At the tea-dance.'

Somewhere, wherever he was, Neville giggled. The relief she supposed. Like being let off something nasty at school. She was losing him. But Susie Till did not want to relinquish Neville Tagg, and the passenger seat in his Ford *Fiesta*, to Hester Jones. He had rung off before she could say so. Susie decided to visit Nev's step-mother and have it out with the woman. 'If you take them tea and toast in bed in the morning,' she would say, 'Nev will only drop crumbs all over the sheets. You don't want to spoil his chances with Hester Jones, not with his mum having been at school with Miss Norah Bird.'

'I don't know what you are talking about!' The second Mrs Tagg would try to close the door but Susie'd be quick to jam the heel of her black shiny boot in the way.

'*I* saw the solitaire first,' she would tell the woman, '*I* have a right to the passenger seat in his Ford *Fiesta*!'

'*You*? You are mad! Look at the mess you made of Miss Quinn's hair – if Neville does not inherit tomorrow at the tea-dance, *you* will be entirely to blame. You will have deprived the poor boy of his Ford *Fiesta*. Kindly remove your boot from my door!'

13

A Couple of Kisses

Veitch said, 'Come on, Louisa, buck up!'

Louisa did her best to smile.

'That's better. Things are going to change round here.' He kissed his wife's hand. In Edmund Veitch's opinion 'things' had got so bad they could only get better. The dead guest had thought so too. Veitch and his wife, the smiling compliant Louisa, had come to the Gallimore Hotel to take tea with their son. Actually, Doris Barr the waitress suspected, the headmaster had come to check up on Hester Jones and make sure that with only a day to go now before the reckoning – when she'd be called out in front of the class and expected to have all the answers – she was doing her homework.

'I have befriended her,' Roger Ambrose told his mother and step-father. 'Just as you said.'

Doris put the tea-pot down smartly and took up the silver tongs, as Mrs Mason had shown her. With elaborate care she then placed a scone on every plate. As she busied herself apportioning out the jam and cream – not too much, but there again, not too little – Roger moved his foot and touched hers.

'Where is she now, then?' Veitch asked. Doris Barr had been a hopeless child and had left school without one single qualification to her name. Yet, here the girl was, Veitch observed, wearing a frill-edged apron and deftly serving teas. He had not thought Doris capable of doing anything deftly but she had somehow managed to get herself taken on here just in time. People, with far more about them than Doris Barr, were now queuing up for jobs at the Gallimore. Mason was apparently having to turn away scores of applicants by the hour – even people prepared to work for next to nothing in the run up to Belle Quinn's tea-dance just because they wanted to be in on the action. They wanted proximity to Hester Jones, to see her arrive at the truth.

'Round and about, I s'pose. Investigating,' Roger said. He

licked jam from his knife and wondered when he'd get his chance to kiss the waitress.

Why aren't *you* 'round and about' with Hester Jones, then? Edmund Veitch wanted to ask. His step-son was as dopey as his delightful mother. The whole world seemed half asleep to Mr Veitch. No one snapped their heels to attention any more. The tea-dance would help see to that though. A little pride in the municipality, that was all that was wanting. The guest had felt it too. There would be a revival of spirit amongst the young. It would work its way upwards. Up, from Doris Barr. Eventually the whole town would gather behind the unknown guest and the man, whoever he had been, would be seen not to have died in vain. Veitch smiled and scratched the side of his neck behind his stiff collar. 'Eat up, Louisa,' he said, patting his wife's delicate hand.

For Edmund's sake, and for the sake of her son, Louisa Veitch chewed bravely. The dry scone stuck in her throat. Tears sprang unbidden to her eyes and she dabbed them away with a napkin.

'Why is Veitch so pleased with himself?' other people taking tea asked themselves, noting how emotional also his quiet wife seemed. It'll be that step-son of his, they concluded. For it was rather odd the way Roger Ambrose had suddenly come back to Knibden. Taking a room at the Gallimore for an indefinite stay before anyone else cottoned on and all the other rooms got snapped up and no one else could get in. Word spread – you could not stop it. People talked – you could not stop them. A vast consignment of fresh stock had been delivered to Miss Bird's. People were pouring into the town. Anyone who had ever had anything to do with Knibden was now hurrying back, hoping that by some miracle the stranger's Will might mention them.

Edmund Veitch had not always lived in Knibden, though his association with the town went back to long before he was born. Veitch had been appointed to the school in Knibden shortly before the last Great Lottery. It was an unfortunate coincidence that the job had been in the *one place on earth* Edmund would rather not have moved to. At the time he had been a young man, fresh in the career he had set out on, and recently married. The name of Knibden or any mention of the lottery made him recoil, but the youthful Veitch was determined not to flinch in the face of this challenge. It was such an extraordinary coincidence, Veitch could not believe it was any coincidence at all. His mettle was being tested for some greater purpose he could not yet see. A greater purpose that now, as he sat with his family in the Gallimore Hotel spreading jam and cream on his scone, had become only too evident.

Veitch's father had come to Knibden in 1915 and bought a trumpet in the year trumpets were drawn on Day One of the lottery. But his foolish father, instead of selling on his ticket at a profit, or being content that he was still in with a chance like any sensible trumpet holder, had bankrupted himself greedily buying up as many more trumpets as he could lay his hands on, borrowing money on ridiculously exorbitant terms in order to do so. He was, after all, on his way to the Front. He expected to be killed in some foreign field. He was young and doomed, and entitled in the circumstances to be reckless. Not one of Private Veitch's trumpets came up trumps. Nor was he subsequently to lose his life in that other Great Lottery, the War of Nations. The debts with which soldier Veitch had marched away from Knibden were not easily shrugged off either. For years they weighed Edmund's poor father down, crushing his spirit and destroying the efforts he made to raise himself. As he ground away at whatever employment he could get to pay off all he owed, he cursed the town whose lottery had engineered his downfall. He never returned to Knibden, preferring to settle his debts from afar. It was only late in life Veitch senior had been free to marry and he'd been careful to choose a mean careful woman who would keep a mean careful home. Together they had instilled in their only child the virtues of self-discipline and hard work. Any tendencies that might lead Master Edmund to emulate his father's youthful folly had been firmly stamped on. The name of Knibden had thus been synonymous throughout Veitch's boyhood with the worst iniquity.

By dint of hard work the young Edmund Veitch won a scholarship to the local university. Determined to enter the teaching profession, he shunned the company of his fellow students, sitting through lectures in the front row doggedly taking notes, producing long uninspired essays and gradually realizing that though he was not blessed with the talents that enabled others to shine with less effort, by working hard and long hours, he might nevertheless attain moderate success.

The school at Knibden had been his second post. At the first, he had encountered Miss Harriet Delilah Beales, a teacher ten years older than himself, who had by that time been disappointed in love more often than she cared to remember. Of the many men Miss Beales had loved, not one of them had noticed her so when Edmund Veitch arrived in the staff room, straight from college and blushing furiously, she had seen her chance. And seized it. To the mirth of their fellow teachers, the two had wed. The new Mrs Veitch having achieved her own ambition of finding a husband, at once became fiercely ambitious on that husband's behalf. She scoured advertisements in the *Times Educational Supplement* and encouraged Edmund to apply for promotion without delay, preferably somewhere distant where her long spinsterhood and many passionate one-sided love affairs would not be known about. Thus it was that shortly before the last lottery, Mr and Mrs Veitch had arrived in Knibden. By this time, Mr and Mrs Veitch senior had fortunately passed away so they did not see the treacherous day their son returned to the scene of his father's youthful disgrace.

Edmund Veitch, deeply sensible that he had betrayed the memory of his father by coming to live in Knibden, resolved not to let his parent down entirely. He immediately took a dim view of the excitement caused by the lottery. His wife, meanwhile, took a dim view of anything that gave other people enjoyment. On weekdays Mr Veitch lectured the children sternly at the school and on Sundays, he and Harriet sat in the front pews at St Redegule's to listen to the Reverend Jerabius Hartley preaching against the evils of lottery tickets, nodding their heads and clicking their teeth in emphatic unison. As the climax of the lottery neared, those who had set their faces against its evils, spent more and more time in the church united in their opposition. When the excitement reached near fever pitch on Day One, Edmund Veitch found his knees pressed to the ground. Trumpets sounded, naked women writhed, dragons coiled and breathed fire down his neck as beside him, Harriet Delilah, *née* Beales, heaved and sighed in her righteous indignation. Jerabius Hartley ranted to the Heavens and his unmarried sister, Zillanah, sniffed and jerked. Gilbert

Sibson pressed his hands together in earnest imitation of prayer. Only the beautiful plaster face of St Redegule remained unmoved. Mesmerized, Edmund Veitch gazed up at the saint. How wondrously like Louisa Ambrose she looked! The pretty young girl with a baby who worked at the Gallimore Hotel, helping the elderly Gallimore sisters with the lottery rush. What a shame the sweet creature was already married, Veitch thought, to a foolish man who hoped that by winning the lottery neither he, nor his wife, need ever travail for their living again.

Harriet Veitch became bosom friends with Zillanah Hartley. A married woman now, Mrs Veitch could enjoy patronizing Miss Hartley in the very way that for years she herself had been patronized in the staff common room at school. It was to her friend, Zillanah, that Harriet Veitch confided how she had become pregnant shortly before she and her husband arrived in Knibden but in the upheaval of packing up and moving she had lost the baby without ever having told Edmund she was expecting one. It had been flushed down a water closet in the railway station hotel where they had stopped off for the night on their way. Into Zillanah Hartley's sympathetic ears also, Harriet poured in general rather than explicit terms, the horror she subsequently felt at any physical relations with her husband. The memory of that tiny form, swirling from her body and then cascading round in its own pool of blood before being washed away into the communal sewers of the great brick city, haunted her.

The Reverend Jerabius Hartley did not particularly like his sister's new-found friend, or her husband. Mr Veitch, though a young man, was already a dry old stick. Yet Hartley regarded him as preferable, probably, to that other newcomer, his young curate. What contrast! Gilbert Sibson's very first act on arriving in Knibden had been *to purchase a naked woman* from one of the ticket vendors roaming the railway station. This information the rector's sister had been able to vouchsafe Mrs Veitch in return for those other personal confidences. Zillanah Hartley did not however tell her married friend of her own disappointment. How she had prayed to St Redegule for more from Gilbert Duncie Sibson. Had asked that saint to spare her yet another lost opportunity.

Harriet Delilah Veitch took to spending her days at the rectory, gossiping with Zillanah and returning home in the evenings to the neglected schoolhouse. She found her childlessness weighing increasingly with her and gradually she grew as bitter and discontented as ever she had been before her marriage. She began to blame the loss of the baby Edmund had not known about, on her husband's ambitions that had, to her mind now, uprooted them and brought them to Knibden. The upheaval, and the night in the noisy railway station hotel, had deprived her of motherhood. Living in the schoolhouse surrounded by other people's unruly children, her marriage felt like a mockery. For all that she had yearned for the married state, she now felt no better off than Miss Zillanah Hartley. And much worse off than that slim pale thing, Louisa Ambrose, who looked far too young to be married, but who slaved in the Gallimore's sculleries, nursing her baby (as far as Mrs Veitch could make out) in between doing the dishes.

The excitement of the lottery died away leaving the normal residue of chaos in its wake. Soon after dragons had been drawn on Day One, Louisa Ambrose's young husband had died in a fight, apparently defending the valuable dragon in his pocket from a man who'd owned a worthless trumpet. The mortal injury took place down a dark alley. There were no witnesses. Nor had Mrs Ambrose had the good sense of Mrs Cardew/Vestey/Jenks so there was no Knibden Municipal Insurance Company policy riding on her husband's head. The penniless young mother was desperate. Her work at the Gallimore had only been temporary, helping out with extra trade during the lottery. The Reverend Jerabius Hartley was meanwhile triumphant. He had been proved right. He stood in his pulpit and told the town so and then, out of charity, persuaded his sister to take young Mrs Ambrose on, as servant of all work about the rectory. A living and constant reminder of how right the Reverend Hartley had been.

One Sunday, when the Veitches were dining with the Hartleys, Miss Hartley had rung repeatedly for the girl to fetch something to the table. Edmund Veitch offered to investigate the delay but his wife rose swiftly from the table. 'I'll go!' she said and made her way down to the kitchens where she found Louisa openly feeding her baby beside the stove. The bell rang impatiently again upstairs.

'Let me hold him for you,' Mrs Veitch offered. Louisa was

about to obediently hand across the beautiful little blue-eyed Roger when the child let out a wail so piercing that it brought both the Hartleys and Mr Veitch running in alarm. The sight of his wife snatching the milky babe from the young girl's soft white breast filled Edmund Veitch with unspeakable horror. He cursed the day he had not purchased a lottery ticket. Why had he set himself so stupidly against something that might have made him rich enough to be rid of his wife and befriend this helpless young widow? Why couldn't he have been in with a fair chance of winning, like the foolish husband of this sweet girl who had perished so valiantly in a fight?

The following day, Edmund Veitch went to the offices of the Knibden Municipal Insurance Company and took out a policy on his first wife's life.

No primrose ever survived on Harriet Delilah's grave. Even grass refused to grow. People assumed this was due to bitterness in the first Mrs Veitch at being replaced so speedily by a girl whose growing child then ran about the schoolhouse in which she had so mourned her own childlessness. Bill Parris, odd-job man, grave digger and grave tender, alone wondered further at the bare earth. He had dug the grave himself. He knew the soil was good. Besides, he had liked the first Mrs Veitch. A gentle sorry creature was how he recalled Harriet Delilah, having found her in tears one evening near his hut in the park. He'd stopped to say a few words of comfort but his great lolling tongue could not get round his kindly thoughts and the headmaster's wife had smiled at him sadly, and given him a sixpence. Bill Parris had never forgotten that smile. Or the sixpence.

14

Looking the Part

Belle Quinn's tea-dance was keeping Mrs Mason busy. As if the manageress of the Gallimore did not have enough to do with all the guestrooms occupied and vast numbers of non-residents pouring into the dining room for every meal. The hotel staff could no longer enjoy that traditional short gap between when the beds were all made and preparations needed to start for lunch. Mrs Mason barely had time to train Doris before Doris herself was needed to show other, newer, girls the ropes. Mr Mason grumbled and said it was quite like old times. All the years they'd been at the Gallimore had been a preparation for this. They should have been painting the walls while the donkeys grew fat and the winds howled along the empty beaches, only they had not known it. Eileen Mason barely had time to think about her long-lost baby and when she did chance to recall little Donald, it seemed to her that the dead guest had deliberately contrived to take her mind off her sorrow. Who had the man been, she wondered, that he had done this much for her? She wished now she had *not* waited till first light to go to his room. *If only* she had been able to sit beside him and hold his hand as he'd breathed his last. It grieved her to think of a man who had alleviated her sorrow, dying in a hotel where she was the manageress, with only a wall clock for company. She had sewn him into his shroud. Only she, in the whole town, had properly been with him, washing and laying the dead man out like a new-born baby. Poor Daniel was much too flustered to do more than wring his hands. His employer – dead! When asked what the dead guest had looked like, Mason shrugged and implied professional discretion. In truth, he'd taken no more notice of the dead guest than he did of any of the other customers who had come and gone from premises managed by themselves over the years.

'And yet,' Mason confided to Hester Jones, 'I am sure the man reminded me of someone.' But Daniel Mason was unable to say who. All corpses are pretty much alike with the life gone out of them, he decided. Dr Treadgold had been happy to authorize the death certificate. For anything he knew, he'd told Follifoot and Macready, he *might* have seen the fellow in the last two weeks.

'Best not upset the applecart,' Treadgold said. Follifoot had knocked up a coffin cheap. And the Reverend Duncie Sibson, who'd needed a name on the coffin and in his church records, had been content to understand he was burying a Mr Applecart. No one could read his handwriting anyway.

Eileen Mason sighed. In that first wave of astonishment over the curious Will, procedures had been hurriedly seen to but she was determined now to make up for any shortcomings and she redoubled her efforts, and redoubled them again, in the preparations for Belle Quinn's tea-dance.

Belle Quinn, meanwhile, was also so busy that she forgot she was waiting for a reply from her sister Fleur in Penzance. Calderon's sister, Barbara, had helped her track down the man who had boasted in the Swan that he had played his clarinet in Dickie Paisley's band.

'Yer what?' Albert Hodge took half an hour to open his front door. He'd taken Belle for a woman from a local government department and took exception to her visit. He was just pissing into a tea-pot to empty from an upper window down on to the visitor, when the sound of her flutey voice calling Dickie Paisley's name through his letterbox suggested to him that he had not altogether grasped the true nature of the visit. He invited Belle in and, having wired his teeth into his gums, he made tea in the tea-pot. While she was drinking the peculiar-tasting tea, Hodge said, 'Dickie Paisley, eh? Haven't thought about the man in years . . .' He then told Belle how he had helped Dickie out on occasions during the war when the regular clarinettist had been off doing his bit and Hodge had been home, on leave from the RAF. Between missions, he said. If Belle had pressed him he'd have explained how he had been a groundsman looking after Spitfires between flights. One of the essential many who had kept the valiant few in the air. Doddery and deaf now, Hodge promised Belle to put together a group who could play the old tunes. Dickie himself had died some twenty years back, he told her, over-exerting himself in bed with some singer.

'She woke up and found the man stiff on top of her!' Hodge said with a cackle. 'Dickie died as he lived – the man should have got a medal for his war-work, all them servicemen's wives he kept warm with his baton for when their husbands came home.'

Dickie Paisley had kept his Iris warm. Hodge did not mention this to Belle. Nor did he say how he had bashed the man's nose in. He'd boasted of this in the Swan also, but Miss Calderon had not chosen to pass on that part of the story. Poor Iris Hodge had wept at the sight of Dickie Paisley's bloody face. She had lost weight and lost a baby, and never been the same since.

Belle ticked Music off her list and went to inspect the Gallimore's ballroom floor. It needed repolishing. She called on Mr Williams at the bank and he at once sanctioned the expense. 'There is no time to lose,' he'd said. 'Of course the place should look as it ought.' Later he mentioned what he'd said to his wife so that Dora Williams was now able to picture herself sitting near the door throughout the tea-dance, explaining to new arrivals that her husband – as the dead guest's executor – had sanctioned the repolishing of the floor. Returning the Gallimore's ballroom to the state it had been in when Dickie Paisley and his Band last struck up. Before Albert Hodge had broken Dickie Paisley's nose. Or its state on the eve of this century when the Five Beautiful Gallimores were in their prime and had danced the night away, and never been happy again. On such a floor too, had Madame Bovary waltzed with her unknown viscount. At the first sign of the tea-dance needing a literary allusion, the dead guest's executor's wife would be there sitting on the sidelines, ready to provide one. 'She was only a foolish farmer's daughter,' Dora would say. 'What can you expect?' And there would be those who heard her and heeded the warning, who in years to come would recall her words and say to each other, 'If it hadn't been for Dora Williams . . .' But that would be after the terrible ending, that no one could avert. And after Hester Jones had left them all, and gone wherever she was going.

'The tea-dance should be insured,' Neville Tagg said to Mr Williams who in turn had a word with Mr Mason who repeated this to Michael Milady after which an enormous policy was immediately taken out – whoever inherited the Gallimore must be guaranteed against any damage. 'Just imagine,' Tagg had said, 'if someone should slip and split open their skull on the newly polished ballroom floor.'

'We must safeguard the inheritor's interests, certainly,' Mr Williams agreed. So far, he had thought chiefly about the anonymous guest who had died, but this conversation with the representative from the Knibden Municipal Insurance Company led him to consider how one day, before long, he would be answerable to some rich man, or woman, who was most likely someone he knew already but had no cause at this stage to defer to. For a bank manager trained to treat his customers with precise regard to the size of their deposits in his bank, this was a novel, highly irregular situation. There was no telling yet who your wealthy client was. He might be Neville Tagg or General Bertram Bensusann or – God forbid – Bill Parris! All kinds of names had been mentioned in this connection and the sooner Hester Jones put an end to the uncertainty the better. William Williams wondered if she had found time in her busy schedule to practise the polka. It would be unfortunate if their investigator should be the one to slip and slit open her skull on the newly polished floor before she had a chance to reveal the solution to the mystery of the dead guest.

The premium, insuring the Gallimore Hotel against who knew what catastrophe occurring at the tea-dance, paid for the bell on Neville Tagg's bicycle a thousand times over. Neville looked forward to telling Wilkes-Tooley so at dinner that evening. 'So we are rich?' he imagined Lalla clasping him to her bosom in gratitude for having set her father's company back on its feet. 'You must have that Ford *Fiesta* at once!'

Michael Milady, on behalf of the committee, agreed to pay for the band, the teas, the insurance premium, not to mention the repolishing of the ballroom floor – business at the hotel was booming and since the place was part of the inheritance, whoever inherited the dead guest's fortune could hardly object to the expense. Everyone on the committee would have to put a little more money into the kitty to tide things over. But what of it? – the sum would be repayable, ten-fold, when the time came. The more money they put in now, the more money would eventually be due to them. Milady called an emergency meeting of the committee for first thing in the morning.

Hester Jones, meanwhile, went to visit Norah Bird in her shop.

'They're not the clothes I'd have chosen for myself,' she said tactfully, glancing along the rails Jack Tagg had once installed. Banging away with his nails and hammer, spinning out the job for he had nothing better to do as his wife, Amy, was ill from the baby and the baby, Neville, had a touch of the colic and Jack Tagg had it in mind just then to please Norah Bird.

Norah Bird ran round Miss Jones with a tape measure. 'How you present yourself is how you will be seen. You must look the part.'

This was one of Mrs Cooper's sayings, but Hester Jones replied, 'I am the part!' In the past she had only ever worn black and shades of grey but now she surrendered herself to the frilly good offices of Miss Bird's.

Norah was delighted to have someone so willing to be dressed and, as she displayed the full range of fresh floral prints in select winter fabrics that a Manchester manufacturer had sent by overnight express, Norah Bird told Miss Jones, 'I might telephone Mr Singh again.' He had been so quick to comprehend the urgency of the situation, Norah felt sure Montague Cayke's Imperial Players must have played in that part of the Indian subcontinent from which Mr Singh originated. 'It only occurred to me after I'd put down the phone, Miss Jones. His family probably lived in some out-of-the-way village that has never forgotten a production of *Aladdin*, and the small boy terrorizing the pantomime cat. I shall ask him if he didn't come to England on the trail of Montague Cayke. And then settled in Manchester stitching clothes. In which case, he might like to know about the rebuilding of the Alhambra, and how Michael Milady wants Miss Rose Meldrew, and Mr Chas Fonteyne, fetched from their places of retirement across the Seven Seas . . .'

Before Miss Bird could mention Harry, the Astonishing Prancing Dog, Hester Jones firmly but politely shook her head. With only a day left now to solve the mystery, the import of Norah Bird's telephone conversations with an Indian clothing manufacturer in Manchester could not interest her.

'No, indeed,' Norah Bird accepted this and at once began telling Miss Jones how she had returned to Mrs Cooper's, as it had been then, in a state of rare excitement. Mrs Cooper was not angry Norah had taken such a long lunch break. Nor did she say anything about the liquor on Norah Bird's breath. 'I'm glad you've found a friend,' she said. 'You must bring him in here for me to meet.'

Mrs Cooper, elderly and anxious to sell the shop, hoped Norah Bird whose rich daddy was going to buy the business for her, would not get swept off her feet. She knew a thing or two about lotteries, she'd said to Norah that afternoon. Young men who bought tickets didn't mean a half of what they said.

Norah Bird had laughed. She was already swept off her feet, and couldn't wait to tell her friend Amy Pasco all about her adventure.

Amy had been suitably impressed. 'Well, ree-allee, Nor-ah Bird!' she had said, doing her imitation of Scarlett O'Hara that could be relied on to reduce the girls to uncontrollable fits of giggles. 'Ah doo day-claire!'

'Amy was no film star,' Norah Bird told Hester Jones now. She had been blonde and pretty, but not beautiful. Nor were the Pascos well off. Amy's father and brothers all worked at Mr Bird's tannery. Amy was one of a large family which was why she'd always enjoyed her visits to the Birds' big house and all the lavish teas and outings that she joined in over the years, for Mr and Mrs Bird had been delighted their daughter had such a blonde, pretty friend and took care to include Amy in their plans. Whenever men needed to be laid off at the tannery, Mr Bird told Sharps and Nye to make sure no Pasco was ever on the list. Amy's family, aware of this preferential treatment, tolerated Amy's friendship without comment. Mrs Pasco kept her misgivings to herself though it was not easy to see one daughter singled out for spoiling by rich folk when the rest of her large brood were no less deserving. She tried to treat Norah no differently from the other friends her children latched on to so that on the few occasions, early on, when little Norah Bird had found herself at the Pascos' crowded, untidy house, sitting timid and uncomprehending amid the din and bustle, Mrs Pasco had studiously ignored her. Norah was astonished to find that Amy, so special and pretty, and made such a fuss of by her own parents, went largely overlooked in this teeming household where you even had to push for a place at the table. Norah found the other Pascos rather rough and would have preferred to go without any food and go home, but Mr Pasco always brought his sons into line, telling them surlily to watch their tongues 'in company'. He made a point of calling Norah 'Miss Bird', even when she was six years old. Amy soon learnt better than to ruin the happy chaos that prevailed at home by inflicting her dumpy schoolfriend on her family. And so, from very early in their friendship, it had suited both girls to spend their evenings playing and chatting together at Norah's house.

Norah told Hester Jones how that evening she had told Amy about Jack's clothes, his nice hands, the silvered cigarette case he'd extended to her, the way he had taken her own hand gently in his as he gave her a light. His amusement as she'd choked on the bitter Woodbine.

'Are you going to see him again?' Amy had asked and Norah could not resist telling her friend that Jack would be calling for her at Mrs Cooper's in her lunch hour tomorrow. She expected they would go for gin fizzes again, in the Swan.

'And you?' Norah asked, politely remembering to inquire what had happened to Amy that day. Amy was never short of adventures to recount. It was easier for her, she was not tied down to being in the dress shop with Mrs Cooper, learning the fashion trade. Already since the lottery began that summer, Amy had met a Tom, a Dick, and a Harry – but she had also encountered a goofy fellow called Gordon, a rather foppish Freddie and a Derek who called himself Dirk. There were others, too, who'd stopped her on the streets but Amy hadn't given these unfortunate fellows the chance even to tell her their names.

Amy did not have an adventure to recount that evening. Instead, she said, 'Have *you* any idea what's going on at the tannery at the moment?'

Norah shook her head. She had heard her father telling Sharps that he must crack down on lottery gossip in the works. Production had slumped and this was not something, in the present state of things, Mr Bird could afford. But Norah had no interest in the present state of the tannery. She was thinking of Jack and how he'd kissed her, first on the cheek and then on her lips. He had told her she tasted of water ice. He had tasted, she told Hester Jones now, of tobacco and gin fizz.

The next day, Amy Pasco had come to Mrs Cooper's just before lunch time. She wanted some velvet trimming for her primrose summer coat, and as Norah measured out the required quantity along the brass rule on the edge of the wooden counter Amy said, 'I'm sorry to hear the news.'

Mrs Cooper frowned. Even though she had sold the shop and was only staying on for a day or two to get things straight, she did not like Norah having private visitors during shop hours. And she did not like Amy Pasco.

'What news?' Norah Bird asked. Her father's signwriter was due any minute to paint out Mrs Cooper's and paint in Miss Bird's.

'Don't you know, then?'

'No – know what?'

'No-no what!' Amy mimicked her friend, flicking back her golden hair the way she had once flicked back her plaits, quick as a snake that first day at the Infants' when Norah had persuaded the other child to become her friend by giving her a brand-new pointed pencil. But Norah and Amy were not children now. Nor was it a pointed pencil Amy intended to take from Miss Bird.

At that moment another caller arrived in the shop. One Mrs Cooper did not object to, for no woman could object to the handsome presence of laughing Jack Tagg. 'Hi there, girls!' he said. Mrs Cooper beamed.

'He's gone bankrupt, your dad,' Amy now tells Norah. 'The bailiffs are in the tannery at this moment tying blue labels on all the machinery. The men have been sent home. Without pay. They are all very angry, I can tell you. The name of Bird stinks.'

Norah let the roll of primrose velvet trimming fall to the floor. It slithered away as she rushed from the shop to find her daddy and comfort him in the way that for years he had comforted her. 'It's your little Norah-bird,' she had tried to say to the disgraced businessman in the days before his despair got the better of him and he had shot himself.

Mrs Cooper shut the door behind Norah and told Jack and Amy that it was a good thing Miss Bird's father had already paid her the full purchase price on the shop. She and Cooper wouldn't have anything to live on otherwise as the shop was probably unsaleable, the fashion business being so bad. When the lottery was over and everyone closed their purses again, Norah would find out how difficult trade really was. If the tannery shut down permanently and the Reverend Hartley succeeded in banning all future lotteries, there'd be even less money in the town. Still, at least Norah would be able to fend a bit for herself, and fend for her parents also. 'It won't just be an heiress's bit of a hobby,' Mrs Cooper said. Then she added, 'I hope Miss Bird doesn't imagine there's much money in fashion. Not in these parts.'

Amy smiled. 'I think Norah imagines her daddy buying her this poky shop will be like winning the Great Knibden Lottery! She plans to make her fortune opening a Miss Bird's in every High Street across the land – as if you could possibly sell the kind of frumpy frocks you can pass off in Knibden, anywhere else! She sees herself commended one day for her services to the nation, at Buckingham Palace . . .' Amy laughs. Mrs Cooper and Jack Tagg also laugh. Then the wily Amy suggests to Jack that she and he go to the Swan as she has always fancied a gin fizz.

'And the primrose trimming?' Mrs Cooper asks, retrieving the yellow velvet from where it had unravelled across the grime on the floor.

'Never mind that now.'

Perched on a tall stall in the bar of the Swan, as Norah had described herself doing the day before, Amy tells Jack about the time at school when Miss Pringle made fun of Norah Bird in front of the class. 'The buttons on her regulation uniform wouldn't do up,' Amy titters. 'Miss Pringle told Fatty Bird to cut down on the chocs!'

Next, Amy tells Jack how embarrassing it has been being friends with the tannery owner's dumpy daughter all these years. 'They made me,' she says, of her father and brothers. The Pasco men had needed the work.

Aubrey Wilkes-Tooley and Gilbert Duncie Sibson arrive just then, hoping for a game of poker. 'Another heiress?' they laugh. And Sibson, looking at the pretty Amy's hair gleaming in the sun, intones in irreverant imitation of Jerabius Hartley, 'The streets of Knibden are *veritably* paved with gold!'

'We met on the train coming here,' Jack tells Amy. They had also met up with Mr Edmund Veitch but *that* unlucky man has

Harriet Delilah Veitch, *née* Beales (not yet RIP), keeping him in check.

The three men settle down to instruct pretty Amy Pasco in the rules of bar-room poker. Aubrey Wilkes-Tooley still has his dragon in his pocket. The dragon he will sell shortly, for a small but tidy profit. To Mary Bridgewater's childhood sweetheart, Peter.

'Bravo! Bravo!' cried Mr Milady when he saw the transformation though nothing at Miss Bird's was cheap and even *he* wondered what the committee would say when they met tomorrow morning and saw the bill.

'I've only ever worn black and shades of grey,' Hester Jones tried to say. Norah Bird had been quite determined that nothing less than the best she could offer would do. Mrs Cooper would have said the same, she said. And Calderon could not say anything because the Swan had already benefited to the tune of six hundred pounds while Mr Veitch was too busy envisaging a great revival in the town to concern himself with the minutiae of committee expenditure. When Louisa remarked over tea at the Gallimore that she felt she ought to make herself a dress for the tea-dance, Veitch was beneficent. 'Buy one from Miss Bird's like everyone else,' he told her. If Hester Jones could acquire a whole new wardrobe from Miss Bird's – why, so could his wife! Besides, Louisa's time was spoken for. This revival would involve a lot of organization. 'We must conserve our efforts,' Veitch said. 'We owe it to the dead guest.'

Louisa Veitch left her husband and son finishing their tea at the Gallimore and set out for Miss Bird's. She soon forgot where she was heading for and was scurrying along when she walked smack bang into Chickie Wilkes-Tooley. The second Mrs Veitch apologized for not looking where she was going and explained how rushed things were just then at the schoolhouse and how busy she was being kept with all Veitch's preparations for the new Knibden that would shortly prevail. 'The revival will involve a lot of organisation. Why, I haven't even had time yet to buy a dress for the tea-dance,' she chattered distractedly. 'It is as well I am not keen on dancing.'

'Oh, but I love dancing!' Chickie exclaimed. 'Can I not assist in this revival in some way?'

Mrs Veitch was so taken aback she declined the offer at the time, but mentioned it later to her husband.

'We need all the help we can get,' Veitch said and, since Louisa was a timid thing, he sent Samuel Till, one of Susie Till's younger brothers, with a note up to the Wilkes-Tooley residence asking Miss Chickie to visit at her earliest possible convenience.

Samuel Till handed over the note and then stood gazing up at her stubbornly with his hand out. Chickie felt like slapping the grubby urchin, but changed her mind. Instead, she took her purse from her pocket and rewarded Mr Veitch's emissary with a shining fifty-pence piece.

15

The Two Women of the Revd Sibson

When Aubrey Wilkes-Tooley told his daughters Neville Tagg was coming to dine, the three said nothing. Chickie thought, 'Well, that settles it!' and immediately accepted the invitation Edmund Veitch had sent. Bea remembered how she had heard that the two old Gallimore sisters had returned to the town and planted themselves on Gilbert Sibson up at the rectory, and she now decided it was incumbent on her to visit them.

'How nice that you are both so busy!' Mary remarked wonderingly. She turned to her middle daughter. 'Lalla, you had better help me in the kitchen.'

Lalla Wilkes-Tooley, as if in a daze, did as her mother bid her. Neville Tagg! she thought. So that was it! She might need that wifely bristle brush, after all. As she beat eggs and seasoned a salad under her mother's direction, she contemplated her fate.

The Reverend Gilbert Duncie Sibson, meanwhile, cowered in his study at the rectory of St Redegule's cursing the cowardice that kept him there. He had intended spending the whole day praying to the blessed St Redegule but he trembled to face her. He trembled also to face the aged Gallimore sisters who had spent all day taking it in turns to knock on his study door. 'I have brought you a nice cup of tea,' they would cackle, bustling into his room without waiting to be asked, so that even in here he no longer felt safe. 'You *are* good to me!' he'd hear himself saying, resolving inwardly to take matters in hand next time. Thus it was that when there *next* came a knock, that evening, and Sibson flung open his door to explain that he *did not need* tea brought to him on the hour, every hour – how pleasantly surprised he had been to see Beatrice Wilkes-Tooley standing there! The light on her hair from the old orange lamp in the hall shone like a halo round her eager smiling face.

'Why, er, Miss Wilkes-Tooley! How are you, my dear?'

'I have brought you a nice cup of tea,' she said.

'You *are* good to me!' the Reverend Sibson beamed. He felt

worn out. Like much of the rest of the town, the poor man had not slept in days. Only last night he had awoken from a nightmare in which he'd found himself *married* to one of the Gallimore sisters who had used the death of the guest at the Gallimore as an excuse to declare themselves dispossessed and arrive on his doorstep with suitcases, invoking the name of Jerabius Hartley and his dreadful sister, Zillanah, and showing no sign at all of ever going away. The relief on waking all alone in his hard cold bed and realizing that the repugnant marriage had only been a dream was so immense Gilbert had thrown back the bedclothes and risen at once to open his window and drink deep the cold night air. Across the churchyard outside lay the grave of the unknown guest and Gilbert Sibson found himself gazing into the moonlit darkness, wondering whether the guest's body had already begun the slow, steady process of corruption. He pictured the dead man's flesh rotting away into the soil and hoped poor Mr Applecart, whoever he had been, had enjoyed his time on this earth. Had lived, laughed and danced as, indeed, Gilbert Duncie Sibson had never done.

I *will* go to Belle Quinn's tea-dance, Sibson had vowed at first light that morning. And I will dance with every prettily dressed girl in the room!

And now, by some miracle that proved miracles happen, Beatrice Wilkes-Tooley had come to his room. She contrasted so strikingly with the hideous Gallimore crones, that Bea was rendered miraculously beauteous. Gilbert felt he had himself died and was being admitted into Heaven.

When Gilbert Duncie Sibson arrived in Knibden years ago, he had been a high-minded cheerful young curate, intent on doing good works and making his mark in the world. He had never yet heard of the Great Knibden Lottery and it had not occurred to him, at first, that it was anything but a bit of fairground fun. He had been amazed by the hullaballoo in the town and though he had bought a ticket he'd had no great hope of winning anything and had paid little attention to the draw. Until afterwards. It was only some time later that it had dawned on Gilbert that his ticket had had the *very same number* as the winner but had carried the *wrong design*. If only, instead of purchasing a naked woman, his ticket had been a dragon! How rich he might have been. What expensive good works he would have been able to effect, in the name of the blessed St Redegule. What a mark he might have made on the world! At first he had shrugged off these thoughts as nonsensical. It was childish to go through life dwelling in the dark shadow of what might have been. He had even preached to that effect, in the pulpit of St Redegule's, on several occasions. A long time ago. As time passed, Gilbert increasingly felt he'd been unduly punished. Punished for choosing so unsuitable a motif. It had been youthful whimsy to select a woman, and a naked one at that, given that he was bent on a career as a *man* of the *cloth*! He had written and told his professor the joke. He'd felt daring. A man of the world at last with a curacy of his own and not some student whispering rather saucily in a seminary dormitory after lights out. The professor had written back and inquired what the lottery prize had been. He wrote that he had once won a bottle of cherryade as a child that had exploded and put out his sister's eye. Nothing good ever comes of what we get freely, the professor had said, counselling the young man to desist from all such misguided fooleries in future. There were no short cuts in this life. The sooner his pupil recognized this fact, the better. Sibson had read the missive and crumpled it up, laughing aloud at such pedagogic stuffiness.

Later he felt chastened. As time went on, the fact he had possessed exactly the right number but with the wrong emblem on his ticket preyed increasingly on his mind. Once, a long time back, when he had been dining at the Laurels with the mathematician, Quinn, and Quinn's two daughters, Sibson had light-heartedly mentioned it.

'How dreadful for you!' Fleur said at once.

'It was probably a blessing in disguise,' the pious Belle remarked. 'Winning the lottery never made anyone happy.'

'It was rather a strange coincidence don't you think?' Sibson voiced his innermost anxiety.

'Coincidence?' Harold Augustus Quinn looked up from his plate.

'Having exactly the right number, but the wrong design.' It was all Sibson could do to say the dread words.

The girls' father bellowed down the table, 'There is no such thing as *coincidence* in this world!' Quinn pointed his fork menacingly at the curate. 'Since everything in this universe is actually in reverse, what you see and register as some random event is in fact the inevitable conclusion of earlier action that only *appears* to come later. There isn't a "coincidence" that cannot be accounted for in this way. I have the equations and theorems to prove it.'

Fleur giggled. Sibson heard himself laughing. But Belle had not liked her lover and her sister laughing together at her father and she had treated Sibson frostily from that point onwards.

At night, sleeping in the rectory – even in the days when Miss Zillanah and Jerabius Hartley had still been in residence, asleep in their rooms on the floor below – the naked woman came to Gilbert in his dreams mocking him for having succumbed to her charms. If it wasn't for me! she would taunt so that Gilbert would try and keep awake to avoid her, lying there in the darkness and wondering what sort of a God teased men in this way. Deliberately sending him to Knibden while a lottery was on, letting him purchase a ticket so near and yet so far from the winner that his peace of mind was shattered forever. Gilbert did not blame God, he blamed the naked woman. If it hadn't been for *her* the beautiful old church of St Redegule's could have been restored to something surpassing its former glory. The people of the town would congregate there once more, not merely for funerals but to joyously worship their plaster saint. The naked woman had deliberately deprived the blessed St Redegule of her due. There had been a time when Sibson was so disgusted by the town's apathy towards its beautiful saint, he had gone up into his pulpit and read snatches from an old copy of Sidney Mastermain Bensusann's essays he had found at the rectory. Hardly anyone noticed. Only a Mr Storr who sold Bibles for a living, who was lodging just then with Mrs Willow and had come to the church hoping to shift a box of mildewed volumes he'd had in the back of his car for years. Sibson did not want the cheap Bibles but he'd been glad of the company and had invited Storr into the rectory for a glass of ginger wine and a bit of a chat. In the course of conversation, Storr admitted that he too had bought a lottery ticket at the last lottery, with a naked woman on it.

Sibson stared. 'Didn't that upset you?' he'd asked.

Mr Storr shrugged. 'Win some, lose some – dragons were drawn, so it was back to selling Bibles on Monday morning.'

Sibson envied the salesman his equanimity. But Storr had had less cause to complain – the number on *his* naked woman had been nowhere near the number that won. 'Mind you,' said Storr as he was leaving the rectory. And he'd then communicated something rather extraordinary about his landlady, Mrs Willow, and her daughter. And another lodger of theirs at the time of the last lottery, a Mr Harry Best. Allegations Sibson could not begin to take seriously.

As his nights were increasingly taken up trying to avoid the naked woman in his dreams, so the Reverend Gilbert Duncie Sibson turned more and more by day to the ancient plaster figure of St Redegule set on a plinth to one side of the main aisle in the church. Before he had come to the town he had done some research in the seminary library and discovered that the obscure female saint Knibden had chosen for its own was the Patron Saint of Lost Opportunities.

Gilbert Duncie Sibson spent his days in the church gazing up at St Redegule. She gazed coolly back at him. Eventually her virginity and obscurity came to irk him nearly as much as his own. He felt himself torn apart between her clothed saintliness and the naked woman who nightly taunted him.

One year, after the Hartleys had left – we won't give you our address, we are retiring for good and want nothing more to do with Knibden – and Sibson was running the parish on his own, it happened that the old wooden plinth beneath the saint showed signs of collapse. It had become necessary to replace it in a hurry with something more substantial. Richard Follifoot, sole trader, builder of Knibden, came in with the cheapest quote for the work and though Sibson did not like the man he had given him the job. Sibson looked on as an ugly concrete affair was constructed on which to place the statue. As he watched Follifoot lift the girl down on to the floor, he heard him swear. There was a lot to swear about. The job took longer than Follifoot had accounted for. 'There's more to it than first appears,' the builder told the vicar as if challenging him to ask questions.

One afternoon, Gilbert Sibson had come into the church to find Follifoot's wife trumpeting and carrying on. She had discovered her husband canoodling in a dark corner with a girl from the Swan. Mrs Follifoot now turned on Sibson and blamed him for allowing such things in his church. There weren't many lost opportunities here! she shrieked. Poor Gilbert had been profoundly shocked, not just by the shouting but by the presence of the saint who watched the unseemly to-do with exactly the same lack of concern she had always shown Sibson. It seemed to him that the ugly new concrete plinth was her due for her carelessness of mortal sufferings. 'Stuck-up bitch!' Mrs Follifoot had shouted and Sibson did not know whether it was Calderon's current barmaid, now hastily rearranging her clothes, or the blessed clothed St Redegule that the builder's wife was referring to.

Once the Bishop had offered Sibson another living elsewhere and this he had declined almost before he knew he had done so, such was his attachment he supposed to his obscure and disdainful saint. If opportunities had been lost over the years, these had been because of her. Because of her, he had neglected to woo Belle Quinn.

And now the dead guest had other plans for him. He was old enough to be Beatrice Wilkes-Tooley's father. Indeed, he had come to the town on the very same train as Aubrey Wilkes-Tooley. And Jack Tagg. He had made his way to the rectory attached to St Redegule's having agreed to meet his new friends for more poker later at the Swan.

The Reverend Hartley and his sister inquired what had kept him? They had known the time his train was due and kept a meal waiting on the table. Poor Gilbert was not to know about the fierce crusade that Jerabius Hartley was waging just then against the Great Knibden Lottery which he regarded as the Work of the Devil and preached virulently to that effect from his pulpit every Sunday. By creating a great opportunity right here in Knibden that would be lost to just about everyone but the one lucky winner, the Devil was wickedly setting himself up in direct opposition to the blessed St Redegule, Hartley opined. Lost opportunities were the food on which the Devil thrived. Assiduously did Jerabius Hartley resurrect old stories to prove his point. He ranted and raved to his tiny congregation about Mrs Cardigan Cardew, later Mrs Percival Vestey, finally hanged as Mrs Albert Jenks. He speculated keenly on the fate of Miss Angelica Hook.

He railed against a certain Mrs Burrel, the respectable wife and mother who had taken up a life of drunken debauchery in the arms of the lottery winner over a century back, to be afterwards commemorated when the milestones erected with lottery money on the roads around Knibden became known as Burrels. 'See!' yelled Jerabius Hartley from his pulpit, 'how time and the tide has seen to it that the profane woman who once adorned each stone has long since been rubbed away!'

The Hartleys stared at the new young curate and wondered what kind of creature they had invited in under their roof.

'They were selling them on the platform at the station,' the young Gilbert explained ingenuously. 'I did not think there could be any harm . . .'

In silence had Zillanah Hartley risen from the table and, although none of the dishes had yet been touched, she cleared away the luncheon from under the diners' noses. Tut-tutting her way down to the rectory kitchens, she left her brother to remonstrate with his new curate across the empty dining table. It had not been an auspicious start.

'My dear young sir! I can only urge you to pray to the blessed St Redegule for forgiveness! May she, in her mercy, have mercy upon you for one thing you can be sure of, my sister never will!'

Zillanah Hartley never had.

Last night, Gilbert Sibson had dreamed that his saint appeared at the end of his bed warning him about Beatrice Wilkes-Tooley the way she had once warned him off Belle Quinn. And her lovely, lively sister Fleur. 'You will have to choose,' the blessed St Redegule said. 'Between her, and me.' Bea and the naked woman of the lottery ticket he had purchased years ago became one. They constituted his downfall. He had sat up in his cold narrow bed in the darkness, and wept. Like Zillanah Hartley, St Redegule had never forgiven him for buying that lottery ticket. He was lost – but for all that he had devoted his life to her service, in the hope of making amends, she would not save him. She would look calmly down from her plinth as he waded out into the sea of his enslavement and was sucked down into the watery quagmire, and drowned.

The young Mrs Herbert Vale had walked by the sea in the pouring rain on her honeymoon. She'd been thinking about the summer of Raymond Bast which had also been the summer of the last Great Knibden Lottery and she had wondered what could have prompted her to tell her husband something that had happened so long before. When she was only a young girl, of thirteen. She shivered. 'You're cold, Verity,' the kind man who sold corrugated cardboard boxes for a living had said. 'Let's get you back to the hotel.'

In the lounge of the seaside hotel they had chosen for their honeymoon, an iced cake was being cut to celebrate the nuptials that morning of the manager, Mason, and one of his staff, a pasty-faced Irish chambermaid called Eileen. 'He'll have got her up the spout,' one of the women told Verity so that when she accepted a slice of the cake from the girl, Verity had congratulated her pro-fusely and said that she too had only recently married and also hoped to have children. She did not mention the boy Raymond or the stories about small creatures with human faces that she intended to write for his bedtime.

When the Masons turned up at the Gallimore Hotel ten years ago, Miss Willow recognized the couple at once. She wondered what had happened to Eileen's baby but always felt too shy to ask. The Masons did not frequent Knibden's public library – there being too short a space of time between making beds and preparing lunch in which to take up a book – so they did not recognize Knibden's assistant librarian as the young bride, Mrs Vale, who had said to her husband later that evening at the Sea-view, 'Herbert, I haven't told you this before. I have a little money put by. It was given me by Mr Bast, I mean Harry Best, the man I told you about who stayed with us that summer. He sent it to me after he'd left. By way of recompense. I should like you to have it now to buy yourself a new van. It would help you get about the country, selling your cardboard boxes . . .'

When the two Gallimore sisters retired from their lives as showgirls, they had gone to live by the sea. Unable to afford a smart hotel like the Seaview, they had rented rooms at the top of a tall house. Unfortunately they had lived a lot longer than either anticipated and recently their funds had run low. They wrote to the rectory at Knibden asking for advice. Their letter was addressed to his predecessor, a man whom, even after his retire-ment and death long before, Gilbert did not want to let down again – so Sibson had written a chatty letter back telling the sisters, in passing, about the guest who had died the previous night at the Gallimore. 'A committee has been got up, and Bill Parris has dug the grave, and I am to bury him with all due care and ceremony although no one knows who he left his fortune to. Or why . . .'

'Knibden needs us,' the sisters had agreed as they looked out for the last time at the sheet of cold steely sea they could no longer afford to live beside. The last of the Gallimores packed their bags immediately and returned to Knibden. They regarded the fact that Sibson had written to them as an invitation to stay at the rectory, and the fact he had mentioned the dead stranger's fortune as an indication their money problems would soon be solved.

'If the Gallimore sisters do *not* inherit, how will I ever get rid of them?' Gilbert Sibson asked himself now. Perhaps the pair *did* know something touching the affair that he did not. This would hardly be surprising. He knew so little. Perhaps there would be some money for them after all. In which case, he need have no fear.

'You were *such* a darling young man!' they'd said on arriving back. 'You never married then?'

'No Knibden lass ever tempt you?'

'When you first came, we thought what a change you would make from crusty old Hartley. It is astonishing for us to see that nothing much changed when you replaced him. Even the old orange lamp is still in the hall. Tilda was in love with Jerabius, you know.'

'I wasn't.'

'You can't deny it, Tildie! So inappropriate, of course, but it would never have worked. Few wives have ever managed to fend off Tilda Gallimore the way Zillanah Hartley . . .'

'Have you really been here, just like this, all these years?' Tilda asked Sibson briskly.

Sibson nodded. No wonder she didn't believe him – where had the years gone? Knibden was a quiet place in which to have been so busy.

'And the Gallimore Hotel? You will have to tell us everything. We are obviously connected to this dead guest in some way.'

'We are bound to inherit something.'

'To make up.'

'For all we have lost – Gilbert thinks so, you can tell.'

Sibson shook his head. 'I'm afraid I really don't know what's going on. I'm more in the dark than anyone.'

The sisters both laughed. 'We have been to see his grave.'

'You buried him.'

'So romantic!'

'What a head for sensation this unknown guest had – it's a wonder he didn't organize ringside tickets and side-shows for the event.'

'He'd have made a fortune if he had!' The pair cackled irreverently. The sisters had been disappointed to find the Reverend Sibson was not on the committee. 'Whyever not?' they demanded. 'We were relying on you.'

'I did not think I should pledge . . . It would be a gamble . . .'

'You weren't so set against the Great Knibden Lottery!' Bessie laughed. 'Old Hartley tore you off a strip or two there – you a young curate with a naked woman in your pocket. We laughed at the time – we have been laughing ever since. We were always surprised you were allowed to stay on. We were sure Zillanah Hartley must have had designs on your person – else she and her brother would certainly have sent you packing.'

Sibson blushed. 'It's all a long time ago,' he said. That was the problem with this whole business of the dead guest. People would keep raking over the past. A past so lacking, on his part at least, in anything worth remembering. The sisters were watching him closely. They are disappointed in me, he thought. I have let them down. The thought saddened him and he resolved to pray to St Redegule for one last opportunity to redeem himself. At Belle Quinn's tea-dance tomorrow.

In this frame of mind had Gilbert Duncie Sibson opened the door that Friday evening to Beatrice Wilkes-Tooley, standing there in the full glory of her maroon crêpe dress that she intended to wear for the tea-dance. Gilbert had never seen Bea apart from her younger sisters, Lalla and Chickie, before. He did not listen to the pretext the girl gave for her visit, but flung the door wide open to admit her.

Inside the church that loomed dark and silent beyond the

252

study window, a tiny tear welled in the painted eye of the blessed St Redegule and trickled slowly down her immobile plaster face.

By chance, Bill Parris had wandered into the church to get out of the cold and had come to a halt beside St Redegule's feet. 'A miracle!' he exclaimed when the teardrop spattered the ground at *his* feet. He spat the baccy from his mouth and, throwing himself down on old threadbare knees, he fumbled to light a small candle. 'She weeps for the stranger buried out in her churchyard,' Bill Parris mumbled. 'But well might St Redegule weep for us all.'

16

Family Business

Well might St Redegule have wept just then for Belle Quinn. She was hurrying down the canal towpath that led to Buckworth & Matchett's. The light was fading fast and the brambles tore at her skirts. She shivered and drew her paisley shawl tightly about her. Somewhere along this cold muddy stretch was the spot where Godfrey Buckworth, stumbling home late one night at the time of the last Great Lottery, had slipped and toppled into the canal. As children, Beatrice Wilkes-Tooley and her sisters had played The Drowning of Mr Godfrey, running along here to the consternation of their mother who tried in vain to forbid them going near the old canal. The three had pointed to places, claiming petulantly and with authority that *this* was where it had happened. A different spot every time. Once, when Belle had suggested visiting Buckworth & Matchett's with a view to printing his life's work at last, Daddy had reminded her about Mr Godfrey and said he would not want the same watery fate to befall her. 'If you take the twelve parts along that towpath, one by one,' Harold Augustus Quinn had told his elder daughter, 'something untoward is *bound* to happen.' 'Nonsense, Daddy!' Belle protested with a smile, but Quinn turned unaccountably angry. 'I may not have entirely solved the mystery of the universe, Belle, but *even you* must allow I know a thing or two about the ways of the world!'

And the dead guest, Daddy? Belle asked now. Would Harold Augustus Quinn have been able to take Hester Jones aside during the dancing tomorrow and instruct her in some unique mathematical equation that would clear up the mystery, at least to his own satisfaction? I may not be as clever as Daddy but I am helping Miss Jones every way I can. I am doing all that is humanly possible to make her tea-dance a success . . .

Buckworth & Matchett's was a collection of large, mostly derelict, brick sheds that straggled beside the canal beyond the outskirts of the town. Belle hurried through the rusty iron gates with the name of the firm across the top, Buckworth on one gate, Matchett on the other, the '&' looping over and only in place when the gates were shut. Which they never were these days, now there was nothing inside worth enclosing. The roofs of the sprawling buildings were open to the elements. The gutters had come away, and water cascaded down the walls. All the paint-work was blistering and few windows remained unbroken. Whereas the Bensusanns' luxuriated in its dilapidation, with Otti-lie Vigo's garden growing defiantly alive all round the worn stone house, here the old brick sheds stood windswept, the derel-iction was hollow and stark.

Belle faltered. She gazed about the dank cobbled yard and wondered where, in all this ugly mass of dark deserted buildings, Victor Matchett could possibly live and work. She tried a few doors which were either locked, or opened on to dark cavernous rooms she did not like to enter. Whatever Dick Follifoot, sole trader and builder of Knibden, had claimed, it was hard to imagine the *Knibden Bugle* ever blasting from these premises again. Or *The Cold Sun* by Harold Augustus Quinn being printed in twelve volumes using best paper and bound in calf-leather covers, tooled and gilded, as Daddy would have liked.

Matchett watched the woman wandering about down in the weed-strewn yard like a piece of crumpled tissue blown hither and thither by a careless wind. It has started, he thought. First the oily Follifoot with his clever patter that made no attempt to hide who knew what designs. And now the Quinn woman, beating her way along the overgrown towpath, destroying the privacy he had managed to preserve all these years, shutting himself away, shutting down the old works. Matchett rubbed his hands together and opened a window. By the tea-dance on Saturday evening, you'll easily be the richest man in Knibden. The women would be queuing up to show him their wares. You'll be fighting 'em off, mate! Matchett called to Belle to come up. 'Green door right beneath me,' he yelled, pointing vigorously.

Belle timidly mounted a short flight of rickety wooden steps that had rotted away from the wall. She stood on the unrailed platform at the top and pulled hard at the green door Matchett had indicated. Then she gave it such a strong push, it fell open hurtling her into pitch darkness inside. Before the door slammed

255

to behind her, she had seen that she was at the bottom of a musty stairwell. Sensing light somewhere high above, she groped her way up the stairs towards it.

'You should have used the electric!' Matchett said. He had waited till she got to the top before he flicked the switch beside him. Miss Quinn had dust and cobwebs all over her paisley shawl and short-cropped hair. The preparations for the hasty tea-dance were taking their toll on the woman, Matchett thought gleefully.

The man is malicious, Belle decided as she got her breath back. No wonder Daddy had tried to warn her! 'I brought some copy for an advertisement for the tea-dance,' she explained breathlessly. 'To go in the *Bugle*.'

'Follifoot doesn't waste much time!' Matchett remarked. 'Come through to the office.' He led the way along a corridor and up another two flights of stairs and into a large bare room down one end of which stood a smoky stove surrounded by bits of rough carpet and a few scattered pieces of furniture. Matchett sat himself in one of the old armchairs that had springs and horsehair poking through the upholstery. He signalled to Miss Quinn to sit down also. 'I don't often get lady visitors,' he said, to make Belle blush.

Belle lowered herself and perched very straight, resolving to get down to business and be off without delay.

'Now then, Miss Quinn, you're in the know what with this dance you're in charge of. Who do you think the dead stranger was? What's *your* best guess?'

Belle ignored the question. She had not come to chat. 'It's about the dance I've come. I am considering taking out a full-page advertisement in the new *Bugle*. What would such an item cost?'

Matchett waved a hand, frowned and named a preposterous figure off the top of his head. A figure Belle immediately halved, although even halved it was a sizeable fee for something Matchett had not thought of doing until Follifoot suggested it last night. Matchett nodded, struggling to hide his delight. 'I'm a fool to myself,' he said. 'But you're a fine businesswoman, Miss Quinn, I can see that. The dead guest should be proud of you. Now, let me think. How about we say *two* adverts for the price of *one* – my price that is. That would double what you get for the amount I

256

suggested – I cannot charge any less. The *Bugle* will be expensive to get off the ground after the machines have sat about idle so long.'

Belle nodded. Her main concern now was to know that an advertisement had been placed, and to be on her way.

Matchett went on, 'But, supposing for the sake of goodwill and as a favour to you, and to our dead guest – and since we are both on the committee and the more we spend the more we get back – we double that price. I then let you have *five* adverts for the original cost of only *two*, I would say the both of us have got a pretty fair bargain.'

'But how can I have five advertisements – there can't possibly be five *Bugles* between now and the tea-dance tomorrow evening!' The man was obviously trying it on.

'Pardon me, Miss Quinn! The presses will be rolling all through the night. People will want to keep *abreast* of the latest developments. They will buy every edition as it comes out – we can't possibly print enough copies to supply the demand. Now, if you put a full-page advert in each of the next five editions, I can guarantee you the whole of Knibden will hear about your tea-dance.'

'That sounds reasonable, Mr Matchett,' Belle said hesitantly.

'The voice of reason, the *Bugle*!' Matchett took the neatly written copy from Miss Quinn. 'Music, Dancing, Flowers, Food,' he read. 'Its going to be some tea-dance, eh, Miss Quinn!'

'I do hope so,' Belle said earnestly. 'I am doing my best.'

'I'm sure you are. Your goodness is famous. Even out here, along the towpath. Now, if you would have the goodness to pay on the nail, as it were, Miss Quinn, then you can have that special rate I'm a fool to myself to allow yer.'

Belle was dismayed. 'I haven't got nearly that amount of money on me. I could call back later with it – or would a cheque do? I don't want to delay things.'

'A cheque in your fair hand would do very nicely, my dear Miss Quinn.'

As Belle was writing the cheque, she became aware of an odd, rather acrid smell. Out of the corner of her eye she saw a dead pigeon lying on the ground. It had obviously been there a long time judging by its state of decay. A fly crawled over the remains of its beak and in and out of an eye socket. 'Ugh!' she said, turning away.

'The birds fly in,' Matchett said. 'I cannot stop them.'

'You could mend some of the windows,' Belle suggested. She pulled her paisley shawl about her. It was colder in here than *outside*! Belle could feel none of the warmth from the stove and she could not afford to catch cold, not when there was still so much to do for the tea-dance. She would call in at the Gallimore on her way home for one last check – she had a horrid feeling she was going to be up all night.

Matchett nodded. The cheque would certainly pay for a good many windows, he thought as he took it from her. It was a long time since he had experienced the pleasure of dealing with customers. 'I'll come down and see you out,' he said gallantly. 'I have some business in town I need to attend to.'

He walked back with Belle along the dark towpath, past the exact spot where Godfrey Buckworth had once slipped to his death. Belle was grateful for the company but strode briskly ahead. She parted from the printer in the main Square. As Belle hurried into the Gallimore, Mr Matchett went up to Gary Laffety leaning against his motorbike by the War Memorial. Gary said, Yeh, he and his friends could do with earning a bob or two. They'd need new jackets for the tea-dance!

'It'll be Buckworth, Matchett & Laffety's if you play your cards right,' Victor Matchett said.

'How'll yer fit all *that* on the rusty ol' gates, then?' Gary Laffety laughed.

'We'll get some new gates.' Matchett was surprised how simple it sounded. Henry Buckworth must have said the same to his father once. And his father, picturing the name of 'Matchett' cut in steel on top of the gates, had agreed to the arrangements Buckworth proposed. He sold his soul to the old man, Matchett thought. And he sold my soul, also.

Matchett told Laffety to come as soon as he could round up a workforce and he would show him the great printing sheds where the machines had lain idle for years. The compositors' offices where banks of trays of type stood covered in cobwebs. The flywheels would need de-rusting and a drop or two of oil. It had all been in perfectly good working order when used last so there was no reason why the machines could not be got working again at once. No reason copies of the new revised *Knibden Bugle* complete with Belle Quinn's advertisement could not be sold on every street corner and keep people *abreast* with events, now that there were events. Just as Dick Follifoot, sole trader and builder of Knibden, had suggested.

Gary Laffety did not point out that the technology at Buckworth & Matchett's was bound to be antiquated. Flywheels, trays of type – these days a hundred times the work could be done, at the press of a button. He thought it would be a laugh, though, to get in there with his mates and do whatever it was the old skinflint wanted. A miser, Matchett was known to be. Vast wealth hoarded up who knew where. Hidden in those tumbled-down sheds most like. No one knew *how* he'd made his fortune. Gary Laffety thought this might be his chance to find out.

It had been Henry's and Godfrey's father, the first Henry Buckworth, a man of great energy and ambition, who had founded the printing works. He had come to Knibden shortly before the Great Lottery that resulted in the building of the camera obscura. Timing is as much everything in business as it is in the theatre – and Buckworth senior's timing had been as renowned as Montague Cayke's. He'd arrived penniless and been taken on to work for the *Knibden Bugle*, a small long-established newspaper, run at that time from its owner's front room. The energetic young Buckworth tried to persuade his employer that they ought to concentrate on giving readers up-to-date news on the lottery by seeking 'inside information' from the committee running it. But the *Bugle*'s owner was a lazy man who had, in the true tradition of Knibden men, set his sights on winning the lottery and retiring. It was hard work running a newspaper office and his wife did not like the smell of ink that wafted up to her parlour from downstairs. Nor did that good lady approve of the naked woman who adorned one third of the lottery tickets. This meant that the tickets Buckworth's employer spent more on than he ought, had *all* been either trumpets or dragons. When the naked woman triumphed on Day One of the lottery, the bankrupted owner of the *Bugle* blew his brains out and young Buckworth saw his chance to trade *his* lottery ticket, which had a naked woman on it, with the man's widow in exchange for the *Bugle*.

At once, the new proprietor of the *Knibden Bugle* had set his radical ideas in motion. Countless editions kept Knibden informed of all the latest developments. The latest price of naked women, their availability, rumours and counter rumours whipped into full spin by the eager young Buckworth. Buckworth's new revised *Bugle* became the main source of information in all this whirlwind so that by the end of Day Two, he had been able to sit back in the knowledge that *he* had not needed a lucky lottery ticket to make *his* fortune, hard work and good business sense had been enough. He *could* have sat back, but Buckworth senior did no such thing. Instead he bought a plot of cheap land beside the canal to build a purpose-built brick shed to house a new press he immediately had sent up from London. The *Bugle* did not relinquish interest in the lottery. It carried an interview with the winner and even a series about the losers, wretched men who'd lost all they had and were only too glad of a few coppers to tell of their miserable plight. When *that* rich seam had been mined, Buckworth imaginatively commenced to follow the affairs of the lottery committee intent on spending the funds that had been raised. Cardigan Cardew became a household name. The relative merits of the camera obscura, the super horse trough and Millicent Vantickel's remarkable periscope had been hotly debated in the *Bugle*'s pages. Next, Buckworth built special rooms to house all the typesetters he was obliged to take on – countless women, many of whom had been abandoned by lovers and husbands after the excitement of the lottery and who were now in desperate need of employment. Out of charity he even took on the widow of the original owner of the *Bugle* who had not been lucky with the naked woman he had sold her, but who was now obliged to get over her aversion to the smell of ink. By the time that other widow, the notorious Mrs Cardew/Vestey/Jenks was hanged, Buckworth had made enough from the new go-ahead *Bugle* to expand his premises many times over. He had also married the pretty typesetter of his choice.

Buckworth senior privately relished the notion that his fortunes had been founded on a naked woman. Trumpets and dragons would not have been nearly so appropriate to a man who was thenceforward to provide such ample employment for the females of Knibden. Nimble fingers were needed for handling the tiny pieces of lead type and the girl who became Mrs Buckworth had the nimblest fingers of all. Yet nimble fingers and marriage to Mr Buckworth did not turn out to be quite the stroke of luck they first appeared. Shortly before the birth of young Henry, Mrs Buckworth was mortified to learn that her husband had turned his attentions to another. The birth of Henry was then so painful she afterwards felt grateful to the succession of girls who kept her energetic husband away from her.

Little Henry grew into a hardy robust child, a favourite both with his father and the women who worked for him. He would wander into the compositors' office and be petted by the women. He would help himself to lead Hs from their type-trays, dipping the ends in the ink and pressing them on to sheets of paper. A born printer, his proud father would say. But it was easy for Henry – H is a letter that looks the same, whether on the piece of lead type or on the impression it made. Poor Godfrey, attempting to copy his elder brother, was later to get into terrible confusion over *his* letters, for a G back to front is a very different proposition from the G you are meant to write when you spell your name on a slate at school.

Henry had been five years old when Mrs Buckworth died giving birth to Godfrey, a sickly baby who would grow into a sickly man. Try as he might, poor delicate Godfrey could never catch his elder brother up. The typesetters did not go out of their way to give him sweets or club together to take him to the Alhambra after work, the way they doted on Henry. If Godfrey wandered into their offices they shooed him out. Soon there was nothing the poor orphan boy craved more than to be admitted into their feminine presence and enjoy the embraces that so irked his elder brother. Even at an early age Henry knew, without articulating it, that the girls pressed their attentions on him in the hope of marrying his father and giving up typesetting. Although Buckworth senior always had a current favourite among the girls, usually the newest, youngest recruit, he never married again. A good-looking Knibden girl could always get work at Buckworth's. The requirements of the job meant that Mr Buckworth could, with all propriety as a future employer, take applicants by the hand to examine professionally the strength of their wrists and the nimbleness of their dainty fingers. Henry learnt to ignore the strange cries that emanated from his father's chambers just as later he resolutely chose not to hear what went on in Godfrey's rooms. When he took over from his father, the first thing Henry did was to give his brother separate quarters across the yard so that he could come and go as he pleased, along the towpath to the town.

Like Veitch, Victor Matchett's father also arrived in Knibden for the great lottery of 1915. By chance, this was the first lottery for which Buckworth's had secured the job of actually printing the lottery tickets. Buckworth's having bought up all the other printers in Knibden, there was now no competition for the work. Matchett, like Veitch and a lot of men who had come to Knibden at that time, had delayed enlisting until after he had tried his luck in the lottery. Shying away from anything military, Matchett lost all his money buying dragons and women. In his enthusiasm to do so, he too had got into debt but he had taken work at Buckworth's, working on the presses, and so managed to pay off what he owed. Unlike Veitch senior, Matchett senior had no cause then to curse Knibden and in fact returned to the town after the war, having nowhere better to call home. The shortage of able-bodied men meant he could get his old job back and it was only a matter of time before one of the typesetters – who'd have nothing to do with him previously when young men were plentiful and he had been penniless – persuaded Matchett to marry her. Reading the names freshly carved on the War Memorial that was eventually erected with the proceeds from the 1915 lottery, Matchett senior was able to remember the faces of men he had marched away with. Wilfred and Johnny Dawes Dobson for instance. And Denis Lobb, Lavinia Lobb's brother. But of all that great exodus from Knibden, only he returned.

Buckworth senior, the founder, had by this time passed on and young Henry Buckworth was now a portly man of forty. He took a rather paternal interest in the Matchetts. Mrs Matchett, as it happened, had been the last girl his father had gone for, summoning her from her place among the compositors to undress and lie down beside him. The girl knew other girls who had submitted in this way and did not know how to refuse without hurting the old man's feelings. Besides, all he'd wanted was to stroke her like a kitten, and it had seemed a harmless enough pleasure to bestow. One sunny afternoon she had fallen asleep and Henry Buckworth, coming to give his father his medicine, found the two curled up naked together, the girl asleep, his father – dead.

Henry Buckworth naturally felt grateful to the girl who had eased his father's last moments on this earth. Neither he, nor she, ever referred to the matter or mentioned what had happened to Matchett when he returned from the war. A young man in his early twenties, though he looked far far older, Matchett was very much more to her taste than old Buckworth senior had been. There were few eligible men about so it was easy for her to fancy herself in love with him, despite the disfiguring scars across his body, and those other scars you could not see.

When the girl died giving birth to Victor, Henry Buckworth felt responsible in some way. He took it on himself to teach the taciturn Matchett all aspects of the printing trade and gradually gave him increased responsibility until eventually he had put him in charge of the works. He called in his lawyers and the wrought-iron gatemakers, officially altering the name from Buckworth's to Buckworth & Matchett's. Unmarried himself, and never likely to wed now, he looked on Matchett rather as a son, and Victor, as a favoured grandson.

It was an odd household then that Victor Matchett had grown up in. The elderly Buckworth brothers so different in temperament and barely on speaking terms. The benign business-like Henry and the dissolute useless Godfrey who spent his days in bed recovering from nights of excess in the town. A regular feature of life at the works was the stream of young Knibden women applying for funds to keep their babies in bread, and their own mouths shut. The child, Victor, watched his quiet haunted father slaving for the brothers. He was given to long spells of black melancholy, as dark as the ink on the Buckworth & Matchett rollers, during which he spoke to no one, not even his son.

And when Victor turned sixteen and was about to take the exams that would have taken him away from his dreary upbringing, his father caught pneumonia and died. Victor then found himself expected to take his father's place at the head of the works and it was he who now lived at the old man's beck and call. And he who saw the way Godfrey behaved with the typesetters so that the firm was always short staffed. As quickly as they took girls on they had to replace others who found themselves with child. Victor Matchett had been at the famous school prizegiving when a boy in the class above him had gone up to receive an Attendance Prize and met his father face to face for the first time. Godfrey Buckworth gazed at his son over a prize edition of Mrs Esmerald Dean's *The Good Path* and when the boy died of TB shortly afterwards, the youthful Matchett had opened the packet in which the boy's mother returned the volume.

'Good heavens!' Henry peered over Victor's shoulder and saw the note that came with the book tersely telling Godfrey Buckworth that he could keep it. 'We printed those labels for the school.' He'd taken the book and run his hand professionally over his handiwork glued on the fly-leaf. He tapped the florid red and gold printing. 'Some of Buckworth's best plates, those were.'

Then one day, shortly before the last Great Lottery, Henry Buckworth told Victor he did not think he had long to live and charged him to look after poor Godfrey and after the grand old firm of Buckworth & Matchett's. A few days later he died in his sleep. And not long after, Godfrey drowned in the canal.

'Coo!' said Beryl Laffety to her eldest son. 'You're in the luck, then. A son of mine, foreman at Buckworth & Matchett's – well, I never!' That a Laffety had found gainful employment, with an old respected Knibden firm. 'It's the dead guest's doin',' she said. 'I knew the stranger would see us right – we may not be the only Laffetys, but we are the Knibden Laffetys, after all.'

'Who was he do yer think?'

'Who cares – so long as 'e's left us 'is money.'

Gary Laffety told his mother how Belle Quinn had taken out an expensive advertisement, inviting everyone in the town to attend her tea-dance. His new boss, Victor Matchett, said the answer to the dead guest's Will would be revealed tomorrow evening during the music, dancing, flowers and food. 'Will you be going?' Gary asked his mother.

'Just try an' stop me!' Beryl replied. 'I may be a Laffety, but I've as much right to be there as anyone else. The dead guest will have heard of us Laffetys and decided to do something for us. I told Hester Jones as much, and she agreed.'

'She *agreed*?'

'She said it was "always a possibility".'

'What can she have meant by that?'

'You tell me.'

'I'll tell you, Mum! That Hester Jones 'n't right in the head.'

'How'd you mean?'

'We had all better watch out. That's what I'm saying. It'll be a good thing when this is all over an' she takes 'erself off.'

'Yeh – but it'll only be a good thing if *we* gets the money. I couldn't bear to see anyone else . . . That Hilda Parbold, for instance, who's set her heart on buying up the Bensusanns'.'

'Or Bill Parris,' put in her son. And then Gary Laffety put his hands in his pockets and started whistling.

'You watch it!' she said. 'That's a good job you've got there. Don't yer go and do nothing to spoil it.'

Gary laughed. He put his jacket back on to go out again on his bike. 'Just try an' stop me!' he said.

PART THREE

Friday Night/Saturday Morning

1

The Night Before

It was the night before the day of the tea-dance. By this time tomorrow, the inhabitants of Knibden all said to themselves, and to each other, we will *know* who the dead guest was, and who he's left his fortune to. Hester Jones will have made her announcement and gone on her way. The great fortune in the bank will be distributed. The excitement would be over . . .

Lights blazed from all one hundred and eighty-seven windows of the Bensusanns' – or would have done if there'd been electric light bulbs in every room. The old house looked like a great ship berthed on the hillside. Mrs Parbold had propped her mop in the kitchen and refused to go home. She poured herself a glass of stout and put her feet up. Nothing Desmond Chase could do would budge the woman. When the old General entered the kitchen to find out the cause of the brouhaha, Hilda May Parbold demanded all the wages she said she had never been paid and when the General said there was no money in his billet box she plied him with his own drink. Now the pair sat snoring in front of the cold, unblackened range and Chase was beside himself. So this was her game! The woman had got her great feet under the table by putting them there, and refusing to move.

Desmond Chase shook General Bensusann awake but the sole survivor of the Eleventh Knibdens, that had long since been disbanded, only stared at Chase as if he had never seen him before. He held out his glass. 'A top up, if you please!'

'I'll *top* you up,' Chase roared and tried to pull the old man from his chair. 'Look at the state of you – look at the state of her.'

The General glanced over in Hilda Parbold's direction. 'The last rose of summer!' he said with a wink. Then he let his jaw sag and gave out another great snore.

It was a scandal, Chase repeated, an outrage! Look what the dead guest had done – the sole survivor of the Eleventh Knibdens drinking in his kitchen with a washerwoman! Mrs Parbold was only after the stranger's millions. Couldn't the old man see that?

Of course he could – he was doing this to spite Chase. The General will become the laughing stock of Knibden. And when his army friends find out . . . But the General no longer had any army friends. The Eleventh Knibdens being disbanded. The old man, the sole survivor.

Desmond Chase stood for a moment gazing down at his employer. Could it really be true what Mrs Parbold had said? And would the truth be made public, during the tea-dance tomorrow? Shouldn't he, Desmond Chase, cut his losses, pack up his kit and be on his way, right now? Who had the dead guest been that he had sought out the great General Bertram Bensusann to punish him at his time of life? Only one man that Chase knew of would ever have been capable of such a thing – but the inestimable Lethbridge was dead, and buried somewhere outside, below the overgrown herbaceous borders. Or so the General had told Chase when he'd first come to work at the Bensusanns', nearly twenty years ago.

'I should have gone straight back down into town and caught that bus,' Desmond Chase muttered. He left the pair in the kitchen and began wandering in and out of the rooms and up and down the corridors of the Bensusanns' that once Mr Lethbridge had had charge of, employing a certain Mrs Enderby as housekeeper. As the night wore on, the lonely restless Chase began to think he heard the sound of someone tap tapping along the corridors behind him. He recalled Lethbridge's silver-topped cane. And Ottilie Vigo's dibbing stick. And he moved faster. Then faster, until he was running. Only late into the night did he realize that the footsteps that so terrified him were merely echoes of his own. At last, overcome with misery and exhaustion Desmond Chase collapsed on the stone steps at the front of the house. He huddled in the icy cold to watch the dawn come up over Knibden. The Parbold woman had got the General into her clutches, Desmond Chase thought bleakly, and unless he took prompt and drastic action, the sole survivor of the Eleventh Knibdens would never escape. The Bensusanns' would fall into Mrs Parbold's broad lap as surely as if she'd spread her skirts beneath a ripe cherry tree on a windy day. Or as if she had indeed been left a fortune by the dead guest at the Gallimore. Chase resolved to speak as soon as possible to Belle Quinn and Verity Willow. Good respected Knibden ladies, both on the committee overseeing the dead guest's Will, they must surely be able to make the General see the error of his ways. Besides, Miss Quinn was organizing the fateful tea-dance that Mrs Parbold was bent on taking advantage of. *She* should be held responsible for any abomination that ensued. Desmond Chase resolved to call on Belle Quinn first and insist that she set to at once and sort everything out.

Neville Tagg arrived late for dinner.

Mrs Wilkes-Tooley apologized as she showed him into the Wilkes-Tooley dining room where Lalla and her parents were already eating. 'I'm sorry,' she said, 'we didn't wait.'

Lalla had refused to wait. If the fellow was late, she'd told her parents, he could go without. Start as you mean to go on, she said to herself. She was wearing her peach-silk dress, the one her mother had repaired and sponged ready for the tea-dance tomorrow. As it was Lalla's only dress, it would have to do for tonight as well.

'Chain fell off your bicycle then?' Aubrey Wilkes-Tooley chuckled. 'A wild goose, the other side of town?'

Neville blinked. 'No, indeed, Sir. No.'

At first the boy offered no explanation. He sat staring at the food they placed before him, pulling at his moustaches and scarcely daring to eat. When he reached out to pass a dish down the table, as requested by Mrs Wilkes-Tooley, his untouched glass of red wine spilled over the table-cloth and had to be mopped up amid much suppressed annoyance and confusion.

'The lad is trying to tell you he would prefer a beer!' Aubrey Wilkes-Tooley attempted to make light of the little catastrophe but his daughter refused to hear. She fussed and flapped and insisted that all the plates and dishes and cutlery be taken off the table, the table wiped down and then a new cloth put back on the table and everything returned to where it had been.

Aubrey wondered now why he had invited the lad. He planned to retire to his bed as early as possible and stay there now until the tea-dance was over and whatever happened, had happened.

Neville, meanwhile, was wondering where Lalla's sisters were. Then he realized with a shock that it had already been decided for him: *Miss Lalla* was the one to wait on him hand and foot, and then accompany him to the tea-dance. This was so much in accord with his own wishes, it gave him confidence. Miracles do happen! he thought as she slapped his plate back down in front of him. He immediately began scooping the food up into his mouth. This was not the only miracle! That very afternoon, Neville had put down the bonuses he'd been collecting on all the new policies he'd sold, as a first payment on the Ford *Fiesta* of his dreams. It was sitting outside, even now, in all its glistening winter plumage. When his plate was empty he said, 'I have purchased a car.'

There was a dangerous rustle of peach silk as Lalla leaned across the table and piled another helping of food on to Neville Tagg's plate. Such expenditures would have to stop! She could not have him spending the inheritance willy-nilly, even before he knew it was his. Neville ate his way through the food so that Lalla was obliged to pile the plate high again. Again Neville emptied the plate, and again Lalla filled it. Mr and Mrs Wilkes-Tooley, aware perhaps that they were witnessing a courtship ritual unknown to them, retired discreetly for the night. Neither Neville nor Lalla noticed their departure but when they had gone, Lalla said, 'Well?'

Neville Tagg looked up for the first time that evening, straight into the full glare of Miss Lalla Wilkes-Tooley's gaze. He shielded his eyes.

'I see!' Lalla said. 'You are only prepared to disclose information to Miss Hester Jones?'

Neville shook his head. Hester Jones was the last person he would give information to. 'The documentation will all be at the Knibden Municipal Insurance Company offices,' Neville told Lalla. 'I should very much like to be let loose in there to make a proper search.'

Lalla's pointed eyebrows shot up. The idea of letting Neville Tagg loose anywhere was extraordinary. 'Indeed?'

'The sooner the better.'

'You are asking *me* to steal the keys from my father's pocket, and give them to you, Mr Tagg? You are about to produce a pistol and force me to hand them over so that you can search through confidential company records and discover how the dead stranger's millions might come to you. Is that it, Mr Tagg?'

Neville had no time to reply for Miss Lalla Wilkes-Tooley had risen from the table. 'You have transport outside, you say?'

'My Ford *Fiesta* . . .'

'We haven't a moment to lose!'

Despite the lateness of the hour, Dick Follifoot called on Edmund Veitch to ask how plans for the revival were coming along, and to suggest that the headmaster might care to publish his scheme in the new revised *Bugle*. Everyone was buying up every edition as it rolled off the press to keep *abreast* of the latest developments. Veitch should take advantage of this interest in the dead guest's fortune and the announcement that would be made at the tea-dance tomorrow, to push his revival. 'The time is ripe,' Follifoot said.

Edmund Veitch nodded. He'd expected this, he said.

Follifoot was surprised. He had been shown into the head-master's study by Miss Chickie Wilkes-Tooley, the youngest of the Wilkes-Tooley sisters – and that was surprising too.

'Oh yes,' Veitch assured his visitor. 'Ever since the guest died, I have seen it coming. A new order will prevail, Mr Follifoot. Knibden will never be the same after the tea-dance tomorrow. The dead guest will hail in the dawn of a new . . .'

Chickie Wilkes-Tooley rushed round the room nodding, and reminding Follifoot of one of those little dogs with detached heads in the back of cars, put there to infuriate anyone driving behind. When Chickie came to a halt she offered Mr Follifoot a chair.

As the builder sat down, the headmaster stood up. Clapping his hands behind his back, Edmund Veitch began to pace the carpet. 'Change is in the air! We all feel it. Knibden is waking up to its former glory. Even old men like Bill Parris, and Bertram Bensusann, will soon feel the effects.' Although it was dark and the schoolchildren had long since gone home, he paused beside the window to peer across the school yard and check no one was doing anything they shouldn't. Meanwhile, he said, he would send Mr Matchett details of the revival to go in the paper. Veitch turned back from the window and beamed. Chickie clapped her hands.

Follifoot said he thought Veitch would do well to take out a

273

full-page advertisement immediately. This may cost money but it would encourage tardier, less-public-spirited folk in the town to also show a proper interest in their *Bugle*. And in the revival. He understood Belle Quinn had already placed an advertisement for the tea-dance in each of the next five editions . . .

Chickie Wilkes-Tooley, perched behind an enormous typewriter on a little side desk that was far too small for her, nodded enthusiastically. 'Then we must too,' she yelped. And rolling a fresh sheet of paper into the typewriter, she heaved the carriage return and began typing out the copy straight away. 'I can deliver it to Buckworth & Matchett's on my way home.'

Buckworth & Matchett's was *not* on Chickie's way home – in fact it was a nasty walk down a dark canal path – but Follifoot saw no reason to point this out. He wished the pair 'a good evening!' and hurried to his next port of call.

Follifoot had a team of men starting on the great glass dome of the museum. And another team at the site of the Alhambra. He would call on George Allendale first thing in the morning and then on Michael Milady, also, to collect the monies due up front. Speed is of the essence, Dick Follifoot, sole trader and builder of Knibden, would tell them both. The more work he could get started before the tea-dance, the better placed he and his consortium would be to take advantage of the new situation that would prevail when the dead guest's heir was announced. It was anyone's guess who was going to get it, he'd told Treadgold and Macready. They should spread their options and mop up. (What he did not tell Treadgold and Macready was that he had called at the Gallimore and offered Hester Jones a sizeable sum of money to tip him the wink. The incorruptible Miss Jones had stared at him. 'I'll pretend I didn't hear that,' she had said. 'Furthermore, when I write my account, I will put this conversation into a parenthesis no one is likely to read.' Follifoot grinned. 'You can't blame me for trying,' he said. 'As yet, Mr Follifoot,' Miss Jones had replied, 'I don't *blame* you for anything.' 'Pleased to hear it, Miss,' Follifoot mumbled, and went on his way.)

Michael Milady had been more encouraging. 'The committee will look very favourably . . .' he'd said. Well, of course the committee would look very favourably – Follifoot and his friends were *on* the committee. Hadn't Dr Treadgold signed the death certificate and Follifoot notched up the dead guest's coffin? Milady could see no objection to work commencing right away. The sooner the better, he'd said. Even Mr Williams from the bank was not averse. Head office had been pleased with the extraordinary amount of new business their manager had reported being transacted in the town since his arrival. Fechnie had let the branch tick along, they said. We should have seen it earlier, and put him out to grass. When William Williams repeated this to his wife, Dora laughed at the picture of her husband's predecessor, Theodore Fechnie, as an old horse with large yellow teeth, lazily grazing.

Chickie Wilkes-Tooley typed letter after letter. Her head and fingers ached, but her heart sang. *'A. S. D. F. G. – Edmund Veitch, How I love thee!'* The more she typed the more awake she felt, and the more terribly lovesick than ever. Chickie had spent money from her savings buying a better brand of paper, a crinkled parchment that added extra authority to Veitch's copious dictations.

Samuel Till ran countless errands for Chickie – his alacrity fuelled by shiny fifty-pence pieces from her purse. Heaven knows how he'd persuaded someone to sell him the crinkled parchment at this time of night but the boy evidently had his sources. Chickie had grown used to his freckled face materializing beside her, his small hard eyes locating her handbag as he asked if there was 'Anything, Miss,' he could do 'to help?' She did not like the way the boy jostled her, and stood too close, touching her elbow and picking at the things on her desk but she endured his unpleasant attentions because Mr Veitch was so heartened by the child's eagerness to please. He took this improvement in Samuel Till as a clear sign his own great schemes for the town were working.

'If you had *any idea* of the delinquence of these Tills!' the headmaster said to Chickie who leant towards him as he now described how Mr Till had been a butcher until he'd chopped off one of his fingers while disputing an unpaid bill with a customer. No one wanted meat from Mr Till after that and when the police were called to the shop, it was a while before they realized that the sizeable carcass suspended from the hook above the bench was not a pig, or a sheep, but Mr Till himself. They cut him down with his own cleaver but the suicide of the bankrupt butcher had not put an end to the steady stream of little Tills born into this world. Mrs Till was as reckless with her favours as her husband had been with his fingers. Veitch said he had long ago lost count how many Till children there'd been in the school. 'There's at least one in every class, and they're all as bad as each other.'

Chickie Wilkes-Tooley lapped up the information eagerly. She had never been into the Silver Scissors Salon because she wore her hair long to save the expense, but she now told Mr Veitch that she did have some idea about the delinquency of the Tills because the eldest of the Till children had a reputation. She could not bring herself to mention how her own sister, Lalla, was for some unfathomable reason taking an interest in Susie Till's boyfriend, Neville Tagg. Nor that she herself planned to visit the Silver Scissors first thing in the morning, to have her hair bobbed for the tea-dance. And to sound Susie out about Lalla's interest in the fellow.

When Follifoot, Treadgold and Macready met in the Swan, they debated whether the headmaster had bedded Miss Chickie yet. Follifoot thought he had, Treadgold and Macready were not so certain. He'll be savouring the pleasure, they said. Keeping her back like a tit-bit on the pantry shelf, for some special occasion. Like after the tea-dance.

Calderon did not join in the speculation. He had his own concerns. He and Barbara were doing their best to make Janice Oakes's life miserable, but the barmaid ignored their efforts to send her packing and stood steadfastly behind her beer pumps, a grim determined look upon her face, as if she were a heroine in an old-fashioned painting of a ship going down, all hands to attention on deck. She asked everyone who came through the Swan's swing doors how Hester Jones was getting on. Did she know the answer yet? Who had the dead guest been, and who was going to get his great fortune? Follifoot, Treadgold and Macready stared at the tight sweater that revealed more than it concealed of Janice's shapely bosom, and they asked what possible concern it could be of hers? The barmaid said the three of them would have to wait and find out. Macready muttered that you didn't have to wait, you could see all you needed from where he was sitting. Follifoot slapped his thigh.

*

Verity Willow tossed and turned. The dead guest offered her a whisky sour but she turned from him. Then Hester Jones demanded to know why Knibden's assistant librarian had resigned and when Miss Willow tossed back some answers, Miss Jones refused to listen to them. I don't need to hear what you have to say, she said. I know already.

'Most particularly you are not to tell Belle!' Bast had said. 'Not *Belle*, of all people!' Why was Miss Quinn busily organizing the tea-dance? What had Raymond Bast known all those years ago about her friend, Belle Quinn, that Verity and her mother had not known? I shall call on her first thing in the morning and ask if she remembers our lodger, Harry Best, Verity decided.

Verity went on tossing and turning. Hester Jones has not questioned me! Verity Willow thought. The girl may not be a Poirot, or a Miss Marple or even a Randolphe Shyne but she would know the first law of whodunnits: the most likely culprit is the least obvious suspect. She is lying low waiting for me to give myself, and Raymond Bast/Harry Best, away! One false move . . .

And one thing, at least, was certain, he *would* have been in touch if he could. Verity sighed. He *would* have been there at the Gallimore taking tea that morning, if it had been possible. Verity sat bolt upright in her bed. She was awake now. More awake than she had ever been. She had always assumed he was out there somewhere in the world, her schoolgirl stitches in his jacket, and one sunny day he would come back. Now, of course, she questioned this. If it had been possible to return, he'd have done so. If not to see her, at least he'd have come for the guest at the Gallimore's money. Or perhaps he *had* sent someone. Maybe the dead guest had come on his behalf, with a message that would have explained everything but which the poor man had not had time to deliver. Maisie Vollutu would end her days without ever knowing that Randolphe Shyne had tried to get in touch. It would be a poignant melancholy ending that would have been beautiful in a book. It would make you weep and feel better about your own life.

Now Verity Willow felt angry. As angry as Dora Williams over the fate of Madame Bovary. *It was all very well* in a Bast thriller, but in reality, Miss Maisie Vollutu yearning for Shyne to return, could spend her days doing a routine job that did not tax her but which kept her in some boring out-of-the-way place where she knew he could always find her. The years would pass, she would grow old and infirm, and childless, her fair hair would turn imperceptibly silver – and still he would not come. Eventually she would die with only a clock ticking in the room for company. For all that she had once been loved by Randolphe Shyne, Maisie Vollutu would be no better off than Lavinia Lobb hanging round the public library, complaining about any changes that were made and yearning for the young men who had cheered her goal at the hockey match, marched off to battle. Missing. Presumed Dead.

So where was Raymond Bast if even the dead guest's money had not brought him back? *Either* he was dead – and the death of a loved one is always unthinkable – *or* he had fallen into the hands of an enemy! Tomorrow at the tea-dance, Verity thought, I must be vigilant . . .

And, as she tossed and turned, it seemed impossible to Verity Willow that Hester Jones did not already know what the assistant librarian of Knibden had done to deserve her sorrows. 'I shall confess,' she said bravely into the darkness. 'During a break in the dancing, I will take Miss Jones aside and tell her all she wants to know.'

When the front-door bell of the Gallimore Hotel rang late that night, Daniel Mason woke with a start. He groaned, and visions of another guest coming to die on premises managed by himself, and the whole nightmare starting all over again, were only dispelled when Mason opened the door to find Belle Quinn standing there. He was so relieved to see the good woman he admitted her at once, and returned to his desk to resume his snooze.

Mrs Mason was also surprised, but not at all pleased to see Belle back at the Gallimore again that night, so late.

'I just thought I would take one final look,' Belle said as she bustled in. 'I couldn't sleep if I thought there might be some tiny thing we haven't taken care of.' Belle felt like a bride the night before her wedding, checking and rechecking her wardrobe in readiness for the big day.

'How *good* you are!' Mrs Mason sighed.

Belle smiled. An advertisement was to appear in five consecutive editions of the new, revised *Knibden Bugle,* Belle now told Mrs Mason. The presses at Buckworth & Matchett's would be rolling all through the night. There'd be no one in the town who would not hear about the tea-dance. 'I want *everyone* to feel invited – it is what the dead guest would want.'

Mrs Mason nodded. She had been in the hotel business long enough to know that such an advertisement could cause trouble. The dance would be impossibly crowded, and could easily get out of control. Then Miss Quinn would rush about wringing her hands, while others coped with a situation she, in her goodness, had foolishly created.

Belle Quinn was now mounting the main flight of stairs that led to the great ballroom. 'I thought I would take one more look at the floor. And the chandeliers . . .' Belle was particularly proud of the chandeliers. When the repolishing of the ballroom floor had been finished, its sheen had made the Gallimore's blackened chandeliers look dull. Miss Quinn threw up her hands in horror, and quickly arranged for them to be taken down and cleaned by a professional team of chandelier cleaners. Painters had also been called in to brighten the walls. Gilders to touch up the mirrors. Belle had discovered that by offering large sums of money, people could be persuaded to drop whatever they were doing, wherever they were doing it, and rush to Knibden to perform miracles at a moment's notice. 'I can't believe how much we have accomplished in so short a time,' Belle enthused. In saying 'we' she was, of course, being kind. Mrs Mason may have done much of the work, but it was Belle who had organized it all.

'Do go home, Miss Quinn!' Mrs Mason urged at last. 'You *must* get some rest – or you'll be far too tired to enjoy the dance yourself. Doris and the girls can easily see to what little's left to do in the morning. Why, Hester Jones is already in bed, fast asleep.' The manageress of the Gallimore Hotel gestured down the corridor towards the room where the dead guest had died, and where his investigator was now sleeping. 'I called in and checked on her just now.'

'Did you?' So! Belle thought, she was not the only one checking up on Miss Jones. 'I suppose,' Belle said to Eileen Mason in a whisper, 'since Miss Jones is sleeping, she must know the answer! She must *know* who the dead guest was. And who he left his fortune to.' It was an astonishing thought and both women glanced in some alarm along the corridor that led to Hester Jones's closed bedroom door. The corridor down which the dead guest had walked, and back along which he had had to be carried.

'I am sure Miss Jones *does* know,' Mrs Mason agreed. 'Either that, or she is very close to arriving at the truth.'

Belle shivered. Suddenly Belle found she was barely able to keep her eyes open. 'I *shall* sleep well tonight,' she remarked.

'You deserve to!' Mrs Mason smiled. 'You are a miracle worker.' She left Belle at the top of the stairs that led down to the main front door. Inwardly she sighed. Miss Quinn was too impossibly virtuous. Surely the ballroom floor hadn't needed a complete repolishing! And did the chandeliers really have to be taken down and cleaned quite so elaborately? As for painting the walls and gilding the mirrors – just for a Saturday evening tea-dance! Why had a tea-dance been organized in the first place? Hadn't the unknown guest's death, and mysterious Will, caused disruption enough already? Eileen Mason wondered whether she would not wake up Hester Jones at once and ask to be put out of her misery. Tell me who the dead stranger was? she would plead. And who is to inherit his fortune – whoever they are they will be our new employer. Haven't we a right to know? We should never have allowed Mr Theodore Fechnie at the bank to run rings round us. We see that now. When he offered us the job we should have told him the terms were unacceptable. My Donald would never have allowed his poor mother to get mixed up in these peculiar arrangements, and if he were here today, he wouldn't stand for Belle Quinn bossing me about like this, either. Why has that indefatigably good woman gone to all this trouble and expense? What has she got on her conscience? I have been in the hotel business long enough, the tired Mrs Mason thought, to know that Belle Quinn is a woman with something to hide.

At the foot of the staircase, Belle glanced at the sleeping figure of Mr Mason slumped at his desk, and could not resist entering the Gallimore's lounge for a quick rest before walking home. I am not as young as I used to be, she thought, as she shook off her shoes. She lay back for one long luxurious moment on one of the hotel's deep sofas. Tomorrow morning there might be a letter in the post from Fleur: *I, too, no longer know what we quarrelled about, dear Belle, though we were probably always quarrelling. Sisters do. And as for the little problem you mention, I will certainly make inquiries. I dare say someone here in Penzance must know your Hester Jones. Meanwhile, WHO was this mysterious guest at the Gallimore? WHY did he die – did someone POISON him? Or was it death by suffocation? I am dying to hear more! What fun if you or I should suddenly find ourselves rich. Goodness knows, I could do with the money . . .*

Typical of Fleur. Always quarrelling! It takes two to quarrel but even as children Belle had never had a portion of her younger sister's energy and anger. The first thing Fleur had done when she'd grown her first tooth was crawl across the floor and sink it neatly into her sister's arm. Belle still had a tiny red scar just above her left elbow. If their father had always shown a preference for Belle, it had been because Fleur's temper made her unlovable as a child. She had been equally headstrong as a young woman. Always contradicting poor Father for the sake of it. Making fun of his scientific pronouncements, just because *she* could not understand them. Why had Fleur gone off to Penzance? There had obviously been some reason Belle had not known. A reason that was about to come to light . . .

All those years the Reverend Gilbert Duncie Sibson had accepted invitations to Sunday dinner at the Laurels, and cigars afterwards from her father's box, the man had sat at the far end of the Quinns' dining table eating food Belle had prepared and occasionally making idle conversation which poor dear Father, his head full of his own great thoughts, had done his best to engage with.

Harold Augustus Quinn put up with Gilbert Sibson's empty chatter for *my* sake, Belle thought fondly. True, Gilbert had steadfastly ignored Fleur's ostentatious flirtations, but he had also overlooked Belle's quiet tributes that ought not to have been overlooked. It was as though he'd had something perpetually on his mind that blocked out all other interests. Then one day, Fleur had cheekily piped up and asked Mr Sibson why he had never married.

'Hush!' Belle said, attempting a sharp kick under the table. She caught poor Father by mistake and the old man had yelped in pain. Despite the convenient diversion, Sibson had been frank in his reply.

'If I'd won the Great Knibden Lottery,' he burst out, 'how different my life might have been! I might have married . . .'

'Really?' Fleur's eyes opened wide. She ignored the warning flashes darting across the table from her elder sister's eyes. '*Who* would you have married?'

'Miss Zillanah Hartley, I suppose . . .'

That evening, the young Belle sat down at her mother's rosewood desk to write Gilbert Sibson a letter. Only when her pen was poised over the paper had she realized there was nothing to say. She could make no break since there had been nothing to break. Instead, for a while after, and also after Fleur had suddenly left the Laurels (leaving a note saying she had gone to Penzance and would send an address later), Belle had gone on inviting the man to dine. Out of habit, and not wanting to do anything that would further disrupt the household routine and upset poor Father. On those last Sundays, without the loud presence of Fleur, and unhampered by her own foolish hopes, Belle had been shocked to notice things about the man that she had not observed in all the time when she had thought of him as someone she might marry. Gilbert Sibson drank more than was good for him. And when the drink was in him Sibson talked incessantly about that lottery ticket he'd once purchased. He had been slumbered with a naked woman, he complained, whereas the owner of the self-same dragon . . .

Belle sighed. Belle slept. 'Where there is a man, there must be a woman, don't you think?'

'It seems likely!'

Belle heard her own voice again, 'The dead man, the guest at the Gallimore – I *know* who he was.'

'Are *you* the woman then, Belle?'

Miss Quinn laughed, and said lightly, 'I might be.'

'So might *anyone*, for all that you've told me.'

'Yes,' Belle conceded. 'It still could be anyone. It will be up to Hester Jones, of course, and she – it would seem – already knows the answer.'

'If it *is* you, Belle, what will you do with all the money?'

'First, I shall probably have to pay for this tea-dance! It has cost considerably more than we anticipated. I have never been a woman to do things by halves. Then, if I have any left over after that . . .

'Come now, there are *millions* in the bank. There will be more than enough left, even with all the repolishing, cleaning, gilding and painting to do anything you want . . .'

'I should like to use it to publish *The Complete Works of Harold Augustus Quinn*. In twelve beautifully gold-tooled, leather-bound volumes. It is a project I have long had in mind but, somehow, never got round to. Perhaps I have been frightened of the expense – I have sufficient to live on comfortably of course, but to print the works properly would be beyond my means. I have not had the courage. But now . . . I can see it so clearly – *The Cold Sun, A Work in 12 parts*. Harold Augustus Quinn's ideas will be made public at last. And if ignorant people scoff, I shall be strong enough now to defend him. Yes, I will pay Buckworth & Matchett's to print it all beautifully, in numbered order, and with fine calf bindings just as dear Daddy would have liked.'

'A noble ambition, Belle. You are a good woman. You were a good daughter. No one in Knibden is more deserving. I am sure Hester Jones will see this also. I'm sure there is *nothing* about you that Miss Jones does not *already* know.'

Belle sat up abruptly. For the first time, she looked directly at her companion, who now said, 'And, *I* should so like to share your good fortune with you! Perhaps you could leave the Laurels and come and live with me at the rectory – as you wanted to, all those years ago. I dare say we are too old now to cause a scandal.'

Belle stared. Only now did she comprehend whom she had been conversing with. The Reverend Gilbert Duncie Sibson went blithely on, 'We can end our days together, in luxury. How nice it will be to heat the old rectory properly. And do some of the much needed repairs to the church. The blessed St Redegule deserves better than that nasty concrete plinth the builder Follifoot was pleased to throw together. And when Dick Follifoot rebuilds the Alhambra, you and I can go to the theatre *every evening*, if we choose. Why, we'll take a box – and with it, our rightful place at last in Knibden society. Oh, dearest Belle . . .' The Reverend Sibson grew impassioned. He reached out one of his long dry cold hands towards her. 'Forgive me, my love, my own darling! I made a mistake once, but we were young then. Too young. The dead guest seeks now to put it all right.'

Belle recoiled. She refused to take Sibson's hand. 'Young? Like Beatrice Wilkes-Tooley?' she asked sharply.

'Oh, Belle – you're not jealous?'

'No!' Then Belle softened. 'Well, maybe I am, a little.'

'My own darling!'

How Belle had yearned once for such endearments to pass his lips. 'I gave you my heart, Gilbert. You never even bothered to snap it in two. I loved you for years, but you . . .'

'Don't you see, Belle, I was not nearly good enough for you. The goodness of Belle Quinn was well known whereas I drank too much. I was always so wracked with self-pity and bitterness. I had been stuck with a naked woman when *if only* I'd had the dragon! I have had to live my life with the terrible knowledge that if I had had the *same number* on my ticket, but a dragon instead, *I'd have won*! I'd have been rich – I could have done *anything*. You and I could have married at once, and not had to wait until the dead guest made you rich. I have cursed the naked woman with all the venom in my soul. Because of her I lost you and have had to content myself till now with a plaster effigy on an ugly concrete plinth. But now, now there is money after all . . .'

Miss Quinn took a deep breath. 'Mr Sibson, money should not have made a difference then. It cannot be allowed to make a difference now. Wealth ought only to be won by hard work or accomplishment. If there *is* to be this money, it has come too late. The lives we might have led are closed to us. For ever. Besides, if I *do* inherit the dead stranger's money, if indeed I am to be rich, it is impossible I can ever marry you.'

'Why, Belle?'

'I would know for certain you would only be marrying me for the guest at the Gallimore's money. As it is, I shall be happy to spend it all printing my father's works. The works you and my sister both found so funny.'

'Your sister made fun of me . . .'

'Fleur made fun of everyone. It was her way. She will have been making fun of people in Penzance all these years. She even made fun of the dead stranger in her letter just now. As if the guest at the Gallimore could have been *poisoned* or *suffocated*! She would have made fun of Hester Jones if the girl had gone to Penzance, instead of wandering into the Swan that evening . . .'

A youth put his head round the door. 'Belle Quinn?' he asked.

Belle sat up hurriedly. 'I must have dozed off,' she said as she shook herself. The Reverend Sibson had *not* been there. He had not declared himself. She glanced at her watch: it was past midnight.

'You've let your carriage turn into a pumpkin!' The young man laughed. 'The bloke on the desk told me I would find you in here. He was fast asleep too, I had to wake 'im.'

'Oh dear, that will have been Mr Mason. His wife and I have been preparing for the . . .' Belle slipped her feet into her shoes, and stood up shakily. 'Have you come for the tea-dance?'

'Tea-dance?'

'Everyone is invited.'

The youth laughed again. 'Even me?' He advanced on her. 'I'm Sol,' he introduced himself. 'Your nephew.'

'My . . .' Belle began. The youth nodded and grinned. '*Sol?*' Belle Quinn sat down again quickly. Yes, Fleur *had* had a son. She had written and told them so in one of the few letters that had come a long time ago from Penzance. Belle had not given Fleur the satisfaction of writing back, and asking for further details, so she had never known the child's name. The youth had a great gaping hole in one shoe and there was mud all over his clothes.

'I've been sleeping rough to get here,' he said. He looked rough – his chin was unshaven, his face and hands were engrained with dirt. Belle clasped the edge of the sofa tightly.

'Daddy died in my arms,' she murmured. 'Fleur had gone away. I wrote to the address she had given in Penzance, telling her how ill he was but she did not want to know. I hoped she would come at the last and bring the boy to see him, but we had had one disagreement too many. I have seen that in families, disputes can be patched until there comes a point where the final argument about something seemingly trivial puts an end to all communication for ever. The invisible bonds snap. Love dies.'

'Mum said something similar.'

Belle looked sharply at Sol. 'You will stay with me, I hope? While you are in Knibden.'

'Yeh.'

'Sol – that is short for Solomon?'

Fleur's son shrugged. 'Dunno what it's "short" for,' he said. There was nothing short about Sol. Belle wondered how the lad would fit into the Laurels with all her fine Georgian furniture and hand-painted porcelain. 'Your mother – she got my letter. She sent you, by way of reply?'

'She doesn't know. I don't like Mum knowing my business.'

Belle nodded. It was hardly surprising that with his parentage Sol had a secretive independent streak. She smiled and clasped her hands together. 'So,' she said, standing up. 'You are Harold Quinn's grandson! How proud he would have been to see you back here, in Knibden. And *I* am glad you have looked me up at last. My nephew!' She took him by the hand and tried not to see how bitten down his nails were and grimy with dirt. The boy obviously needed looking after. Fleur would have been as careless a mother as she had been a daughter and sister.

Sol watched her through narrowed eyes. He doesn't altogether trust me, Belle thought. Fleur will have put ideas about me into his head which at least I shall now have a chance to disprove. Belle could not be sorry the boy had apparently deceived his mother and come to Knibden of his own accord to see her. It would serve Fleur right if her son were to find out the truth for himself. Of course Sol was probably only hoping for something from the dead stranger's Will – Belle allowed herself to acknowledge this. And yet, what did people's motives matter if what they *did* in the end was sound? 'It is late, dear. I have kept poor Mr Mason up long enough as it is. We had better be getting home. Where are your things?'

'At your place.'

'You have been to my house?'

Sol nodded.

As they neared the Laurels, Belle fished in her pocket for her key. She was sure she had not left so many lights on. Then she saw the front door open and a figure emerge. 'My girl,' Sol said indicating the scrawny creature who came to meet them down Belle's own path.

'You found her then?' the girl asked him.

Belle stared at the pair, dumbfounded.

'You weren't at home so I climbed in through an upstairs

window and opened the door,' Sol explained. He grinned. His girl smiled.

'Like a burglar!' Belle said.

'If you say so,' Sol shrugged.

'It's kind of quaint this place,' the girl said. She had a thin whining voice that perfectly matched her body. She disentangled herself from Sol's embrace and, seizing Miss Quinn by the arm, steered her deftly indoors. 'And you've got such nice pretty things everywhere. Loads of 'em.'

There was a strong smell of fried food. 'Have you been cooking?' Belle asked.

'Good, I'm famished,' Sol said.

'The kitchen's through here.' Again the girl led the way.

Belle thought, I must be patient. I can spare a little food – it is a long way from Penzance and they probably haven't eaten for days. I will sort all this out better in the morning. She went briefly into her kitchen only to avert her eyes from the piles of dirty saucepans and plates, opened tins and food taken from the fridge and left uncovered. 'I will say "goodnight",' she said tightly.

'Aren't you going to eat with us?' Sol asked jauntily as he banged some of her best china down on the table.

Belle shook her head. 'I have had a long day. I won't tell you to "make yourselves at home" – I can see you've been doing that already.'

'Thank you, Auntie!' Before she could evade him, Sol had clamped one of his great rough arms round her shoulder. He smelled of sweat and grass. An animal smell which reminded Belle of a boisterous kitten Fleur had once adopted. Porgie, it had been called. Georgie-Porgie pudding and pie . . .

'Yeh, goodnight, Auntie!' the girl echoed. If anything, her clothes were dirtier and tattier than Sol's. They clung to her thin little body.

Belle went thankfully to bed. When she woke again it was completely daylight, but the house was quiet. It had all been a bad dream, she thought. Just like that strange conversation she had had in the lounge of the Gallimore with Gilbert Sibson! Brought on, no doubt, by excitement over the tea-dance. The dance was costing a lot more than expected. Michael Milady had called an emergency committee meeting first thing that morning

– she must hurry along. She would offer to pay for all the expenses she had incurred. They probably wouldn't accept, but she would offer in any case. No wonder she found herself dreaming of inheriting the dead guest's money!

Belle bathed and dressed. I must rise above such pettiness, she thought as she dabbed generous drops of lilac scent behind her ears. It was only money after all – there were other more important things to think about. Like what she could possibly have meant when she'd told the Reverend Sibson in her dream that she *knew* who the guest at the Gallimore was? I must have meant *something* by that, she mused, and if I *do* know who the poor man was, it is hardly surprising I have disturbing dreams.

Tonight the whole town would know for certain. It seemed unthinkable. Hester Jones would mount the podium and ask Albert Hodge and his Band for silence. Then she would take the microphone and tell the town who had inherited the fortune. Just like that. But before she did so, she would ask for a vote of thanks for Belle Quinn, for all her sterling efforts to make the evening such a pleasant and memorable . . .

Belle heard a noise across the landing. When she went to investigate she discovered Sol and his girl were no dream. They lay fast asleep, sprawled naked across one another on top of the big bed in Harold Quinn's bedroom. Belle had kept the bed made up fresh each day, though it had not been slept in since Daddy had died.

Downstairs every room had been disturbed. In Daddy's study the glass door to his bookcase stood open. Papers and books had been moved, a few taken out, one manuscript lay upturned on the floor. She picked it up. *An Inverted Universe, fully described and illustrated by Harold Augustus Quinn, Mathematician.*

The boy is after his inheritance, Belle thought. Fleur will have told him of their father's brilliance and naturally he'll have wanted to see for himself. She flattened out bent pages and arranged the neatly sewn manuscripts back into their proper order on the shelves. Young Solomon must always have known he would come to Knibden one day, she mused. It will have been something he felt he had to do before he could go out into the world and distinguish himself in whatever field his talents lay. Not that Sol's talents were obvious yet. But after this visit to the

Laurels they would emerge. For dear Daddy's sake, I must do all I can for the boy.

The prospect of such imminent beneficence being required on her part at once put Belle in a better mood. She smoothed her short cropped hair, tied on an apron and began tidying the kitchen – although it was impossible to know where to begin. She was at the sink bravely scrubbing one of her best copper pans that looked as if it had been dropped on the floor when the girl, wearing Belle's woollen paisley shawl, and nothing underneath it, came in.

'Oh, don't do that!' she said, seizing the dented dirty pan from Belle. 'Sol and I will see to the dishes. D'you want a cup of tea?'

Belle said rather faintly that she thought she did and allowed herself to be hustled from the room. She felt hot and feverish. She had probably caught a chill while sitting in Mr Matchett's windowless office and then struggling back along that dank over-grown canal path. Belle considered asking the girl to pop out and buy her a copy of the *Knibden Bugle*. She would so like to see the advertisement . . .

It was while they were traversing the hall that Desmond Chase appeared like a madman at the front door. 'He has been kid-napped by the enemy!' Chase yelled. 'Before long he'll be com-pletely brainwashed – it may already be too late. The debriefing will be in progress. His resistance weakened by stout. He'll find himself divulging all kinds of . . .'

Belle gazed at the fellow. 'My dear Mr Chase,' she began. She glanced as if for guidance at the girl whose tight lips had settled into a suspicious sneer.

'The General has fallen into enemy hands, Miss Quinn! You must come at once before it is too late.'

'I – I'm not sure I can do that, Mr Chase,' Belle said faintly. 'I cannot go anywhere this morning.' She put the back of her hand to her burning forehead.

'It's a disaster – only *you* can save him!'

'I am sorry you have difficulties, Mr Chase. But I, too, am a little occupied just now. I wonder if you could fetch me a copy of the *Knibden Bugle* . . .'

Desmond Chase glared furiously at Belle and took no notice of the scrawny girl wrapped in a paisley shawl who gripped her firmly by the arm. '*You* will be responsible, Miss Quinn,' he spat nastily. 'It's *your* tea-dance I reckon that has done all the damage.'

'I . . .' Belle faltered. Her head spun. 'If there is any *damage*, Mr Chase, you must speak to Michael Milady, on the committee. Or Daniel Mason at the hotel. Or William Williams at the bank. A large insurance policy was very sensibly taken out to cover any damage. If it is really urgent, you might go directly and see Mr Wilkes-Tooley at the Knibden Municipal Company's offices. I'm sure one of them will be better able to help . . .'

Alerted by the sound of raised voices, Sol came lurching down Miss Quinn's tiny stairs attired only in underpants and vest. There was shaving cream smeared across his face and neck, and he was studiously engaged in sharpening Harold Quinn's razor on a short leather strop. He stared at the visitor and then waved the razor in Chase's direction. 'Who's this then?' he demanded of Belle. 'He giving you trouble, or what?'

'Oh no, no trouble at all,' Belle Quinn said quickly.

'If he's suggesting you ought to get rid of us . . .'

'Whyever would he do that?' Belle was astonished at the idea. 'Let me introduce Mr Desmond Chase, General Bensusann's err . . .' She did not like to say 'manservant' though that was probably what the fellow was. 'And this is Sol – Solomon, my nephew. Fleur's son. He has come to stay.' Despite the difficulties of the situation, the sharpened razor and Mr Chase's disbelieving stare, Belle found herself enjoying the sensation of having a nephew to introduce to people. A young man who had sought her out of his own accord, without Fleur knowing. She felt dizzy.

Desmond Chase was disconcerted. He had not been aware Miss Quinn had any family and he did not like the look of the razor. 'Pardon me, Miss, I didn't know you had guests else I wouldn't have interrupted,' he muttered, backing away. 'I'll not disturb you further.' He turned on his heel and beat a quick, undignified retreat up the garden path.

'Oh, Mr Chase!' Belle cried after him. She hoped she had not offended the man. She wondered what he had wanted.

Sol snarled loud enough for the fleeing Chase to hear. But Desmond Chase's thoughts were already elsewhere. He must seek Verity Willow out at the public library and hope that lady proved more help.

Sol banged the door shut and slid the bolt. 'Can't be too careful, Auntie,' he said to Belle. 'A woman on her own like you! A man like that . . .' He escorted Miss Quinn into her sitting room.

Gratefully, Belle sat down. Here, at least, little appeared to have been moved -although when she looked closely the bureau flap had evidently been pulled down and all the tiny fitted drawers inside taken out and put back, their contents jammed carelessly in. Belle wondered what the pair were looking for – and what they had found.

Sol said, 'He courtin' you, or something?'

Belle bit her lip. Was this the reputation her sister had given her? 'Did Fleur mention . . .'

'Mention what?' The girl came in carrying two mugs of tea. She gave Sol one and sipped from the other. 'Blimey!' she said. 'I clean forgot, Auntie. I'll go an' – no, here! Have this!' She handed Belle the mug she had been drinking from. There were clots of tea leaves floating about on the surface. 'You was saying?'

'I only wondered if Fleur ever mentioned Gilbert Sibson?' Belle struggled to extract a tea leaf that had wedged itself between her teeth.

'Your fancy man?'

'Not exactly – well, in a way, perhaps.' She wished Sol would stop waving Daddy's razor about.

'Oh yeh!' Sol said at once. 'Mum mentioned *him* all right. You and Gilbert Sibson were going at it hammer and tongs at one time.'

Belle stared at the youth with the hideous mask of white shaving cream still plastered all over his face.

'Like a couple of randy rabbits – it was the talk of the town, she said, what with you being so respectable, and the daughter of a distinguished mathematician. A disgrace! She were that ashamed of all the scandal she had to leave.'

'Goodness!' Belle gasped. It hadn't occurred to her before that Fleur had left Knibden because of anything *she* . . .

'I doubt if "goodness" had much to do with it!' Sol and the girl both smirked.

'No, I don't suppose it did,' Belle said quietly.

'You never married, then?' Sol asked. He and the girl were watching her closely.

'No,' Belle admitted. Then, so there could be no further talk on the subject, she added, 'These days Mr Sibson loves another.'

Later, when Sol and the girl were clattering about in the kitchen, tidying up she supposed, she heard the girl's thin underfed voice imitating her own, 'These days Mr Sibson loves another!'

Oh dear, thought Belle. Sol may have come here of his own accord, but even so he has been sent by Fleur to punish me. It is as well dear Daddy isn't about, I would hate him to have seen . . .

Belle clutched her heart. It had missed a beat. She shut her eyes. She would never have thought it possible to be *glad* of Daddy's death. After all these years so steadfastly missing him. Every morning when she opened the curtains in his room. Every night when she closed them and wished him 'goodnight'. Yet now, here she was, actually *glad* he was not alive still to see Sol and his girl taking over the house. They have inherited the earth, she whispered, and all that therein is. They have a right to dirty my kitchen and wear my paisley shawl. She started to weep. You can no more stand in the way of the oncoming generation than you can stop the waves of the sea rushing in with the tide. This was surely a rule of the universe not even Daddy's clever mathematical equations could ever manage to invert.

2

Knibden Breakfasts

The morning of the tea-dance dawned bright and clear. Everyone in the town, except Miss Jones, was up bright and early.

'It's the big day, today!' Edmund Veitch remarked to his wife as he helped himself expansively to several slices of thick toast. These he proceeded to martial on his plate.

Louisa blenched. She had barely slept. Chickie Wilkes-Tooley and her husband had been making plans and typing in the room directly below hers until five o'clock that morning, only an hour or so before. 'I loved him with all my heart,' she thought, thinking of her young first husband, David Ambrose, who had the same handsome bright blue eyes Roger had inherited. He'd been so pleased with himself at having a dragon when dragons were chosen on Day One of the lottery. That dragon had been their undoing. By the evening of Day Two he lay dead in his own blood in the darkness of a back alley, leaving her and baby Roger to make their way in the world, with nothing.

Veitch coughed emphatically.

Louisa looked up. Never mind the mysterious dead guest at the Gallimore, she thought. The large man sitting down the far end of the table, decapitating his soft boiled egg, was a complete stranger also! One with whom she had, incredibly as it seemed to her now, lived in the same house for forty years.

'My dear,' said the man who had come to her rescue. 'There is something you should know.'

For a moment longer Louisa stared. Then she cried out in blind terror, making the crockery and cutlery on the table ring, 'Nnnno!' Clapping her hands over her ears, she rose from her chair and ran from the room as if her very life depended on her not hearing whatever it was her second husband had been about to say.

Edmund Veitch sighed. Shaking his head, he dipped one of the soldiers he'd cut from his toast into the salt heaped to the side of his plate. This he then plunged into the thick runny yolk of his egg. If only she'd listened, the headmaster thought as he chewed. If only Harriet Delilah Veitch, *née* Beales, had also heeded . . .

They had neither of them understood he preferred his eggs *hard* boiled.

Mr and Mrs Williams were up betimes also, although there was nothing unusual in this. Except that it was Saturday morning and the bank was not due to open. 'I have come to the conclusion,' Mr Williams said as he spread Golden Shred marmalade thinly on his toast, 'that my predecessor, Mr Fechnie, was *utterly unfit* for the job.'

Mrs Williams raised her eyebrows and glanced at the clock on the mantelpiece. This was undoubtedly the earliest, yet, this particular subject had been broached. I, too, shall be dreaming about Theodore Fechnie soon, she thought. He will come to me waving his secret files and offering to tell *me* who the dead stranger was. Then I will go and see Hester Jones. 'Doubtless you have heard about my dark pink winceyette dressing-gown,' I will say.

'Look at the legacy he has left me with!' William Williams went on angrily.

'I'm sure you'll sort it all out, dear,' Dora Williams smiled encouragingly. She wished her husband would not talk with quite such a full complement of toast and marmalade in his mouth.

'Of course I will!' Williams was shouting now. Tiny gobs of breakfast flew from his mouth and spattered the table-cloth. Dora watched her husband in horrified fascination. It was a miracle to her how she had ever married this man. But the unlikeliest miracles, and marriages, *do* happen, that was the nature of them. 'I always sort things out. It's men like *me* irresponsible fellows like Fechnie depend on to clear up after them. It's men like *me* that enable the Fechnies of this world to carry on as they do. I cannot think how Mr Fechnie got taken on in the first place by a bank that also employs me. And then left to his own deleterious devices for so many years. When *I* die, I assure you, I shall leave nothing untoward for *my* successor to sort . . .'

'When you die,' Dora said, 'I shall miss you, William.' She thought, If men like *you* enable men like *Fechnie* to carry on as they do, then I would say you are very much to blame, William.

Out loud again, she said, 'I heard that Theodore Fechnie bought a *trumpet* at the last lottery.'

'A trumpet?' Golden Shred slithered unhindered down William Williams's pink chin.

'Mr Fechnie's lottery ticket had a *trumpet* on, but that was the lottery when *dragons* won. So, you see, he wasted his money!'

'Ha, ha, ha! How very typical – Fechnie couldn't even get a little investment like a lottery ticket right! And to think he had charge of other people's money. Ha, ha – that trumpet tells you *all you need to know* about our Mr Theodore Fechnie!'

'Mrs Follifoot, the builder's wife, told me in the queue at the bakery yesterday.'

'The bakery!' What had Dora been doing in a bakery?

'When I bought that nice fresh bread you're eating, dear!' Dora had also been informed about that remarkable Knibden woman, Mrs Cardew/Jenks/Vestey who had done very well for herself out of insurance policies on the deaths of her husbands.

William Williams stared at the bread he'd been about to put into his mouth. Then he looked across at Dora as though he had never seen her before. Of course the woman would go to a bakery. It was the first time he had ever considered what his wife did during the day. Obviously the food she prepared for him had to be fetched. Next he would discover she frequented the local library! William Williams wiped his chin with a napkin, and scraped back his chair. Pecking Dora on the forehead, he picked up his briefcase and hurried out of the flat and down the aerial steps to his bank. The town was bound to be busy in anticipation of the tea-dance that evening. Everyone would come to the bank on some trivial business connected with their accounts. Williams sighed at the prospect of having his neat piles of white paying-in and green withdrawal slips tampered with, his clean floors trodden on and the spotless brass of his door handle covered in greasy fingerprints. He wondered if he might not lock the door to his office and practise a few steps of the polka.

So intent was Mr Williams on his own churning thoughts, he forgot it was Saturday and the bank ought to stay closed. And he nearly tripped over Miss Chickie Wilkes-Tooley. 'Are you waiting for me?' William Williams asked.

Chickie blushed. I might have been, she thought. I have been waiting for some man all my life. Besides, she could do with a loan. To tide her over. She had got through her life's savings, pocket money assiduously put by all these years, completely spent now. Meted out, for the most part, in fifty-pence pieces to young Samuel Till. 'Life has been expensive of late,' she told Mr Williams and he, with his predecessor's fecklessness uppermost in mind, looked severely at the youngest Wilkes-Tooley sister and wondered what the girl could possibly be finding to spend her money on, in Knibden.

'Debt is a grave union between borrower and lender,' Mr Williams told Chickie, like a bishop putting a young bride through her paces prior to her impending nuptials. 'Not to be entered into lightly, nor without due consideration, by either party.'

The extravagant Chickie hung her head. Until recently – until the guest at the Gallimore's death, to be precise – it would have pained her to part with a penny. Bill Parris the tramp, for instance, had never received any coin from *her* purse. 'I . . . ' she began. How could she explain that her love for the headmaster made her feel rich? Or that she intended to go to the Silver Scissors Salon and have her hair expensively bobbed, and that money was as *nothing* in the face of all that must shortly transpire.

William Williams looked the girl up and down. She'd be hoping to ensnare some man during the tea-dance. Only yesterday he had overheard this foolish virgin being linked by some of the bank's customers chatting at the counter, in less than flattering or virginal terms, with the headmaster, Edmund Veitch. Williams took a step closer to Chickie. Perhaps she would help him practise the polka in return for a cheque book. 'Come into my office, my dear Miss Chickie! It's time you and I had a little chat.'

George Allendale heard his mother talking but she often woke him at an early hour, switching on the light and using a cup of tea as an excuse to sit on the end of his bed and engage him in conversation. Only a minute ago George had been emerging into daylight from the hidden entrance to a cave just below Knibden Crags with Arthur Dawes Dobson.

'You haven't listened to a word I've said!' Edina Allendale jabbed her son through the counterpane with a knitting needle. He yelped in his sleep and she resumed work on the lime-green sweater that had now taken sufficient shape to occasion poor George, when he opened his eyes, some alarm. 'Your miserable father was just the same!'

'I'm asleep,' George mumbled, although seconds earlier Dawes Dobson had patted him on the back and said, 'This had better remain a secret between us. Don't tell your mother, but *do* try and dissuade her from visiting my library . . .'

'There!' cried Mrs Allendale. 'All that remains is to stitch up the sides and you'll be able to wear it at the tea-dance. As the town's chief librarian you'll want to look your best . . .'

Men from Scotland Yard were travelling up from London that afternoon to question him about Dawes Dobson's finds. They would search the new museum and must find nothing untoward to rouse their suspicions. They must certainly not find Mrs Allendale clacking her needles and sucking boiled lemon sweets. George rubbed his eyes and then saw the garment his mother was casting off the needles. 'I'll get arrested if I wear that.'

'You ungrateful boy!' Edina Allendale cried. 'Next thing you'll be bringing some fancy woman home. And installing her in my place.'

George groaned. He pulled himself up and lay back against the pillows to sip his tea. This was not a particularly unusual start to the Allendales' day. 'There isn't any fancy woman,' George said, and thought (as he thought every morning) that perhaps it was time there was.

'Miss Willow, then,' Mrs Allendale sniffed.

'She has resigned from the library.'

'I always said the creature was unreliable!' Verity Willow had deserted her son in his hour of need, driven out most likely by Miss Hester Jones, the girl Edina Allendale had designated as her future daughter-in-law.

Michael Milady had called an emergency meeting of the committee. He and Hester Jones breakfasted together in the Gallimore Hotel while they waited for everyone to come.

Veitch sent word – typed by Chickie on crinkled parchment, delivered by Samuel Till for the usual fee of fifty pence – that he had better things to do than attend meetings. Had they any idea how much organization a revival required? Follifoot, Treadgold and Macready told Milady that the building work he had approved of was occupying their every waking hour. Neither Belle Quinn nor Verity Willow even bothered to explain their absences. Calderon telephoned to say he could not leave the Swan but he would be happy to abide by any decisions the others made. Victor Matchett and Norah Bird arrived late and in a hurry, both saying they could not stay long. Their businesses needed their every effort now that trade had suddenly got so busy.

'We are running out of funds,' Milady told the depleted group.

'Then we must raise some more,' said Miss Bird.

'Out of funds?' Matchett was immediately suspicious. 'What have you been spending it on? I hope there hasn't been any . . .'

'No, no,' Michael Milady was impatient. 'Everything has cost a lot more than we bargained for.'

'I haven't seen much *bargaining* going on,' Matchett grumbled.

'No matter,' said Miss Bird cheerily. 'We'll get all our expenditure back ten-fold – I, for one, will be happy to put in more if it's necessary . . .'

'I am not sure I *can* run to further investment,' Matchett said. 'I shall need every penny for the new revised *Bugle*.'

'Perhaps the committee should agree to underwrite the *Bugle*,' Milady suggested. 'Since it is chiefly because of the guest, and news of our search for his heir, that it is starting up again.'

'Yes, of course,' said Miss Bird eagerly. 'The least we can do!'

Victor Matchett was pleasantly surprised. 'Very good of you, I'm sure. As a matter of fact, I have already taken on Gary Laffety . . .'

'Good, good.' Milady then recounted how work had started on the Alhambra. George Allendale was restoring the museum (this at his own expense). They all knew about the improvements at the Gallimore. 'Quite a hive of industry, in fact.' The town was spending hand over fist. Spending like there was no tomorrow.

'Perhaps we could invite others to contribute to the funds,' Norah Bird suggested. 'When we started we did not know how much we would need. I think we all wondered how we would ever spend everything we had in the kitty in only three days. But then – well, *I* had no idea we were getting involved in anything quite so elaborate. I thought we were just employing a someone-who-isn't-someone to go round asking a few questions. It seems a shame not to spend more just because there isn't the money in the kitty to spend, if you see what I mean.'

'But why should newcomers take advantage of the ten-fold payout now, when they weren't interested in putting up money at the start?' Matchett objected. 'Before the scheme looked as if it were going to be a success. There ought to be *some* reward for having had faith at the outset in the dead guest . . .'

'As I recall, Mrs Allendale wanted to invest part of her pension, for the sake of her son – but we were already set up and I had to turn her away,' Michael Milady said.

'I don't know why anyone had to be turned away – we can obviously do with all the funds we can get . . .'

'It should cost people a lot more if they buy in later . . .'

'If anyone new wants to get involved, they should buy out the interests of those of us shrewd enough to put up money immediately.'

'Quite so. And if we make a small profit in the process, so be it.'

'Everybody on the committee should be asked to contribute again the same sum they put in before. That will keep us all liable to benefit in exactly the same proportion as formerly. Then, if anyone wants, they can sell their extra shares to others for whatever they can get.'

'This all sounds sensible.' Matchett folded his arms across his chest. He figured he could sell half his share for double what he'd paid and still be in there. It was a good thing wishy-washy people who understood nothing of business, like Belle Quinn and Verity Willow, weren't here sticking their oar in, coming up with irrelevant objections.

'Have ye solved the mystery?' he asked Hester Jones.

She smiled and poured herself another cup of coffee.

'You'll have to wait and see like the rest of us!' Michael Milady laughed.

'Of course she's solved the mystery,' Norah Bird said. No one could suit the fresh floral prints in select winter fabrics so well as Miss Jones.

3

Done For

'I know you're in there!' Desmond Chase banged loudly on the door.

Verity cowered in her kitchen. Shyne's enemies had tracked her down. She was done for. The banging went on. If only I had a gun, she thought, a Smith & Wesson thirty-eight calibre six shot.

'I know you're . . .' Chase, beside himself with anxiety and desperate to get back up to the Bensusanns' before further damage could be done, peered through Miss Willow's letterbox. He saw movement inside the house so he knocked loudly again. Chase had called at the library but George Allendale informed him his assistant was at home, preparing most probably for the excitements of the evening. 'You know what these unmarried women are like about a tea-dance!' Chase who knew nothing of unmarried women, did know that there was no time to waste preparing for anything. If they acted promptly, the whole thing could be hushed up. Chase had it planned: while Verity kept the General talking, he would plunge a syringe of something into Mrs Parbold's arm and then frogmarch her back down to the council house the other side of town where she belonged.

Verity trembled. If she didn't open her door they would batter it down. Her letterbox rattled violently again and as she turned her face, she glimpsed her own shadow moving behind her on the wall, betraying her. They knew for certain now that she was in here. Taking a deep breath and raising her head high, Verity Willow stepped boldly out into her tiny hallway. The important thing, Miss Maisie Vollutu would have reminded herself at this point, was to show no fear.

'Why, Mr Chase!' Verity stared at Desmond Chase. Just as you never knew, almost till the last page, who the murderer in a Raymond Bast mystery was, so you could never be certain who Randolphe Shyne's enemies might turn out to be. Desmond Chase? The handyman who lived up at the Bensusanns' and waited on the old General hand and foot! As once Mr Lethbridge had done. She must move with utmost caution. On no account let him see she harboured the least suspicion.

Chase saw at once the anxiety in the woman's pale face. The spinster was anxious she wouldn't have any partners, he thought. 'Tea-dance, indeed!' he commiserated. 'As soon as I heard of it, I knew it could only upset all the unmarried women and lead to trouble. The whole town is not itself any more – if you ask me Knibden has gone stark raving mad.'

'Won't you come in?' Verity asked nervously for Chase was obviously stark raving mad. He had already entered her house and was making his way into the kitchen. 'Can I offer you something – to help . . .'

'It's help I've come for!' Chase said. 'He's fallen into the hands of the enemy!'

'Yes, I know,' Verity said. 'But Mr Chase, I think it important we remain calm. We will be no good to the man if we break under the strain. Now, what will you have, a cup of tea, a drop of brandy? A whisky-sour?'

'Very good of you, Miss. Tea – with the brandy, if I may. Thank heavens I thought to come *here*. You're the only one in the whole town with any sense. I see that now. I dare say Hester Jones will see it also. When the time comes. It's him I'm concerned about. It's a scandal, of course.'

'Of course. He is a good man. He has been led astray.'

'Evil, I call it! Plain downright evil. I am not surprised to find you cowering at home, unable to carry on calmly in the library while this abomination takes place . . .'

'I have handed in my notice at the library, Mr Chase. So that I can concentrate . . .'

Desmond Chase gazed in admiration. 'You are the only woman in Knibden worthy of him. I have always said so . . .'

'Have you, Mr Chase?'

'You're far too good to be stuck in that stuffy library all day. I have always said *that*, also.'

'How kind – but I have been perfectly content. He always knew where to find me. Now, though, I feel I should do something before it is too late – I would like to know the truth at last.'

'I'll tell you the truth!' Chase seized the bottle of brandy from Verity and unscrewed the cap. Funny how the General had such a horror of flat-chested women and yet, here was Miss Willow, as flat-chested as can be, doing all she could to help, prepared even to give up paid employment for his sake. Meanwhile that big-bosomed Parbold creature had revealed herself in her full, grasping glory. 'He has been lured into a trap!'

'Oh, I do hope not!' Verity said earnestly. Then she picked up the tray with the tea-pot and cups and calling, 'Come through!' led the way into her sitting room. It had been in *this* room that Verity had said to Raymond Bast, or rather Harry Best as they'd called him, 'Aren't you bored with us?' It had never occurred to Verity until Mr Bast arrived in their house that merry May morning what tedious confined lives she and her mother led.

Bast did not look up, but he took his pipe from his mouth. 'Bored? No. Why?'

'Compared to London. And your literary friends.'

'Oh no – *they* are all very boring.'

'Compared to your books then.'

Raymond Bast lowered his newspaper and eyed his landlady's daughter. 'Life is always boring, compared to books.'

'Even a life as thrilling as yours?'

Bast contemplated the girl for a moment, then resumed his newspaper. He read something that made him take a long hard puff on his pipe.

They were sitting in the tiny front room that Mrs Willow's 'paying guests' used. Verity was meant to be doing her home-work but she could not concentrate. She was aware of a restrained restlessness in Raymond Bast. She stared round at the green china dogs on top of the tiled fireplace, the faded prints, the brown patterned rugs. This was no setting for a man like Raymond Bast. Verity was terrified that one day their guest would see this too. If he had to stop in Knibden, he should be staying in the best suite at the Gallimore Hotel, waited on by the ancient Miss Gallimores.

Verity said, 'I went to the library yesterday.'

Bast looked at her.

'You write the Randolphe Shyne mysteries,' she said.

'That's right,' Bast replied slowly.

'I had a quick look. But I didn't dare get one out – I thought it would be a mistake to draw unnecessary attention ...'

'You're a good girl.'

Verity smiled. She felt immense pleasure in his words.

'You're loyal,' he went on. 'Like Maisie.'

'Maisie?'

'Maisie Vollutu – the girl in Randolphe Shyne's life. She loved him. She'd never let her love hurt him.'

'Maisie Vollutu!' Verity sighed at the beauty of the name. 'But how could her love *hurt* him?' she wondered out loud.

'Women use their love to hurt,' Bast said stonily. 'Loving and clinging, like ivy on a tree. Soaking up, killing off . . .'

'I'm not like that,' Verity said with a little pout.

'I never said you were. You're like Maisie Vollutu, remember. She was special.'

'She loved Randolphe Shyne?'

'She certainly did! However closely his enemies watched her, and followed her, hoping to get to him, she'd never let on. Not even if they took a knife to her throat and started to press it slowly, slowly . . . She wouldn't squeal. Not Maisie Vollutu. And there he'd be, off on one of his terrifying adventures, jumping trains, swimming rivers in the dark, being shot at, and he'd always know that whatever was happening to him, little Maisie was somewhere, loyally loving him.'

'How wonderful!' said Verity.

'Yes, isn't it!' Bast snarled. He looked hard at the girl. He sighed. He would go mad cooped up in this dingy house. Perhaps he was going mad already. Verity Willow – Maisie Vollutu! He eyed a grinning green china dog. Still, it wasn't for much longer. The Great Knibden Lottery would be over in a few weeks . . .

Chase said urgently, 'You must talk to General Bensusann.'

'If you think that would be a good idea,' Verity said.

'Oh, I do!' Chase was emphatic. He helped himself to another big splash of brandy. He did not bother to add any tea from the pot this time. The bottle left a round wet ring on the neat gingham table-cloth. 'I am depending on you, Miss Willow . . .'

I am depending on you, Miss Willow. Raymond Bast's last words to her! Verity gulped. 'Mr Chase,' she said in a quiet wavering voice when she had recovered her powers of speech. 'I will do all I can. You have my word.'

She burst into tears.

Desmond Chase eyed the weeping woman for a moment. He felt like weeping himself and drank openly now from the brandy bottle. 'Two of a kind, you and me,' he said to Verity, belching gently. He waved his hand towards the window. 'They're all of them only after advantage for themselves. They don't understand loyalty. And wanting to be of service. A nasty washed-up town this. I would never have come here but for the General, I would never have spent twenty years of my life amongst such hard grasping people as you find in Knibden.'

Verity stared at Desmond Chase through her tears.

'You should come to the Bensusanns' as soon as possible, Miss Willow,' the man continued. 'I want to see you mistress there. It is where you belong. That Parbold woman pushes her great mop about, effecting nothing. But you, Miss Willow, would have the hundred and eighty-seven windows repaired, and the famous garden shipshape in no time.'

'It *is* a shame certainly that the beautiful garden has been allowed to . . .'

'It is nothing short of a disgrace, Miss Willow! Let us be perfectly frank with one another. That garden used to be written about and photographed in national magazines. No one would want to photograph the place now.'

'Well, no.'

'No national publication would show the slightest interest.'

'I remember the beautiful avenues of trees, great green canopies of leaves . . .'

'You see things my way, Miss Willow. You and I must strive together, to bring the General back from the brink of destruction. Here, take these!' Desmond Chase drew an enormous bunch of keys from his pocket and threw them down on the check-gingham table-cloth. They landed with a clunk in the middle of one of the damp patches he had created with the brandy bottle reminding Verity of the hoop-la stall at a fête. She picked up the keys, and looked queryingly at her prize.

'Those are the keys to the Bensusanns',' Chase said. 'They will come to you anyway, so you may as well have them now. And if you'll take my advice, Miss Willow, you'll get straight up there, and see what you can do. One hundred and eighty-seven – be sure to check that figure. For insurance purposes. Only the inesti-mable Mr Lethbridge has ever before . . .' Desmond Chase stood up, swayed about unsteadily and then sat down again. He reached out and raised the brandy bottle to his lips. Then resting his eyes with great deference on the future mistress and chatel-aine of the Bensusanns', General Bertram Bensusann's handyman finished the brandy off in one long, loud gulp.

4

Every Entry from Day Dot

Chickie turned her head this way and that, appraising the stranger who gazed critically back at her from the other side of the mirror. 'You *are* clever,' she said to Susie. The Silver Scissors was crowded with queues of women all wanting to look their best that evening at the tea-dance.

'A bob suits you!' Susie Till had felt like digging the points of her scissors deep into Miss Wilkes-Tooley's neck, instead she had done a very precise job on the woman's hair. Poor Susie, after all, would not like to be blamed for anything *her* brothers and sisters got up to. Who knew what Sammy was doing running errands all the time for Miss Chickie. With a supreme effort she told Lalla's vain sister what she supposed she wanted to hear, 'Makes you look a lot younger, somehow.'

Chickie smiled. It was not youth she was after. 'Your young man, Neville . . .' Chickie began.

Susie said, 'I wouldn't say he was *my* young man any more. He spent last night with *your* sister.'

'What? Why would anyone want to spend the night with Lalla?'

'You tell me!' Then, Susie added bravely, 'She's welcome to him!'

'Oh?'

'Norah Bird thinks he is going to come into the fortune – I can only assume your sister is after it.'

'Aren't you bothered?'

'Nah!' Susie's breasts shook.

'Then you must be the only one in Knibden not anxious to get their hands on the dead guest's money. Besides, I can't really see Neville Tagg inheriting a bean . . .'

'And Mr Veitch?' Susie inquired spitefully. Sam had told her he'd seen Veitchie with his hand up Miss Wilkes-Tooley's skirt. Sammy said things like that about everyone. He had also told her that Chickie possessed a magical bottomless purse from which an endless supply of fifty-pence pieces was to be had. 'The woman is a witch,' Samuel Till had said, producing dozens of new shiny coins from his pocket as proof. 'She has bewitched old Veitchie.'

'You watch yourself, then,' Susie pinched her brother's arm. 'Don't you go upsetting her or there's no knowing what might 'appen to yer.'

Chickie tipped the girl fifty pence and, leaving Susie with her mouth wide open, Chickie Wilkes-Tooley hurried from the Silver Scissors to her father's offices. It was years since she had been there. She was astonished to find Lalla and Neville Tagg sitting side by side at Aubrey Wilkes-Tooley's desk, poring over ledgers.

'Daddy is at home in bed,' Lalla told her younger sister briskly.

Chickie promptly sat down on one of the chairs used by customers. 'You ought to open a window,' she remarked. When neither of them took any notice, she asked, 'What are you doing?'

Lalla adjusted the tiny spectacles propped on her nose and told her younger sister sternly, 'Mr Tagg and I are *working*.'

'So I see!' Chickie looked about her. Many of the volumes that formed the Knibden Municipal Insurance Company's records had been taken down from the shelves that lined the room. They'd had the dust blown off them and now lay piled precariously on the desk.

Neville Tagg glanced curiously at Chickie. She had none of her sister's poise. She was large in all the wrong places and her big lips had a permanent pout.

'Ooh – I can remember playing with this.' Chickie leant over the desk and picked up the round ruler her father rolled down the page.

'Old-fashioned thing!' Lalla seized the ruler from her sister and tossed it impatiently into the wastepaper bin.

'Bea used to hit us with it when we came in here when we were children,' Chickie said.

'What is this?' Lalla demanded angrily. She felt like hitting Chickie herself now. '*You* may have time to trip down Memory Lane, but Mr Tagg and I are working round the clock. Was there anything particular you wanted?'

'Insurance, perhaps?' Neville put in helpfully. 'For Mr Veitch's revival?'

Both sisters turned on the young man. How *dare* he interrupt them? Then Lalla's face relaxed into a generous smile. 'Yes,' she said to Chickie. 'Mr Tagg is quite right! Edmund Veitch *will* need insurance – take one of our forms away with you, and get him to fill it out.'

'Oh!' said Chickie. 'I wouldn't like to disturb Mr Veitch with anything so trivial.'

'Do it yourself, then!' Lalla smirked. 'If the headmaster's time is that precious, you must do what you can to save it.'

'Yes,' agreed Chickie. 'I must. Thank you for bringing the matter to my attention, Mr Tagg. I shall organize the insurance for Edmund right away.'

'Fix it, will you!' As Lalla handed her sister over to Neville, both women were surprised to note that he had already started filling out the form.

'You can't be too careful,' the insurance clerk said in a professional monotone as he scribbled. 'I understand Mr Desmond Chase from up at the Bensusanns' intends to claim against the Gallimore's policy for damage done by the forthcoming tea-dance. Belle Quinn must be very relieved I reminded your father to speak to Mr Williams who spoke to Mr Mason on the matter. Who knows what expense the person who inherits the Gallimore Hotel from the dead guest might have been occasioned in, otherwise? And as for the organizers of the tea-dance, Miss Quinn and her committee, they could have been held personally liable – such things can *bankrupt* people. We see it all the time in here . . .' He tapped a ledger on the desk with his pen.

'For pity's sake, Mr Tagg, spare us the patter and the pitch!' Lalla banged her hand hard on the table, making all the Knibden Municipal Insurance Company volumes bounce. 'Get that done as quickly as possible, then we can get on.'

Neville coloured violently and bent over the paperwork. He wondered what it would be like if Lalla Wilkes-Tooley decided to kiss him. There'd be no stopping the woman in any course she chose to embark on. He handed forms to Chickie to sign. 'It is quite a large premium,' he said, 'but a lot can go wrong with a revival . . .'

Neville did not like to admit he did not know what a revival entailed so he charged the highest amount he could think of to cover all eventualities. Chickie who had negotiated a loan from

Mr Williams proudly waved her new cheque book and said, 'We are taking a full-page advertisement in Mr Matchett's new *Bugle* – the people of Knibden are to be given the opportunity to join in. You, Mr Tagg, will be able to . . .'

'Neville is far too busy for such nonsense!' interposed Lalla. She wondered how Chickie had acquired a cheque book all of a sudden. 'Follifoot has been here also. The Knibden Municipal Insurance Co must also advertise in the *Bugle* – I will speak to Father.'

'Why bother – *you* are clearly in charge now.' Chickie screwed up her nose.

Neville Tagg and Lalla Wilkes-Tooley smiled at each other.

Ah ha! Chickie thought.

'I have just had my hair done,' she said. 'At the Silver Scissors Salon.'

'It looks very nice,' Neville replied politely, and immediately resumed his work. Susie had deliberately made the woman look hideous, he thought.

'A great improvement,' Lalla remarked. 'Now, Chickie dear, we have work to do. If you would care to write out a cheque to cover the premium, I am sure Mr Veitch will be waiting for you . . .'

Lalla took the cheque and showed her sister to the door. She bolted it shut behind her.

Nev thought, I am locked in. With her! He bent fearfully over a ledger so that his face nearly touched the page.

'Sit up!' shouted Lalla. There could be no slouching. The whole of Knibden's history was in these files. Somewhere in all these great volumes would be the answer. She gazed round the shelves at the rows of great dusty books her father and grandfather and great-grandfather before that had written in. It was unbearably tantalizing. Apart from anything else, there was so much of it! *If only* they knew which volume and which page to turn to, the time that could be saved! With each passing minute the more money the stupid committee would be frittering away and the closer Hester Jones might be getting to the truth. Ahead of them. The only thing to do was set Tagg to work right through from the beginning, and drive him remorsely on till they found what they were looking for. They must remain at their desks – right up to the tea-dance that evening, if need be – until the job was done.

Neville had already passed the chapters containing the Cardew/Vestey/Jenks fiasco. 'What a woman!' he had said, gazing at Lalla who was the only creature he had ever encountered who might match Cardigan Cardew's widow in guile and determination.

'But what happened to Miss Angelica Hook, spinster of Knibden Brook and friend of the widow Cardew?' Lalla wanted to know. Obviously once she'd gained the money from her policy on Cardigan Cardew's life she'd have married and moved away. It was with the Miss Hooks of this world, forgotten creatures who took themselves off into interesting obscurity, that the great hidden truths resided. Even so, Miss Hook was too long ago. Anything of any significance in *this* matter would have happened more recently. 'You really must stop getting distracted,' she barked at Neville.

'I wonder if we are going about it all wrong,' Neville ventured.

'I beg your pardon!' Lalla shrieked, sharp as the points on Susie Till's scissors.

Neville Tagg's lack of sleep made him bold. 'Rather than work our way through every ledger, Miss Wilkes-Tooley, on the off-chance we may come upon something, I think we would do better to start by making out a list of suspects.'

'Suspects!'

Neville nodded. 'And then use the books to see what we can find out about them. Whoever inherits must be linked to the dead guest fairly directly. It would be quicker than working through every entry from day dot like this – and we might just be lucky and hit on the answer straight away.'

Lalla stared at the young man. His ginger moustaches twitched. Like her father she found herself continually amazed by Neville Tagg. Not a young man one expected to be amazed by. 'Who do you suggest?' she asked meekly.

'Edmund Veitch, for a start.'

As Lalla went on staring, the young man half rose from his chair. 'Why, for instance, is the headmaster organizing a revival? Who asked him to? It's too daft for words. He must *know* something about the dead guest to go to such trouble in his honour. Your sister obviously thinks so too. Perhaps she already knows what his secret is – though I doubt if she'll tell us.'

'Who do you think you are, Mr Tagg?' Lalla Wilkes-Tooley cried at the top of her voice. 'How dare you presume to remark on my sister! The impertinence!'

Neville Tagg's moustaches drooped. He sat down.

Lalla stared at Neville. What *did* Chickie know? Why had Edmund Veitch given her her own bank account? She thought of Bea. 'The other person we should investigate,' she said, 'is the Reverend Gilbert Duncie Sibson.'

'The ancient Gallimore sisters are staying with Mr Sibson at the moment,' Neville said. 'Even though they left Knibden for good, years ago. Why have they suddenly returned? What do they know about Gilbert Sibson? What did they know about the dead guest?'

Lalla stood up. 'Chatter, chatter, chatter, Mr Tagg. I feel like sacking you here and now for wasting valuable Knibden Municipal Insurance Company time! I want you to locate *every* reference to Edmund Veitch, and to Gilbert Sibson, in the ledgers by the time I get back. Meanwhile, *I* am going to get some fresh air.'

In fact she thought they were making such good progress she would pop home for some breakfast, and perhaps a hot bath.

5

Pitfalls for the Unwary

'I have never lived in such . . .' Belle wanted to say 'squalor'. She choked on the word 'turmoil'.

Sol's girl smiled understandingly. She was almost pretty when she smiled, with the deceptive sweetness, Belle thought, of an alert young weasel. Belle sipped some of the gin Sol had found for her in a cupboard and wondered how to impress on the young people that whatever Sol's mother might find acceptable in Penzance was not to be tolerated at the Laurels. Sol and his girl had used her pretty bathroom and not only dirtied the whole place but emerged dirtier themselves than when they went in. It turned the laws of bathrooms upside down.

Verity Willow came to visit Belle Quinn. She did not like the look of this nephew, or the way Sol and the girl stood over her, blatantly sizing her up. 'Penzance?' she asked. 'Wasn't that . . .'

'Hester Jones was on her way there,' Belle said tersely. She seemed downcast, defeated.

'Change is in the air,' Verity told her friend brightly. 'Everyone is so looking forward to your tea-dance tonight.'

Belle stared at Verity as though she did not know what she was talking about.

'Why – I have given up my job in the library. And Victor Matchett is re-launching the *Knibden Bugle*. He has already taken on Gary Laffety as foreman. I saw the boy and his friends riding along the canal towpath to work this morning. Roger Ambrose was strolling there with Doris Barr, the waitress from the Gallimore – they both had to leap out of the way. It is nice, though, that we will have a printing works again in Knibden. Don't you think so, Belle?'

After a pause, Belle replied dreamily, 'I always intended to get Daddy's writings printed.' A nearly empty bottle of gin stood open beside her. '*The Complete Works of Harold Augustus Quinn* in twelve volumes . . .'

'Why don't you?' Sol asked his aunt.

'Why don't I what?' Belle looked puzzled. She appeared to have difficulty in concentrating, or focusing her eyes.

'Get on with it,' Sol said. 'Surely you can afford . . .'

'Sol could take all them dusty papers to the printers for you,' the girl put in eagerly. 'Anything we can do to make ourselves useful while we are here, Auntie.' She smiled at Miss Willow as if assuring her of their good intentions.

Verity thought, 'These two are up to no good.' Verity had come to ask if Belle Quinn remembered Harry Best but there was no chance to broach the subject because Sol and the girl would not leave the room. They stood steadfastly behind Miss Quinn and Miss Willow like prison warders at visiting time. Eventually, Verity gave up hoping for any privacy. 'I had better go,' she said. 'I promised Desmond Chase I would call at the Bensusanns'.' She had hoped to ask her friend about that also, but Belle did not reply, and Sol and the girl immediately hustled her to the door. Verity turned at the last moment. 'Take care of yourself!' she called back, but Belle went on sitting, giving no indication that she had heard. 'I'll see you at the tea-dance later, then!'

'So where's this Buckworth & Matchett's?' Sol asked when he came back into the room.

Miss Quinn looked puzzled.

'The printers,' Sol reminded her.

'Down by the canal. Along the towpath past the Swan. Godfrey Buckworth drowned there . . .'

'I think you should go and arrange everything with this Mr Matchett,' the girl urged Sol. 'Harold Quinn was *your* grandfather. It'll show our appreciation to Auntie.'

Belle turned her head towards them. 'Tell Mr Matchett I want the *Complete Works* printed and bound in twelve volumes,' she sang out. 'No expense spared. I want plenty of copies, all with tooled calf-leather covers and gilded edges.'

'Nothing but the best, eh!' Sol laughed.

'Nothing but the best,' Belle repeated solemnly.

When Sol had gone, bearing away Harold Augustus Quinn's life's work in a cardboard box on his shoulder, the girl sidled back into the room and sat down close beside Belle. 'I thought we could have a nice chat,' she said. When Belle did not reply, the girl said, 'I suppose this Gilbert Sibson wasn't good enough for you? I suppose you took pleasure in turning him down.'

For a moment Belle hesitated. 'I never turned him down,' she told Sol's girl truthfully. 'I never got the chance.'

'Do you still love him?' the girl asked.

Belle said nothing. She sipped from her glass.

'Oh, I forgot,' the girl went on. 'These days, he loves another . . .'

At that moment, in the study of the unheated rectory attached to St Redegule's, Beatrice Wilkes-Tooley cast her eyes beseechingly on Gilbert Sibson. He fiddled with the book in his lap. Her open gaze and the low cut of her bodice made him quake. 'I am very concerned about my younger sisters,' Bea confided breathily. 'They have both taken up with unsuitable men. I fear they are being led astray.'

'Your sisters?' Sibson was surprised. From what he had seen of Lalla and Chickie, they were much more likely to lead, than be led anywhere.

'Lalla spent last night with an insurance salesman. A feckless fellow my father only employed out of charity. He has acquired a brand-new Ford *Fiesta* which I believe he has purchased, on tick. Spending extravagantly against his expectations. Expectations that would appear to involve poor misguided Lalla.' Bea shook her head. 'He thinks she is a wealthy heiress – when I know for a fact Lalla has always been very profligate with her pocket money. It is *Chickie* who squirrelled her money away. But *she* – ' Here Bea lowered her eyes, and voice. 'I scarcely know how to tell you this, Mr Sibson. The child has formed a desperate attachment. To a *married* man. And he, though of otherwise impeccable character, does nothing to dissuade her from her infatuation. She spends every hour at his side, typing his letters on crinkled parchment paper she purchased herself. She is squandering her money on him. I know for a fact she has acquired a cheque book, she wheedled it out of William Williams at the bank by agreeing to practise the polka. The tea-dance has gone to her head. For all I know they . . .'

'They?'

Bea spread her hands dumbly before her.

'My poor dear Bea!' Gilbert Sibson shook his head wearily. 'This world is full of pitfalls for the unwary. Cunning traps waiting to be sprung . . .'

'But what are you going to do?'

'Do? Me?' Gilbert had never done anything much.

'I am terrified what will happen to my poor sisters at the tea-dance. My father is unwell, he spends his day in bed, waiting for the worst. Could you not speak to them? Before it is too late. I beg you! As a friend.'

'A friend?' Sibson trembled violently. The book slipped from his lap to the cold stone hearth. It was all going exactly as Beatrice Wilkes-Tooley intended. Outside the study door Tilda and Bessie Gallimore could barely breathe. There was a rustle of maroon crêpe as Bea reached out and seized Gilbert Sibson's long dry fingers. Then she pressed her lips to his and he, accustomed only to cold unresponsive plaster, was astonished by the tight warm clasp of her hands and moist supple lips moving firmly on his.

'I will do anything,' he whispered into the swirling curtain of her thick black hair. 'Everything, you ask!'

When Desmond Chase returned to the Bensusanns' with a promise from Miss Willow that she would come as soon as she'd had a word with her friend, Belle, he found his worst fears confirmed. The General had vanished. Mrs Parbold's mop was missing. The woman had taken advantage of his absence to march the old man down into the town the moment Chase's back was turned. Bensusann was not used to the after-effects of stout and had allowed himself to be led by the arm to Mrs Parbold's comfortable little house that was warm and stuffed with knick-knacks, some of which Bertram Bensusann rather thought he recognized as having belonged at one time up at the Bensusanns'. Mrs Parbold's abode had no garden to speak of. Just a paved area with tubs and a straggly flower border for her cats to piss in.

What a vulgar habitation, the General gleefully imagined Chase remarking. Not at all a fit resting place for the sole survivor of Knibden's own Elevenths, now disbanded.

'Belongs to the council,' Mrs Parbold explained. 'I don't have the bother. They see to everything, painting the doors, repairing the roof.'

'And if a window gets broken?' Bensusann asked, for all of Mrs Parbold's windows were intact. They fitted neatly into metal frames, and admitted no draught.

'They send a man straight round to fix it. Just as well, what with all them Tills and Laffetys throwing bricks and balls.'

'I wish the council would come and fix my windows,' Bensusann remarked.

Mrs Parbold roared with laughter. 'Lor' – I wouldn't want that old ruin of your'n for all the tea in China! Must be worth a few bob, though?'

'I shall leave it to you in my Will, Mrs Parbold.'

Mrs Parbold screamed. 'Don't you dare do no such thing!' she yelled although there was nothing, of course, she would like more. Think what all the neighbours would say – it would be like winning the Great Knibden Lottery, or inheriting the dead guest's fortune, right under their nosy noses! 'You might announce that at the tea-dance this evening,' she suggested. 'You could stand up when 'Ester Jones stands up, and tell the whole town you intend leaving me the 'ouse.'

Matchett said, 'I'm far too busy printing the *Bugle*.' He looked Sol up and down. 'I didn't know Miss Quinn had family.'

'She has me,' Sol grinned.

Matchett thought the lad resembled a great chattering ape at the zoo. It was impossible to believe he could be related to Miss Belle Quinn.

'Now then, do you want to print this stuff or don't you?' Sol stood over him.

'Well . . .'

'She told me to tell you she wants only the best – gildin', toolin', finest paper – you know the kind of thing.'

'I'll think about it,' Matchett said.

'Please yourself, Squire!' Sol tipped the papers back into the box, hoisted it on to his shoulders and started to walk back into Knibden along the old towpath. As he rounded the corner where Godfrey Buckworth had slipped to his watery death, the new foreman at Buckworth & Matchett's came hurtling in the opposite direction. Sol staggered to regain his balance and the twelve parts of his grandfather's works tipped, one by one, into the canal.

'You watch it!' yelled Sol, shaking his fist at Gary Laffety's disappearing exhaust.

'Porgie is buried underneath the third laurel along from the left,' Belle said, when Sol returned. She was pointing out of the window.

'What?'

'Porgie – your mother's kitten.' Things were moving on apace. Sol gawped at her.

'Fleur never told you?' Belle now had one shoe on and one shoe off. 'She came home one afternoon with this kitten. Someone had given it to her – I forget who. Anyhow, it died a few weeks later, while she was out. I buried it in the garden before she got home. So as not to upset her. I had completely forgotten, until now.' Belle gazed hard at Sol as if challenging him to contradict her.

Sol stood silently for a while, his hands in his pockets. When he opened his mouth, it was to let out a long low whistle. He glanced outside, at the third laurel from the left. 'You killed Fleur's kitten,' he said slowly.

Belle hung her head.

'You poisoned Porgie!'

Belle began to sob. Sol and the girl glanced at each other.

'I see it all now,' Sol stood over his aunt. 'Your father – my grandfather, the famous mathematician, Harold Augustus Quinn – was completely taken in by you. You stopped Fleur, my mother, having anything to do with him. You poisoned her father against her the way you dealt with little Porgie. In the end, she was forced to flee to Penzance. She tried writing to patch up the quarrel – but you never replied. She wrote long letters full of her exciting new life, and her new-found happiness. Later, she swallowed her pride and wrote again, telling you how poor we were after my father died. But you did not care. You wanted your precious Harold Quinn and his crackpot ideas to yourself. A cold sun, indeed! An inverted universe! My mother suffered terribly at your hands while your father looked on, saw this reverse of sisterly love that fitted in so well with his notion of the universe. He wrote equations to explain it, but did nothing to stop you.'

Belle was weeping freely now. 'If only I could make amends,' she gasped.

'You'll make amends all right!' Sol laughed. He joined hands with the girl. 'That is why we are here.'

'What is it you want?' Belle gasped. Sol said nothing. 'If it is *money* you have come for . . .'

'Some things you can't simply *pay* to go away.'

The girl said, 'That's right, Auntie. Anything we can do while we are here . . .'

I am to be punished, Belle Quinn thought. My home, despoiled. I am to watch Beatrice Wilkes-Tooley consorting openly with Gilbert Sibson. Sibson who gave my sister a sweet little kitten when he never gave me anything. 'Look what old Gibsey gave me!' she'd taunted Belle. 'Georgie Porgie pudding and pie, Kissed the girls and made them cry.'

'He kissed you?' Belle asked.

'No, silly! I kissed him!' Fleur laughed. 'Of course I gave old Gibsey a kiss when he gave me this little Porgie-pie . . .'

I shall sit in the church and see that great kitten Beatrice Wilkes-Tooley enjoying the place that might have been mine. St Redegule herself will break her long plaster silence on Follifoot's ugly concrete plinth. She will kick her slender slippered feet in the air and laugh uproariously at my fate. I have deserved no less. The dead stranger, the guest at the Gallimore, has seen to it all.

'I told Mr Matchett "the very best",' Sol said. 'The most expensive job he could manage. He was very keen. Said he'd fit it in, in between editions of the *Bugle*. Remembered Harold Quinn, my grandad, he did! Said it was a privilege to shake my hand. And he even offered me a job in the new revised printing works, Matchett & Laffety's – but I have my auntie to take care of, I told him. Oh, and I also told him you would pay however much he asked. Money no object . . .'

I am to be bankrupted also, Belle thought. Victor Matchett will come for his dues and I shall have to sell up. I shall be forced to leave the Laurels and go about the streets, a gin bottle my only companion. Bill Parris on whom I have bestowed little acts of charity over the years will sit comfortably in his hut in the municipal gardens and never again wish to swap places with me. 'There goes Belle Quinn!' they will say. The shoes on my feet full of holes. My hair cut close as a favour to me, to keep out the nits.

My hands will become gnarled and grimy and instead of lilac scent behind my ears, I will stink of the gutter. Children will hide their faces. Dogs will bark and snap at my heels, chasing me down dark murderous alleyways and everyone will murmur, 'That good woman has got her just deserts, at last. And all thanks to the dead guest . . .'

'There is something else you should know,' Belle said to Sol and his girl. She held her head back as proudly as any saint martyred for her goodness. 'I shall confess it publicly to Hester Jones at the tea-dance tonight.'

6

A *Cause Célèbre*

As Lalla Wilkes-Tooley danced back and forth between home and the Knibden Municipal Insurance Company offices, unable to settle to much for all the excitement, Neville Tagg stayed steadily at his desk poring over the books. He was glad he did not have to go out on the streets. He was terrified of encountering Susie Till, and he trembled too at what Miss Lalla might say if she found him slacking. Occasionally, as a treat, he would turn to the window and eye his brand-new Ford *Fiesta* waiting for him like a faithful hound out in the yard. He would have no problems keeping up with the repayments as his labours were constantly interrupted by people wanting policies – the company was taking in money hand over fist. Neville Tagg remembered those teams of young men he had once envisaged, all like himself as he had been only a day or two ago, tearing round town on his bicycle, a great notebook jutting out of his pocket – it was working out *exactly* as he'd predicted. All he had to do now was find the answer, alter the evidence as necessary, and Lalla Wilkes-Tooley would be his. He heard Lalla's bustling tread on the stairs. Then she burst into the room like a river breaking its banks. 'Well?' she demanded.

'I have sold seven policies since you went out . . .'

'Never mind that now! What have you got on the suspect?'

'Edmund Veitch has been married before.'

'Everyone knows *that*!' Lalla retorted scornfully. 'The first wife died and almost immediately he married Louisa Ambrose, a pretty young widow with a baby son.'

Neville coughed. Then made his disclosure, 'Edmund Veitch had *only just* taken out the policy on the first wife when she died.'

'So?' Lalla jabbed a pen painfully into Neville's shoulder blades.

'He hardly made any payments before he collected a nice sum after her funeral.'

'Mr Veitch was lucky,' Lalla said.

There was a pause. Then Neville spoke with stubborn emphasis, 'Miss Wilkes-Tooley, the first Mrs Veitch's death was *completely unexpected*.'

'What are you saying?'

'That Edmund Veitch was a bit too lucky.'

Lalla stared at Neville Tagg, who continued unperturbed, 'I am also saying that the present Mrs Veitch might do well to watch out since her husband has recently taken out a sizeable premium on her head, also.'

'What?'

'Then there is that curious business of Louisa Veitch's own first husband, David Ambrose, father of Roger who was a baby at the time, dying in a brawl over his lottery ticket. Down a dark alley. No witnesses.'

'Someone killed him for his dragon.'

'That was the story put about.'

'Mr Tagg – what *exactly* are you saying?'

'It seems to me far too convenient, that's all. Her husband disposed of in the traditional way Knibden men are disposed of. And Veitch's first wife dying suddenly like that, a big premium on her head. Of course, there could be an innocent explanation . . .'

'Innocent! Edmund Veitch?' The man had sought to impose authority on the Wilkes-Tooley sisters when they'd been schoolgirls and, although they had long since left school, they did not recall his efforts kindly. 'You say he has just taken out a policy on his present wife's life?'

'Well, he isn't the only one – lots of people have been coming in here recently, taking out policies. My bonuses will . . .'

'Never mind *your bonuses*! How can you sit there and selfishly chatter about bonuses – what have your "bonuses" to do with Edmund Veitch?'

'This business over the guest at the Gallimore has turned people's thoughts to their own mortality, and that of those around them. Naturally it has occurred to Mr Veitch that his wife is a healthy woman, and quite a lot younger than him – you have only to look at our tables of risks and mortification to see that if she dies first, Veitch would stand to collect quite a sum. If she dies shortly, it will not have cost him much to do so.'

'Why should she do any such thing? Really Mr Tagg! What can

you possibly know of Mrs Louisa Veitch that makes you think she might die *before* her husband?'

'The man has *every incentive* she should die first – and, when a man has every incentive for something to happen, it generally does.'

Lalla thought her father's employee had completely taken leave of what few senses he'd ever possessed. She wondered if she was safe to be in the same room.

Neville squirmed beneath the withering gaze of Lalla Wilkes-Tooley, but he went on bravely, 'Our suspect, Mr Veitch, will not only get rich by collecting on the policy. He'll also be free to make your sister, Chickie . . .' Neville coughed as delicately as his clumsy manner and the delicate matter allowed.

'Make my sister Chickie *what*?' yelled Lalla. The incorrigible impertinence of the fellow!

'Into the third Mrs Veitch!'

'Well!' Now Lalla was impressed. So that was Chickie's game! That was how the silly girl intended to get herself a rich husband. At least there could be no threat to the dead stranger's inheritance – little Chickie's ambitions did not tend that way. But Bea? Neville must turn his attentions to the Reverend Gilbert Sibson without delay.

'What are you waiting for?' Lalla screamed at her father's clerk. She had a terrible urge to tug his bushy ginger moustaches. 'I will not have you sitting here twiddling your thumbs at the company's expense. Time is running out – Hester Jones will shortly be announcing the recipient of the dead stranger's millions. We have eliminated the first suspect, why aren't you getting on with the next?'

'The Reverend Sibson?'

Lalla nodded. As Neville set to work, Lalla wracked her brains. The first Mrs Veitch! When she, Chickie and Bea had been school-girls, the headmaster's love life had been a *cause célèbre*. A cause celebrated by the three Wilkes-Tooley girls, to whom the first Mrs Veitch's unexpected death, and immediate replacement in the pedagogic marital bed by a docile pretty widow, Mrs Louisa Ambrose, was a matter of great interest.

What a brilliant dumb show it had been – better than the Drowning of Mr Godfrey – with three equally wonderful parts to fight over. First, the angry childless Harriet Delilah, who had hold over the man who held sway over them during school hours. Then the pale ineffectual Louisa, a sickly sweet madonna in need of protecting. And lastly, the third in the trio, the wretched Edmund Veitch trapped in a loveless marriage to a hard bitter woman, forced to conceal his passion for the young Mrs Ambrose.

By good fortune, Harriet Delilah Veitch dies. The husband, observed by Bill Parris, duly kneels before her grave, biting back tears and planting primroses, but all the while rejoicing inwardly that at last he is free of her. Free to wed, almost before common decency can be observed, the fragile young widow whose child he takes for his own. End of Scene One. Scene Two – the peda-gogic bed in the schoolhouse. The spectre of the first wife hangs over the mattress like a dark, dank curtain draped from four posters. Every time the newly weds try to indulge in the sins of the flesh, Harriet appears in the room with a lighted candle. This enough to quell even the most ardent bridegroom's libido, Chickie, Lalla and Bea had agreed. And indeed, as things really *did* turn out between the headmaster and his second wife, no children were ever born. No step-brothers or -sisters for the spoilt, blue-eyed baby, Roger.

Lalla, sitting now in the Knibden Municipal Insurance Com-pany offices that had been her father's, and grandfather's before that, saw that it had taken the fearless, febrile imagination of Neville Tagg, her father's gormless clerk, to perceive the greater truth that had eluded the three Wilkes-Tooley girls' tableaux all those years ago: *Veitch had done away with Harriet Delilah* née *Beales, Beloved Wife of Edmund Veitch, Schoolmaster of Knibden, Requiescat in Pace!* Not merely in order to facilitate a licentious liaison with the young widow *but also* to collect comprehensively from their own father's Knibden Municipal Insurance Company!

If Edmund Veitch were thinking of bumping off his present wife to wed Chickie and collect again, he would have Lalla Wilkes-Tooley to contend with! Chickie was her younger sister after all. Lalla would be there at the tea-dance to do what was needed to protect her. She would inform Hester Jones, and the whole town if need be . . .

'If you want me to go on working here,' Neville said to Lalla, 'you must marry me.'

'What?'

'I said . . .'

'I heard what you said!' Lalla glared at Neville. Then she laughed. 'If you can discover the heir to the dead stranger's millions, before Hester Jones, I will marry you!'

7

Towards the End of Summer

Verity Willow followed behind Desmond Chase as he guided her along corridors, up stairs and in and out of the derelict rooms of the Bensusanns'. 'A woman like you,' Chase said, to encourage her, 'should inhabit a place like this.'

Verity laughed. The rooms were ramshackle and dirty. They had not been cleaned or lived in, in years. Fewer than half had electric light bulbs in the bare dangling sockets.

'It's a disgrace!' Chase went on, mounting a further flight of stairs two at a time so that Verity could scarcely keep up. She wondered where General Bensusann was. 'When you think of all the porcelain and books that used to be here. Books that belonged to the great essayist Sidney Mastermain Bensusann. Porcelain that had been in the Vigo family for generations. Porcelain and books a flat-chested woman like you would know how to treasure, Miss Willow. *You* would never have allowed the house to become so run-down. *You* would make sure the General . . .'

Verity grabbed hold of a bannister. Somewhere above her, Chase sensed that the woman had stopped. He paused also, and called back, 'Are you all right there now, Miss Willow? I'm not going too fast?'

Verity said, yes, she was fine. She asked where the General was.

'He'll be back.'

Still Verity did not move. 'You see, I came here once before when the General was not here,' she called up to Chase, uncertain if he heard.

Desmond Chase, half way up the flight above her, panted quietly. 'Oh?' He was wondering whether, if she tried to leave, he might not force her up into one of the rooms above and keep her there for when the General came back home. Tie her up, if need be.

'I was only young,' Verity said, as if excusing herself for something she had done. 'I was thirteen years old. General Bensusann was abroad at the time. I met a Mr Lethbridge. And a Mrs Enderby. The sworn enemies of a friend of mine, you see. At least, that was what I thought until I came . . .'

Chase peered down at the tall pale woman standing in the half light on the stairs below. Her face was tinged with the green reflected from outside for even in winter the garden of the Bensusanns' grew luxuriantly verdant. 'Mr Lethbridge and Mrs Enderby are long gone,' he assured her. 'You can have nothing to fear from them.'

Verity smiled and shook her head. 'If only it were that easy, Mr Chase. It was one of those beautiful long evenings towards the end of summer, made all the more beautiful because you know the summer will soon be over. Raymond Bast would not stay with us for ever. In a house stuffed with green china dogs. I climbed over the gate at the far end of the long back drive. Then I walked up here. You could see the house through the trees and just make out where Ottilie Vigo's famous avenues of limes and beeches once led off like great tunnels on either side.'

Maisie Vollutu had walked, or rather Verity had crept up to the house. She'd been bold and brave enough at the outset but once inside the locked gate the resolute courage of Maisie Vollutu had melted away so that it had been Verity Willow, thirteen years old with a tear in her navy knickers, who had pressed forward, her heart pounding, terrified of what might happen to her alone in all that green darkness. As she'd neared the house she had heard voices coming from an open window. Raymond Bast – or rather Harry Best – was talking inside to Mr Lethbridge. She had leaned forward, and then leaned too far. She fell on to a cold frame, smashing the glass and shredding the skin on her hands. As she sobbed uncontrollably, Verity knew she was not brave enough to be Randolphe Shyne's girl. The crash, and the sobs, brought the men to the window.

'What the . . .' Best.

'It's Mrs Willow's girl!' Mr Lethbridge.

'She must have followed . . .' Best, again.

'I came to protect you,' Verity whimpered but the two men above her were now shouting at each other.

'I told you . . .'

'Leave the girl to me!' Harry Best said nastily. 'I'll handle her.'

Verity lay amid the jagged glass inside the broken cold frame. Blood dripped from her hands. She was pulled roughly to her feet. Best avoided her eye. 'You had better go with Mrs Enderby to the kitchen, Verity,' he said. And because Mr Lethbridge was standing at his elbow scowling furiously, Verity asked no questions but let herself be led away by the housekeeper.

'What were you doing snoopin' about 'ere then?' The woman wrapped a coarse cloth tightly round Verity's hand.

'I was trying to rescue Randolphe Shyne,' Verity whispered. There was a large gash across her forehead.

Mrs Enderby dashed disinfectant at the wounds so that they burned and stung. Verity yelped. She gazed at the tea-towel soaked in her blood. What if the bleeding never stopped? She concentrated hard on staying upright in her chair.

Best and Lethbridge appeared in the entrance to the kitchen, arguing.

'Verity won't speak,' Best said. 'Verity and I understand each other . . .' He elbowed Mrs Enderby out of the way and bent over Verity, his mouth close to her ear. They had never been so close. 'You've got to help me, Maisie,' he pleaded. 'If you blow this, you'll get me killed.'

'Killed?' Verity sniffed back her tears and gazed straight into Raymond Bast's handsome face.

'You understand what I'm saying?' The man was frantic. He glanced towards the doorway where Mr Lethbridge and Mrs Enderby stood. It was as if he were holding the pair at bay. 'You must be brave. Above all, you must trust me.'

Verity nodded. 'Like Maisie Vollutu?' She gave a final sniff.

'Just like Maisie Vollutu. I'm going to have to lock you in a room upstairs. Don't be frightened. Just stay there quietly for as long as it takes and never say anything to anyone ever, and nothing can go wrong. I am depending on you, Miss Willow.'

Verity nodded again. Bast put a hand on her shoulder and she could hear his breathing as he walked her straight past the housekeeper and the butler of the Bensusanns', out of the kitchen and up the staircase.

Verity followed Chase into the room he had pictured the new mistress of the Bensusanns' making her own. He stood by the door to watch the woman in her new setting. He saw her start.

She went immediately over to the iron bed that had no mattress. Verity sat down on the coiled springs. Chase had had to burn a lot of the old mattresses when they'd become infested. He and Mrs Parbold had dragged them outside on occasions and lit large bonfires. Once, when General Bensusann returned unexpectedly early from his walk, he had screamed at them. The General did not like fires. It was to do with being rescued as a little boy from a fire at the Alhambra, Mrs Parbold had said. Chase did not know where she had got that from but Mrs Parbold was full of useless information that she was good at putting to good use. 'It was Mrs Enderby what rescued the General from the fire. He was about three years old at the time. Other Knibden children died in the blaze. If it hadn't been for Mrs Enderby . . . It was what gave her her hold over him,' Mrs Parbold had said. Lethbridge of course had had a hold over Mrs Enderby.

Verity crossed to the window. Chase joined her. They were right at the very top of the old house. Out of earshot of every other living soul.

'You can see the town from here,' Chase remarked conversationally.

'I know,' Verity murmured. 'I told you, Mr Chase, I came here once before.'

There was a strange light in her eye. As Desmond Chase and Verity Willow stood together in the musty room with bare floorboards and old brown paint on the walls, both stooping slightly to see out of the window, Mrs Parbold and the General appeared in view, climbing slowly up the steps to the main entrance.

'Well, I'm . . .' Chase exclaimed.

For a moment longer he and Verity watched. Then Chase, with a jubilant whoop, made a dash for the door. Verity hurrying after him had a fleeting impression that the man considered slamming it in her face. Bolting her in here as once before she had been locked up in this very room and only let out when Harry Best had fled Knibden and the last Great Lottery was over.

'We thought we'd pop back and fetch a few things, didn't we, duck?' Mrs Parbold said. She was surprised to see Verity Willow coming out of the house to stand with Desmond Chase. This was a complication she had not anticipated.

The General was red in the face from the climb. 'You look worn out,' Verity said.

'I could do with sitting down,' Bensusann admitted. He pulled himself free of Mrs Parbold. 'You can't stop me eating my sandwiches *here*,' he grinned at Miss Willow, who smiled. It was their private joke. Verity always turned a blind eye in the library, but when George Allendale, the officious chief librarian, was there, he would send her over to tell the old man that he couldn't luncheon in the library. Verity was always apologetic which pleased the General. He would try and get her to walk with him back home to the Bensusanns' to annoy Chase, but Verity would glance across at the frowning George and say she could not leave the library just then. The General reckoned Miss Willow on her own would be happy to be at his beck and call.

Mrs Parbold said, 'We had best be getting on, duck. There'll be the long walk back down later.'

'Back?' Desmond Chase asked sharply. 'Back where?'

'To the tea-dance. The General has something important to tell the whole town.'

'I think the General needs to sit down,' Verity said, taking Bertram Bensusann by the arm.

8

A Wanderer Returns

'*More* money?' Belle Quinn asked faintly, when told what the committee had decided.

'Who was he then?' Sol wanted to know as soon as Michael Milady had left.

'No one rightly knows.'

'What?' Sol was incredulous. 'You must know something about a man who comes to the house raising cash . . .'

Belle hesitated. She tried to think what she could say so as not to appear foolish in front of Fleur's son. 'He's a retired theatrical gentleman. I understand he used to come to Knibden on tour in the old days. With Montague Cayke's Imperial Players. He played the part of Aladdin's younger brother.'

'Aladdin didn't have a younger brother.'

'Oh! Well, *we* never went to the theatre, of course,' Belle said quickly. 'It was not something Daddy . . .'

'You should stop talking about the past all the time, Auntie,' Sol's girl said. 'Only the future counts.'

Belle smiled bravely. The girl had just told her she was expecting Sol's child. A baby was to be born at the Laurels. Among all Belle's nice things, the girl had said.

'I do not think I shall be living here much longer,' Belle told them.

Tilda and Bessie Gallimore asked Beatrice Wilkes-Tooley why she supposed Hester Jones had not wanted to know *their* story yet. Time was running out. If an announcement was to be made in a couple of hours at the tea-dance, Hester Jones should by now have apprised herself of all the facts.

'I suppose she hasn't got round to it,' Bea said. 'She only had three days.'

The sisters cackled, and clicked their teeth. 'She can't be much good then, can she, to get so side-tracked all the time. Perhaps, we may escape her eye altogether.'

'We told her all about Gurney, and Monsieur Henri. We set up a smokescreen . . .'

'There's hope for us yet!'

'Miss Jones should stick to what's *important* if she wants to get at the truth.'

'And are you important?' Bea asked. 'To that truth? Did you know the dead guest?'

'It is impossible we were *not* acquainted, Bea dear. We have known a great many men in our time. Anyone of any significance is bound to have crossed our path. You'd have thought Hester Jones would have worked that out by now.'

'She is spending a lot of time with Michael Milady,' Bea said. 'It is obvious he is connected to all this in some way.'

'He is unconnected to any of it.' Tilda sniffed indignantly. 'A man like that!'

'We know the type.'

'He is unconnected to anything.'

'A forgotten face – a name on the cast list of an out-of-date playbill. A man who has rented rooms and played other men's parts all his life.'

'And not played them very well.'

'No roots, no savings, he only came back to Knibden because he had nowhere better to call home. He told us so himself.'

'No one will notice when he has gone for good . . .'

'His own mother abandoned him to the squalls of fate. If she wasn't interested in him, why should the rest of us care?'

'Why should the dead guest lift a finger?'

'Do you remember his mother?' Bea asked.

'It depends who you mean by "his mother", Miss Bea,' Tilda said.

'Oh?'

'The man Hester Jones knows as "Michael Milady" was sold as a young boy to Montague Cayke by *his* mother. From that day on he played the part of Mikey Milady, the beautiful Melinda Milady's orphaned son whom Monty Cayke had stepped in and taken on in the foyer of the Gallimore Hotel many moons before. See there, he pointed; we looked. At a cigarette stain on the floor. A child snivelling on the hard oak settle. The dead Melinda's sisters quarrelling over his head as Cayke removed his plumed hat and, before the boy's family could change their minds, adopted Michael Milady for good. The story he told Miss Jones the evening she arrived – about Melinda Milady bringing him to Knibden and leaving him asleep in the Gallimore – was Michael Milady's story all right, the personal history he took on when he entered the Imperial Players. His own mother having received a ten-shilling note and a glass of ale in exchange for him. Cayke always liked to have a Michael Milady on his books. When one boy died or ran away, or got too old for the part, Cayke simply purchased another to take his place. When Cayke himself eventually died, his last Michael Milady was allowed to grow up and grow old. And retire here to Knibden, the only place he could call home. It was like musical chairs – that man just happened to be in Michael Milady's place when the music stopped. This will be too subtle for poor Hester Jones. Unlike us, she is not used to the cloak and dagger stuff of theatricals . . .'

'But can *you* remember Melinda Milady?' Bea wanted to know. Had she not detected in the last of the Gallimores' story the kind of deception that must be cloaking the solution to the dead guest's Will? If *she* should get there before Hester Jones, and before either of her sisters, what riches might lie in store? How nice it would be to heat the old rectory properly, and do some of the much needed repairs to the church, the roof, that plinth. She would have a husband and she would be rich. She would be generous with cast-off clothing. 'I have always thought puce suited you so much better than me . . .'

How could Bessie and Tilda Gallimore *forget* Melinda Milady! The beautiful, fair Melinda who had run away with the lottery winner, taking advantage of the glorious confusion that followed the excitement of the Great Knibden Lottery of 1916 to disappear in a cloud of golden smoke. Trumpets had won and, while trumpets were sounding across the battlefields of Northern France calling soldier Veitch, Denis Lobb and Johnny and Wilfred Dawes Dobson to battle, the happy couple had left for a brave New World, boarding an ocean liner laden with vast quantities of leather luggage, boxes of hats and dresses from Paris, pink Venetian glasses and a train of servants. It was what people wanted to hear. The dream of every Knibden maiden had come true for Melinda. Her two elder sisters had also vied to be the one to go with him, but Milady had chosen the youngest who had upped sticks without so much as a backward glance, taking nothing with her into her new life. How wealthy, beautiful, hopeful and dream-like the world had seemed to the pretty Melinda then! Her sisters gnashed their teeth and immediately married other beaux, vociferously denouncing the disruption caused to the life of the town by the lottery and seeking to put the tragic loss of their sister behind them. They tried not to think of the gilded life she was leading but the unfairness haunted their every hour. Of course it did. It marred their looks and made the two old and crotchety before their time.

Which was quite unnecessary – since Melinda's true fate was not at all one they would have envied. At first, New York welcomed the rich young Miladys, but it proved an expensive place for a man with money. The carefree Milady ran through his winnings. Not used to having cash, he overtipped. Every hard-luck story found him generous. At every bar he bought every round. Anyone with a clever scheme for investing interested him – he had been lucky against all odds, so even the riskiest ventures seemed sure-fire bets by comparison. Apart from which, like children coming home from a magical party, the young couple could settle to nothing. Milady was increasingly drawn to the casinos for only there, beside the rotating roulette wheels, could he savour again something of the excitement of winning the Great Knibden Lottery.

Six years on found the Miladys back in peacetime Europe, eking out their lives and diminished resources in the South of France. Melinda spent her days in darkened hotel rooms with her small son. Increasingly her husband did not come back at night while little Mikey, the product of this unhappy union, ran about as noiselessly as possible to avoid worsening his poor mamma's headache. Madame, the proprietress, had no such scruples. She called at regular intervals, day and night, to demand sums of money she declared were owing. One evening, word came that Milady had died in an accident on a yacht, an accident that involved the husband of one of the women he had been seeing. I want you out of here tomorrow, the heartless Madame told his widow. While Monsieur had played the wheel, there'd been the possibility of recouping some of her losses. Now she could not wait to see the back of the haughty *Anglaise* and her pasty-faced *enfant*. *She* would not have given ten bob and a glass of ale for *that* child. Melinda pawned what jewels she had left to pay off the maid, and Madame, the proprietress, seized her choice of the couple's things to cover the rent already owing and her 'loss' at losing occupants at such short notice. She took the pink Venetian glasses, and any dresses she thought she could sell. Clad in her one remaining robe, a stiff woollen outfit she had worn while holidaying in the Alps, Melinda Milady set out with young Mikey for Knibden, hoping to throw herself and her son on the mercy of her elder sisters. 'There was a lottery and a war on. We were all foolish,' she would say.

Melinda sat on deck as the ferry plied the stormy English Channel until the Captain took pity and let the young mother and child shelter in his bridgehouse. She held the boy close and coughed fitfully into a handkerchief, concerned only to conceal from her son the blood that welled up from her lungs. 'We are going home,' she told the little boy over and over. 'Soon we'll be home.'

The Captain thought his own great heart would break and when his boat berthed safely beneath the white cliffs of Dover, he arranged for someone driving towards Knibden to give the pair a lift to the nearest big town where they could take a carriage the last stretch of the journey home. Gallantly he warned the driver, on pain of a nautical knot being tied in his landlubber's throat, not to try anything on with the young widow.

When Melinda Milady and her small son emerged into the cold Knibden sunshine, heads turned and stared. The girl who had slipped away in triumph on the arms of the lottery winner had returned, seven years on, a pale spectre from the past. An uncomfortable reminder people could do without. The war was over. Many young men who had loved and lost this girl, had lost their lives. The world had moved on. Here was an inglorious ghost no one wanted to see.

Tilda and Bessie had watched her arrival from their mother's upstairs parlour, standing on tippy-toe and peering out through the wooden slats. Downstairs, Sarah Gallimore received Melinda Milady civilly.

'Yes, Ma'am, the Hall is a hotel now,' Sarah Gallimore

explained. 'My sisters and I do the work. There have been a lot of changes.'

Melinda took the best rooms in the hotel. She penned notes to her two sisters asking them to do what they could for her son and she put little Mikey to bed. Then, under the watchful eyes of the five Gallimore sisters, Sarah, Caro, Charlotte, Elizabeth and Anne, she wandered out into the town to post her letters and breathe for the last time the fresh familiar air of home. Montague Cayke's Imperial Players were showing at the Alhambra. What would she not give to join the throng entering the theatre just then, and to sit in the warm crowded darkness below the brightly lit stage? Like a moth before a candle, the penniless Melinda Milady pulled her lavender headscarf about her and stood by the entrance intently reading a playbill. Just as the bell sounded, indicating the performance was about to start, someone affecting not to recognize her stepped from the shadows and handed Melinda a ticket. Whoever this had been was gone before she had seen them but her face lit up when she realized what she held in her hand. The bell rang again, and with no time to lose, she hurried inside to take her seat.

Beatrice Wilkes-Tooley, as the eldest of the three Wilkes-Tooley girls, did not find the tale of Melinda Milady to her taste. Naturally she had no patience with the way youngest, prettiest sisters are dealt with in fairy tales while the more solid claims of an older, wiser (less pretty) sister are all too often overshadowed. 'And you?' she asked briskly.

'Our lives are nearly over,' Bessie said. 'We have lived them to the full.'

'Money, jewels, men have all slipped through our fingers.'

'What difference could money, jewels and men make to us now, even if we had them still? Which we haven't. We are the very lilies of the field your Gilbert preaches about . . .'

'He would do, if he ever did any preaching. I have heard it said he stands in his pulpit reading from the essays of Sidney Mastermain Bensusann! On the Perils of Love & Literature. Or the famous essay on the Great Knibden Lottery that had Lethbridge dropping everything beneath the lions on Trafalgar Square and hot footing it to Knibden.'

335

'Gilbert does not set himself up over others,' Bea defended her lover.

'He buried the dead guest,' Bessie retorted.

'To my way of thinking he should not have done that,' Tilda remarked. 'You can be sure the Reverend Jerabius Hartley would never have tolerated such nonsense.'

'The Reverend Hartley would have put his foot down. He and his sister, Zillanah, took a firm stand against the Knibden lottery. *They* would not have aided and abetted the dead guest. Or approved of Hester Jones and all this fun people are having hoping they are about to become rich, planning what to do with the great fortune when they are.'

'I have seen them.' Tilda Gallimore waved through the window towards the far side of the graveyard. 'Standing out there hours on end beside the dead stranger's grave, wondering what secrets it holds.'

'When Hester Jones *does* deign to question us about our interest in the man, I wonder what we will tell her.'

'Which of the many versions of our lives we will feel like disclosing.'

'If any.'

'There may be no necessity. They say she has already worked out the answer.'

'And what is the answer?' Gilbert Sibson asked. He had entered the kitchen and overheard Bessie's last remark. 'Who is to inherit the dead stranger's fortune?'

The two old ladies nodded their spritely grey heads in unison.

'They know something!' Beatrice Wilkes-Tooley cried out to her lover. 'It is why the Miss Gallimores have come back. They are waiting for the tea-dance to make their disclosures.'

'Well!' The Reverend Gilbert Duncie Sibson rubbed his hands. 'If there *is* to be money at last, I must hold out for the claims of St Redegule's. The roof, that plinth . . .'

'Money!' shrieked Tilda. 'You can stand there and think of *money* at a time like this?'

'Restoring a worn-out old church when *lives* are at stake!' scoffed Bessie.

'Lives?' Bea and Gilbert inquired together.

'Even now Hester Jones is closing in.'

Miss Beatrice Wilkes-Tooley and the Reverend Gilbert Sibson clutched one another and trembled in violent embrace. 'It is time to go down into town for the tea-dance,' Gilbert said. 'It is time to hear what Hester Jones has to say.'

9

Verity Confesses

'My mother and I used to come to the Bensusanns' blackberry-ing.' Verity Willow thought the old General was asleep so she tucked a thin woollen blanket about his legs and knelt beside him leaning her chin against the arm of his chair. 'We loved this place.'

Bensusann opened one eye, but shut it again quickly. 'Must be going gaga,' he thought.

'There was a small wooden gate we used to climb over,' Verity went on dreamily. 'It was at the far end of the long back drive that leads up to the Bensusanns'. You could see the great house in the distance, a small bright speck like a beacon shining far off, beckoning us through the trees. My mother had found an article about Ottilie Vigo's garden in an old illustrated magazine and she brought me up here one Sunday afternoon to see if anything was left. When we found we could get in and wander about, we took to coming regularly. We didn't have much of a garden at home, in any case Mother would not have had time for gardening beyond growing the potatoes and carrots she needed for the paying guests' teas. Mother thought it a shame the way the beautiful house and grounds had been left to deteriorate. She'd have given anything to be allowed to come up here and put it all to rights – I dread to think what poor Mother would say if she could see it now!' Verity sighed. She looked up at the General's impassive face, and went on.

'After Mother died, I have often comforted myself by thinking of her in a place very like the Bensusanns'. If anyone ever deserved to go to Heaven, she did – and this would be exactly the Paradise my poor mother would have chosen. I only wish she could have enjoyed it in her lifetime. At least a beautiful great house would have been *worthy* of all her housewifely devotion . . .

'I do not, alas, take after my mother. Mr Chase was shocked by the damp stains on my gingham table-cloths which reminded him, though he was kind enough not to say so, of a hoop-la stall at a fête. He obviously thinks the present ramshackle condition of the Bensusanns' quite suitable for a woman like myself, so lacking in any . . .' Verity glanced at her companion.

Reassured by his closed eyes and ponderous breathing, she continued, 'Life was never kind to my poor mother. After my father left she rarely smiled – until the summer of Raymond Bast when we both of us . . . My father had been a pilot in the RAF – he had come back from the excitement of commanding a squadron of fighter planes to a job selling vacuum cleaners. And to an obsessively houseproud wife, by then a complete stranger to him, and a small whingeing daughter who was frightened of this strange man who treated the house like a hotel and her mother like his own personal chambermaid. It wasn't his fault – he had been used to men such as the clarinettist Albert Hodge who serviced the planes, standing to attention and saluting him on sight. Now he had to go knocking at people's doors and listening to the woes of Iris Hodge who had been discarded by Dickie Paisley and did not know what to do with herself all day except keep travelling salesmen from travelling by chatting on the doorstep. Mrs Hodge could no more afford a vacuum cleaner than . . . It will have been like living on in Knibden after a lottery – it was so dull, my poor father could not settle. One morning he climbed out of the bed he shared with my mother, dressed himself quietly, tip-toed past the door of the room where I slept with my dolly, and left the house before we were up. I have often gone over that morning in my mind, retracing his steps. I shall never know if my daddy looked in on my sleeping head, and gave me one last kiss.' Verity sighed audibly.

General Bensusann held his breath. One last kiss! he thought. And when the dance was over, and the mystery of the dead guest solved, what then?

'If we had never known where my father went, if we had never heard from him again, I suppose I would now be wondering if the dead guest at the Gallimore could have been my father. Filled with remorse and wanting to do something for the daughter he'd taken no interest in all these years. I'd be planning what to do with the vast sums of money waiting in the bank. Others would be wondering too. Men like Follifoot, Treadgold and Macready would be making up to me, seeing as how Hester Jones might shortly reveal that I am an heiress. Everyone would be saying, "So! That ne'er-do-well, Jimmy Willow, made a fortune out of his vacuum cleaners, after all!" '

Verity Willow sighed again. 'Still, if I *were* to have money now, I would only be thinking how my mother could have done with it *then*. She had to manage as best she could. Throughout the war my father had always sent part of his earnings home each week – after he left, we did not even have that. Mother had no family to fall back on. Life was hard – but stealing up here to the Bensusanns', carrying a string bag containing a little food wrapped in grease-proof paper and a tea cloth each for us to sit on, made life bearable. I feel sure you would not have begrudged this to my mother, General Bensusann, if you had known her.'

The General heaved in his sleep and turned his head slightly to one side.

'If only you knew how I used to *dream* that one day the great Bertram Bensusann might come along and catch us picnicking under the trees his famous mother once planted. *My* mother would offer him one of our sandwiches, or an apple, and you would fall madly in love with her. And then we would come to live with you up here, and she would use all the energy she wasted frying breakfasts for ungrateful salesmen to make *you* happy, and to transform the Bensusanns' back to what it once was. I used to dream, too, about the wedding at St Redegule's, a lavish affair, conducted rather grudgingly by the Reverend Jerabius Hartley who always took a dim view of my mother, and would not enjoy seeing someone he frowned upon so well rewarded. I'd have been bridesmaid. And worn a satin dress with rosebuds made of netting and lace gloves – like Norah Bird at the wedding of Mr Nye with her teacher, Miss Pringle. And after that, my friend Belle Quinn and her sister Fleur to whose smart house I occasionally used to get invited, out of pity probably, would sometimes be allowed to come and play with me in the great grounds of the Bensusanns'. Mrs Enderby would lay on freshly squeezed lemonade, and there would be tennis. Mr Lethbridge would mark out the lawn and call me Miss Verity . . .

'But my mother could never have said boo to a goose, let alone offered General Bertram Bensusann, sole survivor of the Eleventh

Knibdens, an apple or a pickle sandwich. She was only too ready, though, to be mercilessly exploited by men who paid to stay in our house – they obviously thought they were paying for more besides the room, Mr Harris who sold crumpled hats, Mr Storr with his mildewy Bibles, and the rest of them. They would take it in turns to enter my mother's bed the way they took turns to use the bathroom on the stairs, queuing impatiently and urging one another not to take too long, and leave everything clean and ready for the next occupant. I used to hear the men snigger among themselves that they were making do with old mutton when they would prefer juicy spring lamb. Meaning me. They felt entitled to meat after a hard day's work. My mother obliged them all patiently. I can see her now standing over the stove, frying countless tomatoes, sausages, liver and bacon. She worked hard. Between them, the lodgers paid her just enough to keep us respectably housed and clothed. But, as I say, the Reverend Jerabius Hartley took a dim view. It did not matter to him that paying guests had been Theodore Fechnie at the bank's idea to help make ends meet.

'Our secret trips to the Bensusanns' were like flights into fairyland. I had seen you once, in the town, on one of your rare visits home. You barely noticed us as you held the door for my mother at the post office, but I thought, how much more noble and worthy of my poor mother you were, in your Eleventh Knibdens uniform, than any of her fat bald-headed salesmen. Children can be such snobs . . .

'On my tenth birthday we came up here as usual. The back gate had been left unlocked, so for once we did not need to scrabble over. I was wearing my best frock and I had brought Dolly along. I was getting a bit old for dolls but Dolly made it more of a birthday party without the need for extra food. We should have realized someone was about, because of the unlocked door. Perhaps we had grown too sure of ourselves – Mother and I had come up here so often over the years we'd almost forgotten we were not meant to.

'We had just settled ourselves and spread out our banquet when a man was suddenly bearing down on us, yelling and waving a gun. He began firing at our feet. I screamed in terror but my mother grabbed hold of my hand and started to run, dragging me with her. The man went on firing, peppering the ground behind so that little clods of earth sputtered the backs of my sandals and if we had stopped, even for an instant, his line of fire might have caught up and blown off our ankles. We ran and ran and did not let up till we were back through the gate and half way down the rhododendron-clad hill. It was only as I recovered my breath I realized I had left Dolly behind. We had hardly touched the birthday food and my mother had lost her string bag. Who was he? I asked at last and Mother said she thought it was Mr Lethbridge, General Bensusann's butler, out with his gun. He was only doing his job, she said, but I was inconsolable. My mother had made Dolly for me out of one of my baby dresses. I could remember holding her up to show my father a few weeks after he had come back from the war. Showing him Dolly was my attempt to make friends. Mother tried to tell him that I did not show my special doll to anyone, but I do not think this privilege impressed a man who had flown fighter planes through moonless nights into enemy territory.

'I have often wondered what Mr Lethbridge did with the home-made doll and the string bag containing apples and pickle sandwiches he captured that afternoon. Sometimes I pictured him picking up Dolly and being softened by her sweet button eyes and little stitched mouth. I hoped he might give her a little of the love she was used to receiving from me. But I dare say he went straight back up to the house and instructed Mrs Enderby to dispose of the confiscated items in the Bensusanns' incinerator. It was as if my childhood had been left behind under the trees of our forbidden paradise. And burned.

'After that, there was nothing much to look forward to. I was no longer able to dream of a romantic encounter between my mother and the wealthy handsome owner of the Bensusanns' that might break the unremitting monotony of our lives. I lived in a narrow little world between school and home and the public library. Then came the summer of Raymond Bast. The summer of the last Great Knibden Lottery, when I was thirteen. And dragons won.'

'Dragons?' Bensusann said, waking up. He shook himself. 'Mr Lethbridge was only doing his job, you know! To keep out trespassers from the town.'

'I know,' Verity said. 'I followed Raymond Bast up here – and discovered that the man was only Harry Best. He had some scam going with Mr Lethbridge, though I never found out what it was. They locked me up for hours in one of the rooms upstairs. It had no glass in the window. I had a fever for days afterwards – but by then Mr Best had made his get-away. I never told the police. I never even told Herbert. I have not needed to tell Miss Jones – I am sure she knows already. I expect she has found out the truth and will tell the town tonight how I . . .'

Bertram Bensusann patted the slender hand that held the side of his chair. 'I am an old man,' he said. 'But you have nothing to fear. Lethbridge was a good butler. He spent his life looking after this place all those years when I never came near it. He kept out trespassers like yourselves. Then he died here. He is buried down by the herbaceous borders . . .' General Bensusann pointed towards some thick undergrowth; Verity Willow looked in the direction he indicated. 'Mr Lethbridge would not have wanted to spend eternity in the neatly tended graveyard beside St Redegule's. Even if the Reverend Hartley would have had him – I rather think Jerabius Hartley took a dim view of Mr Lethbridge, also. In any case, I thought, Keep an eye on the old sod, know what he gets up to. I should have kept more of an eye on the fellow while he was alive.'

'Yes, I think perhaps you should,' Verity said with some feeling. 'Mr Lethbridge . . .'

'He was a devil. Just the sort to eat his lunch in your library so sneakily nobody would ever catch him out. *She* was even worse, Mrs Enderby. She'd have eaten the books themselves. What a pair those two were – well matched.'

'If you didn't like Mr Lethbridge, or Mrs Enderby, why didn't you get rid of them? There can have been nothing to stop you after you'd come of age.'

'How simple you make it sound, Miss Willow! After my mother died, I used to come home in the holidays and find Mrs Enderby and Mr Lethbridge sitting in silence at opposite ends of the long dining table in my parents' dining room, not talking to each other but sharing the best cuts. I would eat whatever was left over when they had finished. Mrs Enderby was a thin-lipped, flat-chested, unmotherly, unhousewifely sort of woman, not so

343

very unlike you yourself in appearance, dear Miss Willow, but nothing at all like you. It puzzled me how she came to be doing the job she was in. Lethbridge, on the other hand, was good at being a butler. Too good. I always had a feeling he was not really a butler. Just a man biding his time, acting the part.'

'Oh?'

'But then, I too was in the wrong part, so perhaps I was alert to these things.'

'In the wrong part, General Bensusann?'

Bertram Bensusann nodded his head. 'It will come out shortly, so you may as well know now. I was such a very ordinary little boy. Everyone remarked on it. People openly wondered how Ottilie Vigo and her great essayist husband could have produced a child so unlike themselves. I enjoyed the rough and tumble of ordinary little boys. I had no artistic sensibility. My mother was unable to hide her disappointment.'

'It was a lot for anyone to have to live up to,' Verity observed. 'Being the heir to the Bensusanns'.'

'It was not for *me* to live up to anything!' The General seized Verity's hand and squeezed it fervently. 'When I came home from school that time and found Ottilie Vigo had died and there were lengthy obituaries singing her praises in the horticultural press, I was not so much sorry as relieved. My mother's brother whom I had rarely seen became my guardian, but he lived far away and was happy to leave everything here to the competent Mr Lethbridge. And I was free to get on with my stamp collecting, unhindered.'

'Stamp collecting?'

'It was my schoolboy passion. That, and longing to be rid of Mrs Enderby. I promised myself that on my twenty-first birthday I would fire her.'

'And did you?'

'I did. On my twenty-first birthday, I said "You are fired!" Simple as that.' He went quiet.

Through the window they could see Desmond Chase arguing with Mrs Parbold.

'They look so unhappy,' Verity said.

'They will be happy one day,' General Bensusann said. 'I will see to it personally.'

'Will you?' Verity asked. 'Will you really?'

'Ah, Miss Willow, it is not difficult to make the likes of Desmond Chase and Hilda May Parbold happy. Why, the dead stranger could do it a million times over with that fortune of his! But you . . .'

'Me?'

'For you, and me, to find happiness, Verity, the whole world must first be turned upside down. Even then, such moments as we can enjoy can only be fleeting. Legendary.'

'I feel happy now,' Verity said quietly.

General Bertram Bensusann grinned. 'So do I, my dear, so do I.'

The *reveille* had sounded. It was time to walk down into town and take up position in the Gallimore Hotel. 'Whatever happens, Verity,' Bensusann said as she helped him to his feet, 'you need only give your name, rank and number. You are not obliged to help the enemy. There are international conventions governing these things.'

10

I Never Wished You Dead

Mary Wilkes-Tooley saw her daughters off to the tea-dance and then returned to her kitchen where she sat for a long time with her head in her hands.

'Peter!' she moaned as emotions long suppressed welled from within like liquids boiling in the great black pans beside her. But it was *Peter* who sat in the room beside her. *Peter* was the reason she'd not dared open her eyes to look about her all these years.

'Peter,' she moaned again, angry this time. It had all been his fault, all of it – no wonder he now sought by elaborate and public means to make amends! But Mary was not so easily appeased. 'As if a great fortune *now* could make up for what I lost *then*.' She sighed. And she sighed again – Peter Goodfellow, *dead*? He had been dead to her for years, what difference did his dying make now? 'He used me ill, and continues to do so from beyond his grave . . .' she thought.

Even as she wept, poor Mary knew she could not wholly blame Peter. Her father, the kindly, good-hearted Mr Bridgewater who had run the Knibden Municipal Insurance Company for decades and who took an insurance man's distrustful view of any risk, had refused to allow Mary and Peter to wed until the lad had proved himself. This Peter had naturally sought to do, as all Knibden's menfolk hoped to, by winning the Great Knibden Lottery. 'We have all been victims of that!' Mary concluded. 'I have been Aubrey Wilkes-Tooley's wife all these years. Mother of his three great selfish daughters, when all the while, but for the lottery . . .'

Mary shivered, suddenly feeling the chill. The cast-iron pans were not boiling on the hob beside her; the fire was not lit. She rose and went upstairs to where Aubrey lay slumped on his side, on his side of the bed. A spent husk, she thought looking down at the man. A skin some creature of the sun sloughed off long ago as it went on its way. Where had they all gone, the people they had once been? Where had Peter gone when he'd left Knibden? What had happened to him between that day, and this?

'And what has happened to us?' Mary asked her husband, uncertain whether she said the words out loud. Aubrey, in any case, did not respond. She left the room and returning to the kitchen, wrapped herself up warm and slipped out of the back door to hurry after her daughters, down into the town towards the Gallimore. The streets were packed with people, oblivious of one another, all hurrying in the same direction. It was just like the eve of Day One of the lottery, Mary thought, when every dragon, every naked woman and every trumpet were all still in with an equal chance. Anyone with a ticket in his pocket might win and everyone shared in the general rejoicing that a great fortune would soon come to someone.

How excited Peter had been as he'd taken her hand and hurried her through Knibden's streets towards the dance held *that* evening at the Gallimore Hotel. He had waved his lottery ticket in her face. The poor lad actually thought their lives would come right now – all he had to do, to show her father he was worthy of Mary, was to win the Great Knibden Lottery! He'd had such faith. She had been the faithless one – and she had paid the price.

Mr Bridgewater had not known, though he might have guessed, that his daughter had already promised to marry Peter. It was an engagement that had gone on ever since they'd first exchanged vows with the proverbial curtain ring in the infant class. Since then, the pair had grown to a private understanding by which they understood that when Peter had put together enough to buy himself a small shop, or a travelling business, and had proved to her father – by having sufficient of his own – that it was not merely Mary's money he was after, they would wed. Until then, Mary was content to go on keeping house for her father, enjoying an occasional outing to the Alhambra with her beau, and kissing chastely by moonlight afterwards outside the kitchen door.

Once or twice, Mary had tried to persuade her father to take Peter on. She suggested he might be allowed to join the teams of young men who cycled round Knibden with notebooks jutting from their pockets, chasing Knibden Municipal Insurance

Company business. 'I know Peter's probably not pushy enough, but people will like him and maybe he'll sell policies that way,' she'd said hopefully. Her father steadfastly resisted the idea. Pressed further on one occasion he'd told his daughter that he did not think her young man had it in him. 'I do not wish to displease you, Mary, so I have refrained from saying this before. I dare say Peter Goodfellow is very likeable – but I have yet to see *anything* that suggests he is steady enough either for the insurance business, or to marry you.' Mary could not argue since she also had her doubts. She had known Peter too long not to.

Young Peter, meanwhile, was in an impossible position. He tried all kinds of jobs but they were, without exception, poorly paid and uninteresting. He stuck at nothing. He'd had work in Mr Bird's tannery at one stage but had been laid off after sticking up for a man the foreman Sharps had it in for. Peter was unable to move to another town where there might be more opportunities because he wanted to be near Mary. After a time, he pinned all his hopes and ambitions on the next lottery. It seemed to him his only chance of getting anywhere in life. And of marrying Mary.

The very first day tickets went on sale, he'd spent nearly every penny he could put together buying one. Then he hurried round to show the ticket to his fiancée. Bursting into the kitchen where she was making bread, he waved the valuable bit of paper in her face, kissing her. 'If this comes up trumps, Mary, we'll be able to do as we please! We'll be able to wed at last.'

Mary regarded the naked woman on the ticket briefly, and with amusement. Peter's joy in anticipation of their good fortune was infectious. Despite the flour on her hands and dull pain in her heart, Mary let him tuck his arm into hers and the pair danced round and round the dough-covered table just as they had done when they were children. When her mother had been alive. If only her mother were here now, baking the bread and able to offer guidance. At night, each night then, right up to the first day of the lottery when trumpets, dragons or the woman would be drawn, Mary knelt down by her bed as her long dead mother had taught her and prayed as fervently she could that Peter's naked woman might win. Every day, during that exciting time when tickets were freely on sale and the competition was still wide open, Peter had appeared in her kitchen waving the ticket on which all their hopes rested. What plans Peter had! How she wished her father were at home sometimes to hear her beau speak of them. Every day Peter arrived with a fresh scheme to cleverly turn the winnings, when he'd won them, into something even more substantial. 'I could double it all in no time, and double it again, Mary. All I need is a start . . .' All he needed was to win. Every night after Peter had gone, Mary had given her father his supper, locked the doors of the house, and hurried upstairs to pray.

As Day One of the lottery drew near, the whole town seemed to go berserk. One afternoon Mary had taken tea with Peter at the Gallimore Hotel. It had been an extravagance beyond their means but in those heady days Peter had felt rich and Mary Bridgewater did not have it in her heart to crush his enthusiasm. They had sat whispering together in awed silence, waited on by the elderly Gallimores.

'That's what will happen to you,' Peter had whispered. Mary knew what he meant. When Sir Mayhew Gallimore's fortune was entirely squandered, the second Lady Gallimore, or Florrie Farr as she'd been, had turned the family home into a hotel, and set the five ageing Miss Gallimores to run it. They ran it still. Five stick-like figures in worn ancient clothes, with worn ancient faces. There wasn't a girl in Knibden who did not know that if you waited too long to be married, as the Gallimore sisters had waited, losing your looks and missing your chances, you might end up a dry old stick serving teas in a faded hotel dining room. Lady Florence Gallimore had hung the painting of her step-daughters in their wasted prime on the wall of the Gallimore's dining room to warn the maidens of Knibden against excessive delay.

Sarah Gallimore smiled stiffly at Mary and Peter as she served them their scones with jam and cream. When she left them alone at last, Peter said eagerly, '*Someone* will win – why should that someone not be me?'

'Yes, why not you, Peter?' Mary agreed, touching his wrist lightly with her finger. Didn't the Queen of England wake up in the mornings and lie there and marvel that of all the people who might have been Queen, she was the one with a royal insignia on her dressing-gown and fluffy bedsocks? 'Montague Cayke's

Imperial Players are on at the Alhambra at the end of the week. I've got a little money put by. Couldn't we perhaps get seats in the stalls?'

'We can do *anything*.' Peter kissed her.

Old Sarah Gallimore's hands shook as she returned and asked the lovers if there was anything further they required.

'Only to win the lottery,' Peter said laughing, and without looking up.

Old Sarah Gallimore opened her mouth to say something, but no words came. Mary felt suddenly cold, but Peter noticed nothing amiss.

No one slept a wink the night before the lottery, and yet, in that wink, dragons, trumpets and naked women danced from their woodcuts and clattered along Knibden's streets, hammering on the doors and leering in at the windows. They entered the Gallimore and joined in the dancing. They stepped on Mary's toes as Peter swung her round. And when Peter delivered Mary safely back home after the dance – held on the eve of every lottery to commemorate some Frenchie who had been stoned to death by a mob that hadn't liked a foreigner winning – the girl bid her father 'goodnight' and hurried upstairs to her room. Throwing herself down on the rag rug beside her bed, Mary had prayed, not to Knibden's St Redegule, but to that other woman who might better understand. She could only dimly remember her long dead mother yet Mary turned to her now in her hour of need.

Had that been sacrilege, Mary wondered. Had St Redegule punished her by inflicting on young Mary Bridgewater the worst fate that could befall a Knibden girl? 'It was no more than I deserved,' Mary thought this evening as she stood in the main Square of the town, gazing up at the lighted ballroom of the Gallimore Hotel. She could hear the music and see the dancers but she stood alone outside in the darkness. 'I have been standing alone like this in the darkness ever since you left,' she moaned. 'Poor Peter.' The man had died alone in the room on the first floor that was occupied now by Hester Jones. He'd had with him only enough money in his pocket to pay for his one night's stay – and had left her no clues to comfort her and tell her what had happened to him throughout the intervening years. That was his story, and he had kept it to himself. And this has been my punishment for not believing in him.

The morning after the dance at the Gallimore, news came: dragons had been drawn. Trumpets and naked women were worthless. Mary had not known what she would say to her fiancé. She longed for Peter to come to her for comforting and yet she dreaded his arrival, and his despair. Late in the afternoon Peter Goodfellow staggered into her kitchen. She'd been alarmed to see him, not downcast as she'd expected, but with liquor on his breath and a strange new light in his eye. 'Lend me some money, Mary!'

Mary gazed at her fiancé without speaking.

'I must buy a dragon now, can't you see?'

Mary could not see. She went on staring at the young man, scarcely recognizing him. She was frozen to the spot, unable to speak. Peter came up very close to her and put his hands on her shoulders. They moved towards her neck. Still Mary stared.

'Must I beg? Well then!' Peter threw himself down on his knees before her, his face distorted into a surly sneer. He made a futile grab at her hand – and fell forward on the floor like Bill Parris clumsily lighting candles in front of St Redegule. Then Peter rose again and lurched towards her. Poor Mary managed to step aside just in time, and he then began pummelling his fists furiously on the table. 'Every minute you delay,' he roared, saliva dripping from his mouth, his hair wet with sweat, 'standing there like some simpering virgin, begging for it on her wedding night, the more dragons'll cost when I get back out . . .'

Still Mary hesitated. She had a little money she'd sensibly put by, and she would not mind Peter's having it, but she had been strictly taught that lending and borrowing were equally ruinous: demeaning the borrower, undermining the lender. A grave union not to be entered into lightly nor without due consideration. 'I was planning to go to the Alhambra,' she said quietly.

'The Al'ambra!' Peter shouted, frothing at the mouth. 'You would rather spend your money seeing theatricals than give me the chance to make our fortune! That's all you think of me, is it, Mary?'

'Montague Cayke's Imperial Players are on – I was hoping . . .'

'Screw Monty Cayke!' Peter thundered. 'Bugger his Imperial Players. And damn you!'

Mary winced as though he had hit her. Silently turning her back on the boy she had loved since the first class of the infant school, she reached a glazed jam pot down from the mantelpiece and took it to the table. She shook out its contents. Peter's eyes boggled as her savings spilled across the table. 'Take it, Peter,' she said, without expression. 'Go and buy your dragon.'

Peter glanced quickly at the girl. He would like to have said 'I don't want your blasted money!', but he did want her blasted money. He wanted it very badly. He scooped all the notes and coins off the table, counting them up as he did so. Who knew what her delay had cost him? Still, it might be about enough. Outside the vaunting whoops of dragon owners could be heard above the pitiful yelps of those who trampled discarded trumpets and women underfoot. Peter pulled open the door and without pausing to say 'goodbye', charged headlong into the frenzied night.

Mary picked up the ticket Peter had left behind. She ran her finger wistfully over the contours of the crudely cut naked woman that had, until that morning, represented so much hope. Then the poor girl crumpled the worthless piece of paper and stuffed it into the empty pot which she returned to its place on the mantelpiece. Only now did she notice her father who had noiselessly entered the kitchen and, judging from the grave look on his face, witnessed the entire scene. With a cry of deep sorrow, Mary threw herself into Mr Bridgewater's arms and let him cradle her head on his chest just as he had done, in this exact same spot, that terrible night long ago when her mother had died. 'He's gone!' she sobbed.

I will not always be here, the widower thought, feeling as crumpled and useless to his daughter as the hapless lottery ticket. 'I think I'd better go after him,' her father said then. Mr Bridgewater lowered his daughter gently into a chair. 'Whatever my past differences with Peter, it is not safe on the streets of Knibden tonight. Destinies are being decided – who knows what may happen to a man in his state, and with money in his pocket, out there on a night like this. I must see he's all right . . .'

'Do that, Father!' Mary urged gratefully and, as she watched the beloved elderly figure disappear off into the dark, following the same route taken by her fiancé not a minute or two since, she knew it could not matter to her now whether Peter's new ticket lost or won. Her love for him had been destroyed.

Aubrey Wilkes-Tooley woke with a head that raged as if the dragon himself – the one on the ticket he had sold at a good profit to a chap he'd met in the street – had breathed fire. Mary's father had arrived just in time to witness the transaction. Mr Bridgewater was impressed by the steadiness of a young man who could trade an outside chance of winning the lottery for the certainty of slight, but immediate, solid gain. Such a man with the talent to calculate risk would be an asset in the insurance business. He invited Aubrey to join him in a drink. While Peter slumbered beside them, overcome with exhaustion and relief at having acquired the dragon that now resposed expensively and safely in his pocket, one drink had led to another, leading eventually to Aubrey Wilkes-Tooley being brought home by the proprietor of the Knibden Municipal Insurance Company in the middle of the night to sleep off the excitement in Mary's kitchen.

Mary never forgot coming downstairs first thing in the morning to light the stove and finding her future husband and the father of her three daughters, fast asleep on the bench. She had been staring at him when he opened his eyes and saw her bending over him. 'We married shortly afterwards, and have lived happily ever after,' she told Hester Jones.

'The dance is well underway,' Miss Jones replied, glancing fearfully up at the lighted windows of the Gallimore Hotel's ballroom.

The dead guest's investigator looked drawn, and rather nervous, Mary Wilkes-Tooley thought. And she couldn't help wondering what her three daughters had been up to. Then she noticed that Hester Jones was clutching an official-looking envelope.

'That's not . . .?' Mary inquired.

Hester Jones nodded. 'Mr Williams entrusted it to me earlier. I must say I am rather dreading . . .'

A burst of music came down to them from the crowded ballroom.

'They will be expecting you,' Mary said.

Miss Jones sighed. 'Expectations are high. All Knibden is alight with dreams and desires. There is scarcely anyone who does not . . .'

'I can see why you hesitate to go in!' Mary laughed. 'I would not like to be in your shoes.'

Hester Jones smiled bravely. Her shoes were *not* enviable – the strap on her best pair had broken while she'd been struggling along the railway line, three days before.

'And I don't fancy your chances when you meet my three daughters!'

'I have met them,' Miss Jones said. 'I rather think *they* are about to meet their . . .'

'I suppose, at this point, you wish you'd never started? You must be tempted to pick up your suitcase, and be on your way. Leave the town to sort itself out.'

Hester Jones nodded. 'I *am* looking forward to moving on. But I cannot abandon my task just yet, however much I'd like to. I would only spend the rest of my life wondering how it all turned out. A bit like finding the last pages ripped from a library book. Not knowing the ending would haunt my waking hours, and ruin my dreams. I'd never be able to concentrate on anything else. How much better to go ahead and risk disappointing everyone, than walk away now and leave people to guess what might have been in my power to purvey.'

'You are a brave woman, Miss Jones! If I'd had more courage in the face of the unknown, and more faith in poor Peter, *my* story might not have ended as it has. I should now be telling you how my fiancé won the last Great Knibden Lottery. And then doubled and trebled his money and how my father let us marry, and what splendid children we had, and all the adventures and little disasters along the way. As it is, I have lived my life in the shadow of what might have been . . .'

'Hallo, Mary!' A man stepped, as if at Hester Jones's bidding, from the shadows. The light from the lighted ballroom falling across his face.

'Peter!' Mary gasped. The pair embraced. 'I don't believe it!'

'Miracles happen, that is the nature of miracles, Mary.' Peter and Mary were oblivious now to any third person present. 'I heard about the dead guest at the Gallimore and I . . .'

'I always knew you would come back. But . . .'

'You thought the dead guest was me? Come to leave you his fortune.'

Mary nodded.

'You are disappointed? You looked forward to when Hester Jones mounted the podium and asked the band to hush while she announced that the man who won the last lottery, with a ticket purchased using money lent him by Mary Wilkes-Tooley – only she was Mary Bridgewater then – had come back to Knibden to die and leave his childhood sweetheart a great fortune. His lottery winnings doubled, and trebled. Is that what you wanted?'

'Oh, Peter, I never wished you dead! How can you think such a thing?'

Peter Goodfellow sighed. 'It didn't work out quite the way I intended, Mary.'

Mary smiled. 'I didn't think it would.'

'I halved my winnings almost immediately. Then, without even trying I halved them again. Money, I have found, is a tricky substance to hold on to. Trickier than love . . .'

'Or the peach-coloured silk that slipped through *my* fingers, reminding me of the infant Lalla . . .'

'I could not return to you, Mary, because very quickly every penny was gone. Your father always thought I was worthless – he was right. I now have nothing.'

'You have me.'

'But your husband, your daughters?'

Mary laughed. 'Oh, Peter, you goose!' She linked arms with the man, not to enter the Gallimore ballroom and perform the polka on the repolished floor, but to dance round the dough-covered table of her dreams. Aubrey would be all right. The Knibden Municipal Insurance Company had been set back on its feet. The bell on Neville Tagg's bicycle having been paid for many times over by people taking out policies in the wake of the guest at the Gallimore's death. As for Chickie, Lalla and Bea – those three young dragons were all fired up and would none of them miss her, or even notice her absence. 'If there is one thing you and I have learned, Peter, it is to alter the ending before it is too late.'

'Aren't you coming in to hear what I have to say?' Hester Jones called after the lovers, but they were no longer interested in the mysterious guest who had died at the Gallimore. Or in who would inherit his enormous fortune. And why. Soon Hester Jones was left standing on her own, in the cold. Clutching the official-looking envelope.

'There you are, Hester!' Michael Milady emerged from the Gallimore Hotel's entrance. 'We were wondering where you'd got to. Albert Hodge and his Band are in full swing. Everyone is so excited . . .'

11

Nemesis

Bill Parris staggered through the darkness. He had not had a copy of the unprinted newly revised *Knibden Bugle* so he did not know he had been invited to the tea-dance along with the rest of the town. He knew nothing of the music, dancing, flowers and food – but he *did* know that the dead guest owed him. And he had come to collect.

There had been no family at the graveside to tip him. No grieving, grateful widow weeping her eyes out but about to collect on a Knibden Municipal Insurance Company policy, and so flushed and generous with her cash. No one had remembered the grave digger, and slipped a little something into Bill Parris's pocket. Hester Jones would see him right though. He had come to see that she did.

As he emerged into the main Square, Mary and Peter rushed past him in the opposite direction, so absorbed in each other and intent on wherever they were going, they might have been leaves blown along Knibden's pavements by the late-autumn evening breeze. Bill Parris stared at Peter Goodfellow as if he had seen a ghost.

He gazed up at the lighted ballroom of the Gallimore Hotel, and at the crowds of dancers who were all about to get their come-uppance. It is like the ball at the turn of the century, he thought, when the Five Beautiful Gallimores danced in their prime, and not long after got what was coming to them.

This is a town founded on folly. A town about to pay for its foolishness. And he had been sent there, by the blessed St Redegule, Patron Saint of Lost Opportunities, weeping on her ugly concrete plinth, to seize the moment and make sure that it did.

He mounted the steps that led up to the Gallimore Hotel and, reaching into his pocket for one last swig that would give him the courage to confront Miss Hester Jones, he missed his footing. Bill Parris staggered and fell forward and as he fell, he had time to wonder who there would be now to dig *his* grave. No man is indispensable, he thought as he struck the ground. Except perhaps to himself.

'*I* am the someone-who-is-not-someone,' he told his Maker. And his Maker replied, 'I know who you are. I made you, remember. You are Mr William Parris.'

PART FOUR

The Tea-Dance

'Ladies and Gentlemen! Take your partners for the "Dead Stranger's Waltz" . . .'

The moment I appeared through the Gallimore's ballroom door, Albert Hodge raised his clarinet high and the dancers surged in a great colourful swirl on to the floor. I had no intention of joining them just then. 'There are one or two things I need to find out before I can make my announcement,' I told Michael Milady.

'There are one or two things she needs to find out before she makes her announcement,' I heard him telling people.

I had not forgotten my promise to partner Mr Williams in the polka. I also suspected that the citizens of Knibden would expect the dead guest's investigator to dance with the dead guest's heir. They would therefore set inordinate store by Hester Jones's choice of partner, and it seemed fairer not to raise false hopes. The room was bright and densely crowded – but appeared even more so. The sparkling mirrors that lined the freshly painted walls reflected back the reflections of all the lights and people many times over. When you glanced round the room you saw into other mirrored rooms, a beady-eyed Hester Jones in every corner, looking this way and that.

Michael Milady pointed to the sealed envelope I was holding. 'You don't want to lose it,' he said. 'The way you lost your railway ticket.'

'No,' I agreed. 'I'm to guard this with my life!' The dead guest's executor had instructed me to interrupt proceedings towards the end of the evening. To comply with the terms of the Will – and to ensure I had spent the requisite three full days investigating the dead guest's wishes – I should make my announcement as close to the time at which I had appeared in the Swan, three days ago, as possible. I glanced at my watch. It was just after eight. In scarcely two hours, I would reveal my findings, read the contents of the envelope and then – I'd be free! In the meantime, I had work to do. 'I am hoping to complete my investigation during the next few dances.'

'You are remarkable!' Michael Milady said. 'What a shame Montague Cayke is not here. Why, you could have starred at the top of his bills. Across India, South Africa, Australia and Canada, you would have kept the natives in suspense!'

I smiled, and turned away. It was the natives of Knibden who concerned me tonight. Ever since Melinda Milady put her small son to bed in one of the rooms upstairs, abandoning him for ever at the Gallimore Hotel, Michael Milady's story had been waiting for Hester Jones. It could wait a little longer.

George Allendale sidled up in his lime-green jumper, his mother at his side. He produced a rusty Roman spear from his pocket and aimed it menacingly in my direction. 'Tea-dances are *dangerous* things, Miss Jones!'

Mrs Allendale scowled at his foolery, but I responded, 'Dangerous, Mr Allendale? It would take more than a spear sawn off some cast-iron railing to terrify me!'

'Very dangerous,' the chief librarian insisted. 'Why, someone might ask *you* to dance.' He roared with laughter. It was forbidden, of course to laugh in the library, so here in the ballroom of the Gallimore Hotel he felt free to laugh as loudly and openly as he pleased at his own jokes.

Mrs Allendale raised her eyes to the heavens and offered me a boiled sweet. 'I shall not be losing a son . . .' she started to say as I walked on.

Verity Willow moved steadily through the swirl of fresh flowery dresses, first with one partner, now another. On she danced in all that lightly scented springtime that swayed about her as she went, reminding Verity as so much did these days of that merry morning in May long ago when the whole of her life still stretched before her, but had then been channelled off into a dream. And Verity smiled the secret smile of Miss Maisie Vollutu for somewhere across the crowded ballroom, beyond the heaving tide of dancers and swell of heedless onlookers, sat Randolphe Shyne waiting calmly for her to reach him. She waved across the room – and I waved back, though I do not think it was me she was waving at.

Edmund Veitch, headmaster of Knibden, was keeping strict

time. He danced the first dance with his wife, which was only right and proper, then he took Chickie Wilkes-Tooley in his arms. It is important to keep one's workers' spirits raised, he thought, and Miss Wilkes-Tooley had been working long hours for him lately, helping to prepare for his revival. The frail Louisa did not like dancing, it left her breathless, whereas Miss Chickie was unmarried and enthusiastic, and would fret to sit out. Especially as her two sisters appeared to have such devoted partners. Edmund Veitch glanced stiffly down at the youngest of the Wilkes-Tooley girls, and could not help wishing Chickie had been a little less lavish with the *eau de roses*. He extracted a handkerchief from his pocket and, without missing a step, he deftly blew his nose. 'Ptarmic', he said to a class of boys and girls: a substance that causes sneezes.

Chickie Wilkes-Tooley in flouncy lace, with a cream-coloured ribbon in her bobbed hair and cream-coloured bows on her large flat shoes, thought she would *die* for joy! How keenly she noted that other couples fell back as she and the headmaster stepped their way, and she noted also the bright blue eyes of Roger Ambrose watching jealously over the timid little woman, his mother – Mr Veitch's second wife.

'I would do *anything* this man asked of me!' Chickie said to herself. 'Why, I would *kill* for Edmund Veitch, if that was what he wanted and it gave him the briefest moment's pleasure.' Chickie turned as she danced to smile brightly across at Louisa Veitch and was *astonished* to see that the woman had *turned her back*. Mrs Veitch appeared to be eating *a plate of strawberry mousse*! Well! thought Chickie Wilkes-Tooley indignantly. If Edmund Veitch were *my* husband, *I* would not sit by guzzling blood-red strawberry mousse while another, younger, woman danced all evening in his arms.

Hester Jones will notice my devotion, Chickie thought. She will have seen my crinkled typewriting paper and see to it that I am properly and publicly rewarded.

And Chickie felt properly and publicly rewarded as she leant more heavily on Veitch's strong supporting arm. A verse once chanted by the three Wilkes-Tooley girls as children came irresistibly into her head: *If wishes were horses, beggars would ride* . . . Chickie glanced again in Louisa's direction. *SHE would be dead, and you'd be by MY side!* A thrill, like a sharp stab of pain, coursed through Chickie's veins. Mrs Veitch *dead*! Chickie put her hand to her throat and feared she might faint except that to do so would occasion the headmaster unnecessary alarm. He'd have to lift her up and bear her bodily through the crowd of dancers out on to one of the Gallimore's white stone balconies for fresh air. And there, beyond the safety of the hotel's lighted ballroom, beneath the canopy of stars high above, she and Edmund Veitch would cling to one another, two brave creatures alone in all the endless emptiness of the great sprawling universe. Brought together at this tea-dance tonight, against all odds. As unlikely, magical, and yet statistically possible, as winning the Great Knibden Lottery!

'This is bigger than both of us,' Veitch would bend over her and whisper sternly. 'The hand of destiny is at work. It is what the dead guest willed. Even Hester Jones will give her blessing.' And Chickie Wilkes-Tooley would shiver and smile courageously up at her beloved until . . . until he kissed her! And Chickie would take strength from that kiss to go on. To return to the ballroom, and do whatever needed doing.

General Bensusann looked round the room for Verity Willow but could not see Knibden's assistant librarian anywhere in the great crush of dancers. It was a battlefield, he thought. The main thing was to keep moving forward; the main thing was to stay alive. He glanced up at the crystal chandeliers of the Gallimore's ballroom. They had been taken down and cleaned specially for the tea-dance, the banker's thin wife was sitting by the door nervily telling anyone who would listen. 'I bet *you* have a nice chandelier, or two, up at the Bensusanns'!' Dora Williams had remarked gaily to the General as he'd entered the room.

General Bertram Bensusann had leant on his walking stick and stared at Mrs Williams – and in *that* unguarded moment Mrs Parbold arrived to claim him as her prize. 'Gotcha!' she said, grabbing him by the elbow as if he were her mop. He thought he caught a glimpse of Miss Willow the far side of the room, but when he looked again, she had gone. The General attempted to hold the overdressed Mrs Parbold at arm's length, which was not easy as Mrs Parbold thrashed about, making no attempt either to keep time or steer clear of other dancers. 'Call me Hilda!' she said. The General had no intention of doing any such thing.

Women in *estaminets* he'd frequented had names like Jeanette, Petit Pettu and Mignon, he tried to tell her, but Hodge's clarinet was blasting out down the microphone and Mrs Parbold merely nodded and held him even tighter. 'That's nice, duck!' The moment he could, General Bertram Bensusann, sole survivor of the Eleventh Knibdens, long since disbanded, intended to cut in on Hester Jones and leave this frightful woman to her own devices. Out of the corner of his eye, the General saw Desmond Chase leaning against the wall, smirking with sarcastic pleasure. They are in this together, he thought. Desmond Chase and Hilda May Parbold deserved one another. And isn't that why we are all here this evening, he thought, to get our just rewards from Hester Jones?

'Coo-ee!' shouted Mrs Parbold, waving across the floor to a neighbour who nudged the people on either side so that they all looked over and saw Hilda May Parbold dancing with her General, as she had boasted to them she would. 'She'll 'ave 'im down at the bingo next,' one of them said, 'buying 'er crème de menthe, and scoring 'er card!'

He gazed fixedly up at the Gallimore's sparkling chandeliers (to avoid seeing Hilda Parbold), and as he did so a vision of Mrs Enderby appeared to the General, standing above him at the top of a great flight of stairs. Only this afternoon, Verity Willow had ventured up the main staircase of the Bensusanns' that he had not ascended in years. 'I love her,' he thought, for there was nothing the dear girl would like more than to fetch him apples, and a pickle sandwich. But the love of General Bertram Bensusann of the Eleventh Knibdens, now disbanded, for Miss Verity Willow was a hopeless thing. Shortly, Miss Jones would tell the town the truth and he would find himself unarmed and alone, surrounded by enemy fire on exposed terrain. The thousand crystals of the Gallimore's sparkling chandeliers glinted in the glass of Mrs Enderby's metal-rimmed spectacles so that he could not see her eyes. It has all been a mistake, she is telling him now. 'A *mistake*?' he queried. 'But I . . .'

'You didn't believe that nonsense I once told you?' Mrs Enderby's voice rang out. The other dancers appeared not to hear. Mrs Parbold took no notice. But *she* did not need to listen – she already knew Mrs Enderby's story. And had told it to Desmond

Chase. The pair had laughed just as Mrs Enderby was laughing now, so loud that the thousand crystals suspended overhead shivered and shook, but still no one else noticed. And still General Bensusann could not see the woman's eyes. 'Really, Bertram, you are a very silly boy!'

'It was folly on my part to go along with it,' Mr Lethbridge apologized, materializing at the elbow that was not clutched like a mop by Mrs Parbold. He offered to help the General once again with his stamp collection.

'My stamp collection!'

'Mind yer great feet – that's my bunion you've just trod on!' Hilda Parbold gave the General a playful shove. Couples around them smiled. Bensusann sniffed, but could not be altogether sorry now to find himself in the grip of these safe strong arms.

Hilda May Parbold, meanwhile, was wondering when she should push the General forward and remind him of his promise to announce to the town that he was leaving the Bensusanns' to her in his Will. Befuddled by stout, or crème de menthe or whatever she could ply him with in the interval in the dancing, he would publicly agree that she was his long-lost daughter, fathered on a Knibden maiden years ago. She would get what was due to her *this evening*. Without any favours from the dead guest, or from Miss Hester Jones. And that would be one in the eye to Desmond Chase!

Such utterances could never happen, the General thought. Mr Lethbridge and Mrs Enderby were both dead. Besides, this rather tame *thé dansant* was hardly a fit setting for the pair. She could not turn up now and tell Hester Jones that the story she'd once told him about his mother was untrue. Nor could Lethbridge – who had come to the Bensusanns' after reading a newspaper report about his parents' nuptials while sitting beneath the fountains and lions in Trafalgar Square – ever apologize for going along with the wicked woman's tale. But if the truth were to come to light, this very evening in the ballroom of the Gallimore Hotel, General Bertram Bensusann would face the consequences as resolutely as he had always stood firm under enemy fire.

Down the far end of the room the Reverend Gilbert Sibson waltzed with Beatrice Wilkes-Tooley, the eldest and ugliest of the Wilkes-Tooley girls. He buried his face in her coal-black hair and considered how he had not lived, or laughed, or danced until this moment. On arriving in Knibden he had sought out some other woman of the town to protect him from the attentions of Miss Zillanah Hartley. But the women he had chosen – the naked female on the lottery ticket and the unbending plaster virgin on an ugly concrete plinth – had both punished him mercilessly for his pains. The dead guest had changed all that. Gilbert kicked his heels, and clicked his fingers, and solemnly vowed, 'Tonight, I shall dance with every prettily dressed girl in the room!'

'You will do no such thing!' Beatrice Wilkes-Tooley clutched her partner as if she would never let him go. *If wishes were horses, beggars would ride*, she thought. *If you become rich, I'll stick like GLUE to your side.* The scansion was unimportant. What mattered was that when the dead guest's investigator handed Gilbert Duncie Sibson the fortune, Bea would be there at the ready. Next time a dance was held in Knibden, the glass slipper would be hers, and Chickie and Lalla would wear puce!

As it happened, Belle Quinn was already wearing puce. Albeit, puce-coloured best woollen weave that had not been purchased, off the peg, from Miss Bird's. She suppressed a sigh. Why didn't *someone* ask her to dance? She pressed her hands together and tapped her toes conspicuously in time with the music. She moved her head from side to side and smiled generously at the couples who danced by.

Belle had been escorted to the tea-dance by Sol and his girl but almost at once she had lost sight of the pair. Which was a pity as she would like to have introduced the famous mathematician's grandson to everybody. Belle wondered what the frumpy Wilkes-Tooley girl could see in the stick-like Gilbert. Daddy was quite right, she thought, *I* would never have suited the man. He has never in his life put one single good work into effect – while I, I have brought about this tea-dance. Belle smiled to discover the disappointment she had secretly nursed for so long, erased at last from her heart. Silently she thanked the dead guest for the solace he had brought her and, as she looked round the room for Sol and his pregnant girlfriend, she found herself smiling up at Mr Calderon who had just asked her to dance.

'I'd be delighted!' Belle exclaimed, though quite what Daddy would have said about his favourite daughter dancing with a publican in public she dreaded to think! Belle's trim felt hat – in matching puce – was set rather roguishly now on her short-cropped hair. She wondered if Mrs Mason might allow her a thimbleful of gin. Miss Quinn, herself, had expressly instructed that no alcohol whatsoever be permitted at the tea-dance – but might she not be allowed a little Dutch courage, in preparation for when Hester Jones made her announcement. You are a miracle worker! the girl would say, before she opened that envelope and told the town who was to inherit the dead stranger's fortune. I strongly suggest the heir to the dead guest's fortune gives you – ehem – a little consideration, in consideration of your pains. Not to mention the debts you have incurred. All this repolishing, cleaning, gilding and painting will not have been cheap and it would not be right for you to have to leave the Laurels since you will have been instrumental in seeing that they get what is theirs.

Neither Belle nor Mr Calderon could waltz (Daddy had forbidden his daughters dancing lessons) but they both laughed cheerfully enough at themselves. And others laughed with them, for you never saw such an incongruous couple. Janice Oakes wondered why Miss Quinn put up with the great lumbering fellow. The moment Janice knew who had got the cash, she would be off without handing in her notice. But, as the barmaid from the Swan gazed round the crowds of men who had poured into the Gallimore for the tea-dance, she thought that before the evening was out, one of them might make a proposal she could not refuse. Her days as a barmaid would be over. Why shouldn't the dead guest, whoever he had been, not do this, at least, for Miss Janice Oakes?

'Tea-dances are only a way of saving money on booze,' Janice remarked to the builder, Follifoot, who merely grinned back because Mrs Follifoot was near by, but he made a mental note to go down to the Swan 'for a site inspection' later and see if he couldn't take up where Mr Calderon had left off. Meanwhile, Dick Follifoot went on talking to Treadgold and Macready so that Janice wondered why the three were here in the noisy ballroom when they could talk business far better in the Swan. They were keeping an eye on their interests, she thought. Like everyone else in the room. Even those in reverse in the mirrors! Macready would be hoping to sell the inheritor some of his overpriced jewellery. That great solitaire she had seen these last few days in his window.

Matchett, the printer, danced with Beryl Laffety. 'I hadn't a clue, really I hadn't!' Beryl, talking ten to the dozen, was telling her son's new employer, yet again, how her husband had duped her. And others besides her. And not just the other Mrs Laffetys who had all been done out of their life insurance claims. 'He must have known that the truth comes out in the end – and if it doesn't emerge of its own accord, someone like Hester Jones turns up.'

Victor Matchett nodded grimly.

Beryl waved across the room, and I smiled politely back. It was always a possibility! I thought. Poor Mrs Laffety must be wondering whether, when the time came and all was revealed, the dead guest's investigator intended to involve the authorities. It was probably a criminal offence to help a husband on his way for the insurance money, even if it then turned out you had only shared him with others so there wasn't a penny coming to you, after all.

Matchett let Beryl talk. He felt a bit jittery himself. I will enjoy this tea-dance if it's the last thing I do, the printer decided. He was certainly not looking forward to the long trudge back in the darkness afterwards, down the murky towpath that led along-side the canal. If that Follifoot fellow was so keen to buy up the property, and cash in on its 'development possibilities', why not let him? Then he need never again pass the spot where old God-frey Buckworth had slipped . . .

When at last Beryl Laffety ran out of conversation, Matchett steered her bulky form over towards the refreshment table and seized two plates. *Music Dancing Flowers Food* it had said in the advertisement that had never been printed for the *Bugle* was not yet up and running. That's what came of taking on a work-shy Laffety as foreman. 'Forget the man,' Matchett told Beryl gruffly. 'We must all look ahead, not back.'

'He is amongst us!' murmured Norah Bird as she counted the number of fresh floral prints in select winter fabrics that had been purchased from her shop. 'The spirit of the dead stranger has glided over the Gallimore's ballroom floor and touched us all.' Even Mrs Parbold had lashed out to buy that cornflower frock that had been displayed in Miss Bird's window so long one of its sleeves had faded and Norah had marked it down a couple of pounds. 'A bargain,' she'd told Hilda Parbold, making her try it on, telling her the garment could have been made specially for her, it suited so well.

'We are celebrating,' Miss Bird exclaimed out loud. She wished Mrs Cooper could see her success. She wished Jack and Amy were here.

'What's there to celebrate?' someone, overhearing her speak, yelled above the din of the music, their mouth full of food.

'That we are all eating and dancing, while the stranger is dead. I expect he wanted us to think of that.'

Norah Bird herself was thinking, there will be a Miss Bird's of Knibden in every High Street across the land. Just as she had once told Jack there would be. When people met her, they would turn to one another, 'Well, fancy that! I never knew "Miss Bird" actually existed!' Then Norah would be invited to Buckingham Palace as one who had seen to it that the nation was better dressed. It has been my personal mission, she would tell Prince Philip. Miss Pringle made fun of my clothes so, before my father lost all his money, he bought out Mrs Cooper who had run the shop for years.

'And you have gone from strength to strength?' His Royal Highness would incline towards her and inquire.

'Oh no, it wasn't like that at all. For years I had a steadily declining trade. Young people do not know how to dress. Susie Till at the Silver Scissors Salon wears black boots, and goes braless . . .'

Miss Susan Till, standing across the ballroom floor, watching Neville Tagg waltzing with Lalla Wilkes-Tooley, would never know she had been the subject of conversation at Buckingham Palace.

'It is a sad fact of modern life that people have nothing to dress for,' His Royal Highness observed.

'Which was precisely why I agreed to the extravagance of a tea-dance at the Gallimore Hotel,' Norah Bird would say. She would not bore His Royal Highness with the details. Or tell him about Mr Singh who had chased half way across the world on the trail of Montague Cayke and ended up in Manchester stitching fresh floral prints. Nor about the stranger who'd died in Knibden and left a strange Will. How she had invested heavily and been repaid ten-fold and then put her gains to good use. Expanding her chain across the land.

'Yes, I am *the* "Miss Bird",' Norah said out loud. '*I do* exist!' How rich and regal she felt this evening as she held up the silk drawstring bag she'd borrowed from stock (still priced in Mrs Cooper's writing, at two pounds and sixteen shillings), and accepted HRH's gracious invitation to promenade with him across the repolished floor.

'You ought to dance,' Edina Allendale urged her son who had been standing at her side all this time, aloof to the proceedings. She expected him to suggest that they take a turn together but Knibden's chief librarian, picturing Zoë and the scantily clad Hyena, Calperius's favourite concubines, at a tea-dance, merely chortled. Then George waved to Verity Willow across the floor. She was changing partners and did not see him, at which point he noticed Janice Oakes, the busty barmaid from the Swan (only he had never been in the Swan and did not yet know she worked there), standing rather voluptuously on her own. *Veni, vidi, vici,* thought George.

'I think I *will* take a turn,' George Barrington Allendale told his mother.

Susie Till danced round her handbag. Nev was now clearly besotted with Lalla Wilkes-Tooley and she, for unfathomable reasons of her own, was encouraging his attentions. You had to laugh. Hadn't Nev's step-mother said so. The second Mrs Tagg, the woman Nev's father had married after Amy Pasco's early death who sat at home all day making paper flowers. 'I found a book on how to make them when Jack died. I've been making them ever since.'

'You ought to sell them,' Susie said.

Mrs Tagg looked shocked. 'Oh, no dear, I couldn't bear to part . . .'

Neville's step-mother told Susie she had known all along about her and Nev. 'I think the lad wanted me to act the wicked step-mother and say, "I want you out of the house – you and your hairdresser!" '

'You knew about me?'

'I'd have brought you tea and toast in bed in the mornings – but I thought you'd rather not be disturbed. Neville would only blush and drop breadcrumbs all over the sheets.'

'And Hester Jones?'

'Who? Oh – the investigator! She's the last person on earth he'd give his information to!' And then Nev's step-mother told Susie Till that the boy had dined yesterday evening with Lalla Wilkes-Tooley. The boy was faddish, fickle. His father, Jack, was just the same. It wouldn't last.

'Nev never speaks about his father,' Susie said.

'That's hardly surprising!' The woman who had married Jack Tagg, second time round, laughed. 'Always ready for a game of railway poker, was Jack. He only took up with Neville's mother, Amy Pasco who had been Norah Bird's best friend at school, to get away from Norah Bird. When Amy died, when Neville was little, he married me to look after the lad, and help him avoid Miss Bird again. That's men for you! Not to be taken too seriously. Neville will get his fingers burnt, then he'll be back. Wait and see.'

Susie Till was waiting and seeing. Meanwhile, the new foreman at Buckworth & Matchett's sauntered towards her. Gary Laffety was wearing a new biking jacket he'd bought for the tea-dance. Susie's heart missed a beat. It was just the sort of jacket favoured by the glossy magazines she read over other women's shoulders at the salon.

Neville Tagg trod on Lalla's toes. She smiled coolly down at him. 'You oaf!' she thought. *If wishes were horses, beggars would ride, I shall be rich when you inherit from the guest that died!* If, in less than two hours now, Hester Jones announced that Mr Tagg was the heir, the rich husband she'd always wanted would be *hers*! She'd force her sisters to wear puce. She tightened her grip on the fellow's shoulder and pulled him roughly to her. Neville's bushy moustaches tickled the white expanse of Lalla Wilkes-Tooley's shapely bosom and Neville went bright red in the face, and could barely breathe.

Susie Till, circling round Gary Laffety, giggled.

The General sighed. He had almost managed to station himself in front of Miss Jones and was about to command her to trot the next number with him. 'I want to tell you about my stamp collection,' he was on the point of saying. 'Mr Lethbridge took care of the Bensusanns' for fifty years but you will not be surprised to learn, the man was not all he seemed . . .'

Louisa Veitch watched Chickie Wilkes-Tooley dancing with her husband. She thought, I need not worry. All will be well. When the time comes to speak, I will tell Hester Jones what she needs to know. She tapped her son on his knee. 'Roger, dearest, you don't have to sit with me.' The waitress Doris Barr came darting over to them again, attentively filling their cups with tea and offering to fetch more food. 'The strawberry mousse was lovely dear but I couldn't possibly manage any more.' She is in love with the boy, poor creature, Louisa thought and she smiled kindly at Doris. It would have been more surprising to her if all the girls in Knibden were not in love with her son. His father had been equally lovable.

Dora Williams turned to her husband. No one had requested a literary allusion as yet, but the evening was undoubtedly going well. 'Everyone seems to be enjoying themselves, William. It is a credit to you. And to the bank.'

William Williams nodded. The whole town looked pleased with itself. Expectations were running high. He almost looked forward to writing his report! But the dead guest's executor knew he would feel a great deal easier when the dead guest's investigator had made her announcement and he'd be able to hand out the money and have done. He could not for the life of him predict who Miss Jones would favour – and he did rather wish she would not wave that sealed envelope about quite so freely. Supposing she lost it? Still, the girl had her methods, and he had to respect them. No one could keep their eyes off that envelope. It was almost as if Hester Jones were deliberately teasing the whole town. 'I have been reading Theodore Fechnie's secret files,' he told his wife.

Dora put her hand on her heart. She gasped. Whatever Madame Bovary's trials and tribulations had been, Mrs Williams felt sure that good woman never had to contend with confidential memoranda written by Mr Bovary's late predecessor.

Before William Williams could say anything further there was a commotion.

'Here's looking at you, kid!' Randolphe Shyne met Verity's

eyes over the rim of his whisky sour. A split second later, a bullet zinged past her left ear dashing the glass from his lips. When Verity dragged herself out from beneath the table she dived under for cover, a pool of shattered glass and liquid shimmered on the floor at Shyne's feet. A hollow wreath of smoke lingered above the empty chair.

Eileen Mason had come running into the room closely followed by her husband, the manager of the Gallimore Hotel. The Masons were as white as the starched linen for which they were renowned. Another death, in a hotel managed by themselves! It was unthinkable, unforgivable, Mrs Mason was shrieking. 'It is all your doing,' she yelled at Hester Jones. 'My Donald would never have permitted . . .'

'Donald? Who's Donald?' people wanted to know. 'We know no one of that name here.'

'The dead guest?'

'You promised to find me my baby!' Someone took flowers from a vase and dashed the water in Mrs Mason's face. When she had calmed and the music had petered out – for even Albert Hodge and his Band, who had evidently got hold of something a little stronger than tea, sensed that something was happening – the denizens of Knibden learned that Bill Parris had just been found dead on the doorstep.

It was then discovered that Verity Willow had fainted so that she too had to be dashed with water from yet another flower vase. Belle Quinn tried to intervene. 'Have you *any* idea how much those flowers cost?' she shrieked.

As Verity came round she said in a still small voice, 'I *knew* this would happen.'

'You knew?'

'I told you, but no one would listen. This is just like a whodunnit. You cannot have one corpse without another. And then another. I expect many more corpses before this business is over. The dead guest was just the beginning.'

'Oh, I say!'

'But there's only an hour to go!'

'Someone has probably put poison in the tea.'

'Fleur!' Belle was beside herself now. 'She sent Sol and his girlfriend here to ruin the tea-dance and punish me for poisoning Porgie!'

'You poisoned the kitten I gave your sister?' Gilbert Sibson asked. 'No wonder she went to Penzance!'

The elderly Gallimores pointed at Gilbert Sibson who was standing, dwarfed beside Beatrice Wilkes-Tooley. 'We told him *lives* were at stake and all *he* could do was jibber about how he would spend the dead guest's fortune!'

'But he hasn't inherited the dead guest's fortune.'

'We have all been far too interested in the money.'

'I blame Hester Jones.'

Everyone turned to me. 'Well, *I* blame Harry, the Astonishing Prancing Dog!' I said.

My sarcasm was lost on the people of Knibden.

'Yes, so do I!' said Norah Bird. 'He has a lot to answer for.'

'He's dead,' said Michael Milady. 'I killed him.'

'We must all calm down!' This was the chance Edmund Veitch had been waiting for. A revival would work its way upwards but first he must prize Chickie Wilkes-Tooley from his arm. The girl refused to be prized from his arm. She clung on tight and then she fell to the ballroom floor in a swoon ready for Mr Veitch to lift her and bear her bodily out on to one of the Gallimore's white stone balconies. When he did no such thing, she went on lying on the repolished floor at his feet. He said, 'We must all remain calm in the face of this crisis. Let the dancing recommence. Let Bill Parris be carried up to one of the rooms, and the authorities alerted. We cannot stop proceedings this evening for the sake of a tramp.'

'Hear, hear!'

'Alert the authorities!' gasped Beryl Laffety.

'He had liquor on his breath.'

'Bill Parris always had liquor on his breath.'

'Who was he?'

'Who cares?'

'He never forgot a sixpence, and a smile.'

'What?'

'He was in love with the first Mrs Veitch. When Harriet Delilah died he planted primroses on her grave. They never grew.'

375

Lalla Wilkes-Tooley pushed Neville forward. 'Tell them!' she ordered.

'Tell us what?'

'Those primroses never grew because of all the arsenic in the soil.'

'Arsenic?'

'And bumping off Harriet Delilah was not the headmaster's only crime. In all the turmoil the night of the lottery, Edmund Veitch confronted Louisa Ambrose's husband down a murderous dark alley. My grandfather, Mr Bridgewater, was out that night. He rescued my father and gave him a safe place to sleep these last forty years. But Veitch did not sleep. Having got rid of David Ambrose, he disposed of his first wife, collected on the insurance and then married the girl of his dreams . . .'

Louisa cried 'No!' as if her husband were trying to tell her he preferred his eggs hard boiled.

Roger Ambrose turned on his step-father. 'So you killed my father – not for a lottery ticket but for my mother!'

Edmund Veitch looked fearfully at his step-son and found himself staring straight into the same handsome blue eyes he had encountered down that dark alley. It would take more than a revival of spirit, he reflected. He would hand in his notice at the school. He would vacate the schoolhouse and take a small room at the back of the top floor of the Gallimore Hotel. Louisa would go with her son. The boy had returned to the town this week, not to fish in the canal, but to take his mother away with him.

Lalla Wilkes-Tooley had not finished. She was now pointing at Gilbert Sibson. 'That man has promised to do *anything* my sister Bea asks him to!'

But Verity Willow had composed herself and was speaking again. 'It is what I have been dreading,' she said. 'Bill Parris will have been murdered by someone who expected him to inherit. I resigned my job in the library – I could not concentrate. The returned books mounted up. So too the unfiled cards. Whoever the dead guest's heir is, he has been in mortal danger for the last three days. I do not mean to be rude to Miss Jones, but I have said all along she is hardly a Hercule Poirot, a Miss Marple or a Randolphe Shyne. Unless she could get to the dead guest's heir first, someone else was sure to find the answer. Then all they had to do was alter the evidence to make it look as if *they* were the heir. The easiest way to bring this about was to murder the true heir, fabricate the evidence, and collect the dead guest's fortune in his place.'

Lalla Wilkes-Tooley pushed Neville forward again. 'I knew it!' she said. 'This is entirely *your* doing.' She held the red-faced Tagg before her for everyone to see. 'Only last night this fellow barged his way into our dining room and put a pistol to my head, demanding the keys to the Knibden Municipal Company's head offices. He helped himself to the petty cash – which he then put down as a deposit on the Ford *Fiesta* of his dreams. It is sitting outside even now in all its brand-new winter plumage. He wanted me to find him a dog with a nodding head to go in the back window – he said it would annoy Follifoot driving behind, and remind him of my sister, Chickie . . .'

At the mention of her name, Chickie Wilkes-Tooley sat up. She stayed sitting on the floor, her cream bows covered in dust, her bodice awry as Lalla continued, 'Mr Tagg refused to disclose any information to Hester Jones, and spent the whole of last night and the best part of today combing through my father's confidential files in a bid to get at the truth before anyone else. See how his great bushy moustaches twitch! The scoundrel demanded that I marry him . . .'

Susie Till pushed forward. 'You are a liar!' she told Lalla Wilkes-Tooley and swung out her handbag so that it snagged the peach-coloured silk and Lalla let go of Neville and the gawky youth fell gratefully into Susie's waiting arms.

'There is a solitaire in Macready's window I would like,' she said.

'Then you shall have it!'

But no one was listening. Interest had reverted to Miss Willow's story. 'So, someone decided Bill Parris was the heir, and did away with him?'

'He did away with himself – there was an empty bottle of whisky in his pocket.'

'He needed Dutch courage to face Hester Jones,' Belle Quinn said. She needed that thimbleful of gin herself now. She swayed as she spoke. The landlord of the Swan held her steady.

'It's a disgrace!'

'I am not used to alcohol. Sol – Harold Augustus Quinn, the famous mathematician's grandson – gave me . . .'

'But if Bill Parris *is* the heir – I mean, *was* the heir – then *who is Bill Parris's heir*?' Verity Willow said. 'Poirot, Marple and Shyne would have known immediately who the culprit was.'

'All this talk about culprits and whodunnits – look what *you* have done, Miss Willow! First, we were seeking an heir. Now we are after a villain. You with all your library books – you are putting ideas into people's heads.'

'Now look here!' General Bensusann came to the defence of his lady love.

'You must shut down the public library at once!' shrieked Dora Williams. 'The moment you start reading, you know it can only end in mayhem and disaster. Take Madame Bovary . . .'

'Someone already has,' George Allendale remarked. He was standing with his arm round Janice Oakes. 'I doubt we shall ever see the woman again.'

'*Another* murder?'

'We all felt rich, now we only feel fear.'

This was Mrs Parbold's cue. She intended to feel rich, all right. First she pointed at Norah Bird. 'This dress you sold me has a faded sleeve. I reckon you had it in the window a long time.'

'That was why it was reduced, Madam,' Miss Bird said majestically.

'Don't you Madam me, Miss Bird! I want my money back.'

'You tell her!' someone said.

'Soiled goods!' declared Mrs Parbold, folding her arms.

'Now look here,' began Norah Bird. It was a good thing HRH was not here to witness this. 'You are wearing that dress . . .'

'No, you look here. Cornflower blue, you told me. This sleeve is cauliflower green!' A cheer went up and fearlessly now did the triumphant Hilda Parbold turn on General Bertram Bensusann, sole survivor of the Eleventh Knibdens, now disbanded. 'Will you tell them, or shall I?'

'Tell us what?' people wanted to know.

'He has promised to leave me the Bensusanns' in his Will. Isn't that right, General?'

'Now, lookee here!' Desmond Chase leapt in.

The General held up his hand for silence. 'There is something you all should know,' he said. Hilda May Parbold grinned. Desmond Chase nodded his head.

Verity Willow called out in a thin loving voice, 'You don't have to tell them anything. You only have to give your name, rank and telephone number, as required under international conventions governing such things . . .'

'Thank you, my dear. But the time has come. Hester Jones should know that I cannot give my name. On my twenty-first birthday I tried to fire Mrs Enderby at long last. "You are fired," I said.

' "You can't fire me!" Her voice made the sparkling chandeliers overhead shiver and shake.

' "I can. I have." '

Young Mr Bertram Bensusann stood beneath the newly cleaned chandeliers, his hands in his pockets. It was his moment of triumph. His coming of age. He was free. Any minute now the first guests would arrive for his twenty-first birthday party. The lights of the Bensusanns' blazed from all hundred and eighty-seven windows, defying the dense green gloom outside.

The heartless woman who had been his nursemaid, and then his housekeeper, looked at him in an odd way.

'You had better pack your things,' Bensusann said. He knew his lines. He had rehearsed them often enough during the long miserable years of his growing up when his only joy in life had been his schoolboy stamp collection.

'I don't think so,' Mrs Enderby replied quietly, her smile now openly insolent.

'I said,' Bertram Bensusann began, but the woman was already interrupting him.

'I don't think *you* had better say anything, until you hear what *I* have to tell you.'

The heir to the Bensusanns stared at Mrs Enderby in disbelief. He wanted her gone. He wanted the trap driving her down to Knibden station to pass the carriages bearing his friends up the rhododendron-clad hill to his party. Then she told him. How in the fire when Knibden's Alhambra lost part of its roof, she had been there with her sister's little boy and found herself high up on the burning side of the building. How, in the confusion and

379

panic, she had come upon Master Bertram Bensusann from the big house with the famous gardens, wandering alone in the gods. Deserted by his nursemaid. His clothes on fire. She had tried to take him with her to safety but, when he'd perished in her arms, she had calmly swapped the children's clothes over.

Bensusann opened his mouth to say something, and closed it again.

'I am more than the housekeeper,' the woman told Bertram Bensusann. 'And you,' she sneered, 'are less than Bertram Bensusann. You cannot fire me – you yourself were destroyed in a fire!'

'But my mother, Ottilie Vigo Bensusann – *she* must have noticed.'

'You were both the same age, you both had fair curls and freckles. Besides, you were covered in soot. Mrs Bensusann was always far too busy in her garden to know what her son looked like. If anything you were the sturdier specimen. I ran all the way back up here from the town with you clad in the other boy's velvet clothes, covered in smuts, your face suitably daubed. I was terrified at what I had done. If I had been challenged I would have made a clean breast. The whole household had come out on the battlements to watch the blaze down in the town. As I came up the lane out of the darkness your mother was standing alone on the terraces. "He's all right then," she said flatly. "Yes, Ma'am. I got the lad out just in time." I expected her to commend my bravery. I rather hoped there might be some reward, or that she would send me to the kitchens for a meal. But she turned away as Mr Lethbridge appeared and said something to him about the engines being slow to deal with the blaze. He replied that it was probably because, with all the shortages, the men were hungry. At which she laughed – as only someone to whom hunger is meaningless can. Then she went indoors.

'Later, when she heard how bad the blaze had been, and how many had perished and someone told her it was a miracle I'd got her son out alive when I could have been forgiven for running for my life, she looked very coldly in my direction and said, "Miracles happen. That is the nature of miracles." And there was an end to it. She wasn't exactly thrilled by your survival. It was Mr Lethbridge who took me on. Not out of gratitude, but expediency. To replace the nursemaid who'd run off during the fire.'

'And your sister, Mrs Enderby, the woman *you claim* was my real mother?'

'She looked at the charred corpse they presented her with. "No!" She refused to believe it. "Tragedies happen – that is the nature of tragedies," I told her, in the manner I had learned from Ottilie Vigo Bensusann. Of course, I knew this tragedy had *not* happened to her. I thought when she calmed down I might tell her the truth. I even thought that, after some consideration of the advantages I had put her child's way, she might thank me. Before that could happen she drowned herself. She left a note asking that her swollen sodden corpse be buried with the child's burnt one.'

'You must have felt sorry then?'

'Sorry? Me?' Mrs Enderby grinned. It was the moment of triumph *she* had spent years waiting for.

'And no one knew?'

'Mr Lethbridge knew. When we were on the terrace that night with the burning Alhambra glowing orange in the distance he glanced from Ottilie Vigo Bensusann to the child, and then over at me, and in that quick icy flicker of a stare, I knew he knew. For some reason he chose to say nothing. And because *he* accepted the situation, so did the other servants.'

'And others. Outside the house?'

'No one guessed. Only . . .' Mrs Enderby took a deep breath. There had been one witness. Aladdin's younger brother, decked in a costume of red and orange with bells dangling from his tunic, had come running into the little changing room with one of Montague Cayke's famous prancing dogs nipping at his heels. 'I had the clothes off the living child and was putting them on the corpse. He must have seen what I was doing but when he saw the room had no other exit, he ran out again. The dog, though, came prancing over. It took its little pipe from its mouth and sniffed at each of the children. Then ran after the actor's jangling bells. I lived for weeks in fear that someone would come up to the Bensusanns' from the town and say something. Perhaps I hoped they *would* come and expose what I had done. But no one came. After a while I wanted very much to go down into Knibden myself. I told Mrs Bensusann I wanted to visit my sister's grave. I took you with me – her son, the Bensusann cuckoo – and we went to the churchyard and I gave you flowers to lay on your mother's grave, and on the grave of the little boy you had replaced, the real Bertram Bensusann RIP, only it said Percy Potts on the stone. For *that* is your real name. Well, Knibden was tranquil. The lottery was over. The Imperial Players had moved on. I wanted to know who the boy was who had played Aladdin's younger brother, but the wagons had been loaded with what few props survived the flames, and Montague Cayke and his men had departed. For Canada, India, South Africa, Australia. The Alhambra stood there, blackened but more intact than I expected. It had only lost half its roof. And I have watched you ever since, Percy Potts, growing up to lord it over us.'

'She roared with laughter – the nastiest sound you ever heard,' General Bensusann recounted sadly. 'The glint of the Bensusann chandeliers, which had been taken down and cleaned specially for my twenty-first birthday party, reflected a thousand times over in her little round metal-rimmed spectacles.

'That evening the party went ahead. And I went through the motions of being myself. And have done so ever since. There was no going back to being little Percy Potts – and if I established I was not Bertram Bensusann, who could I be? As soon as Mrs Enderby opened her evil mouth I knew what she was saying was true. I'd never felt as if I were me. The responsibility for the great house with its hundred and eighty-seven windows should *never* have been mine. Finding Sidney Mastermain Bensusann shot dead on the floor of his study had not affected me as the death of a father ought. The fearlessness attributed to General Bertram Bensusann of the Eleventh Knibdens *was* unreal. The worst that could happen to him had happened already, in the changing room at the Alhambra. If Bertram Bensusann perished in battle, so be it. Bertram Bensusann had already been destroyed.'

No, indeed. The child had not been himself since the fire. Sidney Mastermain Bensusann saw this and attempted to pen an essay, 'On Trauma'. Bertram was quieter and more stupid which was hardly surprising, given what the little boy had been through. The degree of transformation disturbed the man none the less.

'He seems a different child, Tilly,' the essayist remarked to his wife. Ottilie Vigo shrugged her shoulders. A young woman was coming from *The Lady's Garden* and some of the rose arches required a little twisting and training before a photograph could be taken.

Bensusann was unable to keep away from the nursery. Little Bertram refused to come near him. Cheerfully articulate and affectionate before, his son now sat on the floor, emitting ugly little grunting sounds. 'He's changed,' the essayist remarked to the new nursemaid, Mrs Enderby.

'Yes, Sir,' she said. 'He is a different child.' He looked at Mrs Enderby and saw the softness of her flesh beneath her blouse and wondered if he mightn't write an essay 'On Temptation' instead. Trauma was too upsetting.

Things did not improve. When the child slowly regained his speech it was as if he needed to learn everything again from the start. His father haunted the nursery, fascinated by this horror that eluded his pen. Sidney Mastermain Bensusann felt as wordless and confused about the matter as did the boy. And he took comfort, as did his son, in Mrs Enderby's arms. 'I love you!' he whispered into her dry wispy hair that smelt of custard and carbolic.

Then one day the child found them. Left to his own devices, he had followed the strange sounds until he'd come upon his semi-clad father heaving on top of a naked Mrs Enderby, her flat chest flattened beneath the moving weight of the man. Little Bertram Bensusann found his tongue then, letting forth a stream of deeply remembered language, more suited to an urchin from the town than the product of a Vigo/Bensusann alliance.

'Shut up, Percy!' Mrs Enderby yelled, and in the confusion Sidney Mastermain Bensusann stood up, pulled his trousers back on and went downstairs to his study. Not to pen another essay, but to shoot himself.

There was a long silence in the Gallimore ballroom, broken at last by Mrs Parbold. 'So the Bensusanns' is not, strictly speaking, *yours* to leave?'

'If you believe Mrs Enderby's story, Mrs Parbold, it is not *mine* at all. It belongs to a little boy called Percy Potts who is buried in the churchyard near where the dead guest lies.'

Hilda May Parbold made up her mind at once. 'But I don't believe a word of Mrs Enderby's story! The woman was a liar. *You* are General Bertram Bensusann, only beloved son of Sidney Mastermain Bensusann and Ottilie Vigo, the famous gardener. One only has to look at you, to see that! The Bensusanns' is most definitely yours to dispose of as you please – and you will please to tell the town, this instant, that . . .'

General Bensusann laughed, a hard hammering laugh like a burst of rapid machine-gun fire. 'Mrs Parbold, I *will* leave the Bensusanns' to you in my Will.'

She looked suspicious. Her victory, too easy. Wealth ought only to be won by hard work and accomplishment but here was that valuable great house falling into her lap like ripe cherries blown from a tree on a windy summer's day.

The General went on, 'I can do better than that! On condition you and Desmond Chase marry each other *immediately*, and undertake to mop the floors and repair all hundred and eighty-seven windows for the rest of your natural lives, you can have the house forthwith. I wish never to return there. Meanwhile I will take up residence in your comfortable council house. It may not be a fit resting place for the sole survivor of the Eleventh Knibdens, but since it is already stuffed with knick-knacks pillaged from the Bensusanns', I shall feel quite at home there.'

'Gracious!'

'Gotcha!' Hilda May Parbold pounced on Desmond Chase. 'It's an offer we can't refuse.'

'The last rose of summer – eh, Chase?'

Desmond Chase looked at Hilda Parbold with complete distaste. She glared at him. There was no doubting they deserved one another, but more than that, they both felt certain they deserved the great house. Their destinies were locked together as surely as the thorny intertwined branches of Ottilie Vigo Bensusann's overgrown roses.

'We have a very nice range of engagement rings at the moment,' Macready murmured to the happy couple.

'These private arrangements are all very well,' Michael Milady intervened. 'But can I remind you all, a man has *died* here. I propose in the circumstances we ask Hester Jones to tell us the contents of the dead guest's Will without further ado, and have done.'

'Yes, before anything else can happen.'

'Poor Bill Parris.'

'I could not possibly do that,' I objected. It was only a quarter past nine. 'There are rules to contracts of this kind, strictures that must be strictly adhered to. I shall make my announcement at ten o'clock, and not a minute before!'

Mr Milady looked at me in the same way he had done when we first met. 'Who are you?' he had asked so that the crowd fell back as his question boomed over their heads. Now he said, 'I am surprised. I would not have expected . . . I mean, whoever the dead stranger was, and whoever he has left his money to, it is hardly any concern of yours, Miss Jones. Aren't you taking the whole business a wee bit seriously?'

'I am employed to take it seriously. It's not a game of Cluedo, you know! Or one of Monty Cayke's fantasmoragical bills.'

'Well said, Miss Jones!'

'I want nothing for myself.' Belle Quinn had persuaded Mrs Mason to find her that thimbleful of gin. She was waving the bottle about. 'But if you could see your way to allowing some of the dead guest's fortune to be spent printing my father's works at long last. Why, the whole world would benefit. You would learn equations and theorems that would help you calculate the answer. You could stand before a class in that long blue skirt you talked of, chalking countless numbers up on the blackboard . . .'

'Steady on, Miss Quinn. We don't want her taken on at the school so that she settles in Knibden.'

'The sooner she leaves the town and takes all this bother away with her . . .'

'I hope you don't mind my asking, Miss Jones, but I would so like to have a little memento. A little something to remind me of the dead guest . . .'

'We don't know who he was or how he came to be here, but just a little something . . .'

'It doesn't have to be valuable.'

'It's not the money that counts.'

With only three quarters of an hour to go, people were pressing round me, urgently asking for favours before it was too late. I held on to the envelope tight. I was pretty sure now I knew the answer. Then Michael Milady drew me to one side. 'The committee have asked me to have a word,' he said.

I raised my eyebrows. The committee was in serious financial trouble. Anyone could see that. Its liabilities far outweighed its kitty.

'Perhaps you and I could come to a little arrangement. As chairman of the committee I thought I would mention it. Before anyone else does. You must understand this whole enterprise has cost us a pretty penny. We have all found ourselves putting in far more money than any of us ever intended. To tell you the truth, I would never have thought it *possible* to spend so much in only three short days! Not that I'm blaming the cost of your tomato, egg, lettuce and radish luncheons. Obviously we none of us yet know what you have discovered – and maybe there is no problem, but I was thinking . . .'

'You were thinking?'

'Perhaps you could give me a hint how things are going so that I can take any action necessary before it is too late. I could shore up the position of the committee before you make your announcement. I know we are expected to receive a ten-fold return on our outlay, but I would say that is not very much, in view of the great risk . . .'

'Mr Milady – what exactly are you asking me to do?'

'In return for a little consideration, that might – ehem – help see you on your way to Penzance. Shall we say a small percentage . . .'

I drew myself up, outraged. A hundred Hester Joneses in the regilded mirrors did the same. 'Mr Milady,' I said coldly. 'We shall *say* no such thing! You forget, I am the someone-who-is-not-someone. I have been a goody-goody all my life. When called on to comply with adult ridiculousness, even the ridiculous wishes of a dead man I never met, I have done so to the best of my ability.'

Michael Milady inclined his head. 'So I cannot persuade you . . .'

'Ever since I arrived in this town we have been looking at each other, you and I,' I remarked. 'I am not at all sure what I see. I have learned less about you than almost anyone else.'

Michael Milady smiled slightly, and bowed. This was his cue.

'Take your partners now for the "March of Time!" ' yelled Albert Hodge. Edmund Veitch had instructed him to carry on as normal.

'Normal! Do you call this normal? A tea-dance should last from three o'clock to seven. Dickie Paisley would never have countenanced . . . We shall expect overtime. And then there is the not inconsiderable matter of our expenses . . .'

'Oh, I am sure the committee . . .'

'Pot of gold, eh, this committee of yours, Miss Quinn! Eh, eh?' Albert Hodge cackled and leered. 'Take your partners! Take your partners!' he bellowed into the microphone although the dancing was underway, and there was no need for shouting.

Michael Milady tried to blot out the raucous conversation and beery laughter coming from the nearby tent. He sat on a wicker basket, gazing up at the flying fish, watersnake and lizard glittering far above. These constellations offered no consolation since they did not shine down also on his mother's grave in far-away Knibden. Monty Cayke's Imperial Players were now in the Southern Hemisphere, touring Australia. Knibden's Alhambra, the Gallimore Hotel and the small unmarked pauper's grave where Melinda Milady reposed in peace lay half the world away, beyond the reach of the flying fish, watersnake and lizard that sprawled high above him across the great night sky. Too exhausted to weep, or sleep, the young Michael Milady fingered the tin locket that hung about his neck. Inside, a small photograph of Melinda Milady had been glued on card and cut to shape. The light from the unfamiliar stars was not enough to enable the boy to snap open the locket and look at the beautiful woman, but he did not need to. Her features were imprinted on his mind. The first thing Cayke did when he acquired a new Michael Milady was to hang this tin locket about his neck and instruct him in the personal history the locket conferred.

'One day, Michael Milady, you will grow old and retire,' he would say with a chortle. 'Then you will go home to Knibden, having nowhere better to call home. You will be able to blackmail Mrs Enderby, and end your days in luxury . . .'

Until then, the boy must slave for the Imperial Players. When he wasn't acting, he tended the prancing dogs. When the company moved on, Michael Milady travelled with the animals and when the wagons stopped *en route*, he would walk the dogs on their leashes, guarding the valuable creatures from the attentions of curious onlookers. What little time the boy had free, he attended to the dogs' elaborate outfits. The Imperial Players' costumes were stored in the wicker baskets and were, for the most part, old and tatty. The great Montague Cayke's own costumes and those of his famous prancing dogs, were completely different however – on these no expense was spared.

Michael Milady did not eat with the other Players but licked what was left on their plates. Sometimes the dogs lost their appetites and Mikey was able to supplement his meagre diet with scraps of good meat the dogs could not stomach. The rest of the time, across India, South Africa, Australia and Canada, he went hungry.

When Montague Cayke visited his famous dogs he would test young Mikey on his lines. 'Gave you away like an unwanted pup!' he'd remark, referring to Melinda Milady's sisters who had not wanted the expense of a growing boy. A living reminder of losing the lottery winner to their younger, more beautiful sister. Cayke would stroke the ears of Harry, his favourite dog, who wore a tailored red jacket trimmed with gold braid until Harry rose on his hind legs, turned a complete circle and swivelled his snout. Then he'd receive a lump of sugar from Cayke's pocket. How Michael Milady eyed that sugar! What would he not do for a lump of the stuff. Harry slept at Cayke's feet on a nice warm mattress while Mikey lay on hard bare earth beside the other dogs just beyond Monty Cayke's tent flap, ready to fetch anything the great man required in the night. Ready in the morning, before slopping out and feeding the dogs, to empty Cayke's great smelly bed-pan.

And woe betide Michael Milady if he were tardy or negligent in his duties! The great man was not above delivering a severe boot up the backside or clout on the ear. It was said that after such a blow rendered a previous Michael Milady too deaf to hear his cues, he had been put out of the wagons somewhere along a dirt track in India. The boy had been ceremonially deprived of his tin locket and left to fend for himself.

The features inside the locket grew more faded with each new orphaned Milady. It was whispered among the Players that it *could not possibly* be the same tin locket that the first Mikey Milady had brought with him away from Knibden. The third or fourth child to assume the role was reputed to have absconded with the original. Cayke had not minded the lad running away – he'd been getting too big for the part, in any case – but stealing a prop from the Imperial Players was unforgivable. 'I will *murder* the rascal, if I ever catch up with him!' Montague Cayke had roared. A replacement boy had been found and, with more difficulty, another cheap locket. Some other woman's faded features were then cut to shape and mounted on cardboard to hang about the replacement child's neck.

Tonight, the Players were packed up, ready to move at first light to the next fleapit on tour, in Wagga Wagga. The kegs of beer that marked the end of a successful run had been rolled out and the child Milady set to sit on one of the great wicker baskets containing the costumes and props, guarding the company's possessions. Michael Milady kicked the wicker basket beneath him and watched the exaggerated shadows moving across the walls of the tent. Tonight he was too tired to be amused by the lengthened noses and vast distended tankards the Imperial Players raised to their enormous lips. The plume of Cayke's hat tickled the ceiling, rocking to and fro like a bird up a tree as Cayke roared and bellowed.

The flap of the tent lifted and one of Cayke's leading female Players, Miss Rose Meldrew, came outside. By the light of the Antipodean stars, she glimpsed the tears in the boy's eyes. The kindly Miss Meldrew sat down beside Mikey and tousled his hair. 'You'll start me off,' she said.

'You?' Mikey stared at her. The pretty Miss Meldrew always seemed so cheerful. The life of an Imperial Player suited her.

'An old trouper like me, you mean?' Rose laughed.

Mikey nodded.

'How *old* d'yer think I am, then?' Rose asked him, pretending to be offended. The boy stared. The Players all seemed ancient to him. Even the prancing dogs had been around donkeys' years.

'I am twenty-three – but feel more like forty!' Rose sighed. She had been an Imperial Player longer than she could remember.

Her mother was one before her. And whomever Mr Meldrew had been no one now knew. 'I think Monty got the name off a bottle of Meldrew's Soda Cordial,' she confided. 'Horrid stuff – I tried some once.'

Mikey nodded.

'I remember the seventh Michael Milady,' Rose told the boy proudly.

'What number am *I* then?' Mikey inquired, and Rose had to admit she had long ago lost count. Across Canada, South Africa, India and Australia it was hard to know anything for certain.

The boy whimpered. 'You missing your mum?' Rose asked.

Mikey nodded. He was missing something.

'You're young to be so far from home,' she said.

'I have no home,' the boy replied.

'Everyone has a home. *Your* home, Mikey dear – if you don't want to be abandoned to the turkey vultures along some dirt track in the middle of nowhere – is Knibden.'

Michael Milady nodded obediently. The Players were under strict instructions to reinforce whenever possible the story of the boy's past. In the child's own interests, this Rose now did. 'Knibden is a wonderful place to have as a home to go back to,' she told him. 'A place where all things are possible. I dare say we will go there ourselves at the time of the next lottery. Cayke will bill the show as *The Return of Michael Milady to his Native Alhambra*. The whole of Knibden will turn out to welcome you. He will make a fortune in ticket sales . . .'

The tent flap lifted again and another Player came in search of Rose, a Mr Chas Fonteyne. Mr Fonteyne told the girl Monty Cayke had noticed her absence. Rose sighed and immediately climbed down off the wicker basket and hurried back inside. 'Bloody cur!' the man snarled. Mikey thought Mr Fonteyne was referring to Harry, the most famous prancing dog of all, who often nipped the Players for fun so that they turned on Mikey, blaming the boy for not exercising proper control. No one dared blame the prancing dogs.

But Mr Chas Fonteyne did not mean Harry. He was in love with Miss Rose Meldrew, the current recipient of Cayke's attentions. Mr Fonteyne paced the turf in front of the tent, occasionally kicking out at the wicker basket beneath Mikey. At last, he too hurried back inside. On his own again, in the darkness beneath the unfamiliar stars, the boy actor felt more alone and lost in the world than ever.

It was a sell-out in Wagga Wagga. 'Aladdin's Younger Brother' was opening for seven nights. And seven nights only. Standing room only – and not much of that. Tickets were already changing hands on the streets at double, treble face value. Many of those being sold, as if sold on at exorbitant prices because of the short-age, were being flogged by Cayke's own men – Cayke had been in the business long enough to know every trick in the trade. And *this* was a production in which Innumerable New, Never Been Seen Before, tricks were promised to the folk of Wagga Wagga.

The curtain rises on trumpets, dragons and naked women for sale – the cast cavorting exuberantly round the stage in the guise of Great Knibden Lottery tickets! This was not one of the Imperial Players' most sophisticated productions, but it went down well in out-of-the-way parts. The settlers gasp and gawp at the painted backdrop – more Knibden than Knibden could ever be. A man might fancy himself back home, the other side of the globe, as he looks at the Market Square, the Gallimore Hotel and the church of St Redegule's set on a small grassy mound above the town. The grave of Melinda Milady is obscured in darkness at this point, for that lady has not yet died. Indeed, no. Here we see her very much alive on the arm of Milady at dawn on Day One. Trumpets are drawn. The trumpets all jump in the air. The orchestra – an old man and his son, set beside countless reflecting mirrors, cleverly giving the impression of a full pit – strike up with vigorous dance music. The trumpets perform the 'Victory Waltz'. Abject dragons and discarded naked women fade to the wings. Victor Matchett's father who had shunned anything military goes to work for Henry Buckworth, and sells his soul to have his name cut in big steel letters on top of a pair of gates. Edward Veitch's father, meanwhile, buys as many trumpets as he can lay his hands on, borrowing at ruinous rates to do so. Lavinia Lobb scores her goal at a hockey match, and her beloved brother and his friends all throw their caps in the air and then march away to battle. At last on the evening of Day Two, one trumpet alone emerges tri-umphant and cavorts round the stage with Melinda and Milady until at last the couple depart from Knibden in a cloud of tulle, embarking for the New World with pink Venetian glasses and coffers crammed with gold (the Imperial Players' wicker baskets, stuffed with shredded foil). They are waved off by the Five Beautiful Gallimores – who, for the sake of convenience and economy, are represented by only two.

We watch Milady and his bride enjoy New York society, holding cocktail glasses and handing out shreds of foil from the wicker baskets to all-comers. And then the impoverished return to Europe, in a different part of the ship, Melinda now nursing a bundle in her arms. We see the desperate Milady beside the roulette wheels. Some of the naked women from the lottery ticket dance, redeployed as casino *femmes*. They drape themselves on his arm. We know we are in France from the bits and bobs sewn on their costumes. Meanwhile a dragon has been redeployed as the unpleasant *Madame* in the cheap hotel who keeps banging on Melinda's door demanding money. Then comes the Tragic Demise of the Lottery Winner – a bit of a cliché, this one, but the settlers of Wagga Wagga love it. A husband returning earlier than expected to his yacht (the ocean liner, redeployed), draws a pistol and shoots the dissolute, impoverished Milady in the head so that he topples overboard backwards to a splash backstage (the settlers cheer). Now the lovely Melinda, deprived of everything in the world, save her pasty-faced *enfant*, heads for home. Or for the only place she can call home. Knibden. How the settlers hiss the *Madame* as she exits, stage left, the pink Venetian glasses clunking under one arm.

Sometimes Cayke does the scene with the Captain (redeploying the ocean liner/yacht as a Channel ferry). The settlers like the bit where, as Melinda clutches her son and coughs bucketfuls of blood into a handkerchief, the swashbuckling Captain enjoins the man to whom he entrusts the young widow and her son, on pain of a nasty and nautical knot in his throat, not to try anything on. But Cayke, impatient to get to Knibden, often skips this bit. Continuity and plot are not important in Wagga Wagga.

Aladdin's Younger Brother is showing at Knibden's Alhambra. The great Montague Cayke himself is seen as himself, bestriding his stage, cloak flowing, tight twirly moustaches quivering beneath his plumed sombrero. He mounts the steps of the theatre, opens a door painted in the backdrop and, as he goes inside, the fair Melinda arrives, driving up from the station, shielding her little boy from staring eyes. The only addition to the scenery from when she was in Knibden before is the War Memorial erected in the main Market Square. On it we can see the names of Denis Lobb and his friends. The two Beautiful Gallimores (representing the Five), with even more make-up to make them look even more haggard, hand Melinda the keys to her room.

'The Hall is now a hotel,' Sarah Gallimore explains, the whole of her history in those words.

You could hear a flea hop as we see the young consumptive mother putting her son to bed upstairs in the Gallimore Hotel. She tucks Mikey up for the night, sings him a lullaby and, when the boy turns over to sleep, blissfully unaware that he will never see his mother again alive, there isn't a dry eye in Wagga Wagga. Watched by the Gallimore sisters, Melinda Milady goes forth to breathe for the last time the fresh familiar air of home. She walks towards the Alhambra, and stands in the entrance tying a lavender-covered scarf about her head, reading a playbill. As the evening's well-dressed audience push past her to take their seats inside, she forlornly examines her empty purse. A bell sounds, indicating the performance is about to start. A shadowy figure, in cloak and sombrero, steps forward to press a ticket into Melinda's hands. Her eyes light up – but when she looks round, the cloak and sombrero have gone. Melinda Milady enters Knibden's Alhambra just as the curtain rises.

Aladdin's younger brother is given three wishes from his elder brother's magic lamp. Three wishes and no more, Aladdin says firmly before leaving the boy centre stage.

With the first wish, the child asks the genie of the lamp for a pussy cat. The lisp barely leaving his lips before a vast ginger creature with cardboard claws bounds on, terrifying the child and younger members of the audience. Aladdin's younger brother wastes no time in wasting his second wish, calling for a dog to chase the cat. Harry, the astonishing prancing dog, comes to the boy's aid. The two do a double act, mercilessly teasing the big ginger fellow until finally the cat's tail comes off. Whereupon Aladdin's brother cries at what he has done and wishes the cat's tail were back on. Harry, puffing at his little china pipe, produces a pot marked GLUE and, daubing the cat's injured backside, he reattaches the big ginger tail. The dog does a nimble dance, then prances off to rounds of applause. Aladdin's younger brother, who has used up *all three* wishes, finds himself alone with the marmalade cat who now taunts him mercilessly, pointing out that he could have asked the genie of the lamp for *anything*. He could have wished to win the next Great Knibden Lottery, and become a millionaire. Or, more modestly, he could have asked for Harry to lose his appetite so that he might enjoy a nice slice of meat. Here, Mrs Helen Willow's lodgers let out a round of applause of their own. They like a nice slice of meat themselves, they say, nudging one another. And Amy Pasco, who later became Amy Tagg when she pinched Jack Tagg from under Norah Bird's nose, howled like a wolf until little Norah Bird sitting beside her thought she was going to sick up the chocolate she had been scoffing and had to be taken outside by Mr Nye. Who later married the fearsome Miss Pringle. And served him right. And serve us all right – performances across Canada, India, South Africa, Australia and through all time roll into one for Cayke's timing is famous. Elsewhere, high up in the front row of the upper circle, Mrs Enderby eyes the boy playing Aladdin's younger brother. 'Strange! Very strange. *Very* strange, indeed!'

She had obtained an old playbill after the Imperial Players departed following the fire. Cayke, fearing he might be held responsible in some way, had packed up at once, and moved on. The Knibden Municipal Insurance Company might have ruled some of the Players' theatrical effects in contravention of the terms of the establishment's policy, and refused to pay out. From the old playbill, Mrs Enderby had learned the name of the boy actor playing the part, and this name had become indelibly imprinted in her mind. When the bills had gone up, advertising *The Return of Michael Milady to his Native Alhambra*, poor Mrs Enderby naturally thought her number was up. The boy who had worn a red and orange costume with bells jangling would make his way to the Bensusanns'. He would hammer on the door and demand an audience with the General. 'I can explain the whole thing,' she would say, describing the terrible scene in the changing room. The flames, the billowing smoke coming at her like a Great Knibden dragon. Then the nasty sniffing dog who'd come hoping for sugar lumps but found only two children, one alive, one dead.

She would make out that in the confusion and the flames they had got swapped over. *She* had never meant any harm.

But Mrs Enderby saw that she would not need to explain anything. This Mikey Milady was *another* small child! In the same costume, and, more remarkably, with the same name! Whatever had happened to Michael Milady was every bit as remarkable as what had happened to the infant Bensusann. The lights of the green genie's lamp glittered a thousand times over in the metal-rimmed spectacles of the housekeeper at the Bensusanns'. There were clearly more things in heaven and on earth than were dreamt of in Mrs Enderby's philosophy.

And indeed, shortly before the great Montague Cayke died, the Imperial Players had done *Hamlet* in Canada. Not that Cayke knew he was going to die. Why, at Medicine Hat, he'd produced his most magnificent *Hamlet*. 'The man is remarkable,' remarked the inhabitants in that part of the world painted pink. But can it truly be the same man? Could not another Montague Cayke take over where the last Monty Cayke left off, over and over, for ever and ever, across the globe until the end of time? Like regilded mirrors in the Gallimore ballroom. It had seemed that he might, except that something happened at the next stop on tour, in the back streets of Moose Jaw.

It was a scene Cayke himself would have enjoyed, and doubtless re-enacted over and over, the world over, his nose distended, his plume tickling the ceiling as he rocked to and fro like some bird up a tree clinging on for dear life in a storm. It was the scene in which Cayke died. As the ghost cried Remember me! over the lightning machine and the canvas battlements, the Imperial Players' lighting system failed. In the darkness, the great man toppled forward. Only when lights were restored did everyone see the bloody tomahawk embedded in his skull. There was wild applause. Naturally people assumed this was an improvement on Shakespeare, designed for a Canadian audience. The blood looked real. Harry mistook the clapping for his cue to come on, prancing round the great man, hoping for a lump of sugar from his master's pocket. In vain did Harry lick Monty Cayke's face. It was some time before the rest of the cast, and the audience (now wildly cheering Harry), realized anything was amiss.

*

'Alas!' said Michael Milady. 'We went on, after Cayke's death, valiantly posting up playbills, but without Monty, or an empire any more, it was not the same.' He sighed a sigh of such sorrow I felt myself shudder. The whole room shuddered. And then, drowned by the music of Albert Hodge and his Band, he told us. 'Eventually there was nothing for it. I took the dogs to the deepest point in the great Chattaveechoo River and one by one I weighted them with rocks. I had no choice. We had scarcely enough to feed ourselves, let alone the prancing dogs who, to make matters worse, were all used to a sumptuous diet. Montague Cayke may have known how to whip up an audience in the middle of nowhere, selling tickets at double or treble the printed price. And he always managed to be in Knibden at the time of the lottery when trade was so brisk with everyone feeling rich, he made enough in a few performances to tide us over across the rest of the world. Without him, it was impossible. Harry was the last to die. I walked ahead of him along the path to the river. He pranced behind me puffing his pipe, swivelling his little busy snout and doing the merriest dance you ever saw. When we reached the water's edge, I hadn't the heart to remove the little red jacket with gold braid. The bubbles gurgled up. He took a long time to sink and when he did, I could still see the red and gold far below. "Heigh-ho, away we go!" I thought, and wished with all my heart that I had one last lump of sugar to throw him. After that, of course, the Imperial Players had no hope. Those who had come to the shows to laugh at the famous troupe of ill-trained, moth-eaten dogs stayed away. Eventually we all went our own separate ways. I do not know what became of Miss Rose Meldrew, or Mr Chas Fonteyne. I came home to Knibden, stepping into the backdrop Monty Cayke had painted for my life. I intended to confront Mrs Enderby. And demand that she pay for my silence. It was to be my pension. Instead I found *she* had been silenced. She is buried you know, up at the Bensusanns', alongside Mr Lethbridge in unhallowed ground. I cannot help thinking the dead guest would wish to compensate me for my loss,' Milady said. But Victor Matchett was now talking.

'And what about *my* loss?' he asked.

*

Lethbridge had put his head round the door. 'Victor Matchett?' he asked.

Matchett jumped. 'That's me,' he said. Matchett knew at once that his visitor was the stuffy butler from the Bensusanns' though he had never spoken to the man before.

Lethbridge advanced into the printing office. 'Lottery soon,' he said. 'Tickets printed yet?'

Matchett stared.

'All the trumpets, dragons and naked women?'

Still Matchett stared. How did Mr Lethbridge know that Buckworth & Matchett's printed the lottery tickets? It was hush-hush.

Lethbridge smiled, a butler's discreet superior smile. He rested his weight on his silver-topped cane.

'Ah!' said Matchett. Since the late Mr Buckworth bought up all the other printing firms hereabouts, it was obvious to any fool when you thought about it. And Lethbridge was clearly no fool.

'Stands to reason,' Lethbridge said.

'Was there anything particular you wanted?' Matchett asked. In those days, not long after the death of Henry Buckworth and just before the last Great Knibden Lottery, the flywheels on the presses still flew, girl typesetters still came tripping early every morning along the towpath.

'Mr Godfrey about?' Lethbridge asked.

'He'll be somewhere in the town,' Matchett said.

'He'll be enjoying himself,' Lethbridge added.

'I dare say,' Matchett replied slowly. The two men looked at each other. Then Matchett said, 'Sit down, why don't you?'

Lethbridge sitting very upright, began telling Victor Matchett how he had once sat beneath the lions and fountains in Trafalgar Square reading the *Daily Mercury*. He'd read about the Bensusann/Vigo marriage and how the couple would be living in the ancient family home in Knibden. He had read something about Miss Vigo having already passed the night in a bed Good Queen Bess had slept in. (A little like you, Hester Jones, sleeping in the dead guest's bed.) 'And I don't mind telling you,' Lethbridge went on, 'I underlined *that* part of the account in red ink.'

'Ah.'

'I read the extract from Sidney Mastermain Bensusann's essay "On Trumpets, Dragons and Naked Women", and I read about the clever goings on of Mrs Cardew/Vestey/Jenks, and I thought Knibden the sort of place all things might be possible. A place I might care to call home. That was when a scheme came into my head. Right there, beneath the fountains and lions . . .' This scheme Mr Lethbridge had now laid out before Victor Matchett. 'I have bided my time.'

Matchett paused as the import of Lethbridge's story began to sink in.

'Well?'

'I'm not sure.'

'If the whole thing were guaranteed foolproof?'

'Foolproof!' Matchett had been a fool not to turn the man out of the printing works then and there. But he had known immediately that he would go along with the scheme. To fix the Great Knibden Lottery! And have a sizeable share in the sizeable prize money! Why, with Lethbridge's scheme, *any* pauper could become a prince overnight, without even having to *win* the lottery. What would it matter about the works then, and taking care of Mr Godfrey?

'It's agreed then,' Lethbridge said.

Matchett barely nodded.

'I have an associate,' Lethbridge told him. 'A man who does not mess about. A Mr Harry Best who has already taken up temporary residence in Knibden . . .'

'Good idea!' the old lecher had croaked, demanding to be let in on the scam. He wanted his share of naked women, was how he'd put it. Godfrey Buckworth had *not* been in town the afternoon Lethbridge called – he had heard every word from an adjoining room and thought the scheme a splendid idea. 'All my life I have hoped to put one over on the Great Knibden Lottery,' he cackled.

'Yes, Uncle Godfrey, of course you must have your share,' Matchett agreed. There would be plenty of money and he saw no reason why Godfrey Buckworth should not have some of it. He consulted Harry Best and Mr Lethbridge. 'Leave it to us,' they said. 'I left it to them,' Victor Matchett concluded.

Meanwhile the thirteen-year-old Verity had picked up a Raymond Bast at the W H Smith's bookstall. '*Death of a Loved One*,' she read. The latest two-shilling thriller. She put the book down again. Unlike the Basts she had glimpsed at the library, under Lavinia Lobb's beady eye, this book still had its dust-jacket. With a photograph of Raymond Bast on the flap. A man who looked *nothing like* Harry Best. 'Tread warily,' Verity thought. Randolphe Shyne's enemies came in many guises, hadn't Best told her so, himself? Impersonating Shyne and Maisie Vollutu's author – could anything be more inimical to the pair, than that?

Next time Raymond Bast left the house, Verity followed her mother's paying guest up the steep path that led to the Bensusanns'.

From the window of that small attic room where she had been locked in, Verity Willow had watched the drowning of Mr Godfrey.

'I could have told the awful little Wilkes-Tooley sisters *exactly the spot* where the man slipped,' Verity Willow confessed now. '*And* I saw the presentation copy of Mrs Esmerald Dean's *The Good Path*, float free from his pocket, the red and gold of its beautifully printed Buckworth & Matchett label swirling about in the water. Years later I received a package from Mr Best. It contained money. Plenty of it. I knew I should have turned the money over to my mother, or to the police, but I kept it secret, every penny, not wanting to betray the man. In the end I gave it to Herbert Vale to purchase a little van to help him sell his cardboard boxes. You see, there only ever was the money. No crushed hats or mildewed Bibles. I cannot help feeling the dead guest . . .'

George Allendale threw his rusty Roman spear in the air. 'Listen to this, Hester Jones!' he cried excitedly. He had just learned from Janice who had once had it from Calderon, who had been told by the previous tenants of the Swan, and George now told the whole town. At the time of the last Great Knibden Lottery Mrs Edina Allendale had worked at the Swan! Behind the bar. 'Just think!' George exclaimed. '*My mother* in that den of iniquity!'

Edina Allendale began choking on her boiled sweet. Someone thumped her hard on the back. It would seem that when Mr Allendale had arrived in the town to try his luck at the lottery, the future Mrs Allendale had also come to Knibden, hoping to better herself. She had been lucky – first, in securing employment at the

Swan, secondly in marrying Allendale. And she had certainly bettered herself – since she was now the respected mother of Knibden's chief librarian. 'You never told me,' George said to his mother.

'And I bet she never told you Mr Allendale only married her because she was pregnant.'

'Pregnant!' George gasped. 'My mother?'

'With you. Though the poor man could never be sure he was the father. "I will stand by you," Mr Allendale said. "I will do the decent thing." '

'You mean – *some other man* might be my father! It *is* possible?'

'It's always possible.'

'I might be in the running, after all – for the dead stranger's fortune?'

'You might indeed!'

'Well, well!' George grinned. 'And to think of *Mother* working behind the bar at the Swan!'

'What's so funny about that?' Miss Janice Oakes, a girl who was most definitely not one of the favoured concubines of the conqueror of Vintniorum, asked.

'Nothing, my love!' George kissed his bride-to-be on her brightly rouged cheek.

Janice refused to be kissed by a man wearing a lime-green jumper. She insisted he took it off at once and put on his sensible chief librarian's grey cardigan. 'Arthur Dawes Dobson would never have worn lime green!' she said, tweeking his nose.

'You're putty in that girl's hands,' Mrs Allendale shrieked across the Gallimore's repolished ballroom floor. She rushed from the room, scattering her sweets as she went.

She went straight home to pack. *You must stop work on your stupid museum, at once!* she wrote, in a note she would leave on her side of the coal-effect electric fire in their living room. *I shall need all my savings now that I must make way for your fancy woman, and eke out my days at the Gallimore Hotel* . . .

Matchett was shouting above the din of the music. 'I never agreed to anything. I did not know what they were up to. As far as I was concerned, Harry Best had come from London to buy the printing works. I was only too happy to sell up and move away. The only thing keeping me in Knibden was Mr Godfrey. "We'll see to him," they said. The next thing, I heard a splash. Of course I was suspicious. But I had no proof. I must tread very warily, I told myself. *I* did not want to end up in the slimy canal. I think Best and Lethbridge intended to buy the only remaining printers in Knibden and work a major scam at the *next* lottery. As it was, all that happened was that a large consignment of tickets were stolen from the works. And sold on the black market. The pair thought they had been rumbled by Verity Willow. Best locked her up while he made his getaway. By the time the police did anything, he had gone. Mrs Willow had been thoroughly taken in by her paying guest. General Bensusann, of course, vouched for his long-serving butler.'

'I vouched for him all right,' Bensusann chuckled. 'I cracked him over the head with his silver-topped cane. Buried him myself, beside Mrs Enderby. How *she* met her fate, I never knew. *That* cannot be laid at my door, though goodness knows, I was glad to be rid of the woman. She had had a hold over me, and he had had a hold over her . . .'

'You all deserved one another!'

'That's as may be. It was when I saw the sodden copy of Mrs Esmerald Dean's *The Good Path* with its Buckworth & Matchett label, I realized Lethbridge had got Henry Buckworth to print all the stamps I'd treasured since boyhood. Every spare penny I ever had, I'd spent buying beautifully printed, exotic stamps from Lethbridge. I intended to sell the collection when I retired from the army, and restore the old family house. Perhaps have a family of my own. Marry Helen Willow and let her little girl play in the gardens with her dolly. Then I discovered my stamps were worthless. Prettily printed frippery, turned out by Buckworth & Matchett's and sold to me for exorbitant sums by my butler. I couldn't even afford the Knibden Municipal Insurance Company insurance policy on the house. In the end, most of the hundred and eighty-seven windows were broken, the roof was leaking. Mrs Parbold and Desmond Chase are welcome to it . . .'

Bensusann wept. Verity Willow cradled him in her arms. Follifoot made Matchett an offer he could not refuse. One man was delighted to acquire what the other was delighted to be rid of. 'I need never walk back along the canal towpath again,' he said.

'My son's out of a job, then?' Beryl said sadly. 'Just the luck of the Laffetys, even if we are the Knibden Laffetys.'

And Mr Matchett, with Follifoot's money in his pocket, asked Beryl to marry him – on condition she did not take out a life insurance policy on his head!

'Take your partners,' shouted Albert Hodge. 'Take the partner of your choice for the "Last Waltz on Earth".'

A ripple of excitement ran through the packed ballroom. One more dance! It was as if the good folk of Knibden, past, present and putative crowded the floor. They rose from their tombs and came down from their portraits. The five Beautiful Gallimores twirled in and out of one another, for there was no one else good enough for Sarah, Caro, Charlotte, Elizabeth or Anne to dance with and they had lived and died old maids. Gus, their deerhound, chased Harry the Prancing Dog who teased the marmalade pantomime cat and between them, caused quite a commotion over by the food.

'I promised to partner you in the polka, Mr Williams,' I said. 'But I do not think Albert Hodge and his Band know how to play the polka. I am not at all sure from the music I have heard, that they know how to play anything!'

William Williams looked at me. I am dancing with *her*, he thought. I am actually dancing the 'Last Waltz on Earth' with the dead guest's investigator.

William Williams smiled politely. I clutched the sealed envelope tightly. When this dance finished I would go up on to the podium and reveal the truth about the dead stranger's Will. I was now looking forward to getting my task over and done with. William Williams smiled to think of the troublesome blank cheque that would shortly clear. He turned towards where his wife had been sitting close by the door all evening, and as he watched, the dead guest's executor saw Dora stand up and stretch out her arms to a man he had never seen before. The Gallimore's ballroom floor was crowded. With difficulty, Williams attempted to steer the dancing in his wife's direction but Dora and her unknown partner were soon lost to view, swallowed into the great sea of dancers that rose and swelled between them. Wave upon wave swept past Mr Williams and in vain did he seek among the faces for his wife. She is gone, he thought, I shall never see her again.

Dora slipped on the polished floor. Her partner caught her. He held her close, steering her with expert ease. 'Ridiculously slippery!' the man remarked.

'My husband sanctioned the expense,' Dora heard herself telling the man.

'Indeed?'

'My husband is the dead guest's executor,' Dora gushed in an effort, she supposed, to sound like a woman worth dancing with.

'Let us not speak of William Williams now,' her partner said. 'It is you I wish to hear about. You are the one I've been longing to meet.'

'Have you?' Dora gazed up at the man's obscured face but the bright lights of the newly cleaned chandeliers cast such strong shadows Dora was unable to see his features.

'I have had to wait till the "Last Waltz on Earth",' the man said. Then added, 'Call me Theo!'

Dora danced with difficulty, gasping for breath. 'Not *Theo*dore Fechnie?'

Her partner whisked her through a complicated series of double reverse turns, then whispered in her ear, 'I know all about you, Dora!'

Dora nodded. 'You know then, how for thirteen years I loved Mr Parker. When he called me into his office to inspect my figures and explained in a matter-of-fact voice that his visits to my bed-sit were no longer convenient, I went home as soon as the bank closed, lay down on my truckle bed and swallowed a whole bottle of sleeping tablets for I wished never to wake again. "Excellent, excellent!" were the last words I heard and I tried to rise and present him at the door with his briefcase and umbrella. When I did not appear at the bank next morning and inquiries were made, I was discovered, stone cold in my dark-pink wincey-ette dressing-gown. The colour of uncooked meat before it is thrown in the pan and laced with its own blood. I dare say they'd have buried me like that. For the sake of convenience. Mrs Parker would have walked to the funeral, without aid of a stick or chair, clinging tight to her husband's arm, indignant that such a thing

403

should have happened to his bank. Instead I recovered and married Mr Williams. And Mr and Mrs Parker came to our *wedding*.'

'I was disgusted such a thing could happen at the city. To a female clerk on the front desk.'

'It was one of life's little tragedies no one noticed.'

'I noticed, Dora. Far away in Knibden, I sat down at the desk Mr Williams sits at now and, using the pen he writes with every day, I left confidential memoranda in my files. If the dead guest's executor were ever to take a mirror to his ink blotter he would discover Parker's doings recorded there. In reverse.'

'I wanted so much for something to happen,' Dora confessed, 'that now it has.'

'Of course it has,' Mr Fechnie said soothingly. 'Did you really imagine *no one* cared? Oh, my poor Dora! There are some things that cannot be blotted out or reversed, not even in Knibden. Nor is it always possible to avert the tragedy of the ending. But at least *I* noticed, and made a note. You cannot be thought to have passed through this world unregarded.'

Dora smiled. I shall be quite content in the future if nothing ever happens. And while the 'Last Waltz on Earth' was playing, she felt as young and pretty as she had been years back, before Mr Parker began calling at her bed-sit after work, sitting himself down at her little corner table to consume the delicacies she had purchased during her lunch hour, joyfully carrying them home with her in a brown paper bag. Only that morning, William had realized that the bread he crammed into his mouth at breakfast each morning had been fetched fresh from the bakery. She would visit him in his office at the earliest opportunity and remove the blotting paper where Fechnie's memoranda might be read in reverse. Fortunately her husband was not the type of man to take a mirror to his predecessor's scribblings. How she loved William's boring ways!

Albert Hodge clutched his clarinet and blubbered like a baby. Iris should be here! Hodge thought. He'd not even mind if she danced the 'Last Waltz on Earth' with Dickie Paisley, *if only* the dear old girl were here this evening, and he could see her again, once more.

Amy Pasco clung on Jack's left arm, Norah on his right. 'Now then, girls!' Jack Tagg laughed. He winked at Dickie Paisley who waved his baton and laughed also for Jack had a way of making you laugh. Iris Hodge was waiting for Dickie behind some flowers over by the food. She was wearing new nylons, and chatting happily with her friends. But Amy and Norah were not smiling and chatting. Nor did either girl intend letting go of Jack's arm. They'd kill one another first.

Hodge raised his clarinet high in the air. And barely heard above the noise made by the rest of his band, he blew a long shrill blast and wished with all his heart that Dickie Paisley could see him now. He demanded another bottle of barbary rum. 'Roll up! Roll up! Take your partners for the "March of Time"!'

'What, again?'

'Dear me!' someone said. 'Where *did* Miss Quinn get him from? The man sounds as if he's selling off a market stall.'

Dickie Paisley reeled backwards, clutching his nose. Blood cascaded down the front of his white gold-trimmed jacket as Hodge let fly another punch.

'It is dangerous to cross me,' thought Norah Bird. In a corner of the Gallimore Hotel heavily hung with coats, Miss Pringle had handed her pupil the bridal bouquet of flowers. Had the foreman at Mr Bird's tannery later recalled those yellow blooms when that noddy van came out of nowhere, mowing Mr Nye down on the way to his wife's and child's funeral? It is dangerous to cross me, thought Norah as she and Amy danced round Jack. When the last Great Knibden Lottery was over and Amy had won the man poor Norah lost, Norah Bird had waited in dread to see what would befall her friend.

She had been peeking out all morning from behind the ugly mannequins in her shop window, hoping to catch a glimpse of Jack. He hadn't yet finished her clothes rails. 'He is spinning out the job in order to charge me more,' Norah thought.

'It's Amy,' Jack says as soon as he arrives. His wife is unwell. This is nothing new. She has not been right since Neville was born.

'Amy?' Jack's face is grey. He loves her, Norah thinks. He would not look so distressed if I was unwell. Amy has a fever. The doctor says it is nothing serious. Norah, of course, is disappointed. Wasn't it about time something *was* seriously wrong with Amy? Wasn't it meant to be dangerous to cross Norah Bird?

'I had better go and see her,' Norah says, preparing to close the shop at short notice – something Mrs Cooper would not have approved of, any more than Mrs Cooper ever approved of Amy Pasco.

'Yes, do that,' Jack urges Norah. Any comfort Norah can bring her friend, it is the least she can do after Amy had stood by Fatty Bird, the most unpopular child in the class, ever since their first day together in the Infants'.

Norah enters Amy's bedroom. Amy is lying propped up on the pillows. Despite her overbright eyes and blonde hair pinned out of the way, she looks pretty. With the clever coiling prettiness of a snake slithering in the grass. She is dozing. In a cot beside her slumbers Neville, a mass of ginger hair on a tiny pillow. Norah remembers the great ginger cat. If a genie had ever given *her* three wishes she would not have wasted them. Miss Bird wastes no time now. She pulls the coverlet up over Amy's mouth until her breathing stops. Then leaves the Tagg residence by the back door and hurries round to the front where she makes an elaborate show of ringing the bell and calling to her schoolfriend through the letterbox.

The neighbours gather. Eventually Jack returns. He has with him a couple of the rough Pasco lads. It looks like being a bit of a party – till someone goes upstairs and looks in on Amy.

Jack Tagg married the next woman he met in the Swan. Anything to elude Norah Bird! He never even finished putting up the new dress rails, for Jack had learned how dangerous it is to cross Norah Bird and he refused to set foot in her shop again. It did not save him. The second Mrs Tagg, Neville's step-mother, was a practical-minded woman in the true tradition of practical-minded Knibden women. She did very well for herself out of the Knibden Municipal Insurance Company policy she took out on Jack's head. And if the circumstances of the demise of that jovial chancer, Jack Tagg, were in any way suspicious, she made up for them, taking good care of Neville. And when the boy grew older, encouraging him to bring his girlfriends home. Carrying them tea and toast in bed in the mornings, and offering to share with the young women her skill in making tissue-paper flowers.

'You promised to do something for Nev,' Susie Till tells Norah Bird. 'But you already had – you *killed* his mum!'

Norah Bird wondered if Prince Philip ever visited Her Majesty's prisons. Most likely he did not. So she said to Susie and Nev, 'You don't want to believe a word of it. Hester Jones is just a troublemaker and Amy was my best friend all those years. I'm delighted you're getting engaged. Business has been so good this week, can I not help with a little cash?'

'To buy the solitaire in Macready's window?' Susie asked.

'To buy anything you like.'

As Susie kissed him, Neville thought rather wistfully of the Ford *Fiesta* of his dreams and concluded he would not be altogether sorry to be back on his bicycle and free from Lalla Wilkes-Tooley. It had been like dancing with one of those disdainful mannequins in Norah Bird's shop window.

'Your brown baggy suit,' Susie said.

'What of it?'

'I love it,' Susie told him, nuzzling into his shoulder and playfully tweeking his big bushy moustaches. Neville was Neville. He didn't need transforming. Tagg held Till. Till held Tagg.

The elderly Gallimores giggled. They said it reminded them of when Lavinia Lobb scored her goal in the last hockey match before the Great War. They watch her now, dancing with Johnny Dawes Dobson. 'You'll never guess what happened,' Lavinia says, and before she can tell him how Arthur Dawes Dobson's portrait has been reinstated in the library, Johnny throws his cap in the air.

'You should never have wasted your life working in my father's stupid library,' he rebuked her.

'It was the only place I could feel close to you. With your name, Missing in Action, Presumed Dead, out on the War Memorial, visible through the main window. Just above Denis.'

'Poor Denis, I was with him when he died – he made me promise that if I returned from the trenches, I would take care of you.'

'Did you, Johnny? Did you promise?'

'Before I could do so, I came under fire – not a great enemy offensive but a stray sniper's bullet. A bit of a fluke, my death – like when you scored that goal.'

'A fluke!' Lavinia stamped her foot indignantly. 'My goal, a fluke? How dare you say such a thing!'

If I had lived, Johnny Dawes Dobson thought, I'd have had to marry Denis Lobb's spoilt little sister and spend a lifetime with her. That lone German bullet did me a favour, after all.

Or, if I had lived, I might have put my papers into another man's pockets. A man who'd had his head and limbs blown off. They'd report me Missing in Action. Presumed Dead. And I would be free to get on with my life. Until the last Great Knibden Lottery, when I could not resist returning to the town. I did not win the lottery, Miss Jones, but by avoiding the public library, I was lucky not to run into Miss Lobb.

He had run into Mrs Allendale though.

Edina was unravelling the lime-green jumper as vehemently as she had knitted it. For all her efforts, George had turned out just like his father. As if there were some knitting pattern you could purchase and follow the instructions to produce an exact replica. Who his father had been she wouldn't like to say. She certainly had no intention of disclosing her information to Hester Jones. The boy had betrayed his mother in front of the town. Edina thought Hester Jones would probably know by now how the housekeeper at the Bensusanns' all those years ago had come drinking in the Swan. She had leant across the bar, and confided, 'You see that man over there.' Mrs Enderby pointed at a fellow who'd just arrived in town for the lottery. Stepping down from the very same train as Jack Tagg, Edmund Veitch and Gilbert Duncie Sibson. He too had played railway poker and annoyed poor Harriet Delilah Veitch. Mrs Enderby put her mouth close to the barmaid's ear. 'I reckon 'is name is up on the War Memorial. Presumed Dead. Presumed nothing – avoiding his responsibilities most like. They say he was once promised to Miss Lavinia Lobb!'

The wretch had decamped the moment the lottery was over, avoiding his responsibilities in the town yet again and leaving Mr Allendale to stand by Edina, and do the decent thing. George would be glad if he knew. But Arthur Dawes Dobson's grandson had always had his head buried in some thick book the other side of that coal-effect electric fire. Mrs Allendale, for all her attempts at conversation, had never managed to tell her son this particular version of events.

Chickie Wilkes-Tooley paid Samuel Till fifty pence. The boy

tapped his pocket. He could go on collecting fifty-pence pieces for ever, he reckoned. Chickie had slapped him for saying something foul mouthed about Mr Veitch and he reckoned his silence on the matter of the slap would be an expensive commodity, worthy of its purchase price. 'Anything I can do to help?' he would ask, and the witch would dive, ever after, into her magical bottomless purse. Serve her right.

Chickie wondered why a child had been permitted at the tea-dance. Not to mention the bandsmen openly swigging rum. Albert Hodge had got into a fight and given a dapper man in a white jacket a bloody nose. It made you wonder if the Masons knew what they were doing, running a respectable hotel. And as for allowing a guest to die in his bed. And a tramp to die on their doorstep. That wanted investigating. Chickie gasped, and pointed. Hester Jones was having a word with Mr Hodge. The music subsided as one by one the bandsmen put their instruments down. Any minute now Miss Jones would tell them who was going to get the fortune.

I stood on the podium clutching my envelope. I accepted a swig of barbary rum from Albert Hodge's bottle. I tapped the microphone and asked, 'Can you hear me?'

They could hear me all right. You could have heard a pin drop or a flea hop.

'First, before I make my announcement and open this envelope, I . . .'

'Get on with it . . .'

'I should like to thank Belle Quinn, daughter of the famous mathematician, Harold Augustus Quinn, for her sterling efforts in bringing about this occasion this evening. You are a miracle worker, Miss Quinn! To organize all this music, dancing, flowers and food in only three days . . .'

And then Susan Till broke free from Neville Tagg's bear-like embrace. 'It's not fair to deprive Nev of the inheritance just 'cos I ruined her hair. I didn't mean to make you look like a common criminal, Miss Quinn.'

'But I *am* a common criminal!' that good woman cried. 'Sol and his girl have left now they know I shall have to sell the Laurels, and their baby will not be born among all my nice things. It is as well I am bankrupt. I can only thank the dead guest. At least

Harold Augustus Quinn's grandson and his girl will leave me in peace. I have had no peace. In the end, he said, Fleur, my pet! *Those* were his last words. Had he said *anything* other, almost anything at all, how different these years since his death might have been.' Belle wept. She had not written to Fleur about Daddy's death. How could she? 'Fleur, my pet,' he had said, so that for an instant the goodness of Belle Quinn deserted her. She'd jerked the coverlet up over his head, and held it there.

There was a long awkward silence. 'My, my! It's like the Book of Revelations tonight!' someone said.

'Three cheers for Miss Quinn,' someone else – who had heard my vote of thanks down the microphone, but not Belle's reply from the repolished floor – yelled out. 'Hip Hip . . .'

'The time has come . . .' I began, as soon as the cheering died down.

'And about time too!'

'Time has been a long time coming.'

'Three full days.'

'If I may be allowed to proceed without interruption?' I took a deep breath. All I wanted now was to get this over with. 'Right from the start, it seemed to me you all have a claim on the dead guest,' I said. 'When I began, I knew nothing about any of you. Now I know more than I . . .'

'How long's *this* going to go on for?'

'Just give us the answer!'

'Give the girl a chance.'

'Miss Jones has her methods.'

Through the windows of the Gallimore's ballroom, I looked past the white stone balconies to where a great fire blazed across the town. I pointed. They looked. Knibden's ancient church of St Redegule's was engulfed in flames.

'It'll have been that Bill Parris with his candles!'

'There have always been conflagrations in Knibden. The camera obscura. The Al'ambra . . .'

'It'll cost a bloody fortune to rebuild.'

'It won't be insured – the Knibden Municipal Insurance Company is bankrupt.'

'We are all bankrupt.'

'But there *is* the dead guest's fortune!' I said. Silence fell. 'The dead guest wanted everyone to get their just deserts,' I said. 'And it seems to me that over the last three days, that has happened.'

'Now look here!'

'What?' There was much yelling. The sound of fire engines approaching could be heard outside, while inside the ballroom of the Gallimore Hotel, a clamour rose for me to open the sealed envelope.

I did so.

At first I thought there was a mistake. The envelope was empty. When I looked again, I found a thin slip of paper. On it was written a single sentence which I read aloud: *The one whose voice now speaks my words must decide how my fortune shall be spent. Signed: Theodore Fechnie.*

'The devil!'

I looked up. I saw the flames of the burning St Redegule's dancing in the distance. Little Hester has designs on the whole world. She is bent on causing havoc. Always has been. I told the people of Knibden that they should spend the dead guest's money rebuilding and repairing the damage that had been done.

PART FIVE

Finale

Reader, I ran for it. Straight to the railway station. If a train did not come at once, I intended to make my way back up the tracks and get a connection at the next station. I was meant to be some-one-who-was-not-someone – not someone instrumental in determining people's fates. I was meant to dig out their stories, not fashion their lives. The dead guest had had other plans for me. I see now what I should have known all along. *Things barely remembered, things forgotten that ought not to be, things that ought to be forgotten but cannot be.* Theodore Fechnie had kept secret files his successor could not be expected to understand. The former bank manager had been a law unto himself. There are always rules to contracts of this kind – *he* had made them, and broken them all.

As I raced on to the platform, a train was slowly coming into the station. I stuck my hand out.

'Where to?'

'Penzance!' I shouted the furthest destination I could think of. I did not hear the reply. I was on the train, and the train was moving, before I even realized I had opened the door and climbed in. You would think Hester Jones had learned her lesson but fortunately this train was not being taken out of service for cleaning. The carriage was crowded with standing room only, and not much of that.

'Hasn't stopped at Knibden Halt in years,' someone was saying.

'Must have been an emergency.'

'In a town like Knibden!'

'Never been there . . .'

'I thought I saw a fire . . .'

I pushed my way down the corridor.

While the citizens of Knibden crowded the Gallimore's white stone balconies to watch the church of St Redegule burn, I had taken advantage of the confusion that followed my announcement to run to my room, seize my cardboard suitcase and leave the hotel. The last thing I heard as I tore through Knibden's

415

streets were the plaintive cries of Gilbert Duncie Sibson, wailing into the night for his lost plaster love.

At last I found a seat facing the direction the train was going. On it lay a colourful paper windmill. I picked this up and put it with my suitcase on the rack overhead. It might have been left there for me, I thought rather fancifully as I sat down. If the train had not stopped at Knibden, Edmund Veitch and his first wife, Harriet Delilah, would have carried on, and made a life for themselves elsewhere. They might have taken a holiday beside the sea and returned to Knibden only when the lottery was over and the schoolhouse had been prepared. They would never have stayed in a small back room at the top of the Gallimore Hotel. Jack Tagg would have gone on playing railway poker and wreaked havoc in other girls' lives in other towns. Norah Bird and Amy Pasco might even have remained friends, discussing Amy's adventures every evening, to this day. Young Gilbert Duncie Sibson would have zealously performed his good works elsewhere and, who knows? He might now be Archbishop of England. Aubrey Wilkes-Tooley, a venerable white-haired captain of industry. Mary could have married her Peter all those years ago and Mr Bridgewater been pleasantly surprised by his son-in-law who, though not steady enough for the insurance business, had certainly loved Mary steadily throughout the intervening years. As for Johnny Dawes Dobson – he should not have come back to Knibden and fathered a chief librarian to make tea and conversation in Arthur Dawes Dobson's library. Or, if he had to return, he should have sought out Lavinia Lobb, and cheered her on until she scored a goal that was not a fluke.

I yawned. The carriage was stuffy but fortunately plenty of people got out at each stop and plenty more got in. I almost laughed to think of the scene following my departure.

'But our investment!'

'The ten-fold return on our shares!'

'We are bankrupt!'

'I told you it was fishy.'

'We are no better off . . .'

'We are all a lot worse off.'

'I would say, William, that you are very much to blame. It's men like you that enable the Fechnies of this world to carry on as they do.'

'Except . . .' Verity Willow hesitated. Knibden turned on her *en masse*.

'Except *what*, Miss Willow?'

'Well, it has been better than any whodunnit. We have enjoyed ourselves wondering who the dead guest was, and who he left his money to. It has been rather fun.'

'Fun! It was a funeral. The party afterwards was a wake.'

'It has been like a game of Cluedo.'

'*I* have enjoyed myself, in a way I never thought to again . . .'

'It has been like the Great Knibden Lottery,' trilled Norah Bird. 'All this upheaval, excitement and expense – all for *nothing*!'

'I wouldn't say for nothing,' General Bensusann took Verity's hand. She smiled shyly at him.

'Now I know the truth,' she said quietly, 'about Raymond Bast – Harry Best, I mean – perhaps I can forget Randolphe Shyne and Maisie Vollutu. I can put them behind me and live my own life at last.'

'You can be my Maisie Vollutu,' the General said gallantly, a twinkle in his eye.

'Nothing ventured, nothing gained,' put in Edmund Veitch cheerily.

'We are all as penniless as Bill Parris!'

'God rest his soul!'

'Who was he, do you think?'

'A man who always had sixpence and a bottle of Scotch in his grimy pocket.'

'I shall miss him.'

'At least Miss Jones has gone. And taken her plain little pancake face with her!'

'But we are all exposed! Our innermost thoughts made public property.'

'It's a scandal.'

'She should be strung up.'

'Prison's too good for people like her.'

'Do you think Prince Philip ever visits Her Majesty's prisons?' Norah Bird asked.

'I doubt it!'

'I reckon that's where *she* came from.' This was Veitch.

They all turned to him.

He nodded. 'She'll have been in prison. For deception.'

'She deceived us all.'

'Or impersonation,' Veitch added.

'Impersonation?'

'I reckon she was impersonating herself,' he said. 'She told us who she was and where she'd come from *far too readily* for my liking. My name is Hester Jones, she said almost as soon as she came through the Swan's swing door. She might equally well have said Esther James. Or Alison Jones. Heather Jenkins, Amanda Jackson – or any of those many other aliases she'll have used in her time.'

'It wasn't very convincing.'

'I remember the moment she arrived, a great gust of wind and rain blew in, and there she stood, dripping wet all over the floor. Leaves stuck to her clothes and tangled in her hair. She looked like a creature out of ancient mythology with glistening serpents all over her head. An augur of doom – a foretaste of something to come.'

'She had blood on her hands, and pretended *red ink* had run on a newspaper.'

'Blood on her hands!'

'Are you saying Miss Jones *killed* someone, Mr Veitch?'

'She was a murderer, I knew it all along!'

'When you think about it, she was very keen to establish that *we* were all murderers and impostors.'

'People always accuse others of their own crimes.'

'At the very least we know she was a thief – she stole our stories.'

'And scarpered without paying her bill. That, in itself, is a criminal offence. All those tomato, egg, lettuce and radish salads she ate. Even the dead guest – Theodore Fechnie, I mean – managed to pay *his* bill, posthumously. To the exact penny!'

'How did he do that? No one knows the hour of their death.'

'I reckon Mr Fechnie planned to go to the bank each day and draw out the cost of another night at the Gallimore Hotel, however long it took. That way he would always have the exact amount of money he owed in his pocket. Not a penny more, or less. But when he saw the state his hotel was in, he had a heart attack!'

'Shhhh! Don't let the Masons hear you. You know the pride they take.'

'You'd have thought Daniel Mason would have recognized the guest.'

'He was swathed from head to toe in a greatcoat . . .'

'Mason said the man reminded him of someone!'

'All corpses are pretty much alike . . .'

'Fechnie had it all planned. I reckon he deliberately employed people to run his hotel so unprofessional he could depend on them not to recognize him. He spent every spare hour at that bank all those years, plotting and scheming. It's a quiet country branch. He had nothing much to do all day . . .'

'The devil makes work for idle hands.'

'The devil made work for Theodore Fechnie! He knew the private business of everyone in the town. Perhaps the burden of that knowledge was intolerable.'

'It was obvious it was Fechnie, when you think about it. If Hester Jones had had any sense she would have known immediately.'

'I told you she was not a Poirot, a Marple or a Randolphe Shyne.'

'It was only a prank on his part – she did not have to take the whole caper quite so seriously.'

'I don't know who to blame more, Theodore Fechnie or Hester Jones.'

'We never really asked her who she was. Or how she came to be here. Perhaps that was the problem. If we had once said, "Who are you, Hester Jones? How did you come to be here?" If we had listened to the account she then gave . . .'

'She was right though. She was someone-who-was-not-some-one. We never allowed her to be anything else.'

'I expect a favourite uncle gave her a box of Cluedo as a child. She became addicted to solving mysteries – even ones that aren't there.'

'She insinuated her way into all our lives, exposing us in this shameless way. Knibden will never be the same again. We will never . . .'

'No!' cried Edmund Veitch then. This was his chance to set an example to those whose moral fibre was not as strong as his own. 'The excitement will die down. Hester Jones, or whoever she was, has gone. It is just like after the Great Knibden Lottery. Damage has been done but, in time, we will return to normal.'

'Call this normal! We are all bankrupt.'

'We will have to leave our homes and take rooms at the Gallimore Hotel.'

'I shall be happy to leave the Laurels.'

'The church has burnt to the ground . . .'

'The church can be rebuilt. There is the dead guest's money, don't forget. The best thing is if we all agree, here and now, that Hester Jones had an over-active imagination. As the dead guest's representative in the Land of the Living, she made up stories about us all.'

'Yes, yes. She did! She made them all up.'

'I cannot bear to think of her moving on from here,' the good Belle Quinn exclaimed, her puce felt hat now set very firmly on her head. 'Doing the same thing to another group of unsuspecting people. Innocent parties, as yet blissfully unaware. The stories of their lives drawn out of them, their characteristics closely observed and then tightly drawn into her own strange scheme of things.'

'The general public should be warned.'

'We should write to Penzance!'

'Given she made it all up – and we are all of us agreed on that – you'd have thought she could have been more outlandish.'

'*Outlandish*, Miss Willow?'

'The stories she gave us are really rather mundane. Given that Hester Jones had a completely free hand. I mean – why couldn't Herbert Vale have been something more exciting than a purveyor of cardboard boxes? If, for the purposes of her story, he *had* to be a travelling salesman, why couldn't he have dealt in some more exotic ware? Pungent Eastern tobacco or . . .'

'I see what you mean, Verity,' General Bertram Bensusann squeezed her hand. 'It is rather insulting, when you think about it, not to have . . .'

'She should at least have made our stories come right in the end.'

'But, here we all are! Safe in the Gallimore Hotel . . .'

'Where the state of the linen is second to none!'

'I can think of worse fates.'

'It is not exactly a fairy-tale ending!'

'It could be a lot worse,' Belle Quinn said quietly. 'We might be out on the streets snapped at by dogs. Half a bottle of gin our only companion.'

'How dare Hester Jones bring this down on the Gallimore Hotel!' Mr Mason had entered the room. His wife stood in the doorway.

'She promised to find me my baby,' Eileen Mason said. 'All these years I have spent looking after the Gallimore, and never once has *anyone* but Miss Jones ever thought to stop and think about *me*. And the tiny, downy-haired little boy I handed over all those years ago in a whitewashed room. You!' she pointed at Miss Willow. 'You ate a piece of my wedding cake, yourself a young bride, also, but when we met you again here in Knibden, you never once inquired . . .'

'Now look here!' spluttered General Bertram Bensusann.

But Verity said gently, 'I didn't like to, Mrs Mason. Not in the circumstances.'

The manageress of the Gallimore glared at her husband. 'And you, Daniel!' she said. 'You never even knew Donald's name.'

'I thought it for the best,' Mason mumbled. He helped his wife to a chair. Then stood beside her patting her shoulder. 'This is our family now,' he said, glancing round the old worn room that had seen better days, at the guests who eked out their lives in the faded splendour of the Gallimore Hotel. The retired headmaster whose step-son, Roger, visits occasionally. And the man who once ran Knibden's Municipal Insurance Company, before it was bought up and incorporated into a larger conglomerate – his wife apparently walked out of the family home one night, and never came back. Miss Willow; the impoverished genteel Miss Quinn. The military man whose former batman has a thing going down in the town with a Mrs Hilda May Parbold who had once cleaned for him. The pair sometimes, in view of past services rendered, induce the old General to pay the Masons a few pounds for the bother of setting two extra places at the table so that they can come and tell coarse tales about the old man s family home, now lying derelict on the hill overlooking the town.

'We have had enough excitement,' Daniel Mason said firmly. 'I am going to lock up now – and, if anyone rings the front bell, at whatever hour of the night, and in whatever desperate circumstances, I am not going to open the door. We can do without more guests arriving, disrupting things.'

'We don't want another Hester Jones.'

'As if we would ever have asked her to solve our mystery for us!'

'Astonishing presumption.'

'Let us suppose, for one minute, that we *did* have an anonymous guest dying in our midst, leaving an enormous fortune to someone in the town. Why would we ever employ a complete stranger with no qualification or recommendation to her name, who walked in out of nowhere with some fiction about a train to Penzance! Why would we open our hearts and our lives to her. And *pay* for her to stay while she completes her investigation. It's astonishing that she could even have *thought* of such a thing!'

'Her own parents didn't want her with them in their grave – so why would we put her up in our best hotel?'

'For three days.'

'Like Jonah wallowing in the belly of the fish!'

'Most objectionable.'

'She had a very high opinion of herself.'

'She fancied herself omniscient.'

'A common mistake.'

'A dangerous one. She has been the author of a lot of heartache.'

'Yet, how convenient, when you think about it, that we can blame her for everything. Send Hester Jones packing and send our troubles away also. Rebuild the church. Wipe the slate clean. Start afresh.'

The inhabitants of the Gallimore Hotel nod. How very convenient, they are all agreed, that they can bolt their doors, and deny everything.

'You know who she reminded me of, now I come to think about it?

'Who?'

'Harry, the Astonishing Prancing Dog – a tame creature in a jacket and cap you could never quite trust.'

At that point in my musings, the ticket collector came down the train. Everyone fished in their pockets and their purses, and so did I. I held out my ticket to Penzance rather wonderingly for inspection. The railway official took it, stamped it and handed it back without even looking at me. 'You'll have to change twice,' he said. I was about to tell him I had changed once already but he was already moving down the train.

'Nice weather for this time of year,' the man beside me remarked. I have a shrewd idea where such conversations lead, so I reached down my paper windmill and clutching it stolidly, I stared stonily ahead.